CLIFFORD'S BLUES

CLIFFORD'S
BLUES

JOHN A. WILLIAMS

20367070

COFFEE HOUSE PRESS

MINNEAPOLIS

20367070

PORTIONS OF THIS NOVEL HAVE BEEN PUBLISHED IN:
Another Chicago Magazine, 1987
Syracuse University Magazine, 1988
Love, a Babcock & Koontz broadside, 1988
Black American Literature Forum, 1989
Rutgers Magazine, 1992

Coffee House Press is supported in part by a grant provided by the Minnesota State
Arts Board, through an appropriation by the Minnesota State Legislature, and in part
by a grant from the National Endowment for the Arts. Significant support has also been
provided by The McKnight Foundation; the Lila Wallace Reader's Digest Fund; Lannan
Foundation; Target Stores, Dayton's, and Mervyn's by the Dayton Hudson Foundation;
General Mills Foundation; St. Paul Companies; Butler Family Foundation; Honeywell
Foundation; Star Tribune Foundation; James R. Thorpe Foundation; Dain Bosworth
Foundation; Pentair, Inc.; the Helen L. Kuehn Fund of The Minneapolis Foundation;
the law firm of Schwegman, Lundberg, Woessner & Kluth, P.A.; and many individual
donors. To you and our many readers across the country, we send our thanks for your
continuing support.

Coffee House Press books are available to the trade through our primary distributor,
Consortium Book Sales & Distribution, 1045 Westgate Drive, Saint Paul, MN 55114. For
personal orders, catalogs, or other information, write to: Coffee House Press, 27 North
Fourth Street, Suite 400, Minneapolis, MN 55401.

LIBRARY OF CONGRESS CIP INFORMATION
 Williams, John Alfred, 1925 –
  Clifford's blues / John A. Williams. — 1st ed.
   p.   cm.
  ISBN 1-56689-080-2 (alk. paper)
   1. Afro-Americans—Travel—Europe—Fiction. 2. Dachau
  (Concentration camp)—Fiction. I. Title.
 PS3573.14495C54   1998
 813'.54—dc21   98-56278
                                                    CIP

10 9 8 7 6 5 4 3 2 1
first printing / first edition
printed in Canada

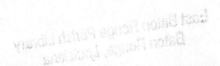

ACKNOWLEDGMENTS

I wish to thank Leroy Graham, who provided me with materials on Germany and black troops in the post-World War I occupation of Germany, as well as other information, ranging in time from 1903 to 1975; Roscoe C. Brown Jr. and Lee Archer, former pilots in the 33rd Fighter Group (Red Tails), for confirming interviews of the unit's actions over southern Germany during World War II; the Hatch-Billops Collection for making available to me an oral recollection by Jacques Butler; the Institute of Jazz Studies at Rutgers University, Newark Campus, for allowing me to research trumpeter Arthur Briggs in its Oral History Collection; and graduate student Michelle Potter, whose German, and that of her friends, helped mightily.

Dedicated to those without memorial or monument

Aguacero
beautiful musician
unclothed at the foot of a tree
amidst the lost harmonies
close to our defeated memories
amidst our hands of defeat
and a people of alien strength
we let our eyes hang low
and untying
the tether of a natal anguish
we sobbed

—Aimé Césaire, "Blues of the Rain"
trans. Clayton Eshleman and Annette Smith

Hey Jayson,   *September 21, 1986*

It's me, Gerald Sanderson—Bounce—and this stuff is for you. Justine and I are practically just off the plane with it. We were in Europe this summer picking up our daughter who was doing her junior year abroad and ran into this old German guy in Flensburg near the Danish border. Strange story. We stopped not far from where we were going to stay that night so I could take a leak. This guy was there. I couldn't really understand him, but it seemed that during the war Black American soldiers hadn't killed him when they could have. He was grateful, but maybe they should have put him out of his misery. I mean, the guy was a mess. He left this box at the desk for us.

Tank suggested we look you up and get this to you, since you're the only writer we know. (Says you owe him for throwing that block of his that let you score the only touchdown of your life in high school.) I know it's been a long time since we've seen each other, but I thought this was important enough to say hello with. What you have is a copy. We have the original if you want to see it, but it's been written on every kind of paper you can imagine—tissue, glazed, schoolkid tablet, wrapping, end pages of books, in pencil, ink, crayon—man, it was a mess to copy. If you even look at the original, it starts falling apart. It had been wrapped in an old smelly raincoat with the rubber dried and cracked off.

You should have seen us coming through customs with it; they probably thought we had 200 pounds of dope. I told customs it was research (I finally did get my master's in history). They rummaged around, asked the boss, made phone calls, and so on. Man, they make it tough for you to get back home. The Germans, when I told them it was research on Black people in the camps, they were glad to let it go.

Jay, this is a diary written by a brother, a piano man name of Clifford Pepperidge. Played with Sam Wooding, which was way before both your time and mine. Clifford was in Dachau. Yeah, Dachau. We drove there and checked it out. Even now the space—it's the size of about ten stadiums; I mean it's huge, and if you include the fringe around it that is now filled with young trees, it becomes a third larger. It's a museum now. We saw pictures of some other brothers, too. Couldn't tell if they were us or

Africans. Now I wonder just how many other Black people we never heard a peep about were in those places. Dachau must have been a bitch. I can't imagine what all those other camps were like. The way I figure it is this: the old soldier giving this to us, our knowing you, is a spooky triple play. Old soldier to Bounce to Jay. Not an accident. Maybe a mysterious way.

You know the Benny Golson tune "I Remember Clifford," with lyrics by Jon Hendricks? I know it was for Clifford Brown who died in 1956, but when I play it now, I think of Clifford Pepperidge. It would be great if you could do something good with this. I'm not trying to lean on you, it would just be great. Justine sends greetings to you, your wife, kids, and grandkids. I'm told you got a bunch of them. Any of them good ball play-ers? My ball club is going to be weak for the next couple of seasons, and if I don't get some talent bopping into this school, I may have to teach history full-time. Maybe it's time for that, anyway. Playing ball doesn't serve the same function it did when you were a kid or even when I was. It's all about money now, not teamwork or building confidence. In any case, I know this season my mind's more on Clifford than anything else and how maybe that bell that rang for him is starting to ring again. I know you know exactly what I mean. For the ball game, except that it isn't a game.

You should know that we've all enjoyed reading your books, especially our daughter, Liz, who would love to meet you. All our best to you and yours. Give me a call when you've finished. No hurry; after all, it's been in the box for forty-one years already.

* * *

Sunday, May 28, 1933

My name's Clifford Pepperidge and I am in trouble. I'm an American Negro and I play piano, sometimes, and I'm a vocalist, too. I shouldn't be here, but they didn't pay any attention to me when they brought me. Didn't listen when I was in Berlin, either. I am in Protective Custody, they call it. They've said I'll be out as soon as they finish their investigation. I hope so. God, I hate this place. As soon as I do get out, I'm hauling ass back home. I don't care what it's like. They never did this to me in New York, and until I left

Storyville, after they closed it down, I managed not to have anything
to do with the John Laws. That's what back home was all about—
playing music and keeping away from trouble because it was always
looking for you. Damn. I'd even go back South to get out of here.
Any place but here. It could be worse. I could be over in the camp.
There's a sign on the front gate: *Arbeit Macht Frei.*

Tues., June 7, 1933

I'm a calfactor, a houseboy, and I am stuck here in Dachau
with no way to get out. Except that if I'm a good enough houseboy
my luck may change. That I doubt since Malcolm, to save his ass,
double-crossed me. That's got to be what happened. Met him after
playing in the Schwarze Kater in the Friedrichstrasse. Then he
showed up at the Kater and usually sent me drinks. We recognized
each other. Well. Malcolm worked at the American embassy. We got
to be quite good friends, as he would say. He had a marked fondness
for me and I played to it. He had money, lots of it. Even a popular
colored entertainer who'd played and sung with the great Sam
Wooding didn't make the money Malcolm already had. Family's rich.
We used to sit around Sunday mornings in silk bathrobes, drinking
champagne, trying to figure out who it was we'd brought home with
us from Kurfurstendamm, where everyone was good-looking, or
from Nollendorfplatz, where everyone was not. It really didn't matter
to Malcolm as long as I was there to join in the fun we always had,
although the cocaine was really hard to come by with the Nazis
running things.

Hitler became Chancellor, so the Brownshirts made it, and
Finck's Katakombe, where the Shirts used to loiter, has become a
very popular place indeed. A-men and Z-men used it a lot. These are
agents and squealers for the Nazis. You never knew when they were
at a party, until the next day when someone stopped by to tell you
that Frankie or Teddy had been arrested with a Protective Custody
warrant as a member of an unpopular category. It was getting awful
around Berlin; it was getting quiet in the Kater. The spirit was gone
from the Friedrichstrasse, the Kurfurstendamm, the Jagerstrasse, the

Behrensstrasse; the Conferenciers didn't make jokes about the Nazis any more, and they introduced the performers with less flair and fancy than they used to. It was like the way it used to be once you stepped across the line from Storyville.

I wanted to get away. I was dreaming of snakes all the time, and anyone from New Orleans knows that when you dream of snakes, you've got enemies. But Malcolm didn't care. He didn't give a damn. Told me I had nothing to worry about because I was an American and he was an American diplomat. And fool that I was, I believed him. We were still in bed on that Sunday morning when they came and found us naked as the day we were born. That was April 23. Malcolm declared "diplomatic immunity." They carried me away while Malcolm was saying, "Don't worry. I'll have you out soon." He took my passport. I haven't heard anything from Malcolm since. It looks like I don't exist. They say the embassy claims it has no record of me. But I was somebody in Berlin. At least I thought I was. So I figure that Malcolm got rid of my passport and the record of my check-ins, and that means I had no contact with him. Of course the cops know different. They arrested me in his flat, but I suppose Malcolm fixed even that. If Almighty God walked into Hitler's office without signing in, then as far as the Germans are concerned, He did not walk in.

Wednesday, July 5, 1933

The camp used to be a munitions factory, they tell me. Some of the buildings and sheds are still standing. There are nine barracks inside the wall and ten outside. The ones outside are fenced around with barbed wire and are guarded. Almost no trees; a few white birches, I think, and pines. Hot sun everywhere. No shade. They expect to keep 5,000 prisoners here.

Dachau is a labor camp. No one here knows anything. Nobody cares to know anything. Never thought I'd be so close to where I played a couple of dates—Munich, in Schwabing. If I'd had any sense, I would have got the hell out of Germany then, with the Nazis running all over. More obnoxious than in Berlin. Goddamn Bavarians.

I came in a van from Berlin. A long drive, and they let us out only
once to piss. Threw bread and sausages in the back. Arrived here
midmorning. Seems like years ago, but it's not quite six weeks.
The SA and the SS cursed us out of the van into the sun. Gangs of
men in gray uniforms, some harnessed like horses to big rollers and
carts, moved back and forth, raising dust; they groaned and grunted.
Most of them had red triangles fastened to the right pants leg; others
had green, and some of those fellas looked as tough as the robbers
and dope fiends in east Berlin. A few wore pink triangles, and when
I saw those and looked into the faces of the men wearing them,
I knew what was going to happen to me. I couldn't work like that.
I played the piano. I sang songs. Everywhere I looked in those few
minutes before my group was called, I saw men working harder than
anyone I ever saw working on a chain gang. I started to shake.
I couldn't help myself. Another group was coming out. I tried to read
hope in their expressions, but there was none, not on a single face.

We started up five steps. I concentrated on them to keep from
shaking so much. My legs were like rubber. The SS were shouting
and pushing. I felt a shoulder lean into my own to lend support.
The man had gray eyes and a big square face; his eyes were the sad-
dest I'd ever looked into, sad but not afraid. The crush of the group
and that shoulder carried me up the steps and inside a room that had
as many SA and SS men as there were prisoners. I wanted to holler
"I'm an American! You've made a mistake! You have no right to hold
me here!"

I didn't say anything, though. I'd said all this in Berlin, said it in
Tegel-Berlin. Didn't help. Not with these jokers. Every official eye
found my face. I shook more. I couldn't stop. The mass of black uniforms and the swastika armbands simply scared the pure-dee shit out
of me.

Then I saw him. I think he saw me first and willed me to find
him. It was Dieter Lange, and he had more reason to be here, in a
gray suit, than me. He'd been a *Raffke* in Berlin—a hustler, pimp,
profiteer, a regular MacHeath, but his lovers were all men. He was
a chicken-plucker who'd always wanted to pluck a black chicken
because they were so rare in Germany, and those he saw were already

being plucked by someone else. But I was with Malcolm then. Besides, I never went out with men like Dieter Lange.

The officer in charge called us to attention and then read from a paper in his hands. All of us had been charged and convicted as dangers to the state, for hostility and immorality to the state, and would be held here in Protective Custody under Article 14 until further notice. We would be notified when we were considered to be rehabilitated and then released. *Achtung!* The thing about Germans is, give them a uniform, give them a little power, and they think they're gods. Yet it was Germans, people like Bert Brecht and Paul Graetz and Joe Ringelnatz, who said I was an artist. I'd never been called that at home, only in Europe. I guess I was so swelled up that I didn't notice other artists going to jail, being fined, or leaving the country. Hitler said the new art was degenerate. Especially jazz music. *Entartete Musik*. But I was an American. How could they do this to me?

When the officer called attention, all the SS and SA in the room began shouting and cursing again, turning us, shoving us out of the door, down those five steps, into the hot sunlight. Then we were marched into a smaller building where we had to squat while soldiers sheared our heads. They laughed at my hair, threw it up in the air, examined it. They were so busy having fun that they didn't notice how much I continued to tremble. Once I saw the man with the sad gray eyes and the great square face. Without hair his head looked like a rock. The floor was inches thick with hair—black, brown, gray, blond, white, straight, curly. In another room, where it was impossibly crowded and everything smelled like vinegar and sweat and stale cigarettes, we filled out forms and listed our belongings and signed papers without having time to read them. In the next room, as we were given uniforms, someone told the soldiers to give me one with a green triangle. It was Dieter Lange.

The SS screamed, called us pigs, bastards, freaks, Communists, crooks, pricks. We peeled off our clothes as best we could and shoved them into boxes and gave them to the guards who gave us the uniforms. Dieter Lange said green again. He gave the man in charge of this business a piece of paper and turned to me. He told me to come with him. The uniform smelled and did not fit, and the SA were kicking me. They told me to go with the captain.

There was a pause like there is just before your fingers come down on the keys, like just before you sing your first note, and it seemed that everyone in the room, prisoners and SA and SS alike, for just a second, looked at me, looked at Dieter Lange. Then I was out in the sun again, Dieter Lange, hands on his hips, looming in front of me. He said I had been detailed to him. He smiled and said, *"Kind Schokolade,"* said it softly. Told me not to worry.

Until I was arrested in Berlin and double-crossed by Malcolm, I thought I was an independent person. I learned my music without benefit of formal teaching. Singing came natural to me; it was a way of saying something with tone and word that expressed more than just plain talking. Older musicians, sometimes when they were trying to conceal techniques, or more often tricks, taught me without knowing they were. I could make my way, find a job, find a stoker, if one didn't find me first. I made mistakes. Malcolm was the biggest. Living in Europe, being considered a strange, exotic creature, gave me, I'm afraid, a sense of being important, and that made me stumble and fall into this snakepit. Maybe it was because of the people I knew and traveled with. Most of them were well-off and didn't seem to notice that I was a Negro. It seemed that way.

But walking behind Dieter Lange, the dust and the shouts merging somewhere near a point in my head that kept lifting toward a faint, I felt alone as I'd never felt before. That sense of independence —it must have come from what I thought was the kindness of people, or from people who wanted something from me, or from people who didn't give a damn about me, really—vanished. I was no longer trembling; I was crying. There was Dieter Lange, now a captain in the SS. But then I remembered, back in 1929, the year Paul Robeson heard us play in the Berlin Zoo Roof Garden, Dieter Lange came into the Troika with his swastika armband half sticking out of his pocket, like he was trying to hide his membership in the Nazis. I never laugh at people. I have never been mean to anyone, so I didn't join in the laughter and the shoving and the teasing. But here he was, now, getting into a car and telling me to hurry because he wanted to fuck me good. I was crying, but I was listening, too.

When he saw me, Dieter Lange said, he'd got one of his friends to give me a uniform with a green instead of a pink triangle because it went hard for queers in Dachau. They were sometimes, if lucky, placed with the political prisoners, the Reds, cutting turf and draining the swamp or working in the quarry, which was worst of all. This way, I was his personal calfactor, his private servant. And he could hold grand parties with me playing and singing and this would get him in good with his superiors. He was the camp purchasing agent—a job with all sorts of possibilities, and he was soon to be in charge of purchasing for other camps that would be opening in a matter of months.

He thought all this was not bad for a better-than-average hustler. He joined the party in 1928 and was accepted into the SS in 1931, about the time he vanished from Berlin. He did it to be on the safe side, and it turned out to be the right move. Dieter Lange was very proud of himself.

(I have just found some extra paper, so now I can finish writing about my first day in Dachau.) The Nazis were growing in power, he said, and there was not a city, town, or hamlet in Germany, and quite possibly Europe, that would not feel that power sooner or later. He said he would make some inquiries for me, see what he could do. I asked how long my sentence was. He said he didn't know. No one knew. He would have to be careful. It would be wise for me to make the best of a bad situation that could have been worse if not for him. If I was nice to him, he'd be nice to me. He'd always liked jazz music and my singing and playing. He would do his best to look after me. But if I became troublesome, he'd have me back in the camp in a prisoner barracks in a flash. As it was, I could work around his home and help him in the office canteen in the camp. These were good jobs. It had been prudent, Dieter Lange told me, for him to marry. Her name was Annaliese. She went to Munich often, he said, to shop and go to the theater, the things women do, for there wasn't much going on in the SS quarters and hardly anything in the town of Dachau. She was not demanding of his time or person. She was the daughter of a farmer and considered herself fortunate to have made such a good marriage. She would not be troublesome, for she knew nothing of life, having left the farm only a year ago, which is when Dieter Lange met her in Munich at a rally. He was sure, he said, she had never even seen a real Negro.

Friday, July 7, 1933

God, I've prayed all night. Did you hear me, God? How can this be happening to me? I know I didn't go to church. I know I lived like You weren't there, like I wouldn't have to pay my bill to You. Maybe You don't want to hear from me because of what I am. I didn't choose to be this way, Lord, You know I didn't. And anyway, aren't we all Your children? Isn't Your Kingdom of Heaven for all of us? Forgive me for what I am. If I could stop right now, I would, but it's not left just to me anymore, Lord. Would it please You if I killed myself? Isn't life Yours to give and Yours to take? Please, God, if You didn't hear me, just read this. Yes, I used to play music on Sunday so people could dance and have a good time, and I drank and took dope, but not out of meanness; for money, yes, to live on or just to have fun sometimes, but not to be mean, Lord. You know I've been more afraid than mean. I've turned the other cheek a thousand times. I've not hurt anyone, because I can't. Doesn't Your word say "Blessed are the meek for they shall see God?" Lord Jesus God, Holiest of Spirits, help this poor Negro so far from home and in the deserts with Satan and the serpents. Don't forsake me, Lord. Hear me, Oh God! I'll do anything You want, anything, that I can do. Just give me a sign. Let me know You're listening or reading, Lord. Or, Lord, is this Your will, visiting trial and tribulation upon Your obedient servant? If it is, Lord, give me the strength to bear this heavy, heavy cross. Thy will be done, Almighty Lord, but why me?

Fri., July 28, 1933

I have written to everyone I could think of, including Malcolm. From America, from France, even Spain, no answer. Of course,

Dieter Lange takes my letters and mails them. He says. But I have no way of knowing whether he has or not. Camp regulations allow us to write. A few prisoners have been released, but the parole conditions are severe. One prisoner named Nefzger, Dieter Lange told me, was found dead. The prosecutor from Munich claims he was murdered by the ss guards. Dieter Lange says that's nonsense. The prosecutor, Winterberger, also claims that three other prisoners— Hausman, Schloss, and Strauss—in spite of what the camp doctor says, may have died from "external causes." I think about running away. That wouldn't be easy. Black skin in pink Germany. Yet Switzerland is only a few hour's hard driving away, I think. I'd have to walk, I think. So near, so far. Like a blues. Mr. Wooding used to say that was the blues, what white folk called a "lament," because what you were lamenting or feeling blue about was what you knew but couldn't do anything about. So you sang or played, and that helped to make things a little better. That was African, Mr. Wooding said, because you were at least saying things were out of your control. I liked Mr. Wooding, but it was coming to Berlin that was like moving up from darkness into the light. (It pleasures me to think back like this, instead of thinking of right now.) James Europe's army band certainly brought jazz music to Europe. I wonder where he got that name. Maybe his folks way, way back, after slavery, just made it up, thinking Europe was the farthest place from Jim Crow they could get. He made this place stomp and jazz.

In New York you could say you were a musician, but they weren't so keen on putting black folks in the limelight, so to speak. They liked all those white mammy singers with burnt cork on their faces. The white companies—Cameo, Paramount, Okeh, Black Swan, Columbia—did record a few colored entertainers, but didn't pay them much, not even Ma Rainey or Miss Bessie Smith, King Oliver or Louis Armstrong, Kid Orey, Fletcher Henderson, or Duke Ellington. Mr. Wooding's band was recorded only by European companies, like Parlophone, Pathe France, and the other French company, Polydor. No, didn't pay as much as they paid white entertainers. There were a few clubs where you could work, but you had to toe the line or those gangsters would put your butt in the street—

maybe with holes in it. Sometimes we had to play behind great big palm plants so the customers couldn't see us.

Most of the clubs were uptown, and unless you were an entertainer of some kind, the most you could do in those places was cook, maybe wait tables, shine shoes, or clean up. But in the end, it didn't matter if you could shout some blues or boot a rag. You were just a jigaboo, and that's all there was to it, and all those white swells from downtown couldn't change things much. Mr. Wooding told me that a lot of times.

Mr. Wooding came out of Philadelphia and got his first band in 1920. Everybody up North had heard of Storyville, but they wanted you to prove you knew what you were doing. I proved it. Mr. Wooding sometimes thought it was more important for him to stand up there with a baton like Paul Whiteman than play the piano. His left hand wasn't a bear, anyway.

We were playing the Club Alabam one night. At the end of the second set, a white man came up and started kissing everybody (and everybody was watching me when it was my turn to be kissed, because they knew I was a fairy). Turned out he was a Russian looking to bring a colored band to Moscow. Couldn't hardly talk English. Can't think of his name now. But that's how I came to Europe, through that Russian and Mr. Wooding's band. We left New York in 1924 when I was 24, and we stopped in Berlin to open a revue called "The Chocolate Kiddies." We may not have been the toast of the town in New York, but we sure were in Berlin. I was slick and sassy and there were more people like me than I could have imagined, and they were plain with it, right out in the open like I'd seen nowhere else. Ber-lin. For me it was champagne and caviar. For most Germans it was starving and people getting shot by the law every day. There were parades and demonstrations. Communists—I didn't know much about them then and still don't—were very busy. There'd been a revolution in Russia and it seemed to spill over into parts of Germany. Their leaders and other people were getting killed, people like Rosa Luxemburg and Karl Liebknecht or those Spartacus people. Myself, I couldn't see why it was such a bad thing for everyone to share equally in everything. My friends who had money were angry with the Communists, but in the poor neighborhoods it was a different story. I guess people with money, or who hope to get money, or to keep what they already have, will always be hot with Communists.

I didn't let all this bother me. I was having a good time. (The band even finally got to Moscow and to France, Spain, Turkey, and Tunisia.) It didn't matter to me that it took a wheelbarrow full of money to buy half a loaf of bread. I was colored and I laughed because for once whatever was bad wasn't happening to colored people.

A colored lady who'd been in Paris tried to open a club in Berlin. They called her Bricktop, a light-skinned lady, whose real name was Ada Smith. But her club didn't last long because her musicians weren't any good. She just barely got out of Berlin with the clothes on her back. I mean she left town about the same time Florence Mills was playing Hamburg.

You had to be a nightbird in Berlin. Mostly I saw things that made the District back home look like Sunday school. Dope fiends everywhere. You could get cocaine anywhere. They sold it on the street in perfume bottles, whores and pimps like Dieter Lange. The more queer you were, the better they liked you. At the new Eldorado in the Motzstrasse, you couldn't tell who was a man and who was a woman, but that didn't make any difference to us or to the high-class Germans who went there. It really seemed to me that there was that thing they called the German Disease, and I guess that was what brought so many pretties from England. But two things couldn't none of them do was the Charleston and the breakaway.

Admirals-Palast was doing what they did back home with the Ziegfeld Follies and the Folies-Bergère in Paris, with the pussy shows, playing the Tillers, the Admirals, and the Paris Mannequins. Good thing they didn't pull the bloomers off a few of those dancers. Josephine Baker turned up on a trip from Paris and set Berlin on its behind. There were as many gangs in Berlin—they called them clubs—as there were bands in New Orleans. They were yeggs, footpads, and cutthroats. One of my dearest friends was killed by a gang outside a dive in the Muntzstrasse.

An interruption. It's the same day. Reading this over, I realized that I've said nothing about Frau Lange. She is young and just the other side of thin. I mean, she could get fat. She has blue eyes and blond hair, like a Kewpie. Dieter Lange was right: she'd never seen a Negro except in photographs. She treats me like a pet monkey. I wonder how the world still manages to produce people as dumb as she is. According to Dieter Lange, she thinks it's perfectly normal for them to fuck every month or two. He doesn't tell her otherwise.

She touches me often, as though to reassure herself that I am a human being. Twice she has found me crying and she sat with me, not knowing what to do, clucking and saying "Shhh! Shhh!" She asked about my father, who was killed in a fight in a turpentine camp; asked about my mother, who, when I was eight, disappeared the same time Preacher Pollard did. My aunt Jordie raised me until she died of the TBs, and then the District took over. It seems to me that Annaliese takes a pleasure I can't describe in watching me. She is very proud of Dieter Lange. Why not? As purchasing agent for the camps in Bavaria and part of the Palatine, he can get everything she wants and maybe never had before—food, liquors, clothing, cigarettes, French wine and perfume, furniture—the cellar is filled with it. The kitchen shelves are packed tightly with cans of everything. This bitch has probably never seen so much in one place in her life. But Dieter Lange travels a lot. When he's gone I have to stay in a rear room of the canteen and go to his house in the morning and return to camp at night. I think Frau Lange is not happy with that, judging from the exuberant greetings she gives me when I report in the mornings. She does not seem to like being alone.

The man with the square face and the sad eyes who lent me his shoulder is a Red, a political prisoner. The red triangle is for Communists and anyone else the government doesn't want running loose. Some are people who just don't like the Nazis—and made the mistake of saying so out loud. The prisoners may shout "Heil Hitler" when the guards are around, but when they aren't, what they whisper is more like "Kiss my ass, Adolph." Werner, the man with the square face and sad eyes, like most politicals, has an indeterminate sentence. He encourages prisoners to be strong. They are making the place bigger, because prisoners are coming in every day. This means Dieter Lange must purchase more food, clothing, and building materials, plus the luxuries it seems the SS must have.

———

Sun., August 13, 1933

It seems that I am a luxury in more ways than one to Dieter Lange. He has plans for me. I will help him advance his career. He will have parties and invite his friends and superiors. In spite of what Hitler and Goebbels say about jazz music, Dieter Lange says, nearly everyone who has ever heard it likes it. Of course, he would only invite those who did. They will be wonderful parties, he says, with me playing and singing, just like in a cabaret. What else can I do? Looks like he can find all kinds of ways to use me, and I can't do a damned thing about it. Nothing. That made me think to ask him, again, if by chance there was any mail for me or if there had been any word about how long my sentence was. There was no mail, he said, and nothing about my sentence, of course, because he'd be the first to tell me about that. I don't believe him, but what can I do? Who can I complain to? Werner said he would try to get some word out, but that I shouldn't be too hopeful. Bert Brecht, he told me, had left Berlin and was probably on his way out of Germany. I asked how he knew, how he managed outside contacts, and he said prisons were just like other societies; some things continued to function in spite of restrictions.

Once he said that, I could see it. Of course! Doesn't life go on for colored people back home, North and South, in spite of Jim Crow and prejudice? When I am in the camp late in the afternoon, and when roll call and the evening meal are over, I see the men sitting on benches outside the barracks talking softly, their washed clothes hung on lines behind them to catch the last sunlight. The intellectuals are together. Werner is among them. There are even prisoners who are Nazis; they cling together. They must have broken some party rule. And there are some army officers, too. In all, there are ten

24

companies of prisoners, each of about 250 men. Number 7 company is the real bad one, for prisoners who need disciplining. These men always look bumped and bruised, with dried blood on their faces. Werner says they are flogged and beaten. Lumped together in 7 are prisoners with all colors of triangles. The members of Number 1 company, the one Werner belongs to, also receive heavy punishment for being Communists, intellectuals, social democrats, teachers, people who made movies, writers, newspaper reporters, and so on. In the whole camp there are fourteen other foreigners besides me. Number 2 company has Jews in it. They are German, just like everyone else here except me and those fourteen other foreigners. Werner says that Hitler has it in for the Jews; that the Nazi party is against Jews and nearly everything and everyone else except "real" Germans and German tradition. Werner whispered to me that the number of prisoners killed in camp is not three or four, but closer to fifty. How can it not get worse? While this place is being enlarged, ten other camps have opened, Werner said: Brandenburg, Papenburg, Konigstein, Lichtenburg, Colditz, Sachsenburg, Moringen, Hohnstein, Reichenbach, and Sonnenburg. Germany has become a dreadful, murderous place, he said, mostly because of the Treaty of Versailles. I don't know anything about that, but he told me the terms of the German surrender were so harsh that the only reaction to it had to be somewhere, sometime, revenge. That time is fast approaching, especially with someone like Hitler in charge, who cries for living space, says Germany must have it.

Werner asked me if I was a *Tappete*. I told him yes because he must have already guessed. He said I was better off than those in the camp, but I already knew that. The thing to do, he said, is to outlast them, no matter how, no matter how long it took, and the prisoners had to work together, did I understand? I said I did, but I didn't know what I could do. Information, he said, is power. Then he said, if each of the prisoners brought just one handful of dirt and dumped it in the Appellplatz (which everyone calls the Dancing Ground), we would have a small hill. That's what information was, when it was all brought together and sorted out.

Thursday, Aug. 24, 1933

Dieter Lange and his wife, Anna, live in a medium-sized house along one of the main camp roads that leads into Dachau. Between the camp itself and this row of pink and white houses are the buildings where munitions used to be made. Like everything else, these are being renovated and enlarged. Today, I had to spend most of the time helping in the canteen. Then, as usual, I started back to the house, checked in at the guardhouse *(Jourhaus)* at the gate between the camp and the staff quarters, in full view of a tower where an SS guard mans a machine gun. The guards know me; there's no problem. I can't escape with my skin. I know it and they know it. My going and coming disturbs nothing. Yet I always feel like the gun is trained on the middle of my back. I wonder, too, if maybe one day a guard, just for the hell of it, will kill me and say it was an accident.

I hadn't seen Dieter Lange all day. Usually, when he's going on a trip, he tells me. So I wondered where he was.

I entered the house through the back door and went down to my room in the cellar. Dieter Lange called from upstairs. I hurried up. You do nothing at a normal pace unless you are out of sight of the SS. The stairs opened on a corner of the large room Anna had not yet furnished, though I had to keep the floor spotless. I came through the door and Dieter Lange swept up his arms. He had a great grin on his face. In the opposite corner stood a baby grand piano. It looked new. I'd never seen such a gorgeous instrument. I always played the box piano, because most clubs couldn't afford anything else, and also the box took up less space. He told me to come look. I guess he had "commandeered" the piano, the way the SS seems to commandeer everything. He asked me did I like it, and I said yes. He told me to try it, so I played a few notes, and they came out so round and pure that they scared me. Too much piano for such a small place; it needed a concert hall. Dieter Lange nodded encouragement. He told me to practice. This room, he said, would be where people danced, that was why Anna had not furnished it. He winked. He patted the goola. Steinway, he said. Hell, I could see the name on it. From Germany, originally, the Steinways were. Two sons in piano manufacturing. One stayed in New York and the other

26

returned. A very special German instrument, he said. And then he left me.

I let myself fold down onto the stool; it fit like it had been made for me. I ran up and down the keys. This was the best piano I'd ever played. I laid on the soft pedal and somehow found myself playing The Duke's "Mood Indigo." That was one of his standards, but it seemed to work for everybody. I had all his records, and hundreds more of everybody who was anybody, when I was in Berlin. I played them right down through the shellac. "In My Solitude": I low-sung that because it was for me, and while I was playing it, I thought how every other slow number I could think of was about love, man-woman love. Only person I think I ever loved was that strange fellow, a writer, from Rocky Mountain country. Never could figure out how his family wound up there in New York. He was sensitive about how black he was, but I always told him "the blacker the berry, the sweeter the juice," and God it was. Called him my cowboy. He didn't love me, though. They never did. "Ain't He Sweet" came to mind and I ran it through kind of bouncy. When I started, my fingers were tight, bunched up at the knuckles, but the more I played, the looser they got. I played some back beat stuff, took it up-tempo, swung through some K.C. stride, and cranked my uptown hand with some bucket-bottom blues. When I looked up, it was dark outside and Annaliese was standing in the dining room doorway behind me. I felt like I'd been ten thousand miles away. Later, after I'd cleaned up, I sat on the floor in my room and thought of the band, thought of the way I'd tell it to a radio announcer or somebody else important: Well, on trumpet we had Doc Cheatham and Bobby Martin. Hank Cooper took over for Doc when we came to Europe. On the 'bones there was Albert Wynn and Billy Burns. Jerry Blake on the stick. Willy Lewis played the alto sax and Gene Sedric was on tenor. Me on piano (when Mr. Wooding and Freddy Johnson were not) and John Mitchell on the git. June Cole on the bass and Ted Fields on drums. I did the vocals. That was the band when we recorded in Paris and Madrid three years ago. When we first got to Berlin, we had three trumpets: Bobby, Maceo Edwards, and Tommy Ladnier, and one trombone, Herb Flemming. Garvin Bushnell was on clarinet. The saxes were the same, Willy and

Gene, like John Mitchell, who was guitar. Georgie Howe played drums then, not Ted Fields, and John Warren played a walking bass. I thought about all of them, smoking muggles, playing the dozens, fooling around with the beat so that everybody would have to catch up, and then someone would run on out ahead and you'd have to do another 32 bars, which was all right. I cried in the darkness, missing it so much and wondering did any of them miss me, if they were asking about me. Then I heard Dieter Lange at the top of the stairs calling me in that tone because Anna had gone out to play Chinese checkers with some of the SS wives. . . .

Saturday, September 16, 1933

Dieter Lange's first party. Oh, I was so nervous. Playing in a club is one thing; the atmosphere is different. If the owner is nasty or the customers mean and you don't need the money, or even if you do, you can always leave. No chance of that here! Dieter Lange got me some black pants, a white shirt, and a tie. He also got me some decent shoes. When I told him how nervous I was, he gave me some schnapps. But, damn, I was nervous. First thing I noticed was how all the SA people stuck together; the SS people did, too. Come to think of it, Dieter Lange was more the SA than the SS type. Wonder how he managed that. I thought I could make things mellow by doodling around with "Falling in Love Again," because the Germans loved to hear Dietrich sing that song. Then I picked it up a bit with "Walkin' My Baby Back Home." You have to play your audience as well as the music, and the second number was bright with a good tempo. I thought that somewhere down the line I'd lean into "I Gotta Right to Sing the Blues." When you're playing, you also listen to the way voices out there start to rise, from a hum to just plain loud. I went into some low-down blues, "Sweet Cat," "Black Cat," and "Weary," and seeing that everyone was now feeling good, joking and calling out, introducing their wives and girlfriends to each other, I did "Tiger Rag" and that got them onto the floor, so I gave them "Bullfoot Stomp" so they could bang their feet, and eased into that neat little "Button Up Your Overcoat."

Dieter Lange was beaming; Anna was high and beaming. The food and liquor never stopped flowing. Dieter Lange kept slipping me schnapps and I kept saying to myself *to hell with it* and romped away. Oh, man, they got to feeling good. They called me "Cleef," and rubbed my head so much I thought the hair that was growing back would come off. There's always a point when the smell of perfume and the smell of sweat bump heads, and that happened. Dicks starting to ease up out of the crotch; tits starting to stand straight out. I mean, the worst dancers in the world thought they could dance to my playing; dancing, fast or slow, seemed to me to be dry-fucking; it was like a Saturday night back home when everybody just cut loose and drank and danced and fucked and fought till daybreak. The floor was creaking with the dancers. Everyone was bringing me drinks, wine, beer, schnapps, rye, scotch, bourbon, splashing the glasses on top of my beautiful new piano. And they rested cigarettes on it, too. I was sweating, getting funky like everyone else, when Dieter Lange calmed everybody down so I could go to the bathroom and get something to eat. While I was in the bathroom, I rammed my fingers down my throat to puke up all that shit they'd given me. Then Anna, pretty drunk herself, made me eat in the kitchen, fixed a plate for me and patted me on the shoulder. I liked that, a pat on the shoulder instead of a rub on the head.

When I went back to the piano, they gave a little cheer and some applause. They seemed less boisterous, and when I looked around I saw why. There were a few high-ranking officers standing in a corner. Dieter Lange was having what seemed to be a pleasant conversation with them. I opened with "Love Me or Leave Me," hung up tight behind "Stormy Weather," and then cut to "Sometimes I'm Happy," and then "You're the Top." I guess I played and sang a lot longer, but I don't remember what songs. I sat on that stool and felt myself going in twenty directions, but I knew that I had to play better than I ever had in my life. Because if I couldn't get out of here, I was going to try to live as comfortably as possible. So yes, I'd do Sambo. Play my ass off, sing my ass off, as long as I could remember a number, as long as my fingers held out, and as long as my voice didn't crack too much. Once, just once, while I played and sang, I felt

I wanted someone to love me, nice or mean, didn't matter. Just wanted to be close to someone, but that passed.

I'm writing this with a hangover the size of New Orleans and New York put together. The house is quiet, but it smells like a Sunday morning in a honky-tonk, a two-bit saloon. God help me if I don't help myself. Is this the way to do it, Lord? I still hear the echoes of the last two songs I played; everyone joined in, drunk or sober. How could they not? The songs were the *"Horst Wessel"* and, of course, *"Deutschland Über Alles."*

Wednesday, September 27, 1933

There's always talk among the calfactors working in the SS and SA homes—gardeners, cooks, tailors, houseboys, streetsweepers, and the like. When details are marched out from the camp to work on the roads or sewers here, even more news is exchanged, like it's getting worse for the queers over there, but we all knew that. A few have been lucky and found protection under guards or block leaders or prisoner foremen. But for the rest . . .

The talk today was about the Munich prosecutor, Winterberger. He's visited Himmler about the killings in camp. Dieter Lange says Winterberger is a Jew who will soon have his eyes screwed in right at the least. I gave a barracks orderly two packs of cigarettes and two cans of sausages to smuggle out a note to Winterberger. Why not take a chance? I can't depend on Dieter Lange, and every little bit helps. I don't think Dieter Lange in no way, shape, form, or fashion, wants me free, especially not now. The party was a great success. I feel like a hog must feel, being treated nice, but there's always a fence around the pig pen, and you're always a pig, and there is always a hog-killing season.

Monday, Dec. 25, 1933

Merry Christmas. Dieter Lange gave me some cocaine for a present. Anna cooked a goose. I heard them fucking. She whined a lot. Maybe she's beginning to think something's wrong, the way they fuck. By evening she was in a better mood because Dieter Lange talked about the New Year's Eve party he's planned. I think Anna likes parties. Merry Christmas.

Saturday, January 6, 1934

Anna had a good time last night. She danced a lot, mostly with a political officer from the Gestapo name of Fritz Bernhardt. The prisoners talk about him. They say he fucks anything that moves. An SA colonel kept rubbing my butt. He was very good-looking.

Thursday, January 11, 1934

Winters in Berlin were not like this. The wind and the dampness lie on you like a suit of clothes. The weather seems to beat men down to half their size. You can see the rain, snow, and sleet pushing down the plain, but it's never quite so cold and nasty until they hit the camp and turn the roll-call area and the streets and alleys between the blocks into mud. No one can play football then. They have had some wild games on the soccer field across from the officers' section, along the road into Dachau. The SS vs. the SA, the guards against the prisoners, the officers against the enlisted men. And then they go right back to doing what they did before, all of them.

Tuesday, Jan. 23, 1934

Dieter Lange went off this week to Karlsfeld, Allach, and Gemering, so I stayed in the back of the canteen and did roll call in the rain and snow. That colonel who rubbed my butt sent for me. Name's Friedrich Schuler. I didn't know until the second time I was with him that he had had Dieter Lange sent to check out campsites. The colonel is a lot of fun and easy to be with. Not rough the way Dieter Lange is. He asked me a lot of questions about myself and how I got there and how long my sentence was. I couldn't answer the last question, of course. He supposed I'd like to get out, and I said, certainly. He plays the spinet. He played for me. He said it was Debussy, and I did recognize "La Mer" and "Claire de Lune." He said he sometimes heard color in Negro music the way he heard it in Debussy's, especially in Ellington. Then he said he would do everything he could to get me out of Dachau. And I believe him! He's a colonel! Of course, he can do it. I don't believe he's lying like the others. Oh, God. Maybe, maybe, maybe . . . ?

Wednesday, January 31, 1934

Werner is now a barracks orderly, so things are easier for him. He is convinced that he will spend the rest of his life in Dachau. He worked on a Berlin newspaper and is a veteran of the World War. He says he often sees Greens being let out, because they'd rather release them under strict supervision than let someone like him out at all. He wrote about the Nazis. He hates them. Something happens to his face when he talks about them. The Greens who continue in crime come back and go right into the prison company in Block 7. Then, he says, anything goes. I gave him a small bag of candy. He told me more about himself. He's married and has kids. Three. He's heard that his family got away to the U.S., "Amerika," he said. He told his wife that if anything happened to him, she should get out fast. He's relieved they're out, but I can tell he wishes they were near. Some visitors are allowed and there's mail, but it's always opened. Werner says he's happy for the prisoners when they have visits from family and friends or get mail from them. We all get stuff from the *Rote Hilfe,* and in spite of the regulations, money does get around, but somehow it all eventually winds up in Dieter Lange's canteen. Whatever happens from now on, at least Werner won't have to worry anymore about his family. He asked me if they would be all right. I told him yes, his family would be all right, that it would be easy for his wife to find work, that the schools were all good and opportunities hung just around every corner. I know that's the way it works for white folks whether they speak good English or not. (Werner said she didn't.) For most of them, anyway.

Sun., February 11, 1934

Sometimes Annaliese's parents come to visit on Sundays. This was one of them. They're a little like farmers I remember back home, except they're white. They're thick and slow and eat like pigs. (Farmers back home got good table manners on Sunday.) But they bring all the good things from their farm, so it's all right. Anna and her mother cook with lots of laughing in the kitchen, and Dieter Lange sits and talks with his father-in-law about the Nazi party and how things are changing for the better in the country now that Hitler's going after the Jews, the unions, the Reds, the Catholics, and the worst kind of Protestants. Anna's mother, no mistake, is fat. Maybe Anna will become just like her. Her father is big, too, but he's not fat. That's muscle, even between his ears. I can tell that Dieter Lange puts up with them. There's always some cute bullshit about Anna getting pregnant, but I know Dieter Lange isn't the least bit interested in having kids. There is a faint odor of cowshit in the house when Anna's folks come, even though they are scrubbed clean and red. Dieter Lange is always relieved when they leave.

A new group in the camp, Jehovah's Witnesses. They say they prefer God to Hitler, so it's their asses, naturally. They get purple triangles for their jackets and legs. They're called Bible students. And there are more than a few ministers and priests here. It's plain and simple: if you ain't for the Nazis, you're against them, and you wind up here. The South was like that. That's why I left it.

Wednesday, Feb. 28, 1934

My handsome Colonel Schuler tells me he's still working on my project. But he seems worried. Where there were no problems, suddenly there are. He assured me that they had nothing to do with me, but with some struggle between the SS and the SA, which he is sure won't last. All very silly, really, he says, this foolishness between the Brownshirts (SA) and the Blackshirts (SS). What a charming, cultured man he is, the kind I used to see in the Berlin clubs. Why he is in the SA and Dieter Lange in the SS, I'll never understand. Shit, I don't understand Germans at all. They've come from being a nation with a culture Americans can't ever catch up to, to a place where they murder not only their own culture but the rest of the world's, too; from a people who sometimes reined in their pride, to a bunch of arrogant bastards. My colonel thinks there are many in the SA who do not agree with Hitler's policies, and that makes for certain frictions between the SS and the SA. The colonel likes to play Bach records for me with the volume turned way down, because Bach is bad, the Nazis say, and Wagner is good. Friedrich says, whispering, that no one's better than Bach; Bach has piety, power, precision, and passion. And I just think to myself that Negro jazz must be pretty damn good to be banned alongside Mr. Bach! And Mr. Hitler isn't doing too hot a job, because some of his people are listening to colored music, and Friedrich can't be the only German listening to Bach.

Thursday, March 8, 1934

Dieter Lange does not like the new SS Gestapo troop leader, name of Adolph Eichmann, and calls him a *Schlemiel,* which was the name of Dachau village's most famous writer, Peter Schlemiel. The town is very proud of him.

There are nineteen regulations posted by Commander Eicke, most punishable by whippings and detention in the Bunker with the Prisoner Company, solitary confinement with bread and water, or death by hanging. But the guards have their own unwritten regulations. They're worse.

Sunday, Mar. 24, 1934

We had another party last night. At first only the SS people showed up. Later the SA came, and as usual, they made two separate groups with their wives and girlfriends. There was a lot of drinking and dancing and singing, just like before, but something had changed. The colonel was very careful not to take the sly liberties he always did, and he gave me no sign, not even a look, that things were going well for me. Dieter Lange had to go out for a while this afternoon, and for the first time Anna came downstairs to my room to talk. I think she caught me watching her and that Fritz Bernhardt kissing in a corner when I looked up from the piano once. She let me know in so many words, all nicely put, that Major Bernhardt liked me and was sorry I was a prisoner. But since I was, he could make life a bit easier for me—or harder. When I asked why harder, she gave me a long, deep look, as if to ask, Don't you know why? But I can play it as innocent as an angel, and I think she was convinced that I didn't see anything. She smiled and rubbed my head and went back upstairs humming. So, a little goose and gander, but shit, why do *I* always have to be in the middle?

Friday, April 21, 1934

I feel like a juggler, tossing lots of balls in the air, not daring to drop even one, because then the act is over. Between Dieter Lange and my colonel, and Anna and Major Bernhardt, who seems to be here whenever Dieter Lange has to make a trip, I'm going crazy. The good thing is that we haven't had any parties in about a month. The camp is growing; more guards and officers are coming in, and maybe it was one of these who complained about hearing *Neger Musik*. My colonel is even stranger these days. Maybe things are falling apart, but I'd be one of the last to know. There's so much fucking going on around here, I don't see how anybody has time to be mad, unless the fuss is about fucking. At least that's what I gather from the news from other calfactors.

I've heard that at Buchenwald they have a slogan on their gates, too: it says: "Right Or Wrong, My Country!" You can have the motherfucker.

Sat., May 19, 1934

We had a party last night. There were no SA. The mood was quiet, so I played soft stuff. There wasn't much eating and not much dancing, either. The wives and girlfriends seemed to be as watchful and careful as the men. There wasn't that rise in the pitch of voices, and not many smiles. Kind of an evil atmosphere, where you want to be near the kitchen door when all hell breaks loose. The weather has been good, although when it rains, it's cold. But the weather doesn't make any difference; the details still march in and out, and of course the prisoners still do roll call in the Appellplatz, ankle-deep in mud. This keeps the doctors and medical aides busy in the Infirmary. I have not been sent for by Friedrich. From what I hear, he and all the SA are in some kind of trouble. Serious trouble. I hope Friedrich isn't hurt by it.

Diary, have I told you about Hitler's speeches? Wherever you are, you have to stop and listen. In the camp there are loudspeakers hooked up and whenever he speaks, everyone crowds outside, pressing against the fences and walls, climbing on rooftops to listen. There are prisoners who cheer when he's finished, and they mean it. Others cheer or make noise because they know they'd better.

A few of the Bible students work out here because the officers would rather have them as calfactors instead of the Reds or Greens. I feel very blue today. With every letter I try to smuggle out, my hopes rise. Then nothing happens and they sink. The colonel was my best hope, and his silence means bad news. I look at Dieter Lange as a burden I have to handle with care. Oh, he got promoted to major. I forgot to write that. Anna was happy. They had champagne and whooped and hollered in bed, but later while she was asleep, he came downstairs, something he'd never done before. He was drunk. My playing, just as he planned, sweetened the way to his promotion. What would have happened if I hadn't been here?

There's a calfactor named Gitzig who works down the street in Major Bernhardt's house. It's Gitzig who says things are going to get worse and that we should start hiding stuff, like cans of food and cigarettes and even old clothes and matches. He's growing potatoes and turnips in the Bernhardt flower bed, hiding them among the flowers so the Bernhardts won't know. Also, he said, we should not throw away old radios or radio parts. He wanted to know if I was a *Mischling*. I told him no, I was not part German, I was all American. He said many Americans liked Hitler, so why was I in Dachau, was I a "race defiler," fucking Aryan *Frauleins*, or *ein Homosexuell*, fucking Aryan *Seigfrieds*, or really *ein Kriminal*? Did I play the *Neger Musik*

36

he'd heard about? He asks one question after another, without waiting for a single answer. Dear God, dear diary, do you know I have been here almost one year?

Saturday, June 2, 1934

Some carving going on for sure. This morning Dieter Lange and a bunch of his friends sat around drinking coffee and schnapps, laughing and shouting. The SA cannot wear uniforms this month. I don't know what it means, but if Dieter Lange is happy about it, it's bad for Friedrich. Haven't heard from him anyway. Know Dieter Lange didn't like taking orders from him that sent him away more often than he wanted to go. No group is as loyal to the Third Reich, they said, as the *Schutz-Staffel*, the SS. The *Sturm-Abteillungen*, the SA, had no discipline, was not devoted. And the army, well, Hitler would take care of those fucking Prussians. I could feel that they were talking themselves up on some *Horst Wessel*, and sure enough, in a couple of hours Dieter Lange called me up and had me play some of those goddamn patriotic and marching numbers while they tried to sing—not a one could carry a tune.

Wednesday, June 20, 1934

When Dieter Lange is away and I stay in the back of the canteen at night and work in the front during the day, I see all the prisoners going and coming, coming and going, always marching, always in step. We do roll call mornings and evenings in the Appellplatz, facing the administration building *(Wirtschaftsgebaude)* where there's also the kitchen and the laundry. (Dieter Lange's trying to get me excused from the roll calls.) The prisoners with their metal bowls march to get their food and march away. They march to details and back from them. They march to build the walls and to dig out the moat. They march to the garden, to the swamps, to the pigsty, to the quarry. They are in step when they push or pull wagons. Only when the work is done, the roll call over, can they sit on benches outside the blocks.

Even so, things go on underneath all the German discipline: money's passed, there's bartering; if you know the right guards you can get almost anything, even sex. Dieter Lange has apparently made arrangements for some women from town to be slipped in. At night the shadows are filled with men shifting and sliding along the blocks to get to the women and to some of the Pinks who are, like me, literally working their asses off to stay alive. I get a lot of propositions—I'm a pretty rare piece here—but they aren't serious ones. Everyone seems to know that I am Major Lange's *Neger,* like in the slavery days (and after, I suppose), when So-and-So was was Mr. So-and-So's nigger. I've heard about that. If you belonged to the right white man, you could kill and the killing would be ignored. You just had to belong—to the right someone. It's the way the Nazis work, too. You have to belong or you wind up in trouble in Dachau. So I guess I do belong to Dieter Lange, but in some ways he belongs to me. He's a busy man and I've learned how to make him reach *the* major key quickly, make him groan and hammer my chest or back to stop bringing him *up* so quick and so good. But shit, I can't have that man romping and stomping in me when Annaliese got to get hers, too. If not, trouble. (I have to think for all *four* of us *all* the time, but she's sure found herself something in that Major Bernhardt.)

Sunday, June 24, 1934

I was in camp yesterday, in the canteen. I was blue, deep down blue, thinking about being here and wondering again if I'll ever get out. I felt like talking to God. I felt He was near and would talk back to me. I thought of church services back home, and singing and the raggedy old piano that Sister Grubbs beat so bad that music actually came out of it while her huge behind hung off the bench. People would get religion like lightning hit them, and they'd jump up happy, jigging in little circles, smiling, crying, and talking to God, and you could almost hear God asking questions because of the answers they always spoke. "Yes, Lord! My Jesus, *yes!*" Answers just laying out there on the air, Sister Grubbs, chin up like she was proud she'd brought God and the people together, playing softly, the congregation humming, not knowing whether to go or stay, but their eyes sure glued to the people touched by the Spirit (including the Loas, the charms, and curses).

In the corner of my room in the canteen I got down on my knees. Before I could start to pray, I began to cry, cried like someone had come along with a big scraper and just jooged it into my soul and dug out all the evil. I must've cried about an hour before I could think of any words. Then I prayed another hour, but that didn't help, either. So I went down to 26, the *Priesterblock*, hoping to talk to one of them. The priests and ministers and Bible students try to put the best face on everything, so it isn't bad to be around them except when the guards have it in for them.

A young man, white as fatback, lean as the first shadow, came out of the block. He saw me and stopped. In good English he said, "Hello, Brother." He gave me his hand and smiled. His hand was thin and long, like something still growing. He said he was Menno Becker and waited like I would know him. He smiled again. He was beautiful. He asked my name and I told him. He looked at my triangle, then into my eyes. "Do they treat you badly, Brother?" His voice was so soft and low that I guessed he had figured everything out just like that. My eyes grew water and I couldn't talk. "God loves you," he said. He took my elbow and we started to walk. Inmates walked up and down, down and up beside us, maybe trying to believe that walking was being free. He asked about America, if I had a family, what I did, how long I'd been here. When I answered with the emptiness of what my life was, recognizing its sound—like a bass drum being hit in a closed saloon—the tears came again. Again he said, "God loves you, Brother." I said that was hard to believe. He said Dachau and the other camps were a sign that the Lord was about to bring mankind to judgment. The Great War, the Depression, Mussolini, Hitler—they were all signs of His coming. Menno said God gave us the signs to give us a chance to repent, to find the Truth and the Faith. Up we walked and down we walked.

He worked in the Infirmary. (It's also called the *Revier.*) He'd learned English from a tutor because he'd wanted to go to America to work with the Brothers and Sisters there. He was named after the man who founded the Mennonite faith, he said. The Mennonites did not believe in slavery and had opposed it. He did not know how he'd become a Witness, but he was sure it had to do with most of his family being Mennonites. He said to me that as a musician, I should try whenever I could to make a joyful noise unto the Lord. "The Lord understands travail," he said, "how a man can be made to suffer. But if a man has music—although Witnesses do not use it—he should use it in the service of God." I asked if he was a minister and he said, "All Witnesses are ministers." Then he took my hands in his. My fingers relaxed; his fingers caressed mine.

I dreamed of Menno last night. He had long brown hair and a soft brown beard and a full mustache. He came near me and his breath smelled like magnolias. I woke up. I stared out at the camp, so silent its walls stabbed by lights, and thought about the dream. I decided that I loved Menno Becker, but there wasn't a damn thing I could do about it.

———

Mon., July 2, 1934

Between catching parts of radio broadcasts, overhearing Dieter Lange and Anna and especially Dieter Lange with his SS buddies, and exchanging news with the other calfactors, it seems that Hitler's man, Ernst Roehm, and Roehm's boyfriend were killed Saturday night in Munich. Gitzig says there were shots way out in the camp swamp Saturday night, too. A bunch of SA leaders were executed at Lichter-fede, and generals have been wiped away like snot, I heard Dieter Lange say. "Hundreds of people killed, leaving the SS in charge and completely loyal to Hitler, and Hitler totally in charge." I always thought he was anyway. Dieter Lange and his friends sang marching songs and toasted each other, Hitler, the SS, Roehm's death, and victory. Victory?

Sunday, July 22, 1934

I have not seen Menno Becker in a month. I can't ask too many questions, and when I am in the camp I can't hang around Block 26 or the Infirmary. But we have exchanged notes—some of them pretty hot—through Werner. Of course, we must destroy these.

Anna almost caught me writing in this diary. She has taken to walking softly about the house, so I loosened a couple of the steps on the stairway to my room; now they creak when anyone steps on them. I am very nervous when she comes down to talk. Suppose Dieter Lange started down, or the Gestapo man, Bernhardt? Anna *still* doesn't understand the way things work. She wanted to practice her English. She always wants to practice her English, since she thinks it will make her high-class. But if Bernhardt caught her down here, there'd be hell to pay. He'd go tougher on me than Dieter Lange, 'cause she could sweet-talk her way out with him. They ought to know I don't want any trouble. But they'd kick *my* ass anyway.

When I heard the creak on the stairs, I just managed to slip my sheets of paper behind the picture of Hitler that hangs on my wall. Then I started to go out and made believe she startled me. She said she had something for me that maybe I could read to her. That would be a good way to help her learn English, she said. She showed me a magazine. I said we should go upstairs where the light was better. The magazine was two years old: *International Literature.* It had a picture of Langston Hughes in it, and some of his poetry. It was printed in Russian, German, English, and French. Would I please read the English? Langston Hughes was the famous writer friend of my cowboy. He seems to have liked Russia, judging from the poems and what the magazine said about him. I hated Moscow. I wonder if Hughes is still in Russia, if I could write to him care of this magazine for help. . . . Of course, I had to try to explain the poems to Anna (not that I understood all of them), as well as the words used in them. She sat very near and paid close attention. When we were finished, I told her Dieter Lange would be angry to find such a magazine in his house, a magazine with "Revolution" appearing at least once on every page. But, I said, if she could bring me anything written in English, we could do much better with her lessons. (And maybe I could find out more about what was going on, even if it was too late to do anything about it.) Anything would be better than that "This is a table, this is a chair" shit.

Thursday, Sept. 27, 1934

Word about Prosecutor Winterberger. Looks like I struck out again. Winterberger's been replaced by Prosecutor Barnickel, and all the cases Winterberger brought against the SS (and the SA) have been dismissed. The SS can do anything it wishes, Dieter Lange said. Anything.

Saturday, November 11, 1934—Armistice Day

It seems that most of the inmates coming into camp right now are fruits. A few Reds and Greens, but mostly queers. "Filth," they're called. Even Dieter Lange calls us that. "Filth."

Tuesday, December 25, 1934

When Dieter Lange and Anna are out of the house, there's not much for me to do. When they are around, they don't care how good I do things, if the things I do look okay. Like playing the piano: you can make shit sound good without trying. Just throw in a lot of din-kles. Arpeggios and glissandos, my colonel called them. Drunks don't care. And I'm tired of playing for drunks. But I can hold out as long as I can play for myself. Like I did today. All day.

They went to Anna's folks for Christmas. Back day after tomorrow. Dieter Lange gave me a bottle of cologne, and Anna gave me a chicken to cook for my dinner, which I did, with stuffing. Of course, I helped myself to the best of Dieter Lange's liquor and wine stores.

About the playing: Dieter Lange thinks that practice makes me play better at parties, but, like his guests, he just likes the beat. He thinks that's the main thing about music, and that Negroes play it better than anyone else, because the beat is like tom-toms. What a dumbbell. Sometimes I ask myself, if this nightmare ended tomorrow, would I be able to make music, to play with a band or be good enough to play in a cabaret? Would I be any good at all?

Today the music started to come out slow. Blues and shuffle, sad stuff. I didn't want to play that. I moved to some faster stuff, but that only sounded frantic and scared, which is how I am most of the time. But I wanted to remember the good times and to hope that this situation won't last much longer. I think I was listening, for the first time, to the echo of the church in my music. Had it always been there, the heavy low-down weeping spiritual for funerals, the happy, ripping sanctified church beat that bounced along all by itself? I let myself out on "Joy to the World," and threw in extra "joys" wherever I found space. And the chicken was cooking and smelling through the house. I filled up my glass again with some Cliquot. Why not "Jingle Bells"? Then I got into the melody of "Joy" with the harmonics of "Jingle." You always hear other music in the music you're playing. I just joyed and jingled up a storm. Let the champagne get warm, too, but Dieter Lange has plenty of it. And the chicken sure was smelling good, man. . . . Chicken. Dieter Lange was really looking over the chickens that came in last month. He told me so. I said to myself that I'd better study this war some more, otherwise Dieter Lange would have my ass right over there in the camp. If he found a better ass than mine. But Anna would say no. She wanted to learn English. Maybe I could even give her more time to be with Bernhardt—if she liked my cooking—and I was sure going to leave them some of my roast chicken with stuffing and gravy. Sir! Play the piano, sing a little, give English lessons, turn a trick, and cook. Shit, The Cliff would be indispensable.

All this time I was bruising the board, matching keys and jumping from one number into another, and I started to find secret places between, before, and after notes and chords. I started a tune with harmonics instead of doing melody followed by the ad-lib, and I thought listeners should be able to track the tune without the melody, just by the harmonics. I felt good when I got up to check the chicken and get myself another bottle. I wondered what those poor bastards over in the camp were eating.

It was getting dark. I saw The Cliff ease outside and start walking into town. Everybody'd be inside having Christmas dinner. No one would see me. Walk clear to Switzerland, into the Alps with the snow on top of them. I could do that if I was white, like that snow up there, just walk until someone asked for my papers. Maybe no one would. I sat down again and discovered sounds between sounds that I'd never played before, because I'd never thought about listening to them. It was like discovering that within a forest the trees had branches and limbs and leaves and roots, and the leaves had veins and the roots had hairs. I played around with some quarter notes, backing the pedal and ending runs up instead of down, so they sounded like questions instead of answers. I put a little stuff on some notes, stretched and bent the tones of some, and squeezed others. I braked, cutting off timbre, and the beat, the rhythm, was there. It has to be, but I found that it could be in no sound as well as sound. I played so long that the chicken got cold, but I think I found something. I know Dieter Lange and his gang won't like it. For me it is a precious fountain. A Christmas tree. A Merry Christmas.

Wed., Dec. 26, 1934

I had this dream when I went to sleep: I had finished my dinner. I was high and feeling very good. I put on every sweater I could find, then put on one of Annaliese's dresses, her heavy jacket, and her hat. I pulled on her everyday overshoes. I stuck bread and sausages and cheese into every pocket. Then I left the house. The road was empty and everything was white with snow and ice. I tried to stay in the shadows. My breath curled out in white balloons. My steps made crunching, squeaking noises. With each sound, a light in a window went out. And, as I passed each streetlight, it, too, went out. Light was always just ahead of me; darkness lay behind me. I smelled myself as I walked. I smelled of Anna's perfume, and I walked like a woman. I felt silk things move and slide on my body, even though I didn't remember putting them on.

The road runs into Dachau, and in my dream I knew I had to keep veering to the west to avoid it, and also Munich or other, smaller towns. I kept walking, and the lights kept going out behind me until, down past where all the ss homes were, there remained one great, bright light, and standing directly under it was a man in a uniform. He was a huge man and the whitest person I'd ever seen. He stood with his hands on his hips and his legs very wide apart. He carried a great sack between his legs; his pants bulged with it. The white circle armband seemed three times the normal size, but there was no swastika in it. I wanted to turn back into the darkness, but I couldn't; the darkness seemed a living force. Then I found myself slipping on the snow, slipping as though it had turned to ice, and I was heading right toward the man. He didn't move. If he had a face, I couldn't see it; there was just a whiteness, very dull and very bright at the same time. The dream ended there.

Friday, December 29, 1934

This morning, about eleven, Dieter Lange came home, stomping and hollering and banging around in that nasty, loud way he sometimes has. "CLEEF! CLEEF!" Scared the shit out of me. Anna looked at him as though he'd gone clear crazy. What it was all about was this: there was a special representative from the *Rote Hilfe* who was asking for me. Dieter Lange was hot on the drive back to the camp.

As soon as we got inside the guardhouse, I saw this tall, slender, cold-faced man. He was very well-dressed, and I could see that he was not at all afraid of the guards. They were walking around on eggshells. They were not joking, laughing, farting, or running around goosing each other. And they weren't beating up the few new prisoners who'd just come in, either; they just led them into another room. The man looked like a Prussian faggot; you never knew they were, though, until they dropped their pants or asked you to drop yours. He said he wanted a private office, and in one minute they led us up the stairs. I could feel Dieter Lange's eyes burning into my back. Could it be he was afraid of losing me? That made me feel good for a minute. The office overlooked the Appellplatz, and I could see the blocks all in a row to my left, and the *Wirtschaftsgebaude*, the kitchen and laundry and storerooms on my right. I could see the guards and inmates bending against the cold, raw wind that blew through the camp streets.

The man told me to sit down. He seemed to be looking for things in the craziest places—inside the lights, behind a picture of Hitler, under a table. He finally straightened up and told me he was Count Walther von Hausberger, which didn't mean a damn thing to me. He had received word, he said, a few months ago from a friend who'd been stationed here. The count sat down and held his hands as though he had a piano in front of him. He moved his fingers, lifted his hands neatly, as if playing in concert, and raised his eyebrows, like he was asking a question. I nodded, yes. He'd heard from my colonel. Then he got up and dug a pencil and a small pad of paper out of a pocket. There was writing in English on the paper: The names of anyone in the U.S. or outside Germany who may assist in getting you out. While I thought, he talked. "Your German is quite good. But let's speak English. They're treating you well enough? I understand that you're assigned to an officer's quarters. Is there anything we can send you that's allowed under the rules?" I told him I wanted to know the length of my sentence. He shrugged and said he didn't know and no one else seemed to know, either. I was writing: Mr. Samuel Wooding, New York City. Mr. Langston Hughes, New York City. Francois Moreau, Pathe Studios and Polydor Studios, Paris. Carlos Bustamente, Parlaphone Studios, Madrid. Malcolm Bradford III, the U.S. Embassy, Berlin. Ada Smith, Paris. Mr. Paul Robeson, New York City. President Franklin D. Roosevelt, Washington, DC. I gave him the list. I expected his sad little smile. "You have no better addresses?" I told him I didn't. He said that Malcolm was no longer in Germany. He sighed as he folded up the list. "We will have to do what we can from Germany," he said, if he could not contact the other people on the list. He would even, he said, through the American Red Cross, try to contact the President, but he didn't think he could. I asked him for the paper and pencil. I asked about the colonel, and he dragged a finger across his throat. Then we went downstairs. Dieter Lange was still looking evil, but not as much as before, once he saw our faces. He made me stay in the guardroom until the count left. Then he made me walk back to the house through the wind, slush, and snow.

But I knew the house would be warm as the blocks were not, because I took care of the stoves, brought in the wood and coal for them.

January 24, 1935

Major and Frau Lange (and me) are in a new, bigger house. It took a little while for it to come through after his promotion. The house is farther away from camp and so a little closer to Dachau —by two or three hundred feet. The cellar stairs don't creak, but I will make them. The cellar is a great big space, about half of which Dieter Lange has blocked off with heavy wire and filled with shelves and storing cabinets. He keeps this space locked and carries the key with him. Even Anna doesn't have one. They have had arguments about this arrangement. In the other house, things were stored everywhere—in the pantry, cabinets, the attic, in their bedroom under the bed, in china closets and armoires. Not even a can of turnips was ever stored in my old room, which was small to begin with, and I was grateful for that because they'd never run in looking for things and maybe find you, old diary, pushing out Adolph's face. Dieter Lange still stores things in the attic, which is larger, but I think mostly clothes and records and account books, stuff like that. The cellar now looks like one great big store, except for a huge new coal bin. In my room, which I think was once the old coal bin, there are plenty of hiding places besides the big picture of Hitler. There are dozens of spaces in the ceiling of the cellar, between the supports and behind the great furnace pipes. Nice and warm down here, and the smell of the hams and sausages that hang in a corner of the storage space is comforting.

Upstairs the piano is in a room that is larger, but then the kitchen, living room, sitting room, and dining room are larger, too. We are still moving things (I've helped Anna with the color schemes), so we haven't had a party yet. I don't think we will have as many now. Dieter Lange was explaining to Anna that the higher you move up in rank, the stuffier the officers and their wives become, because they don't want to take the chance of ruining a good thing, so they become more and more the keepers of Hitler's ideals. Dieter Lange is going to have to be very careful about having me play *Neger Musik.* Looks like foxtrot and croontune time. Now I'll be able to explore that tree I found on Christmas day, the one with all the bright new music on it.

Monday, March 18, 1935

Werner came into the canteen this morning. I sold him some Drummers. (They came from Dieter Lange's storage, so he gets the money.) I also gave him some of my own cigarettes. Smoking is not supposed to be good for Germans now, the Nazis say, but they smoke anyway. "German women do not smoke" is a slogan no woman around here pays any attention to. Anna smokes like a furnace. (We are now working from *Uncle Tom's Cabin,* which she got in both German and English.) Werner says bad business is up. Everyone outside now has to own an employment book. Conscription has started. Everyone has to do service in the army. They want to build up twelve army corps, thirty-six divisions. Unemployed people are being assigned to jobs the government thinks are important to the Reich. Whole gangs of men have been assigned to work on the new *Autobahns* the Nazis are building from the middle of Germany to the borders of other countries.

Werner said he'd been waiting for me to show up at the canteen. I told him I'd been helping Dieter Lange move into the new house. Also, to keep from being sent to the blocks, I was doing a lot of fancy cooking for him and Annaliese. Smart, he said, and then told me Menno Becker was looking for me. He wasn't busy just now, Werner said; he'd just left the *Revier.* He could tell Menno to come over, couldn't he? It wasn't too busy in the canteen. I hadn't had a customer since he came in. Werner kind of smiled. He said, "You scratch my back, I'll scratch yours. It's the only way to get around these bastards." He didn't wait for an answer; he left.

Five minutes later he returned with Menno. He pushed us both into the back. "Fifteen minutes," he said. "I'll take care of the front." For one of those fifteen minutes Menno and I just looked at each other; for the other fourteen we made love as quietly as we could. There was nothing to say. We just hurried. When we were finished,

Menno left quickly. Werner lingered. I felt he wanted something. I waited for him to ask for it. "Could you bring some *wurst* once in a while?"

Tuesday, March 19, 1935

Boy. Just thinking about yesterday gives me goose pimples. It was like we'd rehearsed meeting like that for a long time. And I know *I* had, but I didn't know he had, too. So, now the thing is to—no. Just stay calm, Cliff, cool as a cucumber, Cliff. Don't let The Cliff get excited and let things slip out of control. Wind up in the Bunker where that SS looney Eichmann is in charge. Easy, Clifford. You're thirty-five, more a stewing than a frying chicken. But Menno is so young, so strong. And loving. As fast as it was, I remember his touch, his gentleness, the smoothness of his movements. I could tell by these that he likes me, maybe even loves me, if such a thing can be in a place like this.

Annaliese and I are still working on *Uncle Tom's Cabin*. I've spent *so* much time explaining the colored talk to her. And Legree's talk, too. She doesn't seem to understand that people don't talk that way anymore. Thank God we're close to the end of the book. We just read the part where Uncle Tom dies. Anna cried. I have heard that most Germans cry when they get to this section. I don't know why. "Who—who—who shall separate us from the love of Christ?" says Tom, and right away, boo-hoo, boohoo, boohoo. Christ has given this damned place up.

Friday, April 27, 1935

Now they've gone and done it. Really closed down the Witnesses. They've been banned from all civil service jobs, and they're still arresting the hell out of them. Menno will have a lot more company. Spring is finally starting to come. Poor bastards over in the camp must be happy as hell. Anna hasn't been able to find any more *Negerbuchen* to cry over. With good weather she won't be bothering me quite so much. Thank you, Jesus.

Monday, May 27, 1935

"I don't mind being here after all," Gitzig said the other day when I slipped over to Bernhardt's house. "And neither should you."

It seems that only men with proven Aryan ancestry can go into the services, even if conscripted. As for homos, new laws passed in January, and about to be changed for the worse, are going to make things even harder. The SS magazine we see around the homes, *Das Schwarze Korps,* says we should be executed. Dieter Lange, too? And the others? Ha, ha.

"What's it like, being a queer?" Gitzig asked. "C'mon. I think you are. Is it better that way, better than pulling the pecker when there aren't any women around, or even if there are?" He asks questions like these just to be asking, I think, because he still doesn't seem to pay any attention to my answers. I was talking and he was blowing snot into a bowl of fresh tapioca in the icebox. I could tell he was pleased with himself. "Just wait until it gets warmer," he said, "and they start drinking iced tea and lemonade."

Gitzig looks like his name, sharp-faced, like a rat. "Your Frau Lange," he said. "What a patootie she is. I see her walking and I get a hard-on." He gave me a look. "You sure better be queer." He laughed and slapped me on the back. I told him I knew Bernhardt spent a lot of time away from home, even when he was on duty. How about *him,* Gitzig, and Frau Bernhardt? He laughed. "That bitch? She likes tapi-oca." Gitzig is a Green, and I believe it. Slicker than shit. "Listen, I'd rather fuck you than her, and I'd rather stay here a thousand years without a woman than screw a faggot." I told him time would tell, and that I'd never met a homosexual who would fuck him or let her-self be fucked by him, ugly as he was. And he jumped hot. Said I was the *blackest,* ugliest thing he'd *ever* seen, and then he started to cry. I noticed that he put the highest note on *blackest,* so I changed my spiel a little. I told him, not only had I never met a homosexual who would fuck him or let herself be fucked by him, ugly as he was, I'd never met one who would even *look* at anyone as *white* as he was. (It's true. Three summers, and two bitter winters, and Gitzig never changed colors. He is *white.*) Well, he didn't mean it and I didn't mean it. While he was crying, he blew some more snot into the tapioca, and we laughed. I've seen lots of men who didn't look as good as Gitzig (if you like rats), but I don't think the rest of the world has; a lot of people must have spent a lot of time telling Gitzig he looks like the ass-end of a snake. Maybe that's what had made him a Green.

Gitzig is from Leipzig. He was, he said, a confidence man, a *Schwindler.* "In a city like Leipzig," he said, "where everyone is or thinks he is so cultured, with all that history, it was easy. First, there are all the students, people searching for some truth in the universe. Small potatoes. Last resort, because students never have much of anything. Then there are the artists—the writers, painters, musicians and the like—most of them not better off than the students. Finally, there are the concert halls, the patrons, the money here, the money there, some of it honest, most of it crooked. There were a lot of patrons. Of the *Arts,*" he said, and I gathered that he was making fun of the whole business. "I did very well with them. I was always getting money out of them for some struggling artist who'd been wounded in the war and who, wounded or not, didn't even exist. I was a friend of these explosions of talent that would go unheard, unseen. What are friends for? Most of these patrons were old women. Do you have any idea how demanding old women can be of younger men, especially if the old women have money? Of course you don't. But let me tell you, Pepperidge—what kind of name is that for a black?—they go through friends of artists and sometimes the artists—phoney, naturally—like seaweed through a duck. And you have to invest so much in clothes, luncheons, dinners, proper talk—no fucks, no shits—not like we talk now, and, my friend, more often than you can imagine, sticking your dick into the next thing to a grave about to be filled."

Gitzig seemed proud of whatever wool he'd pulled over anyone, but it sounded like he'd paid a pretty good price, because here he is. "I also leased concert halls and re-leased them at twice the price," he said. "But the best thing for me was theater and concert hall tickets. I had a printer who made up duplicates of concert hall and theater tickets. Counterfeit tickets. This was the racket that got me, but I could have bought my way out if not for these fucking Nazis. The mayor and the chief of police of Leipzig arguing over the same seat.

What fucking luck! Only the second time out on this thing. Shit, Pepperidge, I was almost as famous as the other Leipzigers, or people who'd visited it, Bach, Wagner, Schumann, Mendelssohn, Goethe, Schiller, Napoleon, and Blucher."

But how did he manage to get assigned to Bernhardt? "I'm good with everything except the looks. Numbers and money especially. I'm as good with those as you are with your ass. You have to have something to help you through this shit, and all these officers have their own rackets going. They don't have to pretend too much. Open season, and he knows I can help him on the sneak." The problem is, though, and Gitzig doesn't seem to know it, that once they discover you're good at something here, they want to keep you forever. I asked him what racket Bernhardt had, and Gitzig said he wasn't sure yet. "He works for Goering. Art, I think. You know, paintings and sculptures, shit like that. And coupon books. Lange's got a good racket with the camp canteens. Wish Bernhardt had that. Got a cigarette?"

Thursday, June 6, 1935

I hear them talking about Italy and Selassie and Mussolini and war. They seem to want something like this to happen, maybe because the same old thing goes on here day and night, night and day. But right now I'm getting far away from here, even out of Germany. Anna has found another book. I like this one. I don't know where she got it. It's in English. The few books that are in the canteen are all in German—the ones that aren't banned. I have been in Haiti lately because we're reading something called *Babouk,* about the slave trade and slavery. Maybe the Nazis don't think a book like this can do any harm. This Babouk reminds me of some of those tough guys back home. He's one bad jigaboo. Whipped not only the French, but those dicty *passé blancs* like we have back in Louisiana. Everything Napoleon sent, Babouk cut down, like a machete going through cane. I'd never heard about what happened in Haiti before. Today Anna stopped reading to ask me, after all this time, what I'd done to be sent here.

"I can't imagine you a criminal," she said. She waited for me to speak.

"I sold cocaine," I told her.

"That's all?" she asked.

I said it was.

"That's what Dieter said."

Why wouldn't he? We had long ago agreed on that.

"He said he didn't know how long your sentence was. That's awful."

I said that was just like Uncle Tom, but his sentence turned out to be for life. Anna just looked at me, as if making some awful connection.

She made me nervous just sitting there with the sun coming into the kitchen through the window behind her, probably thinking all kinds of things that missed the boat by a mile.

"But, you're so . . . your playing is so *sweet,*" she said and then sighed. "You must have had German girlfriends, no? How could you not have, a gentle person like yourself, Cleeford?"

I nodded. I had a great urge right then to tell her how very much I want to get out of here, how, if she would, she might help me. But there were certain things in her expression that made me afraid, and certain things I know about her that also stopped me. She is just a farm girl, slowly going to fat, who believes in the rules and in the people in charge; she believes in Dieter Lange and in Bernhardt. It's not a question of getting out with her help; it is a question of staying out of the blocks until something or someone far more important than Annaliese gets me away from here altogether. What I have to do is not get on her nerves. Same with Dieter Lange or anyone else who has the power to send me over there. So I said nothing. I thought of cooking smothered pork chops down-home style for dinner. Anna likes those. There are two kilos of pork chops in the icebox right now.

Tues., June 25, 1935

We had a midsummer party last Friday night. Fewer people than before. I didn't play any up-tempo stuff, just the slow jazz and every now and then Debussy. ("The windows will be open, Cleef, and the doors, so play nice slow jazz and a little classical. This has to be

classy, you know, not like the parties we had at the other place,"
Dieter Lange had said.) I also played some of the soft things that
had been hanging on racks in my head. It was a nice night, with the
sky clear and the moon out. I played "Stardust," "After You've Gone,"
"She's Funny That Way," "You Made Me Love You," "I Ain't Got
Nobody," "Basin Street Blues," "Embraceable You," and did the vocal
on some. My own things had no title. The women were all wearing
sharp-smelling perfume, a lot of gardenia. Seems like that's all they
have around here.

Yesterday and today I had to go to the canteen. Details marching
and singing; details working, raising dust, stinking of sweat and
worse. I slipped by the Infirmary but didn't find Menno, and no one
knew where he was. Werner heard I was in and came by the canteen.
I gave him the soap, cigarettes, and can of fruit I'd brought inside my
clothes. It's easier to smuggle goods in the winter because you wear
more things. Werner thanked me and asked how I was doing. He
asked if I remembered some of the things he'd said before and I said
yes, but I wasn't sure what he meant.

"Well, then," he said. "What do you hear over there? What do
those shit ss people talk about?"

I said, "Ethiopia and the Italians and war."

"We know that. I mean, things about *this* place. What is your
friend Gitzig up to besides hiding things and growing things and
saving radio parts? C'mon, think."

I told him about Bernhardt's connection to Goering. He said that
was good information, very good, but maybe for later. I said they
wanted to kill all the queers and he laughed.

"What they used to call the German Disease. Maybe also the
British Disease? And maybe, too, American?" He patted me on the
back. "It's all right. A man can't help what he is. He just makes the
best of it, like anyone else." He told me that, since he and the others
needed me out there, they'd take care of anyone Dieter Lange
seemed to be interested in over here. He didn't think, though, I had
real worries. After all, I was a rare bird, and while Dieter Lange
might have a fling or two—just as I was having with Menno
Becker—it wouldn't mean that I was out. "Don't worry," he said.

"We *organisieren,* things will work out; we don't, *kaput.*" Werner had heard nothing about his own sentence and nothing from his family. He seemed resigned to this but not to anything else.

Outside, the labor details trooped by, singing or calling cadence. The guards shouted and cursed. We watched as two large vans pulled up on the Appellplatz in front of the *Wirtschaftsgebaude.* Guards descended upon the vans, attacking the men who were tumbling out like store dummies. The men got themselves up and together in time to ward off the tornado of blows the guards were raining upon them. We heard the guards shouting: "Shits!" "Dogs!" "Turds!" "Pigs!" They shoved and kicked the men toward the steps. I could see in the prisoners' faces terror and total disbelief. The details of laborers still marched by singing or shouting "Left, right, left, right."

"It's getting worse," Werner said.

"Yes, of course. It has to get worse. I've heard there are more than 200,000 citizens in the camps already. Where will they stop?"

We watched in silence. The canteen was empty at that hour, which is why Dieter Lange sent me, to sweep up and stock the sad-assed shelves with his goods so he could rake in some of the moolah. Today what I brought is for Werner. On the next trip there will be some American cigarettes: Lucky Strikes in their green package with the red bull's-eye circle. I don't know where they came from, but the prisoners paid a lot for them. Dieter Lange usually sends them over, with other expensive stuff, when the men get their mail—the packages and letters with checks or reichsmarks. There was even wine or cognac for the rich ones whose families sent lots of money.

Werner sighed. Then he asked me if there wasn't any way I could get out of this. I told him that I was waiting to hear from Count von Hausberger. He wanted to know who that was. I told him a friend of Colonel Friedrich. "The SA colonel," he said. He drew his finger across his throat—exactly the same way the count had—and said, "Well, I would not count" (and here he laughed) "on this one, understand?"

Then, just at that moment, we heard the door open with a bang and swing back with a lesser bang. Werner shouted at me, spit flying out of his mouth, his thick arm flung backward, *"Neger! Neger!*

What's that you say?" And as he hit me, as I went down, I saw the look on his face. It sure didn't go with what he was doing to me. So I lay on the floor and looked up at him instead of at the person who came toward us with footsteps that sounded like thunder chasing thunder.

It was Karlsohn, a man I've seen from a distance, but whose reputation preceded him like wind before a storm. He was a bad man—of all the ss in Dachau, he was supposed to be the toughest. Karlsohn looked down at me and spat. "Lange's *Neger*, huh?" Werner snapped to attention, and *"Ja, ja, ja's"* were coming from him like machine-gun bullets. "Keep him in line or Lange or no Lange, I'll kill the *schmutzig Neger*, understand?" More *"Ja's"* from Werner. Karlsohn went behind the counter and helped himself to the remaining three packs of cigarettes. They were Drummers, so there was no great loss. I noticed this just before Karlsohn gave me a kick right in the ass. I felt it swelling as he turned, clapped Werner on the shoulder, and thundered back out of the canteen while I thought to myself, That's the easiest 45 cents that sonofabitch probably ever made in his life. Werner stood stiff and straight as a pine tree until the door swung shut.

He didn't look at me as he bent to help me up. "You're all right?" I told him yes. "You're sure?" I wriggled out of his grip and told him again that I was all right. "You understand why?" I told him I did, but I couldn't help thinking that this was not the same man who had helped me that first day. Werner started to leave, but stopped. "You're sure you're all right? Shall I try to find Becker for you?"

I didn't answer. I put something else in the space Karlsohn had made on the cigarette shelf and picked up the broom again. I glanced out the window. The vans had pulled away. The 'Platz was sizzling in the June sun, and I thought about the new men who would soon be knocked and pushed and kicked into the heat, wearing their lumpy, wrinkled gray uniforms. I heard the door open and close softly behind Werner, and I understood that some new chord changes had developed in the music. The Cliff has learned another lesson.

Thursday, July 4, 1935

Back in camp today. Putting up new shelves because Dieter Lange is supposed to be bringing back more goods from his recent trip to Frankfurt. Werner slipped in, smiling. He slapped me on the back and asked how I felt. I kept working and didn't say anything. "Still mad, eh? Well, Pepperidge, let me tell you how things are changing around here: you know the SS is in complete charge now, under Himmler. No more pretending. The Nazis are going to take us to war. They are going to make Europe weep for beating us in the last war. Europe humiliated us. Shit, every nation that loses a war is humiliated. And it's not only the Nazis. No rump party anywhere ever turned over a country without help, and the help usually comes from people who care more for profit than people or politics. Understand?"

I said I did. Of course, we were both watching the windows and the door.

"Why do you suppose they're starting to fix up those ammunition factories over there? Why do you suppose people like me were the very first ones in Dachau and now in the other camps? People like you and the Greens were just the frosting on the cake. It was us they had to shut up first, understand? So, yes, the guards were always rough and nasty and crude and cruel. Last month, did you hear? Didn't I tell you? Five prisoners were shot dead while trying to escape, *Auf der Flucht erschossen.* More and more each month. Out in the swamp. Why do you suppose they're going to enlarge the SS barracks out there? Hohenberg—you know Hohenberg in the Labor Office? No? It's simple, Pepperidge. More prisoners, more guards, but no jail ever has more guards than prisoners, so they must control them; they do that through—"

"Fear," I said. He was surprised.

"So you do understand. And you know it's going to get worse." He sighed. "I'm sorry I hit you, but I'd do it again. And again. And again. Better me than Karlsohn or any of those other bastards. So, in a backward way, we resist. I brought you something." From under his shirt he whipped out a brand new pair of BVDs. "Very soon, while you are still working, someone from the Infirmary is coming to see you," he said. Oh, God, I thought, *Menno.* He saw the look on my face and told me it was not Menno. Menno is all right, he told me, but he's not coming today. "It's hard with those Bible students. They work them to death. But the next time you come in we'll try to—you know. No, this man's name is Nyassa and he is important to your Menno, for he's a doctor scientist who also is a black man."

Werner left and I returned to the shelves. Then I heard the door open and glanced over my shoulder at the man coming toward me. I looked first at his triangle. It was one I hadn't seen a lot, a black triangle. He was a *Mischling,* the color of a camel-hair coat, and his hair had been freshly cut. Maybe he'd been in camp a week. He stopped when he saw me. *"Ach,"* he said. He spoke in German. "So, you are the man Werner spoke about. Pepperidge, *ja? Amerikan, ja?"* He seemed high-falutin' to me, looking at my green triangle, looking at me. I gave him a cigarette and we talked. He liked it that I spoke German. He was a "race defiler," married to a German woman, as his father, from Tanganyika, had been. He was a biologist, he said, and he had worked with the famous Dr. Ernest Just from Howard University in America; did I know of him or his work? They had worked together in Italy and in Germany. Dr. Just liked Europe, Nyassa said, but had to return to America. Nyassa smiled when he said Werner had told him that I played jazz music on the piano. "I like jazz music," he said in English.

———

Monday, July 29, 1935

In the canteen today I met this Hohenberg from the Labor Office. He's one of the inmates who oversees who gets which jobs and which blocks are assigned to the big details. I guess he is an important man, so it's wise to stay on his good side. He was with Werner and some other barracks bosses. I worked on the stock while one or two watched the windows so they could see who was coming. Hohenberg was telling a story.

They all talk more about sex in the summer than in winter. I guess the juices flow faster when it's hot. "Well," he said. "I'm happy

I did so much fucking before I got here." Hohenberg is a Red.
We waited for him to continue. "I did a lot and I don't mind telling
you about it, as a matter of history, if you will, not entertainment.
Rather like a study, though of course, there was pleasure, too, and
some obligation, for these women, all of them, were not whores, you
know, stick it in and bump-da-bump after you've paid your money.
Then off you go. My first was a lass, quite nice in the ass, who came
from Alsace. She was part French, part German. Leading up to it,
she spoke French; when we did it, she groaned in German. Nothing
fancy there, let me tell you. Pure bread and butter and a cup of hot
coffee. Straight fucking. She was one of my father's secretaries. I
think he was fucking her, too. I didn't ask, though. That was one of
the nice things about being the socialist son of a small manufacturer.
What? Ball bearings. Yes, and if you don't think they're important,
you're a fool. What would roll without them for long? So, she was
my first, and I was twelve. Cute. Already able to quote Hegel and
Marx and some of the others. Precocious. I traveled with my father
on business all over Europe. He knew quite a few ladies and they in
turn knew other, younger ladies. Men don't teach men how to fuck."
(He's sure right about *that*, I said to myself.)

"It's the ladies who teach you how to do it. Do you want to know
how come I did so much fucking? My prick would not go down
most times. It just didn't. It hurt, but once I was fucking it was all
right. I had to tell my father. He thought I was lucky and wished he
had the same condition. He took me to doctors. They called it satyr-
iasis. You know, like a satyr, half man and half goat. Just the sight
of a decent-looking woman would send the thing quivering to
attention. If I'd been raised differently, I probably would have been
a rapist. What? *Now?* Oh, God, no." (And a good thing, too, I
thought.) "Since being here I've been beaten on the prick so much
that the poor thing is even afraid to piss sometimes. But I'm not
sorry; I've had more than my share. Italians, Greeks, French, Germans, Dutch and Irish, Danish and Polish, Swedish, Norwegian,
and Indian, Spanish and Algerian, American and Brazilian,
Tanganyikan—yes, black, like Pepperidge there—and Belgian,
Russian and Czechoslovakian; Catholic, Protestant, Jewish, Moslem,

Hindu . . . I can't remember whatever else. Those are the main ones."
Someone said he thought Hohenberg was supposed to have been out
organizing strikes. "That, too," he said. "But one didn't organize
twenty-four hours a day." He stopped to take a cigarette from one of
the others. "All men," he said, inhaling deeply and blowing out the
smoke in a straight blue stream, "wonder what it'd be like to fuck
this kind of woman or that kind of woman, to have this kind of *puss*,
but I tell you, God is great.

"All men are built the same and so are the women. I found more
socialism, more fundamental democracy, in fucking than I found in
all the radical philosophies. Color, Pepperidge" (here he raised his
voice and looked at me, and so did everyone else), "made no difference whatsoever. There were Catholic women, and still are, I
suppose, who felt that the only sin in fucking was to get fucked
where you're not supposed to before marriage. Any place else is okay.
And after marriage even that's okay, and with a certain passion that
Eskimos must have when they get to the tropics, understand?"
(I'm not as old as Hohenberg, but I can say that lovers I had who
were Protestants were not as vicious as Catholics. I don't know why.)
We all laughed, but we were still watching the windows.

Then someone asked, in that voice they used back home when
asking such questions, "Which, Hohenberg, was the best?"

He said, "There is no such thing as best. I know you would like to
hear that the Jewish ladies are best, but that's not so, anymore than
African ladies or Spanish ladies are best, or any other ladies. You were
not listening to me. Fucking is basic. It is the one thing the richest
and the poorest can do alike, the blackest and the whitest. The prick
goes, or should go, in the same place and is received by that place.
Do you know of people who fuck in the armpits? Tell me these people.
Where do they live? What are they called?" *(Amen,* I thought, *Amen.)*
"You would like to hear that black ladies are best? There were for me
differences, but that did not make the ladies better or best, and I tell
you that, blessed or cursed with my affliction, I searched with utmost
diligence for the *puss* that would lay low that ailing prick of mine.
More than the ladies, I remember the places where I had them—
the country beside haystacks, in the Grünewald, a Schrebgarten,

Freienwald" (he was, then, I thought, from Berlin), "beside Lake
Como, in the sweet grass of the Transylvanian Alps, the plaster-and-
fresh-croissant smell of a room in the Latin Quarter of Paris, the
wind-squeezed compartment of the Milan-Berlin Express, the Bois
de Boulogne—oh, I remember the places."

I could tell they were getting bored with him because he wasn't
really talking about fucking, so they started to leave, slipping out the
door one at a time or in twos. Through the window I could see that
they walked differently outside than they had in here. I guess we all
did that. Then they were all gone, even Werner, and I was alone.

The next time I looked up, at the sound of the door opening,
Menno Becker was creeping across the floor. "I haven't been able to
get away," he said. I told him I didn't think he'd tried hard enough.
He said they'd been watching him very closely. I asked why, had they
caught him with someone else? He shook his head in very slow and
soft movements. "There're so many Witnesses coming in now, and all
this is such a shock. Someone has to talk to them. I talk and they
watch. They tell me if I'm not careful, I'll be in the Prisoner Company with a target painted on my back." He was motionless; the sun
came in through the windows and shone on his face. The light
seemed to gather right around him.

I kept on working. I told him I had met Nyassa, and he said he
was a nice man, but very sad, as he had a right to be. Menno worked
with him, since Nyassa had scientific training and he'd had none. Not
that Nyassa's training was like a real doctor's. I told him I'd missed
him, just told him right out. Hadn't Werner told him when I was in
the canteen? He said he could do nothing at those times. I told him
I was tired of hearing that, and what made him think his neck was
more precious than mine? And he stood right there, like a cow about
to be clubbed. Right then I felt I had the pat hand. It was almost like
playing in a joint when you knew everyone was feeling good enough
to get on the floor when you hit the chords for the opening of "Body
and Soul" or "Stardust." You *made* them get up and two-step, foxtrot,
or whatever. You had power over them.

All this time, from the corner of my eyes, I'd been watching the
windows. Nothing moving. "C'mere," I said, and I pulled him behind

the counter and into the room where I stayed and let him know
that I didn't give a damn just then about Karlsohn or anyone else.
The wooden building smelled of sap leaking out, and he smelled
of sweat, and the dust outside had its smell, and whatever was growing just beyond this prison had a smell, and we did it with those
sounds you think are quiet, but you remember them forever. And
once it was over, all the badness was suddenly gone. I lost that earlier
feeling that if Karlsohn had walked in, I'd have just kicked his ass
and thrown him out on the 'Platz. Menno was shaking, I was shaking and rushing him out, and there were no nice words between us,
nothing like the ease and wonderful sense of being so goddamn special that I'd last had with him. When the door closed behind Menno
I felt okay, I mean relieved and then, right away, I wanted to be with
him again.

Sunday, Aug. 11, 1935

Dieter Lange sent me to the camp today to push the stock
around. He just wanted me out of the way while he played one of his
wild games with Anna. They've been doing that lately, and I'm glad,
because it takes his mind off me. I've heard them running and jumping, whooping and hollering, screaming and laughing, and then it
gets quiet. I guess I've become like a piece of furniture. They never
used to carry on like that. Fat bitch.

In the camp, after looking through the canteen and seeing nothing to do, I took a stroll around. Oh, shit. I headed right for the
Infirmary. Menno wasn't there. Nyassa told me he was down at the
Priesterblock ministering to the new Witnesses. I sat down. Nyassa
looked sad. There weren't too many patients around. There never are
in summer. It's the winters that kill people. I asked how it was going
and he said all right, but his wife would have to divorce him. Kids?
He said no. It was tough enough in Germany for a black adult.
Why have kids go through that, too? Me? Not married, no kids,
I told him. Had I really been in Dachau three years, he wanted to
know. I knew why he was asking, of course. He could see himself in
here for three years or longer, too. He didn't know his sentence.

Then he started to talk fast, I mean up-tempo. He said he'd just written to his wife, telling her to go to America and wait until he got out. They all want to go to America. Me, too. I asked what made him think it would be better for him there than here. Told him that where I came from, if you even looked at a white woman, you'd be dancing at the end of a rope. He said he'd heard that, but didn't believe it. Why? he wanted to know. I said that's just the way things were. Wasn't he in jail for being black *and* marrying a German woman?

Ernest Just was involved with a German woman, he said, and would probably marry her and take her to America, Washington, DC. I said the man must be crazy. He said some people thought so, but he himself had found him to be a brilliant scientist. He was always struggling, though, to find money and places where he could do his work, which was difficult to do in America, but not so hard here. At least they did let him work right here in Germany at the Kaiser Wilhelm Institute, before he went to Naples. Nyassa was talking even faster, his eyes bucking bigger. And Just could have worked in France, too, if he'd wanted to, Dr. Nyassa said. "Brilliant!"

Man, he ran on with this Just, throwing out all this stuff—marine biologist, head of the department of physiology (or did he say psychology?), mostly working with worms, had reversed the sex of some worms (oh, yes?) in an experiment, made more chromosomes (?) in animals, reproduced the histological characteristics of human cancer cells (or did he say historical characteristics?). Then he asked me if I'd ever heard of a Dr. Domagk, but didn't wait for me to say no. This man had invented a miracle drug, Nyassa said, to kill bacteria and therefore infection.

"Hummm," I said.

Then he said it was called Protonsil, sulfanilamide. Domagk was the director of the I.G. Farben Research Institute, and Nyassa said he'd written to him for his help in getting out. I said I wished him good luck. What was his own work about, I asked, and he said it was cellular physiology (or philosophy?).

I didn't have one damned idea what he was talking about, but I could see that it made him feel better to talk about such things, so I sat there for an hour, thinking, Here are two darkies stuck in the middle of a cotton field, a concentration camp, and one is talking about all these ologies, and the other is hoping his officer is having a good time with his wife so he can go back where he lives and slip downstairs to his bed in the cellar and not be bothered. Didn't neither one of us say anything about how strange it was for us to be here. When I got up to go, the glaze went out of his eyes and he suddenly started talking like a normal person. He asked me to tell him about jazz music, how it was played, how it felt to play it. He sounded just like white folks. I sat back down and I asked if he'd ever gone back to his father's home in Tanganyika, and he said he had not, that he was sure he'd find it too primitive for him, but he liked jazz music because it was American. I said it wasn't like any other music, because it was always changing. Not like playing Bach, I said. But is it fun playing? he wanted to know. I said it sometimes wasn't.

He smiled when I spoke. My German was street German, Berlin Alexanderplatz German, and I guess that's why he smiled so much when I talked. Then he wanted to know if I knew Bessie and Jelly Roll, or Duke and Louis and Sidney, and I told him I'd met them, of course, and then went into Mr. Wooding and how I came to Europe with him and stayed, and now wished I hadn't. He excused himself and came back with some "medicinal brandy," he called it, and I said it was good for the Dachau Blues. Then I told him about this music running around in my head, new sounds, and then he said all this reminded him of music by an Austrian named Schoenberg, who developed a 12-tone scale. He wasn't blue anymore. Nyassa poured some more "medicine," and we just sat there, looking out the window at the Appellplatz.

Nyassa asked me about my crime. He said real quick that he'd never known criminals until he came here and that I didn't seem to be like the rest of them. I stroked my face with my finger and said "Black." Then I got up and left.

While I was walking across the 'Platz, through the *Jourhaus* gate and through the section where they were rebuilding the ammunition factory, and down the street to the officers' quarters, I wondered, maybe for the first time with my dumb ass, if Malcolm would have done what he did to me if I'd been white. I cried when I got in and went downstairs without running into Anna or Dieter Lange, cried because there are some things you never let yourself know, even when you do know them.

Sunday, Sept. 22, 1935

Last night Dieter Lange had me playing the piano along with some new records he got somewhere. Know he didn't buy them. But he had Charlie Barnet's "A Star Fell out of Heaven" with "When Did You Leave Heaven" on the flip side, and a Cab Calloway, "Avalon" up and "Chinese Rhythm" over. Dieter Lange loved them because they were new, but they weren't nothing special, even though Doc Cheatham was playing lead trumpet. It was nice playing with Doc again. Made me homesick and sad. Benny Payne was on piano, but I cut him good (or at least it sounded that way to me, because mine was real music and his was on a record). It's been a little while since we had a good house-rent kind of party. Sometimes it just isn't too good to move up in the world.

So this morning, while Anna and Dieter Lange stuffed themselves with ham and eggs American style, and with biscuits I'd made and strawberry jam Annaliese's mother had made, he talked about the latest new law. Every time you turn around, these Germans've got themselves a new law or two or three. Can't do this, can't do that, can't do the other, just like living in a colored section back home. Jews can't vote any more and, on top of that, the government took away their citizenship. Jews can't marry anybody who's not a Jew, and Germans can't marry anybody who isn't German. Can't cross the line, boy, can't even diddle a liddle. Do you suppose the Nazis—that means everyone who isn't in a camp—been studying with some of those crackers like Bilbo and Vardaman and Ben Tilman and Hoke Smith? "Racial desecration"? Well, that's what they got old Nyassa on—even before they passed the goddamn law. Nothing changes. Wherever you are, if you're colored it's all the same.

When Anna wasn't watching, Dieter Lange looked at me and winked. I knew what that meant. Fuck the Nuremberg Laws. He was going to fuck me whenever he wanted to, and, as he once told me, he didn't have to worry whether or not I had "the rag on."

Thursday, Nov. 28, 1935

Yesterday Dieter Lange came back from a trip to Amsterdam. (Annaliese had a good time while he was away, and I'm glad she did.) He brought a Brunswick-French record and a Decca-Dutch record, both cut by Freddie Johnson. And he had another one cut by Willy Lewis. "Freddie Johnson and His Harlemites." "Willy Lewis and His Orchestra." Both had been in the band. Both were free. Now, I never liked Freddie because he played the piano too sometimes, when Mr. Wooding didn't want to. Mr. Wooding figured it was best to have two other piano players, since he thought I was "delicate," and whether I played or not, I could do the vocals. But I could have made a lot more money if it hadn't been for Freddie. Willy played alto, so he wasn't in the way.

Here I thought they'd all gone back home, and the bastards are still in Europe. Dieter Lange knew what I was thinking and he laughed; he laughed and I cried. Did he see them play? Did he talk to them? Did he tell them about me? What did they say? (Being in the sweet life, I didn't pal around with the guys in the band too much. They teased me. Asked if I wanted to dance. Tried to goose me with drumsticks and then pretended they didn't know what they were doing. But this was a different time, different place, and they were free and I wasn't, so I kept on with the questions.) Could they help me get out? Did you tell them to see somebody who could help? The more questions I asked, the harder he laughed, spinning around and pounding the floor with his feet. I knew for real then, if I didn't want to know it before, that Dieter Lange, even after all this time, had never meant to let me go.

I got so mad, I snatched the records and slammed them on the floor. They broke. He stopped laughing then. But that wasn't all. I went crazy, and I slapped him as hard as I could. Spun him around. Then he tried to punch me. I scratched his face. He started hollering that I was going into the camp right away; he didn't have to take this shit from some black fairy. I screamed back that I'd tell the Gestapo he was a coal-digger and that would finish him, too. He said no one would believe me, so I was wasting my breath, and anyway, it'd be nothing to shoot me and tell them I tried to escape, and I said that never happened to a calfactor and they'd certainly know something was funny, and that was when Anna said from behind us, "I believe. I know."

Dieter Lange went red. He was shitting chitlins. Anna was standing in the doorway. She had that look on her face—the one she has when she's been with Bernhardt. There we were, both of us, in her fat little hands. I could see that Dieter Lange was trying to think of something to tell her, *anything* to tell her. She waddled into the room, the big room where the piano is. She walked across the floor to the couch and sat down. She slid her dress up to the top of her stockings, unfastened the garters and rolled them down. Then she reached up behind her dress and loosened her girdle. When she was finished with that, she pulled down her bloomers and threw them on the couch beside her. She pulled her dress way up, letting all that bloated white skin show. She looked like a partly skinned hog, and in the middle of all that was the hair on her pussy. I could hear my heartbeat in my ears. She opened her legs wide and her eyes were like she'd been smoking Mary Jane, or had had some cocaine. She looked at me and smiled. She looked at Dieter Lange and said way down in her throat, "Eat me, sweetheart, eat." She closed her eyes and leaned her head back. Dieter Lange took a couple of clumsy steps forward, collapsed on his knees, and slid toward her. He buried his head between her thighs, and her body snapped up and settled back quivering around him. Dieter Lange was at it like a pig at a trough, slobbering and grunting, grabbing her thighs, and she was working those hams up behind his back and moving his head this way and that. Her mouth was open, her lips wet, and she kept saying "Ahh, yes, oh, yes, yes, ahh." Once, while sucking in her breath, she opened her eyes, looked right at me but didn't seem to see me. It was like I was just a part of the furniture in the room, like I was blind.

I came down here. I closed my door. I heard them grunting and moaning, heard Dieter Lange's feet sliding on the floor. And then there was quiet. Then some moving around, some walking, Dieter Lange's brisk, Anna's kind of clumsy. I know their footsteps better than I know my own. Then they talked, his voice going loud and then soft; hers did the same thing. I'd never heard her being sharp with Dieter Lange before. I sat and shook. I was scared thinking of what was going to happen to me. Then, suddenly, they were shouting and screaming at each other. But there was a new sound in Dieter Lange's voice, like someone pretending he's as tough as he was before he got his behind kicked. I kept waiting for his footsteps on the stairs. I knew he'd never get over that slap I gave him. And I knew as sure as cotton is white that he's sorry he brought those records back and laughed at me.

I thought about Anna. She said she believed, that she knew, and Dieter Lange must sure believe that, the way he did that crawl. The bitch had him. Now, what was she going to do with him—and me? How did she get to know? Did Bernhardt know? I heard them go into the kitchen, heard pots and pans. I waited for the footsteps and Dieter Lange's yell: "Cleef!" The smell of food. One minute I was hungry and the next the smell of it made me want to puke. Voices, then silence; silence, then voices. I crept to the furnace and quietly opened the door. The fire was low. I tiptoed to the coal bin and grabbed a handful of coal and one by one tossed the pieces in. I made four trips while waiting for the sound of his feet on the stairs, his shout. I slid open the vents so the fire could catch and, still shaking, crept back to my bed. I didn't bother to undress. I must have dozed off, finally, because when I heard Anna calling from the head of the stairs, calling for me to fix breakfast, I could see daylight through the cellar windows. And I had to go to the bathroom bad. Thanksgiving Day back home.

Sat., December 7, 1935

Something's changed in the house. Dieter Lange doesn't say much, and Anna smiles all the time like she's got a pat hand. Guess she isn't as dumb as she looks. And coming from a farm where every time you look around you see one animal fucking another, she's probably got lots of tricks she can do. I thought by now I'd be over in the camp, maybe even dead, but things just go on here. They went to some rally in Munich tonight. Yesterday Anna had a bunch of women, officers' wives, over. They sewed swastika flags. That was in the morning. In the afternoon, when they'd gone, Anna wanted to do some more English. Do I think she's really better, or am I afraid not to think that? I don't want her mad at *me*.

She had some *Life* magazines from America. I don't know anything about them, but there are lots of pictures with writing underneath. This beats books. She asked about things in the pictures, too. Sort of like "This is a table, this is a chair" stuff again, but the magazines are more interesting. This was the first time we'd been alone like this in a while, and the first time since the fight. I didn't feel nervous with her, and I thought I could ask some questions.

"What's going to happen to me?"

"What should happen to you?" she asked back.

"But you know," I said.

"And you know, too," she said.

"What?" I asked her.

"Bernhardt," she said. "I know you know. Don't you?"

I didn't answer. It's always dangerous to say you know something about white people, whether they're Germans or Americans, French—it doesn't matter.

Anna laughed. "You're smarter than I am. I shouldn't have said anything last week, but I was feeling reckless, you understand. And anyway, I have him over a barrel and you could have me over a barrel, *nicht wahr?* Paaa! One word to Bernhardt and down the toilet he would go like a turd—but then I must have a husband, Cleef, because Bernhardt has a wife, understand?" She didn't know how well I understood.

"But if you could get me out of here, then you wouldn't have to worry about me saying anything about your husband. Not that I would," I said.

She got up for a cigarette and came back to the table where we were sitting in the kitchen. She blew out a big blue cloud. "I've tried," she said. "If only you hadn't been with that boy from the American embassy!"

I was surprised. "You've known about that all along? How come?" We were becoming like two bitches sitting at a bar exchanging gossip on a slow afternoon.

"Bernhardt," she said.

"Bernhardt!"

She smiled. "Oh, he won't do anything. He wants you here for Dieter, so he can have Dieter over a barrel. It was Dieter who saw you got the green triangle instead of the pink one, but Bernhardt found out about the whole business. See, this thing with *Entartete Musik* . . . and nobody coming to help you, and you not helping yourself with the big names, and the American embassy under quiet, proper blackmail by our government because of you and that boy. . . ." She shrugged and pounded out her cigarette in a cheap ashtray that had figures in *Lederhosen* on it. "You are an example. The prisoners who are released talk about you and the power of the government when it can hold an American, you see? They do not say that you are a *black* American because no one would care, *verstehen Sie?* Yes?" She reached over and patted my hand. "Your skin is so smooth," she said, and she gave me the strangest look and said, "Don't worry. All is in a balance now. Remember, Bernhardt loves jazz music." We went back to studying with the *Life* magazines.

Thursday, January 9, 1936

Christmas and New Year's have come and gone. In the house here, things go on like always. But yes, something's changed. It's like a Saturday night in a saloon, late, when the tough guys start drifting in. You know something's going to happen before the night is out, so you're playing and singing and watching out the back of your head all the time, 'cause you never know. But now I can understand a lot of things. I think Dieter Lange's got over wanting me gone from the house, since he knows Bernhardt and Anna won't let that happen. If Dieter Lange doesn't know about Bernhardt by now, he's a bigger fool than I thought. We didn't have any parties for Christmas and New Year's, but they were out a lot—Dieter Lange had to get the canteens reorganized at Oranienburg and Borgermoor, and Anna's father came down with pneumonia—so I was alone and on the piano many hours and playing the phonograph.

Music sounds strange in this place, stranger when it's empty. But playing what I want to play makes me feel not so blue all the time.

Over in the camp, new ones come in and some of the old ones go out. But the Reds stay. No release for them. Some of the Greens get out, but they're small potatoes. The smart ones like Gitzig they still keep, and sometimes they get good details. When I cleaned the house a couple of days ago, I noticed among the papers on the desk in the small room off the kitchen where Dieter Lange does his work, that 85,000 people were arrested last year, 15,000 more than the year before. Werner likes to know things like this. No wonder Dieter Lange is so busy running from camp to camp. In our camp they are still working, making it bigger and bigger, and details still come out here every day to work on the SS quarters. The SA is back with some changes in their uniform. They aren't so rowdy now; Himmler is boss over everything having to do with the cops and the SS. He can kick everyone's ass, almost.

I feel sorry for the details when they're marched out here singing or yelling out songs. It's bitterly cold. The wind seems to search you out around corners. It's like a knife. Now it's hard to work in the swamps or on the plantation where they grow vegetables. But not too cold to work the quarry. Of course, they have to work the 4711 details all the time to make sure the latrines don't fall apart. In winter the problem is pipes freezing and breaking. In summer it's shit and piss and too much paper that clogs up everything. The prisoners who work inside have it good during weather like this. They're in the SS quarters or officers' homes, like me, or the kitchen, the laundry, or offices; or, like Menno and Dr. Nyassa, in the Infirmary. Then there are those *Koppeln*, the men who pull the wagons. There are attachments on the wagons for two men to pull, like horses, and four men to push from behind. The wagons are filled with rocks and gravel and machinery. Right now the mud is frozen, but they still push and pull, grunting just like animals. The lucky inmates get the wagons that are on tracks, but the prisoners are still the engines.

John A. Williams

This morning when I got up to stoke the stove and start breakfast, I heard the details singing down the road as they marched up to the SS barracks. There was ice on the windows and the sky was growing lighter and bluer. The sun was coming out, shining on the ice and snow. The song, cracking through the cold and icicles that hang from the houses, was *"Moorsoldaten,"* and soon I could hear the footsteps of the men hitting the frozen ground like one big metronone, cr-ump! cr-ump! Louder and louder:

> *Wo-hin auch das Au-ge blicket*
> *Moor und Hei-de nur rings-um.*
> *Vo-gel-sang uns—nicht er-quick-et*
> *Ei-chen ste-hen kahl und krumm.*
> *Wir sind die Moor-sold-da-ten.*
> *Und zie-hen mit den Spa-ten ins Moor.*
> *Dann zieh'n die Moor-sol-da-ten*
> *Nicht mehr mit dem Spa-ten ins Moor!*

Then two details peeled off and came down our street. CR-UMP! CR-UMP! As usual, the men were four abreast. One of the middle two in the very first rank was Menno Becker. Menno! I thought as I ran quietly from window to window to make sure. What'd happened? Why was he on detail and not in the Infirmary? Oh, damn! I hadn't been in the camp for a week. Something was going on. Oh, he looked so cold and red in the face. And was there a bruise or two on his face? Oh, Menno! And the breaths of all of them made a white vapor that drifted back between the ranks. Oh, Jesus, sweet God, I thought.

Sunday, January 19, 1936

For a week Menno was on that detail—it was to lay new sewers for one of the SS barracks. The prisoners marched out in step, their feet banging the frozen ground, their songs hanging like icicles on the morning air. Then I didn't see him again, and I just couldn't get into the camp until today. Things seemed to have quieted down around the house. Dieter Lange has started picking at my ass again

72

and Anna seems friendlier to him, so he sent me to the camp. I walked so fast one of the guards thought I was running. He laughed and said something about how I must still be used to warmer weather.

There wasn't much business. Everyone was trying to stay warm, I guess, huddling around stoves in those drafty blocks. I worked on the stock for a couple of hours and then, because no one came in so I could send word to Werner, I went out to find him. I ran into him and Hohenberg in one of the streets. The wind was *walking* those streets, too. It was *cold.* I pulled Werner away and we went back to the canteen, and before I could say anything about Menno, he said, "They caught him with a *Puppe,* one in that last batch of Bible students. They haven't sent him to the Prisoner Company or given him the pink—yet—because everybody's got the grippe and they need him in the Infirmary. Stay away from him. One whole day they beat him. In the Bunker. Forget him. He's trouble now. They put the pink on the boy. Pink and purple." Werner leaned on the windowsill and looked out. "Everybody's mean," he said. "When it gets so cold and it's hard to stay warm, they get mean."

I had gone back to the stock and the shelves. I asked him about his family, had he heard anything lately. He didn't turn around, just said "Nothing." Then he asked if I'd brought anything for him, and I told him no, because of the problems back at the house. Then he left. He looked older and more tired. Winter does that. I kept working, thinking, I've become an old queen, the most sorry of queers, hauling around age like a chain-gang leg iron, but still thinking and acting, sometimes, like fifteen years younger, always competing, never quitting, deaf to the low rates other faggots put on you, and deaf to the laughing. I thought it was different with us, me and Menno. It was a half-assed, hurry-up, sneak-on-in-here life, but I thought it was a life. I also wonder, again, what Dieter Lange would do about me. He could only do so much plucking now. All he had was me, really, if he wanted to be careful. Hell, he *had* to be careful now. Bernhardt could do us both in. It was very quiet in the canteen; the snow and ice outside made even inside feel cold.

Tues., June 23, 1936

It has been a long, long time. I've been so blue I could hardly hold my head up. I asked myself why I was writing this, what's the point, who cares—but then, for some reason, I began to miss you. I know why. There's no one else I can really talk to. So here I am.

Looks like the cat-trailing-cat game has cooled down. Made me a nervous wreck but also kept Dieter Lange away from me. But I think he's starting to feel his oats again, seems more confident. The rumor out here is that Bernhardt has been assigned to the *Sicherheitsdienst*, the brain boys, the SD—the Gestapo. Not a man to fool with, and I think Dieter Lange has his own grapevine about that. There are a lot of grapevines to tap into around here. Germany went back to the Rhineland and took it, and the French just let them. Wonder what happens now to Hohenberg's lass who's so nice in the ass. Not a shot fired. You'd think the prisoners wouldn't give a shit about what happens anywhere but here, but they're happy; they cheered when the announcement was made, and they cheered when that boxer Max Schmeling knocked out a colored fighter named Joe Louis back in New York over a week ago.

"Proves absolutely Aryan supremacy," said Dieter Lange and Hohenberg and Karlsohn over in camp. Shit, I guess they all said that except me and Dr. Nyassa. Guess they never heard of Jack Johnson and Battling Siki and Joe Gans. They're all so full of shit. Even the guards at the *Jourhaus* run up to me when I go in and out and put up their fists and laugh and shuffle around. "Put 'em up, put 'em up," they say. They sure don't give a colored man a break, even if they're just as bad off—or worse.

Sunday, July 5, 1936

This afternoon Bernhardt and his wife stopped by, then Anna and Lily (Bernhardt's wife) went for a walk down to the soccer field to watch the officers play. I served them some iced tea and Lily said their Gitzig made splendid iced tea and tapioca, too. Better than their cook. This was before they went for their walk. Was all I could do to keep from throwing up. As soon as the women had gone,

Bernhardt and Dieter Lange settled down for a talk. I didn't make myself so scarce that I couldn't hear what they were saying. The talk was about me and something called *Lebensborn,* or Spring of Life, some more of that high-falutin' Nazi shit. I got scared and went the hell away from the window where I was listening. Last person I wanted to catch me listening in was Bernhardt. I went out back and pulled a few weeds from the lawn, waved to some of the other calfactors who were also pretending to work. It was a fine, warm, clear day, and it was Sunday after all, the time to recover from hangovers, for the prisoners to worship.

"Cleef! Cleef!" Oh, shit, I thought. What's he want now? Dieter Lange didn't want me; Bernhardt did. There was going to be a *Lebensborn* club between the camp and the town. A place where strong young ss men and Aryan young women could meet and get to know each other. The women would be the best German types, just like the ss. Bernhardt laughed. They are supposed to make babies. First, though, to like each other and then . . . Well, that was all I needed to know, but he thought a band could play music, not *jazz* music, but swing music. Jazz was, he said, heh, heh, *Entartete,* but swing was all right. "From what I hear from the States there are two or three white kings of swing, so I guess that the music is all right to play here," he went on. What he wanted was for me to lead the band. He could get from camp a drummer, an accordion player, a harmonica player, a guitarist, a cellist/violinist, a man who played the French horn, and someone who could double on clarinet and flute. No saxophones, trombones, or trumpets. What did I think? I would continue to stay with Dieter Lange and Anna and still work in the canteen. At first, there would be rehearsal, of course, so some time would have to be taken from the regular duties, but once everything was in order, I'd go back to them, just like everyone else in the band. Dieter Lange didn't look all that happy, but I guessed there wasn't too much he could do about it. I didn't feel that I had to tell him I couldn't write music; I couldn't even *read* music. But he must have known because he said some of the others could do the arrangements. I could tell them how to make things—uh—*swingy.* But mainly I would just lead and play jazz things like swing. I said okay.

What the hell else could I say? No? Or even dare tell him that both were from the same big old black tree?

———

Saturday, August 1, 1936

It's like party time. The Olympic Games began today in Berlin. And the band was driven to the *Lebensborn* club, which is in one of three connecting mansions way off the Dachauerstrasse between Dachau and Karlsfeld on the road that leads into Munich. It must have taken us close to an hour to get through the woods to the place. It was strange seeing people going about their business as we looked out of the rear of the truck. It's summer, so the women wore light dresses, kids played in the parks, the men wore no coats. We were feeling like special people. We hadn't had to drill, and the sergeant in charge of us said we'd have all the food and beer we wanted when we got to the club. "Just the way musicians ought to be treated," he said. We didn't say anything, but we certainly agreed. We were silent because you never know when these guys are bullshitting you, setting you up for a billy club on the head or hands or kneecaps. We knew we couldn't fuck up. This was too good an arrangement to do that.

We had been reading about the Olympics and how the Americans had a track team with some colored boys on it. Gossip had it that all the freak bars had been reopened in Berlin and the signs against the Jews had been taken down. *Juden Unerwuenscht.* Well. They were still rounding up people, those damned Nazis. They brought a bunch of Gypsies into camp just a couple of weeks ago. I can't imagine what they ever did. They're supposed to not have much to do with people who aren't Gypsies. Most Europeans don't give two shits about them; treat 'em just like colored people back home.

The sign at the door of the building we went into read *Nisten von Gluck.* If what we'd been told and heard about the *Lebensborns* was true, that was sure right. Love nest, yeah. Legal prostitution, we'd heard, only no money was involved. The Nazis were providing free pussy to the SS. The girls only had to be "real Germans," blond, no mistake, or the next best thing to it. Of course, the SS were supposed to be the cream of the crop. I guess the Nazis didn't want to stir that cup too much and turn up all those people like Dieter Lange. We guessed there were a lot of rooms upstairs in the "Nest of Happiness" (we called it the Pussy Palace), but we had a large room to practice and play in, a place where we could rest between sets, and a kitchen with a big table where we'd eat. The icebox was filled with food. We'd be under guard at all times and driven to and from the camp whenever we had to rehearse or play. The hours were going to be long on Friday and Saturday nights and Sunday afternoons, but it beat putting up with Dieter Lange and Anna and their who-struck-john. Looks like old Bernhardt is my angel now, so Dieter Lange better not fuck with me.

The piano is smaller than the one in Dieter Lange's house, but it's brand new, probably from some poor Jew's store. I thought I knew a lot of crooks in Storyville. They stole things and ran away. These Nazis, now, they just take stuff from right under your nose and dare you to say anything: "Gimme that! What? You don't like it? BANG!"

Thursday, August 27, 1936

Now there's a war in Spain. First Italy and Ethiopia and now Spain. Civil war. I liked Spain. I guess Werner's prediction is going to come true, but right now the Games are what everyone's still talking about.

When I saw his pictures in the papers and magazines, I thought Jesse Owens was the most beautiful man in the world. He looked like a black eagle or a voodoo spirit rushing down the track. He's won four medals and set records all over the place. (I'd set some, too, if they just gave me a little running room.) Of course, with all this Aryan superman shit, the Germans were not too happy that this black boy did so well. There are more papers and magazines around the "Nest of Happiness" than back in camp, where you have to hustle and scheme to get them and then they're days, even weeks old. I smuggled a letter out to the U.S. Olympic Team, Berlin, to Jesse Owens. I thought he would get my letter and because he was so

famous and because the Nazis were putting the best face on everything, he might be able to demand my release. I imagined that a
long, official Mercedes-Benz would drive up to the camp, that the
guards would click their heels and salute, and that the American
ambassador, Mr. William Edward Dodd, and Jesse Owens would get
out and go right to Eicke's or Karl's office (Eicke is now also the
inspector of all the camps), and when they came out I'd be sent in
and Eicke or Karl would apologize and I'd drive away with Jesse and
the ambassador. The fact that Mr. Dodd was from North Carolina
wouldn't have mattered a bit. But the Games are over and at thirty-
six I'm too old for this kind of daydream.

At Dachau things go on exactly the same, except this *Lebensborn*
business. Who back home would believe I have a band? Not much of
a band, but I suppose the guys in it haven't caused any problems in
camp, so Bernhardt picked them, even though there are probably
greater musicians here. Today, while workers were fixing up the
dance floor and the bandstand, Bernhardt said we could play blues,
but we shouldn't call them that because, of course, they were
Entartete. "But get ready for the times, Cleef. Get used to them and
you will survive, okay? Make up new names for the old numbers,
understand?" I asked like what. He said, "Something fancy, French,
see. Like, you won't say 'The Man I Love' but—ah—" He snapped
his fingers. *"L'homme que j'adore,"* he said. "I heard that somewhere.
Just make up titles, and when you sing, change some of the words.
You're no *dummkopf,* Cleef. You know what you have to do. No *Neger
Musik."* I got the point. I asked if he could get me some scores—stuff
from Benny Goodman, since we had this guy who doubled on clarinet and flute, and some stuff from Ellington, since he featured a lot
of trumpet with Cootie Williams. That way I could use the guy with
the French horn as a soloist. I could make up the rest. He said he
could. He was rubbing his hands and smiling. He called for a couple
of cognacs and we drank as I listened to the band going every
which-a-way.

Drinking with Bernhardt was like drinking with the gangster who
owns the place you play in. You're always glad when he leaves. I had
enough problems. This band was not going to sound like anything

Freddie Johnson or Willy Lewis could put together in Amsterdam or
Paris. I hoped it would sound bad enough for Bernhardt to give me
some people who he'd let play brass, and more reeds. But he'd made
it sound like this was it and I wasn't going to be fool enough to push
for more. So I set up my front line:

Clarinet/flute. This is Ernst, a joker who looks evil all the time.
Tall and thin. Moves slow like if he doesn't, something will snap
loose. He's heard Benny Goodman, but not Barney Bigard or Garvin
Bushell. Got a tough, pure sound, like for a symphony, which is
where he played. Ernst is a Red.

The boy on harmonica, Oskar, is a Green. Got quick eyes. Scratch
your nuts or flick a cigarette and Oskar's watching. I hear he played
while a buddy worked the street crowds, picking their pockets clean.
Seen people like him all over Berlin. Can't read, either. Short, and
even though he has to keep himself clean like every other prisoner,
he looks dirty.

Moritz is a Pink. He plays the violin. Like Ernst, he reads music.
Chubby fellow. Moody, and we can all see that he thinks his shit
don't stink, even if he is in Dachau. A couple of days ago when we
took a break from practicing, he came up to me and said, "How did
you get *that?*" He cut his eyes to my green triangle. "Who do *you*
belong to?"

I told him right quick, "Shut up, faggot," and for a minute there
he looked confused.

"Sorry," he said, but he didn't mean it. I walked on away. Sum-
bitch trying to fuck up my play just 'cause *he* couldn't get his *own*
arrangements together.

Teodor's a Red. Says he could play trumpet if they gave him one
instead of the French horn (which is all they had in the storage
where they keep things from prisoners who've died or were freed
and left in a big hurry) because he's a pretty good "Hotter," he says.
Yessir, they've all heard of hot jazz and think because I'm colored
I've got to be good. Teodor's got good jaws; it's just the damned
horn that gives off the soft, round sound. And he's a little slow on
the tonguing, but he can sure carry the back line without trouble,
and read, too.

First time I ever saw accordions in a band was here in Europe. Not my idea of a jazz (okay, swing) instrument, but hell, I stuck Alex in the back line because I didn't know where else to put him. He doesn't read, either. Like Oskar, he's a Green. Probably worked the same swindle Oskar did—but maybe with a monkey and a tin cup to help. He can do some crazy things with that Hohner, though.

Fritz is the guy on cello; he's a Red. He's always apologizing. If he plays *doo* instead of *daa,* he hears the mistake if no one else does and apologizes. He apologizes for wanting to speak to you or even if *he* gives you a cigarette. He can saw, though, and read his ass off. I let him do trombone parts.

On the side there's me, piano and vocals, Franz on the drums, and Sam on guitar. Franz is a Black—a vagrant, an antisocial, a race defiler, whatever they want you to be—and behaves like a drummer. Shows off too much; likes to rap hard with his sticks on the high-hat. Told him to make some brushes somehow, someway. But he's tough, got good control, can pick up when the rhythm's falling apart. Takes good direction, because, of course, he thinks I know it all. And he's heard of Zutty Singleton and Big Sid Catlett and Cozy Cole. Does some cute things on the snare.

Sam is a Gold/Red, a Jew, and really works on the gitbox, feeding light-line rhythms in case Franz falls off. Got a strong wrist like a banjo man. Franz acts like colored, tries to talk like colored, because he speaks a little English. Everything is "Man" this and "Man" that. A real wish-he-was hepcat. Sam is calm and careful; he tries to stay out of everybody's way, but he gives the impression that if you push him, you can only push so far.

Saturday, August 29, 1936

I thought by now that every Jehovah's Witness in Germany was in a camp, but yesterday the Nazis had another big roundup. Maybe now they have them all.

We're sounding as good as we possibly can. With what I have to work with, it'd take a miracle to sound better. Some of the local SA men brought in a bundle of black dress shoes and black tuxedos (no navy blue or plum-colored ones), white shirts and black bow ties. Probably cleaned out two or three haberdashers. "This isn't going to be a bumshow," Bernhardt keeps saying. "No one wants to dance to a band dressed in gray prison suits. You must look smart!" Our band-boxes are red, white, and black, the Nazi colors. The red, gold, and black, the German national colors, are sort of in the background these days. The bandboxes also have some of that glitter dust on them. I hope someone takes pictures so The Cliff will have something to remember when this business is all over. "Cliff Pepperidge and His Wittelsbachers." The Wittelsbachs came even before the Counts of Dachau, they say, and everyone loved them. That was a long time ago.

Anyway, we start in two weeks, when all the work on the place will be finished—the rooms, the restaurant, the lounges, the dressing rooms. Ah—a-one, a-two, one, two, three, daaah!

Wednesday, September 2, 1936
"It's the new law," I heard Anna tell Dieter Lange this morning. "Lily told me. Every SS man is to make four babies, if not with his wife, with some other woman." She laughed.

Monday, Sept. 7, 1936
Fire! Man, what a fire! It was Friday morning. I was still sleeping, the wonderful smell of hung hams and sausages in my nose, when I first heard the sirens; they were close, not like the ones over in the camp when a prisoner's escaped, or tried to, and everyone's hauled to the Appellplatz. No, these were close. Outside, I saw when I ran upstairs and looked out the window, there was that early morning fog that's so wet and cold it stings when you first go out. "Fire! Fire!" I heard, and then I saw, boiling through the fog, a busy, black bunch of clouds. From upstairs I heard Dieter Lange shouting, *"Brand? Wo?"* I heard him clomp to his own window; then I heard Anna's footsteps. They went to the window, too. I ran back downstairs and pulled on pants, jacket, and shoes, by which time Dieter Lange was

hollering, "Cleef! Cleef!" I am sure we ran out together with different feelings. He wanted to see what was happening to a fellow SS officer; I wanted to see these invincible bastards burn up. We ran down the street into the fog and smoke through which I could see these big flames licking at the gray sky. More sirens and the fire trucks, but I could see from where we stopped that fire trucks could not save Winkelmann's house. Dieter Lange and the other men grabbed hoses, shouted to each other, hauled the hoses this way and that.

We calfactors grabbed, too, and shouted and waved and pointed, but, really, we weren't doing anything except letting ourselves be moved as the firemen and the SS moved. "Burn!" I heard a guy I didn't know mutter, "Burn!" He wasn't the only one. "Good!" I heard, and "Take that, cocksucker! Sonofabitch! SS!" These were whispers that ran like radio broadcasts for those who were tuned in. And the flames were jumping out of Winkelmann's—Winkelmann, who came to Dieter Lange's for the parties, Winkelmann from Dusseldorf, with the skinny, buck-toothed wife with the high-butt behind. We could see the SS consoling Winkelmann, and the SS wives, still in robes, hair flying everywhere, gathering around his wife. I never loved a smell so much in my life as I did then, of wood, plaster, tarpaper, and things I didn't know, all burning up. Little bits flew away from the house and sank down through the fog and smoke to the ground, or on calfactors and SS alike. Fire. It showed us they could be destroyed. I think we had come to believe they couldn't. What a splendid smell.

Thurs., Sept. 10, 1936

When it was slow in the canteen I slipped over to Werner's block and we exchanged news. He'd heard about the band and asked me to keep my eyes and ears open, to get hold of the *Muenchner Illustrierte Presse* and the *Muenchner Nachristen* whenever I could and bring them to camp. Those are the newspaper and magazine that cover most of Bavaria. He pointed to a detail marching across the 'Platz. "They're going out to clear away the mess the fire made," he said. "Then they'll start building another house. Hohenberg's office has allotted a day crew and a night crew to finish up in a hurry." He smiled. I asked what was funny. He said, "Everything the day crew does, the night crew will partly undo. After all," he said, shrugging, "these prisoners aren't carpenters, not most of them anyway." So they went, in step, and singing, and when the way seemed clear, after I'd gone back to check on the canteen, I slipped over to the *Revier*.

I don't know why I did that. I had the feeling that being in the band, under the control of both Dieter Lange and Bernhardt, nothing could happen to me. Like those bad jokers back home who "belonged" to powerful white folks. I wanted to see Menno, just see him, that was all. I didn't recognize the man who seemed to be the block leader, but I asked for Dr. Nyassa. He looked me up and down. Then I saw in his eyes that he knew who I was. How many colored people were there in Dachau? He's that one, his eyes seemed to say. Still watching me, he called, "Nyassa, come here!" Dr. Nyassa rounded a corner. He looked evil, but when he saw me his face lit up. I gathered he didn't get along with the block leader. No sign of Menno. The block leader pointed to me and went back to his charts. "Come," Dr. Nyassa said, and I followed him to the room where we'd first talked. I could see the canteen from the window. He asked about the fire, about the Olympic Games, Jesse Owens. I asked if his wife had visited and he said she'd been forbidden to do so. But he's gotten some letters from her. She was not going to France or England or America; she was going to wait for him. Dr. Nyassa shook his head. "I don't understand what's happening, even now," he said. I told him he wasn't the only one. "You know, we belonged to the *Schwartz-Weiss Verein* back in Berlin," he said, "about four hundred black people, half of them Americans." I knew about them. Some had come to hear me play; they all lived in the East End and just about all the men had married German women, or German men had married the colored women, and some of the colored married colored. "Now this," he said.

"But you're a German citizen," I said.

"I'm not." Now he smiled. "But I'm not what *you* are," he added.

"Well, then, where's Becker?" I said.

"Out on detail. The swamps."

Oh, God, I thought. "Doesn't he work here anymore?"

Dr. Nyassa said, "Oh, yes. He works the night shift." Dr. Nyassa paused. "It was nothing he did this time, Pepperidge. It's just the SS. They don't like him. They'd like to kill him, but we're shorthanded, and that ass up front only reads charts. He's not a medical person."

So Menno was on detail during the day, and working the night shift here. How long could he last?

———

Friday, September 11, 1936

The truck picked us all up at the *Jourhaus*. Everyone had just come off some detail and was hungry; there hadn't been time to eat supper. There was already some coolness in the air. Around this place it always gets cold in a hurry, even in the summer. I'll never get used to it. I looked around. Ernst, Oskar, Moritz, Teodor, Alex, Fritz, Franz, and Sam. Two SS men on either side at the back of the truck, and two at the front end, plus two in the cab with the driver. Almost as many of them as us, and they all had guns. They smelled fresh-cleaned, and I guessed they'd have their minds at least as much on the girls as on us. They didn't stop us from talking or smoking. They even passed us cigarettes. When we complained about being hungry, they said there was lots of food there for us. We just had to be patient.

The sun was starting to set when we got on the main road. I always wondered how that looked to people who weren't in Dachau, the sun setting all red and gold, down near Bregenz, for example, on the frontier to freedom in Switzerland, 150 kilometers away, they say. The longest buck-and-a-half in the world. The ride to The Nest in the dusk was like sliding through a tunnel without light except for the flare of a match or the red dot of a lighted cigarette. Through the rolled-back canvas door cover, we could see the streetlights and bright shop windows slide back past us, hear the bells ringing on the trams, the car horns, the voices of people talking, without a care in the world, as far as we knew. I wondered if Oskar or Franz or Sam or maybe even Teodor was thinking in the darkness of bowling over the guards and jumping out. Somehow, I couldn't picture Fritz or Moritz or Ernst doing that. I thought about it the way you think about being in a moving picture. Well, there'd be many more rides, so there was plenty of time, if any of us wanted to do it. And then I thought, They know what we're thinking. They're just waiting. Of course. It was normal to think of escape. And it was just as normal for the SS to shoot us if we tried. There were guards who just waited for a *Haftling* to make a break.

Teodor and Sam had helped me with the scores. I learned a lot from them and from Fritz and Ernst. It was terrific, learning music the way you learned numbers, sort of. I'd play the number, they'd write it down. They were almost lost on the solos, when a joker was out there all by himself, playing next to the melody. So I'd hum the riffs (even then they were different from the playing) and they'd write them down, too. First time I ever ran across shit like that. Really sounded like a genuine white band.

When we finally got there it was dark. The guards led us into the kitchen and damned if there weren't some other prisoners there to serve us. Beer and wine, too. But I didn't have to say anything about drinking too much. No one was going to mess up this job. When we were full, we went to the dressing room and got into those tuxedos. We could see car lights whipping across the windows, hear cars running over the dirt driveway, hear men and women laughing and talking. The windows were open. The sounds and the cool night air came in. Until that time we were not a band. I thought that while everyone was loosening up, running through scales or a melody, or tightening up a solo. The prisoners who'd served us came in to listen. They were from the camp, too. They kept up the buildings and the grounds, registered the SS and the women into the rooms. And there would be nursery workers, too, they said, in another nine months. We laughed at that. Then Bernhardt came in; he was in his dress uniform. He pulled me aside and shoved a bottle of cognac into my hand. I took one lick at it and gave it back. He drank from the bottle without wiping the mouth. All the sounds from outside and now inside were like a regular *hummmmm*. I was getting excited, and when I looked around, I could see everybody else was, too.

"First," Bernhardt said, "the anthem."

I knew that. We'd gone over that before. "Then what do you have?" he asked. I was pretty proud of what we'd put together. Yeah, of course we'd play *"Deutschland Über Alles,"* but I had some shit following that would make that dick-licker a memory. I ran down the list and Bernhardt slapped me on the back and offered the cognac again. Europeans had this notion that colored players got drunk as hell and then played like hell. But I took the bottle, tipped it up, and drank not a drop. Shit, you don't say no to a man like Bernhardt.

The guys settled in the bandboxes, lined up the scores. The club was lit with some blue-gray light that seemed almost like fog. We could see them, hear them, smell them, out there. It was almost for real, almost like being free and opening at some club, the cigarette smoke curling up into the spots; the hooch, the beer, the wine; the perfume and the cologne; the flowers and the night air creeping through some of the open windows. The Cliff was on. There was a quick, sharp sound, like everybody sucking in their breath at the same time. The lights came on and we stood to play *"Deutschland."* I remained at the piano. Then the people were whispering: *"Aussehen! Eine Neger!"* We hit the first note and everyone rose, but they sure didn't take their eyes off me! There did not seem to be, as I glanced around, one *Fraulein* who was what you'd call a knockout. It wasn't so bad. There was applause and then that scuffling around when people sit down and move their chairs. But before they were down good, Teodor jumped up and started playing "The Bugle Call Rag":

> De-de-liddle-liddle-de
> de-de-liddle-liddle-de
> da-da-da-da-da-da-daaadaa

Fritz came in: zoom-de-zoom. Then Alex: zeem-de-zeem. Then Oskar: whee-de-whee. And we all jumped in, rounded the melody, and everyone took a solo. These went slow; didn't have that fire you have to have when you're out there by yourself snatching at every tune you ever heard and bringing it in on key. For a minute the audience just sat there, and I thought, Oh, shit, and then they clapped and shouted and got up, eased up near the bandstand. I called out, "A-one, a-two, a-one, two, three, fo—" And we cut loose with "Three Blind Mice" at a good, stiff, marching beat. I saw Bernhardt marching around the floor, and soon couples were following him and before long all those uniforms and dresses were moving to Franz's boom-boom-boom, ba-boom-ba-boom-ba-boom. Me and Sam and Franz laid into the beat; the others came together on the melody. Man, it looked like one of those parades in Berlin we get to see when they show newsreels in camp. We wound down the piece to much applause. "Cliff Pepperidge and His Wittelsbachers!" from Bernhardt. I stood and bowed and let the boys join me. I looked at Sam. His number. Oskar and Alex did the intro and Sam just walked on into "I'm Looking Over a Four Leaf Clover," way up on the strings like his git was a banjo. The rest of us would do a plooey! or dooleoode-doo to back him up. As we ripped along, singing (all songs had to be in German) and playing, I noticed a tall, good-looking, very blond *Oberleutnant* standing just outside the spots near the bandstand. He was stiff and proper in his all-black SS uniform and white shirt and Nazi armband, and I couldn't tell if he liked the music or not, or whether he had anything to do with The Nest. He just stood there. Something in his face reminded me of cynical musicians who'd heard and played everything. A couple of girls got up to dance; they were as big as baby elephants, but surprisingly graceful. We could see they were self-conscious—but determined. They were going to whirl their blond hair and roll their big hips and bounce their tits. Show off their stuff to these SS. They hadn't done more than a half a minute of swirling, dipping, and twisting before the floor filled with people try-ing to do everything from a fast two-step to a camel walk. Before they could sit down at the end of the number, we swung into the "Vienna Woods" waltz; Bernhardt said we should have a waltz or two. Me, Moritz, and Fritz headed out in three-quarter time. I could hear Franz counting: "One, two, three, one, two, three," as he pedaled, Boom, brush, brush, Boom, brush, brush. I don't know how he got the brushes or where, and I didn't ask. Alex and Oskar backed the melody, soft, and Teodor laid off. They loved it. You could see it in their dancing. Every SS man was a soldier from a hundred years ago,

and every *Fraulein* was a princess; they whirled around, erect, barely
touching the floor, some of them, the good dancers who knew what
they were doing. And even the dancers who had to count and watch
their feet knew what they were supposed to do, even if they weren't
doing it right. Time to slow down. My number. I called it "La Vie
New York." It was basically the rhythm section with me doing a solo
(why else be a bandleader?) and Sam and Franz backing. There were
spaces for Teodor: boodle-lee-dee, ba-tha-n-da-daa; and Ernst with
the clarinet: wheedle-lee-whee, bee-dee-doo-bee. Good thing Duke,
Cootie, and Barney Bigard weren't around. A clean steal, and on the
floor they were into a white folks' slow drag; I mean, they weren't all
scrunched up into each other the way colored people would be back
home on a blues piece like that, but close enough. Must be a bitch,
trying to be Siegfried and Hans or Kriemhild and Anna. (My colonel
had told me the story, how Wagner wrote the opera, which ended in
knee-deep blood.)

I swear I didn't know an accordion could sound so mellow, so
right, until Alex did "Falling in Love Again," with some harmony
from Oskar. And they were getting closer together on the floor. I saw
Dieter Lange and Annaliese, Bernhardt and Lily, and even Winkelmann and his wife dancing. Some kind of chaperones, I supposed.
Then we ended the first set and went to the dressing room, after we
grabbed a bunch of sandwiches. Everyone was feeling fine, even
friendly. Moritz told me how well I played. We all exchanged cigarettes and laughed over the beer that Bernhardt had brought in.
He told us how great we were. He whispered to me, "The women
love you!" Behind him came Dieter Lange and Anna and the
Winkelmanns. You wouldn't have thought we were prisoners.

The second set went as well as the first, maybe better. We started
with "Strike Up the Band," so everyone could march again, then did
"Ma Cherie" for a little French flavor, got a request to repeat "Falling
in Love Again," "St. James Infirmary," "A Pretty Girl Is Like a
Melody," "It Had to Be You," "I'll See You in My Dreams," "The
Blue Danube," and me singing "Good Night, Sweetheart," to close
down. All in German. It should have been plain to everybody after
that that they were supposed to go somewhere and fuck.

It was cold on the ride back. The streets were empty, the lights low or out. We passed around a couple of bottles of peppermint schnapps the guards let us have, and we had plenty of cigarettes. We talked as if the guards were not sitting there with rifles over their knees. It was like we'd suddenly discovered each other. We talked about how great the solos were and how steady the rhythm section was; and it had been, after the third or fourth number in the first set. The timing hadn't been bad at all. So we talked and drank and smoked all the way back to camp. Of course, the big thing had been playing before an audience. None of us had ever been allowed out so late. The feeling was good. But once we got inside the "outer camp," where the SS lived with their servants, like me and Gitzig, it was so quiet it made me nervous. Every sound had an echo. I was the only one who wasn't living inside the camp proper, where it's always *Mutze ab, Mutze zu*, cap off, cap on. The rest lived inside, members of the camp band that played when the prisoners went out to work and returned. Or they played at the "concerts" the guards made the prisoners attend. They played when people were marched off to the Prisoner Company. It's a wonder they weren't forced to play when people had to shit.

The guards dropped me off in front of Dieter Lange's house. The lights were on, so I guessed he and Anna left The Nest after the first set. I let myself in and went down to my room, undressed and got into bed. I couldn't go to sleep. I was going over the numbers we'd played, thinking how we could do them better. I missed trumpets and saxes and trombones and a bull fiddle with its soft I-am-the-boss sound. I was about to go to sleep when I heard footsteps coming down the stairs from Dieter and Anna's room. Not Dieter Lange's. I'd never heard Bernhardt on those stairs, but the footsteps didn't sound heavy like a man's; more like a woman in high heels, and not Anna, who made a definite sound when she went up or down the stairs, like a cow. Well, maybe Dieter Lange had got up enough nerve to give her a beating and some SS wife had come over to put cold cloths on her face. Late for that, though, and where was Dieter Lange anyway, if he wasn't upstairs?

Sunday, November 28, 1936

I'm on a schedule, torn between Anna and her English; the housework and the cooking; Dieter Lange and the canteen; Bernhardt, the band, and The Nest. Dieter Lange is gone very often now because they're still expanding camps all over and planning new ones, so I'm in the canteen a lot, but there's a prisoner, a Red named Baum, who's taken over a lot of the work. I think Dieter Lange wants me there mainly to keep an eye on Baum, so he doesn't mess up a good thing. It's sort of funny. Dieter Lange doesn't come to me nowhere near as often as he used to before Anna walked in on us. But we have made our peace, I think, so those times when Anna's visiting or just plain out somewhere, we have fun. Nothing like before, but pleasant enough. He says he's as much a prisoner as I am, because if he crosses Bernhardt, he's in trouble. And he's brought me records, a lot of Brunswick/Berlin, but he says they aren't allowed to make as many as they did before. Some are from Paris and Amsterdam and Copenhagen. Can't get any from Spain now because of the war down there. Drugs are hard to get, so we don't have them often, but Dieter Lange seems to have connections. People like Goering never have any problems getting theirs, or fine big homes and cars. "Not much has changed," Dieter Lange says. "I guess there'll always be big shots. At least bigger than me." But he has already done far better in the SS than he ever did before the Nazis took over. And he knows it; he just wants more. So does Anna. Too bad for Dieter Lange that she is smarter than he thought. Werner was right about the Winkelmanns' house; they had to move because it never got finished.

Now the band rehearses Friday and Saturday afternoons, after which we eat and rest until we begin the first session. When the second set ends, it's the long ride back, and it's growing cold now. Sundays are out since word came down from Heinz Baldauf—SS and Gestapo, like Bernhardt—that there could be no swing music on Sunday. Rest and worship. That's copasetic by me. Sunday is the only day I have mostly to myself.

Anna and Ursula Winklemann have become good friends. Anna visits Ursula often, or says she does. She's a farmer's daughter like

Anna, only her father's a rich farmer to hear her tell it. Big farm,
I heard, with lots of people working for Frau Winkelmann's father.
Only thing Anna's got over her friend is her English, which is not so
bad now. She likes to show it off when Frau Winkelmann visits here.
Thank you, Jesus, that's not often. Anna stays with the magazines
from America and England; books are too much trouble and anyway, the ones around here are old *Tom Swift* and *Rover Boys* books.
It's funny watching them, their chairs pulled together at the kitchen
table, and Anna reading: *"Ja*—yes—'the Cherman leater, Herr
Adolph Hitler, continues to urge rapid'—*schnell*, Cleef, yes? 'hex-
span-sion'—*Ausdehnung*, Cleef, *ja?* 'of the Cherman air corps . . .
Kink Edward de eight is a weakling'—*Schwachling*—Cleef, yes?
'mit Volley Seempson . . . Bruno Hauptmann vill go to de electric
share—' *elektrisher stuhl, ja*, Cleef?" It's easier to read for her: "Heavy
fighting in Spain with the rebels preparing to go on the offensive."
It's something to see, Anna's big butt and Frau Winklemann's high
behind, jiggling in the chairs and sometimes rubbing against each
other while they read, drink coffee, and eat cake.

Tues. Dec. 30, 1936
    Back to Christmas doings. The Nest was decorated for Christmas
—*Weihnachten*—and it was Christmas Eve. So we played a lot of
singing songs as well as the jumps and drags. We drank maybe a bit
more than we should have and Franz got so happy, looked like he
was trying to put holes in his drums. Fritz tried to pluck his cello
like it was a bass, and on "King Porter Stomp" *("La Musique du Roi")*
everybody took a solo at the same time, like New Orleans, and came
back home on schedule. We hadn't tried that before and maybe if
we'd been completely sober we wouldn't have. But everybody else in
the place seemed to be half high, so it didn't matter.
    Christmas morning, before I got up, Dieter Lange came down to
my room with a package. He and Anna were going to visit her parents for the day. Everybody goes to be with someone on Christmas.
He said, "I've taken advantage of you, and that you know, Cleef.
But you've managed well for a prisoner at Dachau, too. I told you

how that would be, but you've done better than I thought. Here's a package that will surprise you, I think, and maybe you won't think so badly of me after you open it. Listen: I thought this was all some kind of wonderful game and I would make money and be a little prominent and after a while find a way to leave it. I never thought you'd be around this long. That would have been sad for me, but good for you, and I'm not such a pure shit as to not want something good for you sometimes. Anyway, here. And there's a bottle of Napoleon brandy to drink while you go through the package. Merry Christmas." He kissed me quickly and went back up the stairs.   ·

This was getting to be too much. The man was going through some kind of change, or maybe it was that quiet pressure Bernhardt put on him just by knowing about us. I couldn't wait until they left the house after Anna fixed breakfast. Once in a blue moon she did that, and she knew I'd had a helluva Christmas Eve. When they left, I got up, dressed, washed in that itty-bitty sink in the cellar (sometimes when I had to piss late at night I went there, too, like you sometimes have to go in a bidet when you can't make it to the toilet in the hall), and went to the bathroom upstairs.

I wasn't in a hurry to open Dieter Lange's present. Anna's was a couple of pairs of socks and some handkerchiefs. I knew hers wasn't as important as Dieter Lange's. So I took my time. Played the piano, with his present sitting right there on top. I poked through their room and the closets, his office and other rooms where so many boxes of papers were stored. I found several writing tablets and took a couple for myself. By the time I got tired of snooping and playing, it was the middle of the afternoon. Outside it was already starting to get dark and snow flurries were falling. I started the pork roast that was for my dinner and also for when they came back, and I opened the brandy and then Dieter Lange's present. The box was filled with papers, documents, and envelopes addressed to me with letters in them. They'd all been opened. I began to tremble because I knew this stuff was going to tell me once and for all that I was in Dachau forever. I knew it. But I started reading the papers. The first one:

Secret State Police
Secret State Police Office   Berlin, sw 11 / April 3, 1933
SA III B H.NR. 3003

PROTECTIVE CUSTODY ORDER

Christian name and surname: Cliford Peperidge
Date and place of birth: June 6, 1900, USA
Occupation: musician
Status: single
Nationality: American
Religion: Protestant
Race: Neger
Domicile: Friedrichstrasse, 18

Is to be taken into protective custody.

Reason: Police evidence shows that his criminally indecent activities constitute a danger to the existence and security of state and people. Because of his previous activities it is feared that when released he would continue his criminally indecent activities. Custody is indeterminate.

Attached was a snapshot of me with a sign that read:

K-L Dachau
1933
3003

All I recalled about that day was being afraid and shaking and going wherever I was pushed, doing whatever I was told. And Werner. It seemed like a thousand years ago. There was another document. The same document, I thought, when I scanned it, but there was a difference under "Reason":

> Police evidence shows that his criminal behavior constitutes a danger to the existence of state and people. Because of his previous criminal activities it is feared that when released he would continue his illegal criminal endeavors. Custody is indeterminate.

The second one carried the same date as the first. I figured that Dieter Lange had substituted the second for the first so he wouldn't be suspected of being a queer, too. Nifty. Was nifty before Anna walked in, before Bernhardt got his nose into the wind. Well.

I pulled out a letter. The envelope was plain, with no return address. But it was from the U.S., Boston:

> Dear Clifford,
>
> I'm sorry for what's happened. I heard from Count Walther von Hausberger about your predicament. I'd hoped by now that you'd be out and even back home. I did the best I could before I had to resign and leave the Service. I did try very hard to get help for you. In fact, I paid a lawyer to get you out, but I couldn't stay. I had to take a train to Paris the next day. I couldn't get into specific details with the lawyer, but he assured me that he understood. I've felt badly about this. But I am still trying to effect your release. I hope it hasn't gone too badly for you and that, when this catches up with you, it will find you safe in Paris, Amsterdam, or Copenhagen. In the meantime, here is a draft for $500 U.S. to make things somewhat easier for you wherever you are, if that's at all possible.
>
> Fondest regards,
> Malcolm

The letter was dated June 15, 1935. There was no draft in the envelope, either. I took another drink and got up to put on the potatoes and cabbage and turnips. In Germany there's never a shortage of this shit. I staggered, but just then I didn't give a damn if Hitler walked in. As bad as they been fucking with me, I'd rip his goddamn nuts off, fucking with The Cliff this way. I cried while I peeled the potatoes and scraped the turnips. I basted the roast. Then I went back to Dieter Lange's Christmas present.

> Dear Monsieur Pepperidge:
> It is shameful what is happening to an artist of your eminent stature. I have heard from a Count Walther von Hausberger

about your situation. We have spoken to the American ambassador here and he hopes to advise the American ambassador in Berlin about you. However, we have been told that you are subject to German law. If we can be of further assistance, please let us know at once.

Sincerely,
François Moreau
Pathe Polydor, Paris

Moreau's letter was dated August 2, 1935. I opened the letter with all the Spanish stamps dated July 28, 1935, and read:

Dear Señor Pepperidge:
This is truly a great misfortune, sir. One hears many distressing things from Germany these days. I've written to a friend at Brunswick Berlin to see if anything can be done even though it is our understanding that foreigners living there fall under the laws of Germany, just as would be the case here. But we have advised the American ambassador here of your predicament. We have written to Mr. Wooding in New York, the editor of the new jazz magazine, *Downbeat,* and Mr. James C. Petrillo, president of Local 802, also in New York.

This letter was from Carlos Bustamente of Parlaphone Madrid. The brandy was half gone. I dragged myself to the kitchen to lower the heat under the food, stir it. I wondered what Gitzig was doing today. Probably nonstop meat-beating. I returned to the package. I was numb not so much from the brandy as from the letters and documents, another of which I picked up to read. It was a form letter and had been sent, it looked like, in response to inquiries about me. There were several of them under different dates:

Dachau Concentration Camp / Political Department

In answer to your inquiry, we wish to inform you that the Protective Custody prisoner Clifferd Pepridge is in good health. He is unable to send you a message because the intrigues of a few criminal scoundrels have made it necessary to impose a post ban. It is not known here when he will be released. Each case will be dealt with by the Bavarian Police in Munich. CAMP COMMANDANT

Why had Dieter Lange given me this stuff? Because way down deep he really cared something about me and wanted me to know what I hadn't known? I couldn't think of any other reason. I was crying pretty good when I got to the last letter. There was no envelope, so I couldn't figure out where it had come from.

Dear Cliff,

A goofy drunk German came into the place here where I work. Drank like sixty and listened, pounded his feet, and clapped like a screwball. When we were finished he came up and said he wanted to talk to me about Cliff Pepperidge! I thought you were back home, Jackson, and there he was telling me you're in Dachau! I just finished reading a book by a joker escaped from there name of Hans Beimler. What you doing in there, man? Place sounds like a bitch. The drunk gave me an address that wasn't the prison. Said he'd see you got this letter. What's he? A friend? A cop? Somebody they just let loose? Anyway, can you write and tell me what's going on? Maybe we can get in touch with somebody who can help. Can we visit—I got Johnny Mitchell and Ted Fields with me—and bring you whatever you need? Let us know. I hear things are jam-up back home. The Savoy's supposed to be jumping in New York, and the Renny, too. But times are hard, they tell me. Don't know how Mr. Wooding does business with all the competition. He's with Moe Gale on the Upstate New York circuit. Billie Holiday's got a band: Bunny Berigan, Artie Shaw, Joe Bushkin, Dick McDonough, Pete Peterson and Cozy Cole (!). Let me know if you got a phonograph. I'll send you some sides. Let me know everything, Cliff, whatever it is, so we can scheme up on how to help. I know we wasn't aces, but anybody winds up where you are needs some help, Jack, and that's a fack won't break back. Oh, yeah, Freddie Johnson's in Paris. Your buddy there said it might be possible to buy you out. How much? Write quick.

The letter was from Willy Lewis in Amsterdam. I turned off the food. I wasn't hungry any more. I finished the brandy. Goddamn! If I hadn't popped Dieter Lange . . . eleven months ago . . . because he was teasing me so hard, I could have been in touch with Willy by now. Maybe that sonofabitch Dieter Lange . . . Aw, shit. If I hadn't popped him, things would be the goddamn same.

Wednesday, Jan. 13, 1937

It was last Thursday, the 7th, when I woke up listening to my thoughts and the conversations in my head. This was when I was sick. I heard myself from a long way away, in a place I didn't know. I could see myself seeing: in the night sky, fat speeding clouds, red, black, and white, tumbled through each other, the way clouds come running in from the Gulf over New Orleans. The clouds gave off a strange, flickering, gray-pink light that made dogs I couldn't see bark and snarl. I thought I heard a voice like thunder crackle and snap with the naming of numbers and names through a great wide place like the 'Platz, which became the Dancing Ground when some voices did not echo in response to the thunder clapping across the sky. Men danced the slow death of complete exhaustion and fell with a splash, one after the another, into the knee-deep blood that had seeped through the marsh underfoot, the dirt, turf, gravel, stone, concrete, and asphalt. Splash, splesh, splish, splosh, splush. The spotlights, bright as the eyes of God, did not follow their fallings. Those who remained standing as the night caterpillared down, wavered until at last, to the north, as usual, the shots rang out or did not ring out. The reprieve was always the truck that sped up and unloaded its cargo, live or dead. The first to be battered with club and fist and foot into the blood; the second to be heaped before the wavering thousands as examples of "pieces"

that had gone astray and would dance no more anywhere, except in heaven or hell.

I heard myself hear music, the music I saw myself playing without a mistake, without nervousness; it bounded out of the Steinway, louder and cleaner than the barking dogs, the rifle shots, the moaning men, the snarling guards, and the sirens; the music leaped beyond the blocks and the SS noncom barracks, the electric fence with its low, mean hum, beyond the newer, higher walls, the moat. I heard my music angling south on an upward slant toward the Alps, then above them, soaring higher into a darkness that was becoming lighter because it was speeding toward the brightest thing in the southwest sky. Oh, I heard myself play melodies I'd never ever heard, and chords that should not have been possible on any piano, and I approached that brightness on an impossibly fast beat, saw myself look at that incredibly bright ball with smaller balls caught in their own rhythms rounding it, and I heard myself say, "How fine it is."

Yes, it was last Thursday when I started to get better. I don't know why I was hearing myself so good that I couldn't forget what I said or what I saw, heard, and did when I was sick. I was in my room in the basement. It smelled like medicine. When the door was open I thought I was in a hospital because the walls were white, too. Then I knew that wasn't so; Dieter Lange must have hung sheets over the fence where he kept his stuff locked up. I must have had visitors.

I said to Dieter Lange (we must have been alone) "I hate you."

"Don't hate me," he said.

I wondered where Annaliese was. Hadn't there been someone with her when she came—I think they came—to visit?

"Why didn't you tell me about the letters? Why did you take Malcolm's money?"

"I didn't take the money. Someone in the camp post did. I know you'd have felt better if I'd given you those things earlier, but it was too much of a risk. And now, you see, they didn't make you feel better after all."

"I really do hate you, Dieter Lange," I remember saying again. I remember feeling hungry just then, and I knew somehow that was a good sign.

Dieter Lange was sitting on my stool. I said, "You changed the records."

"Yes. I had them changed, and you know the reason for that, too."

"Was I in the *Revier?*"

"No, because you might have said something to get us into trouble. And Bernhardt didn't want you to die over there. He needs you."

"Everybody needs poor old Cliff," I said. I watched us from somewhere. "And all I got is a big asshole and can play the piano."

He didn't say anything then, but it occurred to me that we were whispering or seemed to be. I said, "What's wrong with me?"

"The grippe," he said. "Pneumonia."

"Bad?"

"Bad, but better. Twenty people a day die of grippe or pneumonia in the *Revier.* I didn't want that to happen to you. Neither did Bernhardt. Neither did Anna. So Bernhardt arranged for the black man in the *Revier* to come and bring you medicine and look you over, and for Gitzig to help, too."

I remember myself thinking that I didn't want Gitzig to be mad at me because he had handled my piss and shit and washed me. But if he hadn't put something in my water he must like me.

"And Anna has been looking in on you, too, and Ursula and Lily."

I thought then, *Anna and Ursula,* and I wondered if Dieter Lange heard my thoughts, they seemed so loud. He lit a cigarette.

I said, "Did anyone else come to see me?"

"No one. Just that Gitzig and the black man from the Infirmary. I found those letters I gave you at Christmas. I destroyed them."

"You don't care about me, Dieter Lange. I hate you. I meant for you to find them."

"Is that so. Well, anyway, don't be such a sissy," he said, his voice getting thick. "You got yourself here. I found you. I saved you. The SA would have ripped your ass open all the way to your heart if I hadn't. And if they hadn't killed you, the swamps would have or the quarry, and if they didn't, you'd have been drowned in shit on the 4711 detail —and you wouldn't have been the first fairy to vanish like that."

He honked his snot and swallowed it.

"I want to die, Dieter Lange."

"You love music too much to die. You will die, sure, but not now."

"You told Willy Lewis he could buy me out. I'll buy myself out."

"You can't. You've only earned 80 marks. Oh, your guitar player, the Jew, he got bought out. But Bernhardt's got another guitarist. Claims he's a cousin of Django Reinhardt. Never met a Gypsy who could play anything who didn't claim to be related to Django."

I remember thinking, the thoughts bouncing off the drying hams and sausages, the rows of canned goods and glass jars behind the white sheets, that the rhythm section was going to need work with a new man. "How much for Sam?" I asked him.

"Seven thousand five hundred marks. Fifteen thousand dollars. U.S. Jews have money."

"How much for me?"

"Ten thousand marks. Twenty thousand dollars U.S."

I thought, Sam is worth $15,000, me $20,000.

It seemed that I heard snowflakes hitting the ground. "Twenty thousand dollars," I said. "Get me out of here and I'll send it to you." I thought, The price of slavery has gone up.

"You see," he said, "the Reich wants so much per head. The middlemen who arrange such things must have so much. Bernhardt's a middleman. So am I."

"Dieter Lange, get me out."

"It's too late. It's not like the old days. I can't get myself out. That's why I have to pull so many strings to cover me and you."

"Run, Dieter Lange, run. You travel. You can run. Paris. Madrid. Rotterdam. Copenhagen. Zurich. Stockholm."

"And what would happen to you if I did? Besides, Cleef, in five years' time they'd catch up with me. They mean to have it all."

"I hate you, Dieter Lange, and your fat pig wife."

"I thought you liked Anna. I know you like Anna. She likes you. You don't hate her."

He put out his cigarette then and I thought of Anna and Ursula, who'd come to visit me, who'd chased Gitzig out, and who'd pulled down the covers to look at me, measure me, feel me, put their mouths to me; Anna, and Ursula with the high heels and high butt, taking turns playing the clarinet, causing me to rise through my sickness; who exchanged comments between vigorous wet riffs and tiny, musical, secretive *Ohs!* And then I knew who had come down the stairs the night I got home after our opening at The Nest. (Oh, Anna, Oh.) The house was full of Tricksters.

So, I was saved even as I was lost in the funhouse. If I hated, I hated with the reserve of the rescued and measured myself against those in the camp who surely would have died and been buried, or who, within a few months, would have their bodies cremated and their ashes sent home in urns at 50 marks a pop.

"Would you like to hear some music? I can bring the phonograph down."

"No."

He sighed, or seemed to.

"Why did you give me those papers, Dieter Lange?"

He lighted another cigarette from the pack of Camels. Business must be good, I thought.

"I guess I wanted you to know I was looking out for you. But that day after you slapped me and Anna walked in, the last thing I was ever going to let you know about was Willy Lewis. I could have killed you then and even later, because that's when Anna got the upper hand. I know about her and Bernhardt. I'm not a fool, so I know he's got me—us—right under his thumb." He played with his cigarette before crushing it out half-finished. "Just a little bit prominent, that's all I wanted to be, but, shit, Cleef, the whole thing's like a quagmire. There are already over 275,000 Germans in jail. This gang means business." Dieter Lange stood and dipped a cloth into a wash basin and wrung out the water. He wiped my face with it. He was very gentle. Then he bent and kissed my forehead and left.

That day, rising out of my sickness of both body and mind, I think I understood that Dieter Lange was afraid.

Monday, February 1, 1937

Today I got back into the house routine. Anna's insisted that Dieter Lange not send me to the canteen. I need my health for the band; I do not yet need to go out to get sick again, she says, and that's all right with me, because January, February, and March can cut your butt a duster around here. I thought of that guy, Hans Beimler. How had he got away? Why hadn't I heard anything about it? The place was big; you could never know everything that was going on. Some rumors ran around like rats gone crazy; others never went anywhere. Everyone hoped Beimler's book would make things better, even get us out.

Gitzig sneaked over while no one was home. "Now that you're almost well, they don't want me about," he said. "That's all right with me, because I was getting tired of cleaning up after you. You know, your shit's the same color as mine. I always thought black people had different color shit, and piss, too." I told him I always knew the colors were the same. And the smells. He said the tailors were making new uniforms, with stripes, and I told him that's what they wore on the chain gangs back home. He wanted to know what chain gangs were. I told him. Then he wanted to know if I was getting much before I got sick, and I just looked at him and asked if *he* was getting much. He didn't answer.

"It's a mess in Czechoslovakia," Gitzig said. "Next year the Nazis'll get what they want. Bet you."

I kept on dusting the furniture.

"I hear they've got some Gypsies in over there. Brown triangles with 'z' on them."

"What's that mean?"

"*Zigeuner. Sinti.* Gypsies. 'z' for Gypsies, 'J' for Jews. They got a letter for every nationality, don't worry." He took one of Dieter Lange's Gauloises from the pack I held out to him. "Is it true about *Lebensborn?* They have a club? They just go to drink, dance, and fuck? Really? It's enough to make you wish you were SS."

He fidgeted. "I'm glad you're well—or almost. I didn't mind being your *Pfleger.* If things go bad out here I could work in the Infirmary. From what I hear, I'd be better than any of those other nurses in the *Revier.* Knock on wood I don't get sick. You can die over there."

I finished dusting and sat down. I was tired, yet I hadn't done that much. I wondered if I'd be better by Friday.

"Frau Lange and Frau Winkelmann are *very* good friends," Gitzig said. He looked at his cigarette before putting it out.

"They did come to see me, didn't they?" I asked.

"Oh, yes, they did. Threw me out, they did, so they could have you all to themselves to clean and coo over."

He gave me a sharp look; I looked somewhere else. He said, "I guess you had a wet dream after they left, and you with a fever of 103."

He smiled, but it was a kind of jealous smile. "Well, Pepperidge, if you ever have a spare, or need a bit of help, I wouldn't mind delivering a quart of milk to a housewife once in a while, okay?"

"Why do you think I—"

"Pepperidge. It's crazy; it's all crazy and it's not over yet." He came close to me. "You see Werner, tell him I've looked at Bernhardt's list of museums in these cities. Listen. Vienna. Salzburg. Amstetten. Graz. Linz. Okay?" He was slapping the air with his finger at each name. "Prague. Pilsen. Brno. Bratislava. Ostrava. Kosice. Okay? Warsaw. Czestochowa. Breslau. Stettin. Danzig. Cracow. Poznan. Torun. Okay? Austria, Czechoslovakia, Poland. Okay? I've got to get back. Remember: if there's more milk than you can deliver . . . "

Tues., March 9, 1937

He blows that horn like Coleman Hawkins, a wide, sweet coolness on the slow pieces, and on the fast ones he's like a jackhammer biting up a road laid with diamonds. *Oberleutnant* Eric Ulrich. He's that big blond guy I spotted the first night we played at The Nest. The first time he played with me was on a Friday afternoon. We'd come in from the camp for our usual early rehearsal. I wasn't hungry, so I left the guys in the kitchen feeding their faces like eating was going out of style—which, in the camp, it did sometimes. He was already onstage. Older up close than he looked standing near the stage. Looked like he was waiting. Didn't have on no jacket and his shirt was open and he was twisting the mouthpiece and licking the reed. When I came out he pulled up a chair. Ain't said shit yet. Neither did I. I tickled on out with "Tea for Two." Lightly: da, da-da, da-da, da-da . . . He took counter as we moved through the melody. Out of the corner of my eye I saw him lower the horn, that big gold Selmer, and he just tapped his foot while I ran through a whole lot of bars, changing up as I went. Then I led him into his solo, throwing him a handful of dinkles and chord changes. He jumped on them like a starving dog. He was calm and collected and once or twice his eyes seemed to twinkle when I turned to look at him. When he came to the end of 8, I upped the tempo to jump and took off again. Cut this sucker's ass a duster, I said to myself. By this time Franz had come out and leaped on his stool. The *Oberleutnant* nodded and the shit was going socko when Teodor came out and pushed through the small crowd of workers. He grabbed his horn, turned the bell away until he found a fit on his chops, then turned back. Damn! It was like a jam session! Then Danko—we called him "Little Django," the one who'd replaced Sam—somehow was on stage, too, with his guitar and moving fast on the beat. Reminded me of Teddy Bunn and Eddie Lang rolled into one, so I figured big Django must be copasetic. I led them around again and Teodor took a solo, then "Little Django," who could have cut Sam with just one string, and then Franz with his hepcat moves, all shoulders and hands and very little wrist; then the *Oberleutnant* again. We jammed on the same piece for the better part of an hour. The workers applauded real loud, and I had a feeling that we let ourselves get carried away and maybe that was why the *Oberleutnant,* a big smile on his face, stood and nodded to each of us, unhooked his horn, put it in the case, said *"Morgen,"* and left the stage walking fast. He was back for our first and second set dressed in his uniform. Later Teodor told me who he was: Eric Ulrich, the best jazz player in Germany, who had played in America and France as a guest with Ellington, Webb, and Lunceford, and I thought, Damn, no wonder! He only played the Friday and Saturday rehearsals. He never showed any emotion, except maybe a smile, a twinkle in his eyes. On Fridays when we finished he only said, *"Morgen,"* which meant he'd see us the next day. On Saturdays he said *"Wochenachst,"* which meant he'd see us the next week. Sometimes I saw him talking with Bernhardt. We thought he had to be careful with his *Neger Musik,* and, yeah, we did notice that when we jammed after that first time, the workers weren't around. I could never understand how he got such feeling for the music. Didn't seem right he was a Nazi, and maybe he felt what we were thinking, because he had a phonograph brought into the dressing room and a shelf full of the latest records from back home, like "One O'Clock Jump," "Cherokee," "Every Tub," and low-down nasty blues, stuff we sure nuff didn't, *couldn't,* play during the sets.

Wednesday, March 17, 1937

On the roof of the *Wirtschaftsgebaude,* in big letters, they have posted these words:

THERE IS ONE ROAD TO FREEDOM. ITS MILESTONES ARE: OBE-
DIENCE, DILIGENCE, HONESTY, ORDER, CLEANLINESS, TEMPER-
ANCE, TRUTH, SACRIFICE, AND LOVE OF ONE'S COUNTRY

Inmates can see the sign from the end of the Lagerstrasse, way down where the gardens and the disinfection hut are. Can't miss it. From the canteen window the words jump out like giants.

I don't like Baum. I don't like him because he is friendly with Karlsohn, who is really the only guard who gives me trouble. Doesn't seem to matter too much to him that Bernhardt is my patron. Even Dieter Lange, still a major, can't have Karlsohn done in. Karlsohn's only a corporal. Only a corporal! But the plainest soldier—hell, a free civilian—has the power of God where we prisoners are concerned.

Dieter Lange is very busy now with planning a canteen for a new camp to open in July. I think he said it's near Weimar and is called Buchenwald. He has also been able to arrange for a regular detail from the camp to be trucked out to his father-in-law's farm to turn the soil and ready it for the spring planting. He's not the only one who makes such arrangements.

Coal has been scarce this winter and we've had to switch to coke. Dieter Lange is in charge of ordering it for the crematorium and he has got himself a good racket with the dealer. I guess the dealer himself is doing pretty well, since he knows the potter who makes the urns for the ashes. They all know each other, like anywhere else.

Monday, May 10, 1937

The Blacks have come in by the hundreds, and Dieter Lange has raised prices on everything—cigarettes, candy, gum, biscuits, canned goods—everything.

"These are the crazy ones, the Blacks," Werner said, "but some are crazy like foxes. They're all meat for the Institute for Racial Hygiene and Population Biology."

The Institute deals with people it calls asocials, like the Blacks. "But in the meantime," Werner said, "they can help finish the camp, drain the swamp, cut stone from the quarry, rebuild the factory buildings, and all that other shit. The Nazis have got a pretty good slave system here. By the time they finish, with the forced labor and the slaves, Germany will be as big as America became with slavery, eh?"

We were looking out the canteen windows watching the trucks unload yet another batch of Blacks. They didn't have their black triangles yet, but we knew what they were. When I told Werner about Bernhardt's list that Gitzig had seen, I knew something was going to happen to the museums. I didn't know, though, that getting news of that list gave Werner time to get word to "his people," as he called them, to get out of those cities fast. The Reds seem to have a smooth-running organization that reaches outside the camp, even to America, where, I heard, Werner has learned that his wife is very sick. "His people" in New York are looking after her, helping out. I thought that was kind of strange—after not hearing anything from her or even about her for such a long time and now . . .

I've seen Dr. Nyassa a couple of times lately. I thanked him for his care when I was sick. He has the blues. His wife can't get any answers. They've offered to pay whatever money they have and leave Germany, but they don't have what the Nazis want—15,000 marks for him and 30,000 for her. That's $22,500! She's written to Dr. Just, but he can do no more than write to people he knew in Germany. Now it seems safer for her to leave, and that's why he's so blue. She's off to Paris. Dr. Nyassa said he was doing better, even getting along with that evil-looking *Revier* block leader, because he's been treating his friends with the clap and syph with the sulfa powders, and they're grateful. He knows it cures, but they don't, so he said he goes into a lot of mumbo-jumbo about maybe it'll work and maybe it won't, but it'll be better than running that thing down their dicks, huh? He gave me some medicine, just in case of a slight relapse, and a swallow or two of the old medicinal brandy. This, he said, he has to keep hiding, moving from one place to another so the block leader can't find it and either drink it up or sell it.

Becker? They can't break him, Dr. Nyassa said. So they've eased off a bit, but they'll try something else, he said, watch and see.

———

Thurs., May 27, 1937

I've noticed that Karlsohn doesn't holler at me anymore in the canteen unless we're alone. Oh, he's got the meanest look, the kind that says, Let me catch you on a dark night in an alleyway and your ass is mine, boy. My Aunt Jordie once told me about this Negro man who hurt colored people. White people didn't pay him much mind as long as he wasn't bothering *them* or *their* favorite colored people. Did just what he wanted to do, cut people with his razor, beat them up, was fresh with women—anybody's woman—and he would walk right into someone's yard and help himself to a chicken or a watermelon or a burlap sack of pecans. Karlsohn treats me like that sometimes. For a prisoner, I've got a little "prominence," as Dieter Lange calls it. I didn't think there was such a thing in Dachau. Now I know different. That's only because I'm a musician and a freak. I know just being a freak wouldn't be enough to keep Karlsohn and some of the others off me, but being Bernhardt's and Dieter Lange's musician so far has done just that. Thank you, Jesus. I am a *Prominenter*.

Dieter Lange was right about Baum. He clips cigarettes, the expensive foreign ones like Gauloises, Luckies, Camels, Benson & Hedges, Players, and so on. So I said to him yesterday in the canteen when we were alone, "We're lots of cigarettes short, Baum." He turned twenty different shades of white. He thought I was dumb, couldn't count, couldn't read the invoices; that I could seemed to

surprise him. He's a fat little man who jokes all the time. When he
farts, he holds one of his legs way up like a dog. He's lucky. Don't
know how lucky he is, because a fat man in prison is like a red cloth
to a bunch of bulls looking to stick him. I've told him that. Wanted
to put that fear in him, because it's there in every man, the idea of
going to prison and having your nature bent south. 'Course he went
into a lot of labba-labba yabba-yabba. He *knows* if I tell Dieter
Lange he'll be sent to the Prisoner Company, where they put targets
all over your clothes and work you to the bone. Fat man like Baum
probably wouldn't make out his time there. Thing is, I've learned—
and maybe it works even outside a concentration camp—that to have
something on someone is like having money in the bank. And that's
only the beginning; once you have him, yank the hook, again, again,
like you got a channel cat on your line. Too bad he's not taller and
good-looking.

"An error in the accounts is all," he said.

Then I said, "But where are the cigarettes? They should be here
even if there is an error. But they aren't. I guess I better have the
major go over the cigarette invoices. But he'll be mad. That's *our* job,
not his. He expects the pieces to match the money, Baum, and they
don't. Now what am I supposed to do?"

At that moment I knew he hated me as much as Karlsohn does—
but there wasn't anything he could do about it. Nothing. "Well?"
I said. Baum had been in the plumbing-supply business, I'd heard—
not *plumbing*, but supplying the parts—and had made a little fortune
on brass and copper parts. They caught him, so he was here claiming
his boss was the one who got rich, not him. That was probably true,
but I guessed he was closer to grand than petty theft. The big shots
always got away.

"I don't have the money to put back," he said. He choked on the
words. He knew what he faced, and here was this black faggot who
was gonna do him in. I asked if he was willing to make a bargain.
He said yes. Anything. But he didn't mean that. Anything reason-
able.

"Your wife comes once a month?"

He said yes, oh yes.

"She comes next week?"

He said yes again, and I could see he was trying to think what I would ask. I said, "I'll give you a letter. She must smuggle it out. In my letter I'll ask the person to write back at once, addressing the letter to your wife, and that letter she will bring when she comes next month."

"Well," he said, "I don't like to get my wife involved, you know."

I said, "Okay." I went back to checking the invoices.

"But I'll do it," Baum said. "This once."

"No," I said. "You'll have to do it whenever I say. That depends on the kind of answers I get."

"To America?"

"Holland. Why?"

"I don't want to make trouble for my wife. I think they check all the mail from America and going to America."

"You already made it," I told him. But I didn't tell him how I'd cover up his stealing. I'd simply not say anything until Dieter Lange was up to his neck in work in the room he used as an office, and then I'd tell him some of the guards came in and helped themselves to the cigarettes, which they did often enough anyway, but we were supposed to keep count of what they took. Sometimes we couldn't because there were customers and sometimes we didn't even see them. Things haven't gotten better with four eyes instead of two because there are more people in camp now. I can handle Dieter Lange. Hmmm. Could even suggest to him that he keep an eye open for Karlsohn and the guards on his watch. He could pass it up to Bernhardt that Karlsohn was making trouble for me! Now the ss Prisoner Company was a solid dick-licker, Jack, like gods booted out of heaven into pure-dee hell. Heh, heh. Slick score, Cliff.

"You'll take care of it then, Pepperidge?"

"Yes."

"No money?"

"No money. But Baum, you won't steal anymore, will you?"

"No. I won't. Thank you."

"Don't thank me yet, because if your wife doesn't bring me a letter next month . . ."

His face turned a color again, this time somewhere between red and purple. "But—suppose the Hollander does not write back?"

"He will. And move the cigarettes to the back shelf, so Karl-sohn and his buddies can't reach over and help themselves. Now."
I think he also hated me because I could talk to him in his language. My German isn't great, but it isn't bad, either. Having to translate English lyrics into German has helped a lot. Knowing someone else's language is something like being a spy. Oh, in a restaurant they'll pat you on the back and say your German or French or Italian or any other language is great, but they don't really want you to understand the bass notes.

A small group of asocials (ASOS, we call them) crept into the canteen and looked around in surprise like every new prisoner does, and you could see in their eyes they were thinking, A canteen! Well, not so bad. Like a store on the outside. And they were used to stores.

After my talk with Baum, I slipped in to see Werner. He's now got both sections of his block under his "command." His block is still made up of *Roter*, the Reds. In his block there is the "Committee," or *"Familie,"* which tries to look after the guys who don't have their rabbit's foot with them. They gather information from all over—workers in the Medical Office, Political Office, Labor Office, the SS homes, the SS and SA barracks. What they gather, they pass around. They try to get their very sick people off the tough details. They keep a record of who's missing and when he was first missed and which guards were with him, and they try to help the newcomers get used to things like the commands and keeping track of their bowls and spoons. They've even been known to try to talk the guards into going easy on jokers who aren't yet used to the slavery.

Werner told me that there are a few Thaelmann Brigaders in camp now, picked up as soon as they hit their front porches after being sent home from Spain with wounds. The Germans fighting with the Spanish Republicans named themselves after Ernst Thaelmann. He lost in two elections in 1932. Thaelmann's a Red, one of the first the Nazis put into a concentration camp. It was kind of strange, Werner telling me that, because I had a bunch of magazines from Italy and France to give him and they carried stories and pictures about the Spanish war. He thumbed through them looking at the pictures. He doesn't speak French or Italian, but there are a lot of people in his block who do. "Well," he said. "They sat on their hands when that idiot Mussolini went to Ethiopia, and they're still sitting. But now the Germans and the Italians are in Spain. Why is everyone so goddamn blind?" He was so disgusted he spat on the floor. Then he got up to hide the magazines. In Dachau, everybody hides everything. From the guards and from each other.

Monday, June 7, 1937

The summer uniforms feel good, but tuxedos feel even better, like you're somebody, not a prisoner. The guys in the band have a feel for each other now. Moritz and Fritz and me sometimes play some of their stuff. I struggle on the piano (I'm reading more now because of them) with stuff like Beethoven's Concerto for Piano and Violin and Brahms's Violin Concerto, which is mainly for Moritz. If I lose my way they just go on ahead without me, hearing a piano where there should be one until I catch up or plain drop out. Mostly they like the Brahms Double Concerto for Violin and Cello. I've heard Moritz many times off in a closet of The Nest playing his favorites, Mendelssohn's Violin Concerto, Vivaldi's Concerto in D Minor, and Mozart's Fifth Violin Concerto. And he'll go on as long as he can with violin sections from a lot of Bach.

Sometimes Teodor's in another room running through Haydn, Vivaldi, and Purcell. The first time I heard him he stopped to explain that Bach had a guy named Gottfried Reiche playing trumpet for him, and Handel had Valentine Snow, and Henry Purcell had John Shore. "Now," he said, "Cliff Pepperidge has his Teodor Loeb—with a French horn." He waved up his circle of brass and valves and grinned. This guy Haydn also did a lot of things for cello, so many times Fritz sits in with Teodor and then does "Clouds" and "Festivals" from Debussy. They say they're jamming when they play Berlioz's "Roman Carnival," because it's fast.

Then there's Ernst; I know he prefers the flute to his clarinet, and he woodsheds with Bach, too—Sonata in A Minor and Sonata in C

Major. Thing that gets me about their music is that if you put down
the right time to it, it can swing, which is exactly what my colonel
once said. Seems like two thousand years since I knew him. Lord,
how long? Maybe once I start writing and hearing from Willy Lewis
on a regular basis, who knows what might happen? Who knows?
All this made me think of Sam. Long gone by now, with his guitar,
without looking back once, and I don't blame him. I hope his whole
family, if he had one, got the hell outa here. The Germans are death
on Jews, the way Americans are death on Negroes. I really don't
understand that shit, but I know I can't like it, don't like it. I just
wish I had the geetz, the *gelt,* the money, that Sam was able to come
up with. I hope he can do another book, like Beimler, tell about
Dachau, get us out of this place. But, you know, mostly, when a
joker's got his, it turns out he's not too worried about anybody else.

It's Eric Ulrich, though, who intrigues us the most. When he sets
up we don't have no time to worry about no Sam or anything else.
The music is all. Did he really play with those jokers? We can understand that he's gotta be careful. He don't say shit but see you tomorrow or next week. Then gone. Then back again. Last Friday I
thought I'd put some questions to him. I mean, who the fuck he
think he is, just slipping in and pulling up a chair? Didn't nobody
invite him to sit in. Sure, Bernhardt probably told him it was okay,
if he was careful, but Bernhardt's probably already got some kind of
bag to put Ulrich in by now. Like I got Baum.

So here he comes. I saw him. But I just took myself another sandwich in the kitchen and let him wait out there. Of course, when I
went out and found him sitting on the stand, I pretended to be surprised. All right. I sat down and ran up and down the keyboard and
he ran up and down his stops. Franz sneaked up and settled his
cheeks. Danko just sort of floated up beside the drums. Oskar and
Alex grabbed their Hohners, and Ernst and Teodor sidled up a
respectful distance from the *Oberleutnant.* Moritz stayed in the
kitchen with Fritz. I never said what I'd be playing because I didn't
know myself until I was already into the intro. Friday it was "The
Man I Love." I played that intro like a lawyer laying out his case,
slow and serious, heavy on the chords to let the *Oberleutnant* know

they were questions I wanted answers to. In the dim house lights—
Ulrich never sat directly under lights—I saw from the corner of my
eyes (it's not only in Dachau where some things are better seen from
the corners) his head turn toward me, his bright hair, like new hay
tossed in going-down sun, sparkling as he moved. I finished the
melody, statement, and questions, and started a series of ad-libs.
The first was "What's Your Story, Morning Glory?" How come you
play like you know the *lyrics,* the kinda poetry in the words some of
you jokers don't even know are there? And if you *are* the greatest
thing since fried chitlins because you played with Duke, Chick,
and Jimmy, how come you wearing that Nazi shit, and how come
you can't understand my—and here I gave him some melody from
"Mood Indigo"—? And I kept playing, finding melodies within crazy
long lines of improvisation, losing everyone on the changes but
Danko, throwing him "They Didn't Believe Me," "Body and Soul,"
"You Rascal You," "I Ain't Got Nobody."

Even with all the Chinese—the band trying to find the changes—
I heard Eric Ulrich's feet slide into a wider position. His lips went
funny into a little smile when he inhaled around his mouthpiece.
Right in between Danko's beat he blew very quickly the seven notes
that intro "I Cover the Waterfront," then back into the melody of
"The Man I Love." But before he finished that, I *thought* I heard
(and I looked around quick to see if anyone else thought he heard,
too), *"Deutschland, Deutschland, Über Alles,"* played hard like running
over stones, and cynical and made-fun-of, the way some of those
Masters of Ceremonies sometimes introduced acts in Berlin: daaa-
daaa, dee-dee, dum da do-do. I *thought* I even heard a goose step in
there. But before anybody could know for sure, he found a spot to fit
in "Way Down Yonder in New Orleans." He loved jazz and where it
came from and how it made him feel. He hit some notes that were
solid and on time (da da da-da da, ba tha ba da-ba da) . . . "I can't
believe it, it's hard to conceive it . . ."

Danko swiveled his head from me to the *Oberleutnant* and back;
he scowled at the others, What's going on? I know he didn't get any
answers. Franz was whisking those brushes around so soft that I knew
he didn't want to miss any answer that might come. It was just me

and Ulrich. In phrases that just ran beside the melody (and I knew he was searching), he found the reprise of "My Buddy." "Buddy" my behind, I thought, and threw him "I'll Never Be the Same." He got to his feet and planted them, and damned if he didn't cut the rhythm right in half to play um humm-humm da da da-da da dummmmm, um humm-humm da da da-da da dummmmm . . . "Nobody Knows the Trouble I've Seen, Nobody Knows My Sorrows." I led him back to "The Man I Love" and gave everybody time to get in, and we closed out. The *Oberleutnant* sat back down waiting for the next number. Everyone else sort of shuffled around trying not to look at each other. We had been doing some good things with "Tea," so we worked out on that and then "Honeysuckle Rose." Never forget that session. With the exception of Teodor soloing on "I Can't Get Started With You," me on the vocal, of course, the sets didn't go so hot that night, not that anyone but us knew it, because we were all thinking of Ulrich getting to his feet and the way he played and what he played. Everybody in the band knew I knew what he was saying, but they knew better than to ask. Maybe Bernhardt did notice. He thought we should add a conga and a rhumba to our repertoire.

Wednesday, June 30, 1937

Dieter Lange isn't fooling me. He's spooked because Himmler said not long ago that ss men caught in homosexual acts should be "shot while trying to escape." But he also said that actors and other artists who were caught plugging the hole or anything like that could not be arrested unless he approved. I been peeking at Anna; she sure doesn't look like she's anywhere near pregnant. I thought that last edict would have scared her and Dieter Lange into making a baby, but maybe they can't. And, even if she did get pregnant, dime to a dollar it wouldn't be Dieter Lange's kid. Hell, I *know* she's not pregnant.

I've managed to keep him off me a few times just by saying, "Shhh! What's that noise?" Or, "Listen—is that Anna?" There are always those times, though, when, whatever happens, I have to get mine, too, and there's no one else but him to give it to me. Yeah, he's scared. But he's been scared before.

Wrote this long letter to Willy Lewis telling him how much I cost and did he know people who could help get me out without the money, maybe because they got connections. Told him not to send anything because I wanted to keep the mail simple and not suspicious, and that he should send his letters to the woman whose return address is on the envelope. She would see I got his letters. Gave the letter to Baum in time for his wife's visit. He told me she was nervous, but he'd told her if she didn't take care of the letter, the answer, and other letters that would be going out and coming in, they'd bury him under Dachau. She just had to do it, he told her, and the less she knew why, the better off she'd be.

The new crematorium is finished.

We put in the conga and the rhumba. Then we threw the rhumba out, but kept the conga—da-da da-da doomp da, da-da da-da doomp da. ("Am-per Riv-er Con-ga!" "Am-per Riv-er Conga!") We got some maracas and gave them to Fritz. He found a sassy line inside the rhythm, and the conga line formed at least twice each set. I made up lyrics in my head, like the "Amper River Conga" and (also in my head) "Shake Yo Booo-ty *This Way*, Shake Yo Booo-ty *That Way*." Or, "Girl You Got Some *Big Ones*, How You *Get* Such *Big Ones?*" Or, "Hit-ler Is a *Fag*-got, What a Big Mouth *Fag*-got." New words came whenever we did a conga. It got to be fun. I was explaining the conga to Dr. Nyassa. When I finished, he said, "They do the same dance in Western Africa, only they call it the "High Life." Africans carried the dance to South America when they were made slaves." He laughed. "And look at the supermen and superwomen, the Aryans, dancing," he said growling, "like *niggers.*"

Friday, July 9, 1937

It's a hot bright day and it's quiet in the canteen where I'm writing today. Found myself a hiding place for you under the floorboards in the back room where we keep most of the stock. It gets very, very hot in here. There are no side windows, just front and back, and when they're open all the dust from the work that's always going on drifts in and settles everywhere—even under the floorboards. Outside: singing, running, marching, working, the loud-speaker, sometimes, and the dogs snapping at prisoners, right along with the guards.

The only time we hear the radio over here is when the big shots speak, but in Dieter Lange's house we listen to it just about every night. Goebbels, Hitler, this one, that one, some news of the fighting in Spain, a lot on how great Germany and the Germans are. The news about Martin Niemoeller being arrested and brought to Dachau was never broadcast. Werner told me. This man was captain of a submarine during the war and was pastor of the Protestant Free Church in Berlin. An anti-Hitlerite. Werner doesn't think he'll be here long. This is just to teach him a lesson. And if he doesn't shut up when he gets out . . .

Dieter Lange has everything set for the opening of Buchenwald on the 16th. He hates the work he has to do when a new camp is opened, but he likes the money he can rake off. And he and Anna have lots of that now, which is another reason why, whatever happens, they have to stick together. I even know where they hide the lock-box.

Baum should be due at any minute, so I've got to end this and gather the other sheets I sometimes have to leave here, and get over to Dieter Lange's. As usual, there'll be a session with Ulrich and two sets at The Nest tonight.

Tuesday, July 13, 1937

As soon as I came in the door last Friday, Anna called me from upstairs. She sounded high. "Cleef, Cleef! *Kommen sie hier!*" Something told me this was going to be trouble. "Dieter is in Munich, and it is two hours before the truck picks you up. Come!" she hollered. She would listen to no excuses. I wondered why she didn't come to the head of the stairs at least. I wasn't too happy walking upstairs. She had her head stuck out of her bedroom door, and it seemed to me, since I couldn't see any collar around her thick neck, that she might not have anything on. I stopped and said I was not feeling good and that I should rest before the truck came, but she kept saying, "Come on, come on," signaling with her finger. I asked what she wanted. "Come here," she said, "just come here."

I said, "But I'm afraid." And I was. Now I was close and she took my hand (I could see by her bare shoulders that she wasn't wearing clothes, at least not on top) and pulled me into the room she shared with Dieter Lange. I tried not to look at all that heavy white flesh and so looked elsewhere in the room and damned if Ursula Winkelmann wasn't laying there without so much as a button on. She smiled and held out her arms. Anna pushed me down to the bed and followed me there. "Frau Lange—" I started to say, but she shushed me.

"You remember our visit downstairs?" Ursula said. "When you were sick?"

I told her I didn't. They laughed. Anna began undoing the buttons on my clothes. She pressed hard on my skin and slid her hand over it. Ursula was at my shoes. I felt like I would throw up. "There," Anna said when they were finished. "Lie here between us." I was barely able to control my heaving stomach, but I knew I couldn't get up and run out; I knew what they could do and say. No different than back home, and they knew it.

First Anna kissed me with her thick lips and heavy tongue, and she was waiting for me to give her mine. Then Ursula, humping her high behind, wanted a kiss, too. So there I was, flat on my back while they crawled over me like bugs, panting and slobbering and grabbing my piece and jacking it up and down, first one, then the other, and then without a word, just all this breathing and sighing, took turns on the clarinet until I thought it would turn into a bar of steel. Then they shifted around on the bed, snatching and pulling at each other and me until Ursula was flat on her back and Anna was flat on her stomach, crawling right up into her with her mouth, while Ursula jacked me and thrashed around, legs flying, spit spattering, *"Mein Gott! Mein Gott!"* until she took one great breath and then, shuddering, let it out. Quick as a flash, Anna twisted over and Ursula was on top, burrowing between those heavy thighs. Now Anna was jacking and muttering, mumbling, licking, sucking. I thought to grab my clothes and leave, but Anna really had me,

and the closer she was to coming, the harder she squeezed as
she jacked. I kept looking at Ursula's behind, the sassy way it
curved up and out. (There'd been times when I thought mine
looked like that.) I unloosened Anna's hand and I felt her tense.
She looked at me, her eyes glazed. But I got up on my knees and
moved around behind Ursula. She felt me coming and raised herself up high. Anna was like some heifer now with all her racket
and bouncing around. I pushed my hips forward, brought up the
clarinet, fiddled (I'd never done this), found the place and ran it
in as Ursula tightened like I'd nailed her to a board. But she never
left off what she was doing and she was about to come again,
which she did as she forced her butt as far back on the stick
as it'd go. After that round we had to have another, but the clarinet
had to play Anna. When they finally let me go I went downstairs
and threw up.

All my life white women had been like bad voodoo; you simply
didn't have anything to do with them, not even if you worked at a
hotel where they were hooking and asked you to bring a bottle of
hooch into a room where they were with a "client." You didn't look,
or if you did, you made sure nobody was watching you. It was
different with white men; you were a man and so were they, and
so it didn't seem to matter if both of you were freaks. But this
business with Anna and Ursula was like all of us shuffling toward
the end of the world, and since we were on our way, nothing mattered. I didn't understand why they felt like that more than I did.
Maybe it was the camp, where so many things went on that nobody gave a damn about, and if nobody cared who was missing,
who drowned in shit, whose arms got pulled out of their sockets on
the pole, whose head got smashed in the quarry, why would anybody
care what a couple of SS wives were doing with each other? But they
would care if they knew I was with them, jooging them as they
tongue-whipped each other. I wasn't shuffling toward the end of
the world; I was being dragged there. I knew that because I was
scared about the fix I was in, so scared that I was shaking. I hated
them and myself. Them because they had the absolute power to do
anything they wanted; myself because I couldn't do anything about

it. I threw up again and got ready for the truck that was coming for the afternoon and night at The Nest.

———

Thursday, July 29, 1937

Everybody wondered about that new building put up behind the *Wirtschaftsgebaude,* at the south end of the camp. It's the place for the civilian "Prominents," the "Honored," and so they call it the "Honor Bunker." It's where they put Niemoeller, according to Hohenberg, and it will be the "Ritz Dachau" for other big shots who are yet to come, Werner says. (Werner has started taking trips down to the Puff, and so has Dr. Nyassa, who is popular with the farm girls who sneak in to work there. A colored doctor of anything must be pretty exotic, and besides, he can get the medicine to cure whatever ails them.)

Baum gave me a letter from Willy Lewis yesterday, and how good that felt! After all this time! That goddamn Dieter Lange! This'll show up his little red wagon. In my letter I had explained how I got here and how I was the houseboy for that German drunk who first told him about me. I also told Willy about the band, and asked if he'd ever heard of this Eric Ulrich. As I imagined, the question of the money is absolutely out. Willy said he would write to the union in New York, but that probably wouldn't help since he wasn't a member and neither was I. He does not have an address for Mr. Wooding but is trying to get the address for the Moe Gale Agency because they might know how to get in touch with him. He was surprised that I got picked up for "funny business," since people in Europe don't seem to get excited about that kind of thing. He hadn't heard that Germany was getting snotty about it, because lots of Germans who come to Holland are quite open about the way they are. Maybe, he wrote, they come because things have changed in Germany. No, he hadn't heard of Ulrich, but he'd been away a long time, too. Being a houseboy and leading a band didn't sound as bad as it could be. But prison is prison and he understood my wanting to get out.

Couldn't he visit and bring something, even if he wasn't a relative? Couldn't something be worked out? In the meantime, he would write to anyone he thought might help get me out. He was also sending letters to the *Chicago Defender,* the *Pittsburgh Courier,* and the *Afro-American.* There was a 100-mark note in the letter.

Reading Willy's letter was like opening a door on the first warm spring day to air out a house that had been closed tight all winter. I cried when I finished reading it, not because of the hole I was in, but because I'd managed to reach through almost five years and get someone to respond. Remembering Willy and his alto sax, he seemed more like Gabriel with his trumpet, not on Judgment Day but Jubilee Day. I prayed there in the back room of the canteen. Hadn't done that in a long time because there didn't seem to be Anybody or Anything to explain my situation to. I asked the Lord to forgive me. He knew the things I'd done I had to do. And some of the people I did them with were supposed to be real Christians. Christians, yeah, but as far as I knew, it was Christians who were running this part of the world. I prayed anyway, including to a Loa for good measure, and I gave thanks for reaching Willy.

Werner's "people"—they were teachers, doctors, lawyers, clerks, scientists, reporters, plumbers, carpenters, toolmakers, masons, bricklayers, labor leaders, officeholders, writers, students, musicians, painters, and the like—are worried about what's going on in Austria. Some of their friends have been killed by Austrian fascists. Over four years ago 1,000 were killed and 3,000 wounded when the workers' buildings in Vienna were shelled. That was during my first year here, and my thoughts were mostly about myself. Being with Werner is like being with a teacher.

The Europe he talks about isn't the same one I knew when I was a free man. He thinks Britain and France should stand up to Hitler and Mussolini—especially Hitler—but bets they won't. In the meantime, he said, you can see for yourself what's going on in Germany: new roads, new air corps, new ships for the navy, adventures (he calls them) in Alsace and Spain, and talks with the Japanese that have to end in a treaty; conscription, concentration camps—these started with the British in the Boer War, he told me, in Africa, but they sure didn't stay there, and when these in Germany are finished, there'll be camps elsewhere, because people are stupid and their leaders lie.

"Give the people other people they can be better than," he said, "and they'll be happy. Make Communists and Jews 'bad Germans,' and the people will certainly hate them because it'll be legal to do so." He said the leaders change the laws so people they don't like will be outside them—the way it is for colored people in America—then they are not only outside the law, they are no longer citizens of the nation that made the law that put them outside it. So they have no citizenship. They are stateless persons, not covered by law, and are *Dreck, Scheiss.*

"You can do whatever you wish with words like 'citizen' and 'national' because in Germany they don't have to mean the same thing." He said the Americans had done it during slavery and after, and the Russians had done pretty much the same thing after their revolution. "The Germans just picked it up, and you can bet your last pfennig the method will be used again. And again."

Werner's talks always left me feeling blue, like the future was going to be just as bad as it is right now. But I'd get over the feeling after a while; now his words just hung around, like mist from the swamp.

Monday, August 20, 1937

A band can only play well if the musicians come together as one while allowing a single player to take a solo and run. But he must return home, be welcomed back, and then let another take the trip and come home. Sort of like sending a child away to grow up by improvising his way through a life he knows he can always return to—the melody. I'd never played with white musicians before, never wanted to. Training's different and so are the experiences we put into our music. Few white musicians can describe pain or joy in their music, or at least not the kind of pain or joy Negro musicians know. That's the mystery, I guess. They want to know about it, not live it. In Dachau all that changes. Fear gets to be a kind of pain you have to live with—everybody, all the time.

On Fridays and Saturdays it's different for us musicians; we get to do what we love, even with the restrictions on what and how we can play, even with the instruments we're stuck with. Every weekend I thank God for Bernhardt, and also for Dieter Lange, because it was through him that Bernhardt got to know my music. My life here could have been a shit storm like so many other prisoners'. Instead, I've played music, learned to read music (a little), learned to appreciate the violin and what it can do through Moritz (who doesn't seem so moody anymore, maybe because—I think—he's got a friend, another prisoner who works at The Nest). Moritz is almost funny now, sometimes. And Fritz has stopped apologizing for everything. Ernst doesn't look so evil anymore, and he's found that he can do things with both the flute and clarinet he never thought of before. Oskar and Alex have learned when to go and when not to on their instruments. They're blending in very well now and both do sweet little solos, with a French atmosphere that everyone seems to like. They've also both found girlfriends from among the maids that work in the Pussy Palace, and when they don't take the time to eat before rehearsal, I figure they're knocking off a quickie. Teodor is more than confident; sometimes he's so arrogant (that's when he makes lots of mistakes, thinking that French horn can do everything a trumpet can) I have to sit on him. "Little Django," Danko, has the kind of personality everyone likes. He's only nineteen, and if he ever gets out of here, he's got a great future. About Franz, I don't know; he's more showman than musician, and his set isn't complete. I guess he does the best he can. He just can't seem to learn that there are times when the drums should be seen and just barely heard. There are rhythms still to be explored, but he's not too interested. Timing, phrasing, knowing what the other guy's going to do, have made us a band.

Right now, I don't think anyone even gives a thought anymore to trying to escape on the truck rides to and from The Nest. The jokers in the band even walk different than when we first got together. Compared to the average *Haftling,* they too are "prominent," even if they are inside the walls. Things seem swell, copasetic. This is a good life by Dachau standards, but it's not a *free* life. Things can change at any moment.

Speaking of escape, Werner was right. Niemoeller wasn't held very long. He's out. Maybe there is power enough out there to make the Nazis think twice.

The Winkelmanns have moved into a new house on a street where other new houses have been built for the SS who are married and have families. Ursula has been so busy getting settled that she hasn't been over; instead, Anna visits her. It's nice and quiet around the house when she and Dieter Lange are gone. The SS has been expanded again, I guess because the increase in prisoners means more guards. In place of the rickety wooden watchtowers, new concrete ones have been built into the walls. There are six: two at the south end, two on the east side, one on the north wall, and one on the west wall. The top of the *Jourhaus*, also on the west, serves as still another watchtower. There are armed guards in these all day and all night.

Just inside the wall is the electrified fence, and inside it, a few feet of earth with grass. Then the moat they're finishing up; that will be about four feet deep and eight feet wide. On this side of it there is more earth. Nobody is supposed to be on that. Inside the second strip is where the camp streets begin. Thirty-four barracks, seventeen on each side of the Lagerstrasse, the main street, and spread across the front of them is the roll-call square, the Appellplatz.

To the west of the camp, where the little Amper River forms another moat, are the restored factory buildings and, beyond them, the married SS compound where I live with Dieter Lange and Anna. Inside the walls at the north end are gardens and a greenhouse and the disinfection hut. Northwest, outside the walls, is the crematorium. The SS rifle range, the swamps, and the quarry are all outside the north walls, and beyond the walls, north and east, are the farmlands that many prisoners work for the neighboring farmers. I never heard of a southern plantation during slavery that was run more efficiently.

Annaliese has found a place in SS society, I think. She impressed Ursula with her English, but that done, thank God, she doesn't seem to have much interest in it anymore. In fact, the bitch surprises me when she comes up with some English. Now, that's a burden, knowing about her and Ursula, but they carry it off okay. I don't think Dieter Lange would care if he knew. I don't know Captain Winkelmann that well. Maybe he'd care and maybe he wouldn't. But *I* know something Dieter Lange doesn't, and that's like having lead in the bank, because I can't cash it anywhere.

Wed., January 5, 1938

I have been busy and lazy, and it's already the New Year. I guess I have to catch up—except there's nothing much to catch up on. I've written three letters to Willy and got three answers. Baum's wife seems to be getting used to the arrangement. Whenever Baum gives me a letter, I slip him a few packs of cigarettes so he can carry on trades, get those little extras they don't allow you to have. But I invoice them as "missing," so there's a big chunk of inventory in cigarettes unaccounted for. Baum doesn't know that if he messes up, I'll just hand the list over to Dieter Lange, tell him Baum (and the guards) took them, and it'll be Baum's plump round behind. Of course, I'll say nothing about my own nest egg under the floor-boards—cigarettes, candy, canned fruits, and meat. For a rainy day.

Willy once suggested that he write directly to the camp comman-dant requesting my release. When I wrote back, I told him it would be better if someone representing an organization did that, but through offices in Berlin, otherwise these brutes could make me vanish. (A prisoner name of Kurt Schumacher had the woman he's engaged to, an American from Chicago, write directly to Hitler. Schumacher's a Red, a newspaperman, and was a Social Democrat M.P. They liked to have beat his ass to death and put it under Dachau!) Willy has already written to *Downbeat* and the NAACP and the colored papers, but hasn't heard anything from them yet. It's so frustrating! He could get things we need for the band, but if he sent them to Frau Baum . . . So, I mostly tell him what life is like here, my routine, the band. He writes about Amsterdam or Paris or London or Copenhagen where he goes to play, and how most people don't even know about camps like Dachau. Willy says there's a lot of war talk, but it doesn't bother him. As far as he's concerned, it's

white folks' business and they could all do each other in and he
wouldn't lose any sleep. Sure, he wrote, it's better than home, but
don't peel the banana back too far. It's only their fascination with
Negroes that's kept the Europeans from treating them the way
Americans do—so far. Had I heard anything about how the Nazis
took the kids of the German women and colored American soldiers
who'd been stationed in the Rhineland right after the war and made
them so they couldn't have children? They hadn't done anything like
that to me, had they? What's all this stuff about blood and honor
and Nuremberg laws?

I like for Willy to ask questions because they make me think
about things I put out of my mind. Then I ask questions, talk to
Werner and the other Reds and Dr. Nyassa and Gitzig. Oh! Gitzig
got him some. Down at the Puff. Bernhardt, it seems, decided to let
him go once a month. Gitzig looks forward to it, but I know he'd
rather deliver milk closer to home. (Gitzig is also coming into camp
once in a while to work in the Political Office.) While they haven't
given him "Prisoner Foreman" markings, Dr. Nyassa now seems to
be in charge of Infirmary Two. He's pretty free again with the medicinal brandy. That evil-looking block leader in One has nothing to
do with Dr. Nyassa now, but both, along with the helpers, report to
doctors—doctors who are very blasé about patients, whether they
have colds or fractured skulls.

It's the time of year nobody likes. It's the time of the snow commandos and the worst time for roll calls, especially the evening ones.
The snow commandos are the prisoners detailed to clear the snow
from the entire camp, not with shovels, but with boards nailed to
planks. Snow is as forbidden to exist in camp as flower beds are forced
to be in camp. Flower beds. In this hellhole. I watch the snow commandos shovel from the canteen window; shovel, while the prisoner
foremen and detail leaders and the ss holler and scream, kick, hit, and
beat them. But the snow gets cleared and then everything is ice and
frozen mud. Clothes freeze on the prisoners, become as stiff as the
boards they shovel with. Their eyes water with the cold, and their noses
run—but, at least at five o'clock, they can quit and march to their
blocks singing to the music the band plays (some of my boys playing).

The *Strafappell* is punishment for every prisoner in the camp if even one man doesn't answer the roll call. Some prisoners are too tired to move. They hide and sleep. Some have tried to escape. Others are too sick. But for any roll call, the prisoner has to be in his place on the Appellplatz. If not, then 6,999 other prisoners stand *Strafappell* until the prisoner clerks can present to the roll-call officer a tally that shows all prisoners present and accounted for. I watch the roll calls from the canteen window. In warm weather even the *Strafappell* isn't bad; sometimes the sunsets can almost make a man forget that he's standing at attention, his hands along the seams of his pants, his cap tucked under his arm. Of course, people fall out on the ground, or get sick standing up, or even, as I've heard but never seen, die right there and keel over. Winter makes it worse. I look out the window and thank God for Dieter Lange. Seven thousand men standing like posts pounded into the ground, the winter night wrapped around the outsides of the searchlights. When things go well, roll call takes an hour and a half; when things do not go well—*Strafappell* can last all night with the lights on, the dogs barking, the guards shouting and cursing, the prisoners answering weakly or falling out, freezing, turning blue. And for the men who caused the *Strafappell*, there is pure, distilled hatred and maybe a beating in the shower, maybe even an "accidental" killing—a push from the top of the quarry stone, a push into the sewer or marsh, a falling tree, a gravel-filled wagon run over a foot or hand, and so on. For one man, or two or even three, cannot be allowed to make thousands suffer. That is how the ss keeps order, by placing the responsibility for keeping order upon the prisoners themselves.

I'm always afraid there will come that night when they call me out and stand me in a place to be counted just like the others, like so many heads of cattle or sharecroppers needed to pick cotton. Cross my fingers. Knock on wood. Turn three times. Call on the Loas. Pray.

Monday, January 24, 1938
On Saturday I watched a group of prisoners move a pile of frozen gravel from the far end of the 'Platz. Yesterday another group, the

Punishment Company, which works even on Sunday, was putting it right back when the whistle and sirens began to sound. "Roll call for Jehovah's Witnesses. Roll call! All Bible students! Roll call!"

They came out of their blocks shivering in the cold, sliding on the snow and ice and frozen mud, their purple triangles crinkling on their knees and chests as they approached the Dancing Ground, where leashed dogs and hollering guards surrounded and pushed them into formation. I know the other prisoners were relieved they weren't being called out, too. Especially the Jews and the freaks. Everyone in the canteen who was not a Witness crowded to the windows, yet tried to stay out of sight; wanted to see but not be seen, because who knew what an SS guard might take a notion to do?

I saw Menno!

He looked *bad.* His eyes had that narrow, crafty look every other Protective Custody prisoner in Dachau has. Dr. Nyassa tells me they are still working his behind off in *Revier* One and on various labor details as well. He was shaking with the cold. I studied him as if he were a stranger. The kind of joker I wouldn't want to meet in an alleyway after the last set. I couldn't even remember our making love; that seemed to have happened a long time ago. He might have been younger than me, but I knew I now looked younger. This place can age you in no time flat, no time at all, and faster if you've really done the hard time. When the Witnesses were in formation and the roll taken, over the loudspeaker the roll-call officer shouted:

"On this German Christian Sunday we offer you nonbelievers an opportunity to pledge allegiance to the State, after which your sentences will be reconsidered, with release a probability. You will repeat after me. I, say your name!" (We heard the dissonance of 1,500 names being called out.) "Born, give your birth date!" (Again that ragged, splattering sound, this time of numbers.) "In, the town, the town!" (The sound was like a thousand different birds squawking at once.) "*One!* I acknowledge that the International Association of Jehovah's Witnesses advocates a false doctrine using their religious activities as a pretext in their subversive aims. *Two!* I have therefore totally rejected this organization and have freed myself emotionally from the sect. *Three!* I hereby undertake never again to work for the International

Association of Jehovah's Witnesses. I shall report any persons who approach me with the false doctrine of Jehovah's Witnesses or those who in any way display sympathy for them. Should I receive any Jehovah's Witness literature, I shall surrender it immediately to the nearest police station."

"Police station?" they were saying in the canteen. "That means they'll be freed! You think they'll agree? Bet? How much? How many cigarettes?"

"Four! I shall in the future observe the laws of the nation especially in the event of war, when I shall take up arms to defend my Fatherland and strive to become a wholehearted member of the national community. *Five!* I have been informed that I must expect a further term of Protective Custody if I fail to observe the present opportunity made today." The ranks remained still, straight, and stiff. They can get out! I thought. Go free! And once out, keep truckin' and never look back.

"Those accepting the opportunity presented by the Fuhrer . . . two steps forward!"

I know they were dying to look at each other, to read each other's eyes, to see how strong was the faith. But the ranks stayed the same —for three or four seconds, the balloons of breath drifting above them. Then they broke. There was a man who stepped forward and hung his head; and then two, three, four others, and others followed until fully half the Witnesses had taken the two steps forward, among them Menno Becker. Almost at once, the guards and dogs closed in, dividing the two groups, herding those who'd accepted to the east side of the 'Platz and those who hadn't to the west.

I went into the back room and left the running of the canteen to Baum. In the front the customers were murmuring, "War, did you hear him? 'In the event of war,' he said. Oh, shit. Then they *are* serious with this *Lebensraum.* . . ." I was thinking, Austria, Czechoslovakia, Poland, Austria, Czechoslovakia, Poland . . . And after those, what? Who?

Thursday, February 10, 1938

The morgue is in *Revier* One, in the back. It's where they keep
the bodies before examination. Then they take them to the crematorium and burn them in the incinerator and pot the ashes for
sending home. I never had anything to do with morgues. But yesterday Dr. Nyassa came into the canteen and asked me to come with
him. There was something he wanted to show me. There isn't
much heat in the blocks, only a small stove in each barrack living
room. The stove is smaller in the canteen, but when you have to go
out in the snow and wind, you grow to appreciate what little heat
you do get. And we just had to cross the Lagerstrasse. Dr. Nyassa
wasn't very talkative. He was bundled up. His nose and eyes were
running from the cold, which had turned his skin more gray than
black, and he seemed frozen in the blues. We went through the
ward—there're always more patients in the winter; everyone's
sick from the cold—and into the back. When it's this cold, they
don't turn on the machinery that keeps the bodies cold; they don't
need it.

It was dim in there, and very still. The windows were iced over.
Dr. Nyassa reached up and pulled the light string. Bodies lay in rows
on the floor, each fixed in position as if molded in plaster, with just
enough space to walk between them. In spite of the cold, there was
a heavy smell, like you get when you walk into a butcher's freezer.
"Here," he said. We'd reached a corner where the smell seemed to
have collected. Menno. Menno, without a stitch of clothes on.
I could hardly tell it was him, his face was so beat up and swollen.
His head was twice its normal size. I looked at his body. There were
long purple welts on it, from his head down to his ankles, each raised
so high I couldn't believe it. His whatchacallit was black, blue, and
purple, big as a salami, frozen blood still on what was left of it.
I began to shake. What would they do to *me* if they found out, if I
had no protection? Dr. Nyassa said, "When they get mad at you
fellows, they do anything. He's not the first." He lifted his foot
and pointed it toward Menno's crotch. "They are animals, *animals*.
They wouldn't do this to a pig."

"I thought they were letting him go," I said.

Dr. Nyassa turned me and gently pushed me out. "They were never going to let him go, Pepperidge. Make an example of him. He had hard time coming. He was doing hard time," he said. "They were supposed to take his body to the oven so nobody would see this, which is what they usually do. But something must've come up, so they put him here until tonight. Your friend Werner got word from someone who heard it all in the Bunker last night. Worst thing they'd ever heard coming out of that place."

Dr. Nyassa said, "God help us. I live in fear that because I put my penis in a white woman, wife or not, they'll take it off, and yet, you know, even with that fear I keep going to those farm girls at the Puff."

I returned to the canteen. It was starting to snow hard. Baum could tell something was wrong, and he didn't bother me. I stared out the window and thought of voodoo revenge. But I didn't have any eggs to tie to Menno's hands, and there was no coffin to put him face down in, and I sure didn't have and couldn't get seven red candles for the bottom end of his coffin or nine white ones for the head. I couldn't spend the two days and nights called for to do these things. And there would be no burial, with fresh-turned dirt on which I could throw broken eggshells. Even New Orleans voodoo took a whipping from the Nazis. So I stared out the window and could not cry. "God loves you, brother," Menno had said the very first time we met, and I thought, He's got a damned funny way of showing it. Even you must be surprised, Menno.

Monday, Mar. 14, 1938

Gitzig told me last week that it looked as though he might be going off on a brief trip soon, out into the world for a spell. But that was all he said, and I figured he was full of shit and was feeling his oats because he was moving in and out of the camp, doing his private work for Bernhardt, and managing to get some pussy now and again. But I guess he knew what he was talking about because yesterday was the "Joining." I should have known something was going on because there was a strange atmosphere in The Nest when we played

Friday and Saturday. We got requests for marches and the old
German songs. A kind of excitement about something nobody really
knows, only guesses at. Hitler is supposed to march into Vienna
today. Hitler's going to Austria and Dieter Lange is going crazy trying to figure out canteen supplies for the 80,000 Austrians who will
be coming to the camps in Germany or going to camps already
planned in Austria. "Sure, we can make money," I heard him tell
Anna, "but will all this planning never end, and how can I stop all
this infernal stealing? Most of the goddamn SS ought to be wearing
green or black triangles."

I told Baum to question his wife very carefully about the mail
from Holland. He said she said nothing had come. So I asked Baum:
"Is she destroying the letters? Did you tell her to destroy them and
say nothing had come? Did you tell her to destroy my letters?"

"Ah, no, Pepperidge. Please believe. No. You think I want
trouble? Maybe your friend just doesn't write anymore. Maybe he
went away. Maybe he's sick. I would never tell my wife to do as you
just said, never."

Willy Lewis owes me two letters, so I decided not to write until
I hear from him. The SS might be smelling something, so it's best
to leave it be for now. If he writes, he'll probably talk about Austria.
After that conversation with Baum, I learned that a lot of people
aren't getting mail anymore—Dr. Nyassa, Werner, and others. But the
prisoners who get fine packages from home have no trouble. Of
course, they have to divvy up with the guards and the "seniors" who
run the blocks and the camp and details. But the big thing is Austria.
The Reds are about the only prisoners who aren't happy. Maybe the
Witnesses, too, but for different reasons. Everybody else is strutting
around like mugs. The English did nothing, the Russians did nothing, and the French did nothing. Well, the Germans weren't shitting
on *their* doorsteps.

Sunday, March 20, 1938

Gitzig didn't go any fucking place. Saw him this afternoon carrying lumber into Bernhardt's house. Sneaked over and peeked into the

cellar window. Bernhardt's got him building the same kind of compartments Dieter Lange's got in our cellar—except that instead of wire screening, Bernhardt's got wooden walls. Looks like some of the loot from Austria will wind up down there, and I guess he doesn't want anybody to see what's behind the partitions. I rapped on the window and when Gitzig turned around, I grabbed my dick and shook it at him and left. Gitzig may not have gone to Austria, but I'd bet a dime to a dollar Bernhardt did, because he hasn't been around The Nest in a couple of weeks. I let Werner know that. I was feeling pretty goddamn put out this afternoon, too, because I was walking toward the gatehouse, on my way home, when I saw Ulrich. He was coming toward me, right toward me. I stopped, took off my cap, the way you're supposed to, and he went right on by without even so much as a "Kiss my ass," and I wondered where did he get off with shit like that, after always wanting to play with us, hanging around, waiting, until we knew that we were the best thing that'd happened to him in a long time. We knew he enjoyed playing. This was the thanks. Well, I thought, I will put this motherfucker through some changes the next time; he'll think he was wallowing lip-deep in shit. Fix his hincty wagon.

The guards are all talking about "new guests," and I suppose they mean Austrians. This place is now so big that you can't know what's going on from one end to the other, from one side to the other, from one day to the next. People come and people go; some walk out, and some don't, and the more prisoners come, the more guards come. Before I left camp, I ran into Hohenberg from the Labor Office. There are a lot more prisoners working there now. All tailors, he told me, have been detailed to make Jewish stars until further notice. He drew his finger across his throat and whispered, "Hitler wasn't kidding."

———

Wednesday, April 6, 1938

I still can't believe it. At noon today Karlsohn comes into the canteen. I'm wanted at the gatehouse. *Schnell!* I want to ask him why, but that's dangerous, and of course, he doesn't tell me why. Just to get my ass over there quick. The last time I was in that place was to see Count von Hausberger, almost four years ago. That wasn't during regular visiting hours and neither is this. I start thinking, Oh, shit. The letters. What else could it be? I'm walking fast across the 'Platz, thinking it might be my last walk. Spring's on the way, the time when you start to feel like a human being again. I'm hoping it's not my last spring.

I get to the gatehouse and the guards are smiling at me the way people smile when you're the butt of a joke, or like you're some kind of clown, or a joker with two heads. "Your mother's here," Reckse whispers. He's a sergeant of the guards. He's okay. I think to myself, *Mother!* He points up the same stairs where I saw Hausberger, and up I climb. At least it's not about the letters or Reckse would not have been so nice. I was trembling. *Mother?* I smelled perfume that wasn't gardenia before I got into the room, and then I saw in the great light that sweeps from the sky across the 'Platz, a small round figure in black, packages on the floor beside her.

The woman seemed to be weeping softly. "Oh, Lord Jesus, thank you. Oh, sweet Jesus, Amen," she was mumbling between sobs. Behind the desk stood the duty officer of the gatehouse, a captain.

I came to attention again when I crossed the threshold. "Captain—" I said, but before I finished, the woman was on her feet rushing toward me, crying, boo-hoo-hooing, and shouting, the fat on her jiggling like jelly.

"Clifford! Oh, Clifford! Great God Awmighty! My son, my son. Thank you cap'n. Thank you boss," and as she closed to embrace me, she winked and wrapped her arms about me, still sobbing, still thanking Jesus.

The captain cleared his throat. He was watching a minstrel show and it pleased him. He could afford to be kind, because he was being amused. "Prisoner Pepperidge, number 3003," he said. "I have been ordered to allow this woman, your mother, just from America, this special visit because of her age and illness." The woman and I backed off just enough to study each other. Behind her tears she winked again and—Damn! Ruby Mae Richards! "You have one-half hour, and you may keep the packages."

I stepped back from Ruby to attention as the captain went out. As he did, I said, "Mother, I didn't know you were sick, what's wrong?"

She opened her mouth to talk, but I put my hand over it and led her back to the seat. I pulled up a chair beside her. "Whisper," I whispered. "If I talk out loud then you talk out loud." She nodded. Ruby Mae Richards was a fat little woman some people called "Little Bessie" or "Princess of the Blues," since Bessie Smith was "Queen of the Blues" and Clara Smith was "Moaner of the Blues." She had sung with Louis Armstrong, James P. Johnson, and Fletcher Henderson, last I heard, back home. Sang "Nobody Knows the Way I Feel Dis Mornin'," "Broken Busted Blues," did a couple of duets with Bessie, and so on. She was bad, too, could punch out your average man, and that made people wonder just what she carried between her legs. Right then I was so glad to see another colored musician from outside that I didn't care if she had cannonballs under her dress. Didn't know her well, but our paths had crossed, like they always do with musicians.

"I'm so happy you could come," I said aloud and then whispered quickly, "How'd you get here?"

"Oh, son (boo-hoo) it's so good to see you," she said, then whispered, "Willy asked me to come and see what the hell's going on here."

"Can't the doctors *do* anything?" I hope I sounded mournful. "But how'd you manage to get in *here?*" I whispered.

"They tryin', son, they tryin'," she boomed, and then whispered, "I just laid some of that old ignorant mammy shit on them, a little Jesus-Christ-will-bless-you business, you know. It worked all the way from the French border and right into this slammer. You know how *that* goes. Just play the nigger. Niggers can't hurt you. They're funny. I also got some phony statements from doctors and a joker works in the embassy in Paris." She paused to let loose a moan and some more boo-hoos. Then in kind of a half-scream she said, "Clifford, what did you do to get in this place? Didn't I raise you better?"

She put her arms around my neck and I put mine around hers and we rocked and whispered. "Willy came down to Paris and told me the letters he sent you through that German woman were coming back stamped 'Unknown.' We figured an old black woman doin' your mammy could do better than a black man trying to get in here to find out if you were dead or alive. Are you in here *forever?* How much time you draw? What you done?"

Last time I saw her she didn't have any gray in her hair, but that was a long time ago. I suppose I looked a helluva lot older than *she* remembered, too. I told her what had happened and what was going on now. This was between a lot of boo-hoos and moaning and groaning and sometimes we even laughed. I cried, too, because here was some home-folks, after all this time. But what she finally had to say wasn't very funny. Whenever anyone made an inquiry, and Ruby Mae said Willy had said there weren't too many of those, the response from Germany was that no record had been found of a Clifford Pepperidge. Everyone, she said, was afraid of the Germans, even the Americans, and nobody's about to lay their bottom dollar or play their hole card on a nigger faggot, she whispered, any more than they would for a bull dyke. She smiled and I knew that what people had gossiped about for years was true. "I don't know what we can do," she said. Nearly everybody who's colored had left Germany, and some are leaving Europe. Had she run into this German joker, tenor man, who'd sat in with Duke, Chick, and Jimmy?—Ulrich? I asked. But lately I'd been thinking, There's a big difference between *playing* with someone, as the rumor went with Ulrich, and *sitting in.* She said, no, but that name sounded familiar—a big blond German supposed to be a friend—maybe the only one around in this part of Germany. Then she asked if I'd heard anything of Valaida Snow, who used to sing with Fatha Hines and was now running around Europe somewhere?

I said, "What can I hear about anything in here?" But I was thinking, If Ulrich's a friend, he sure got a funny way of showing it.

The captain returned and stood holding the door open, waiting. The minstrel show was over. I hit the floor, ramrod stiff. The half hour had gone by like a minute. Ruby Mae, crying, embraced me again. (Ah-boo-hoo-hoo.) The captain assured me that they'd get her to the station and see she got the right train back to France. Poor old nice little mammy like that, but no additional visits would be permitted. I thanked him. Ruby Mae dropped to her knees like a bag of fertilizer and thanked him, too, and told him God would bless him for being so kind to an old mammy done come all the way from Down South, United States of America. It's wise to thank all the SS and even the few SA for any break they give you. The captain said my mother had told him this was the only camp she knew about and so she came here. Wasn't it remarkable that she got to the right place the first time? I said yes it was, but my mother had always been lucky that way because she trusted in God. I thanked him again for his kindness. And that was it. I had made some contact. Willy knew I was here and alive, if not well in spirit. I hadn't vanished. A few people thought about me, and one even cut through the shit and visited me, but I was thinking, Oh, that fucking Baum! Oh, Baum's fucking wife!

Thursday, April 7, 1938

   Dieter Lange called me right up to his office the first thing in the morning. Before I could fix breakfast. Anna wasn't even up. I took the invoices with me. He couldn't talk too loud, because he didn't want Anna to hear. He wanted to know who the woman was who'd come yesterday; he knew I didn't know if my real mother was dead or alive. He was mad and he was nervous. I told him some of the truth, that she'd been sent by Willy Lewis to see if I was all right. It was all his fault, after all, because, if he hadn't been running his mouth in Amsterdam to Willy, none of this would have happened. Not even Anna would have known about us (except that, knowing her the way I do now, she would have come to know). And who was the woman? It turned out he once had a couple of records by Ruby Mae. We went downstairs and I started breakfast while he worried. "No more visitors," he kept saying, "no more visitors. Too risky." I said what was I supposed to do if, *if* I ever got another visitor, and he wasn't around? Was I supposed to tell the guards to kiss my ass?

That brought the worry lines back to his forehead. He wondered what they knew at the camp commandant's office. He was glad that Eichmann had gone; too snoopy, too quiet. Better off working on the "Jewish Question." The more he talked, the more confident he became that nothing would come of Ruby Mae's visit. The "mammy visit," he called it, after I'd described to him how she'd behaved, and how she'd looked. "She'd be great with the Gestapo," he said, and the worried look came into his eyes again. Once he seemed calmer, I went after Baum.

"Baum's a crook," I said. "Look here. See?" I placed the invoices on the table where he was having the breakfast I'd fancied up. He glanced at me, and then the sheets, but he didn't miss a beat shoveling the food into his mouth. "This goes back a little while," he finally said. I told him I wasn't sure at first, what with Karlsohn and the others who always take what they want. "But see," I said, pointing, "what they take isn't anything like what Baum takes, and besides, what can I do if the guards steal the goods?" Baum was another story, I said.

"All right! All right!" Dieter Lange said. "Let me go over these invoices." I saw that he was checking the imported cigarettes. "That fat little fucker," he said. "That two-bit crook—"

Anna's cry from upstairs startled us both: "What're you two faggots doing down there, huh?" Dieter Lange rolled his eyes at me. I started Anna's breakfast in a light-hearted mood. Baum's ass was mine.

Wednesday, April 13, 1938

Last Friday at The Nest I was fooling around on the piano, not really playing anything that could be recognized for more than three or four notes. Ulrich came into the hall. He always comes at the same time, and I recognized his footsteps. They stopped. I had a feeling that he was trying to guess what kind of mood I was in from the way I was playing. He started walking again, but it wasn't his usual walk. The rest of the band was in the kitchen, of course, finishing up the meal. Ulrich climbed up, sat down, and opened his case. He strapped on his horn and waited for me to lead him into something. But I didn't stop what I was doing; I just acted like he wasn't there. Through the open windows I heard the babies crying in the nursery, and I damned them to death right then, not when they would become part of Hitler's 600 new regiments, but then and there. Didn't need any more Germans like those already grown.

If there'd been music for hate, I'd have played it because of that meeting in the 'Platz that had been more pass-by than meeting. I was still salty about that. Ruby Mae and Willy Lewis were wrong. This wasn't the joker who was a friend. This was a Nazi, a superman, who was supposed to just appear and the machinery would be turned on right away for him. Oh, no, not anymore. I didn't turn an inch. It was just me and him, with everyone in the kitchen or somewhere nearby, fucking, trying to fuck, or getting fucked, as they always did, until the beat and swing of a melody reached them. Ulrich waited. I gave him nothing, just like last week and the week before that. He shuffled his feet. I didn't hear them, or pretended not to. He tapped them. I gave him shit. The only music I know about that's got mad in it is the classical stuff. The music I was brought up with and played didn't have it. I was looking for something that would tell Eric Ulrich to kiss my ass, but it wasn't in our music. Our music signified, it was sassy, it was joyful, and it was blue. There was no hate in it. There should have been a lot in it. Maybe one day there would be, if not hate or anger, then the low-down gospel truth, the I-am-tired-of-taking-your-shit truth. Couldn't call that hate music or mad music, just getting-ready-to-get-even music. I hit a chord that had so many angles in it, Ulrich stopped moving his feet, trying to figure out what it said. I kept creeping up and down the keyboard, thinking about our music and how this Nazi thought he could lay hold of it and still be the sonofabitch he was.

I heard doors squeaking open, felt eyes boring through the dim. This was the third week of this, and the guys in the band thought he must be good and mad by now. Maybe they heard something strange in the dissonant sounds Ulrich was now tootling. I was throwing out notes and smothering or snatching them back in favor of other ones. Our music never celebrated death the way white folks' music did, I was thinking; our music rose above it or at least didn't take you to

Valhalla where you killed all day and ate all night and didn't even have time to make love. James Reese Europe took all the fighting songs and built joy into them; the Europeans sensed that. For us, death was a Rambler, an Easy Rider; when the music took you through the St. James Infirmary, it remembered what love had been like. So I noodled and Ulrich tootled. We could have been a hundred miles apart. The bark and bite of the red, white, and black never came. Ulrich packed his horn and left without a word, once more, and the band came on for rehearsal.

Moritz eased up to me and whispered, "Is this wise, Pepperidge?"

I said, "Look. Fuck wise. Let's work on 'Lady Be Good.' Give you a chance to work off some of that bitchiness." Some of my anger was catching; rehearsal was a mess until Teodor just went off the scales with some bleedily-blee shit and I had to holler at him. They were mad at me because they didn't know what Ulrich would do to us, but I knew he had to be Double C, calm and collected, because of Bernhardt. That's exactly why I showed my ass the way I did. I ain't no fool. I don't have to let these jokers know everything *I* know. But we did the sets as we always did, a little weak now and again, and more sweet than swing, and I was wishing for the biggest brass section in the world to cover up the faking. But, however bad we are, if I cut the fool now and again, got down over the keyboard like it wouldn't let me go, or sang with my eyes closed like the shit is even good to *me*, why, we got by.

The day after Dieter Lange and I had that little talk about Baum, Baum was gone. Baum was on the *Baum*, the "Tree," hanging up there with his hands behind him. I didn't see him; Dieter Lange told me. When they cut him down, he couldn't use his arms, but they took him to the shower anyway so the prisoners who keep the place clean could help him wash. Unfortunately, poor Baum couldn't use his arms to break his fall when he slipped, hit his head on the concrete floor, and died. Dieter Lange told me this after we'd made love. Anna was at a meeting to plan larger flower gardens throughout the SS quarters. I don't know why I use that term, "made love." I don't love Dieter Lange and never did. He doesn't love me or anybody else. What we do is fuck, that's all. We are different men in strange times—but I never thought so strange that people would be killed to protect us, or that I would have to play along with his wife and her friend also to protect us. It had often crossed my mind and Dieter Lange's that if Anna wasn't around we'd be safer. But it was too late for that. So we didn't make love, we fucked, sometimes with all the passion of men trapped by what and where we were. He had to save me to save himself.

I said to him, "A *Badeaktion*."

He said, "Yes. It had to be that way. To protect us. You heard then?"

I laughed. I knew before he did. I said yes, I knew. A *Badeaktion* is a killing in the shower. You don't need the ss to do that; there are always Greens or Blacks willing to do a favor to get a favor. Dieter Lange, stupid man, seems to think he is the only person who tells me about what goes on in camp, like my ears are stopped up and I am blind. There is a knowledge and a kind of talk that the prisoners and the guards have that no one else shares or speaks, and Dieter Lange is no guard. He likes jazz music, but playing it and sharing it with other musicians is still another world he can't get into.

I lay there and considered that Dieter Lange, with the exception of my colonel and Menno, was the only lover I'd had in five years. But, here we were, growing older, old queers who on the outside would have fewer choices anyway, but here on the inside had almost none. We were a bad habit. But . . . Dieter Lange traveled. He had power. He could take what he wanted. How could I know what he did or who he did it with? My own urges seemed to come slowly, sometimes with blazing heat, most times not. Then I'd have to be warmed up, and we were not in a situation where that could take a lot of time.

Thursday, May 5, 1938

Yesterday I walked from the garden near the north fence up toward the main building where, in the showers, Baum got his brains splattered on the concrete floor. It was a nice day. There was a column of prisoners marching south about a hundred yards ahead of me on one side of the 'Strasse, and two other columns, one in the middle and one on the far side, marching north, facing me. At the head of the column on the far side were about fifteen Negroes or Africans—I couldn't tell—and I was so surprised my mouth fell open. I *know* it fell open, because when I closed it, it was filled with dust. The colored men were carrying rocks down to the new wall. I knew they'd just come because not all of them wore the new striped uniforms, and they weren't marching in step, and the old prisoners knew that whatever they did, they had to do it in step, whether the command was called or not; they had to watch the detail leader and fall in exactly as he did. I had to talk to Dr. Nyassa about the colored men, where they were from, what it was they were supposed to have done. There was another very large bunch of Gypsies brought into camp from Austria, Burgenland, wherever that is. But colored men?

I was still pooting in my pants with the fear that any moment now I could be in one of those columns, marching out to work or marching back in from it, marching down to the main hall to get my bowl of food, standing roll call, fighting to keep whatever I had from being stolen, worrying about lice and typhus and just catching a cold from another prisoner, worrying about bedbugs and time to shit. These days, I am afraid, running scared, even though the other prisoners believe I'm still lucky, still "prominent." If God lets me through this one, He's got a deeper believer. There isn't a moment when I'm not praying or thinking of praying, and I have been since April 23.

We'd had two good sets; rehearsal had gone well, with Eric Ulrich sitting in. Things had gotten a little better between us. You could feel spring getting up in the air, and there was a smell of good green things out at the Pussy Palace. I didn't even pay attention to the babies crying in the nursery. All the *Frauleins* looked good that night, and of course all the SS were turned out in their dress uniforms. That night made me feel kind of sad and sweet both. Everybody in the band felt it. Alex, Fritz, Oskar, Franz, Ernst, Teodor, Danko, and Moritz; all their solos were like nothing else I'd heard them play before that night, and I know I was the best jazz music piano player in the world. You can feel things like that, that you could cut the piano player at God's right hand. And when we finished each solo, we came back together better than Germans marching, because that's the

way music is; it fits into where it came from, some place without a
name, but some place we know is there. There were numbers we
couldn't ever play at The Nest, of course, and keys we couldn't play in,
but we were as close to the music as we could get, and that made us
know we could do better if we had the chance. During some of the
numbers I had the distinct feeling that this, being a prisoner of
Dachau for all this time, was a mistake that any second would be discovered and made right. I suppose we all had feelings like that, and
maybe wearing tuxedos twice a week helped. Maybe some of the way
I felt was because Ulrich, before the guys joined us for rehearsal, had
spoken to me for the first time in English.

"I understand why you were angry with me," he said. "But I have
to be careful—don't stop playing." I played and he apologized out
of one corner of his mouth, while his sax rested in the other. Then
we got into a groove. Just before the band came out, Ulrich said,
"Bernhardt's given his permission for me to drive you back to camp
tonight. We can talk more then. Meet me near the front of the Park-
platz. Black BMW, plate number DAH829. Then he led me into
"Sometimes I'm Happy."

I was feeling mellow after the second set. Usually, the thought
of being driven back to where I would have to put up with the
who-struck-john of Dieter Lange, if he was home, or of Anna and
Ursula, if they were home, turned my stomach the way taking Black
Draught without baking soda did. No one seemed to care much anymore about me being in the house alone with Anna when Dieter
Lange was away. That was because, I am sure, Anna said she'd be all
right if Ursula was with her. Yeah, I guess so. The ride with Ulrich
would be a pleasant change, a comfortable way to get "home."

He had a girlfriend, and she was as tall and as blond as he was.
She was "class." She wasn't wearing any gardenia perfume, I could tell
that right away. Her scent was French. She was very beautiful, but
there was something standoffish about her, and nobody can be that
way more than upper-class Germans. But she tried to be friendly as
we got into the car, me in the back seat. I wished I looked like her.
I wished I *was* her. She had a bundle resting on her lap. Her name
was Maria. Ulrich started and I leaned back in a corner of the car,

waiting for the talk we were supposed to have. But he didn't talk and neither did she. Halfway to the main road, Ulrich suddenly pulled off to the side, turned off the lights and stopped. Maria began to rip and snatch at the bundle. The smell of new clothes filled the car.

"Change, Pepperidge, now." Ulrich was handing things back to me: a shirt, trousers, a jacket, a tie, a pair of shoes, a fedora. I was amazed that I recognized such things by touch, but my heart was galloping right up into my throat, and as tired as I was, I came wide awake. I asked what was going on, and Maria said, *"Freiheit,* my friend."

"Change! Change!" Ulrich was saying. He sounded like a camp guard, and you do not argue with camp guards—or anyone else who's not a prisoner. But—

"We go to the Swiss border, Mr. Pepperidge," Maria said. She spoke English with a British accent, like Ulrich. She seemed to struggle to find words. I was pulling off the prison suit, with Ulrich's help, but it was hard in so little space. "We have got papers for you, so now, when we get there, you can be free—"

"Come *on,* Pepperidge," Ulrich was saying. Everything I managed to get out of he handed to Maria. I wanted to say, Wait, suppose— but Ulrich was speaking almost with a growl, "Quickly, quickly." What a lovely smell the clothes had. I was out of my old pants and into the ones they'd brought. I slipped on the new shoes, pulled on the jacket, and got the tie around my collar while Ulrich mashed the hat down on my head, adjusted it, and pulled down the brim. Maria was already wrapping up my old shoes and uniform. "Let's go!" Ulrich said. "Freedom can't wait!" I was still feeling for buttonholes and fastening buttons when he started up and got back on the road with the car lights on. Wasn't no need of me playing around. I told Ulrich I was scared and wanted to go to the camp. This was like a movie, or a dream, and I had the feeling both were bad.

"Don't you *want* to be free?" Maria asked.

"Yes, but—"

"Don't be afraid. Eric's got everything fixed." She passed me a heavy silver flask, and I turned that baby straight up and poured the cognac down my throat. I returned it and she held out a cigarette case. I took a cigarette and she lighted it. Of course, I wanted to be free, free to walk the streets of Paris or Amsterdam or New York—streets anywhere but in Germany. I couldn't stop the tears from starting up. I could see me and Willy Lewis, me and Ruby Mae Richards, me strolling along 125th Street or Lenox Avenue, me in an apartment somewhere on Sugar Hill, me playing the best piano of my life. I also saw me hanging from the "Tree," in the Bunker getting the shit beat out of me, saw myself standing alone in the center of the 'Platz under the hot sun until I passed out, me dead in the same corner of the *Revier* where I'd seen Menno. Hell, yeah, I wanted freedom, but God knows I was afraid to take it, so these two who wouldn't listen to me would have to take me to it and hand me over.

"It'll be all right, Pepperidge," Ulrich said. Maybe, looking in the rearview mirror, he'd seen my tears as we passed an occasional light. At another main road, he turned south and a buzzing started in my head. "There's a blanket back there. Wrap yourself in it if you get cold." I didn't move. "I understand you had a visit from Ruby Mae Richards," he said.

I told him yes, I had, and that she'd told me he was a friend. "You sure didn't act like one," I said. "Bernhardt didn't give you no permission to drive me to camp," I said. "Did he?"

He gave a little laugh. "Well, Pepperidge, one has to be careful, very careful. All this will get worse before it gets better. And no, Bernhardt didn't give me permission, and I'd never ask him anything like this, anyway. He's just waiting for me to make a mistake. He's my enemy; he's the enemy of whatever good is still in Germany. And yet, I don't understand—he loves jazz music, loves to listen to it." He went on talking to me in English. I was thinking he had the same puzzlement about Bernhardt that I'd had about him. "Strange," Ulrich said.

"Anyway, Colonel Bernhardt's away," Maria said.

I asked Ulrich how he could get away with whatever he was doing if Bernhardt was watching him. Ulrich said, and he and his girlfriend laughed as he said it, "We just have to be smarter than he is. For example, right now I am in my quarters, already asleep."

They laughed a little louder. "And of course we have friends. So we have until noon tomorrow to get back, by which time you'll be free in Switzerland and we will have put another one over on Bernhardt." I didn't say anything about that "another" business.

Maria said, "On the other side it would be wise if you said nothing about an SS officer, Mr. Pepperidge." I said all right. She said it was dangerous work, what they were doing, and she was sure I appreciated that.

Ulrich put his arm around her shoulders and said, "Sure he does." She leaned her head against his arm and her hair fell like a patch of moonlight down the back of the seat.

We took side roads around most of Munich—we could see the city lights now and again—and then followed the sign to Starnberg. Ulrich stepped on the gas and we rushed through a tunnel of light, passing only a few other cars, until we got to the town, then slowed as we went through it. I was pressed back into my corner, the hat pulled down so that I could just barely see. We passed some SA patrols, but they didn't stop us; Ulrich was wearing his uniform. Outside the town, we drove on toward—the signs had said—Landsberg and Kaufering. Ulrich picked a road that seemed to go right between them, and another sign read To Buchloe. Ulrich told Maria to give me the papers. "American passport," she said, "and money. We got your picture out of an old magazine from Berlin, re-shot it, and there you are. There's enough money to get you to Paris." In the few dim lights we were passing I saw that my occupation was—musician!—and that I'd entered Germany from Colmar, France, on business a week ago and was returning via Switzerland. My residence was in Paris. I remember how officially solid the passport and visa read, and how good that little book felt, and for how long I'd wanted to hold one just like it in my hand. Ulrich said, "Feels better already, doesn't it?" I told him it sure did. But I was still afraid, and when we came around a curve near Buchloe, we almost ran over two old SA, and they flagged us down. They saluted when they saw Ulrich's uniform, and started backing off; we slowed, but didn't stop. Ulrich, who'd rolled down his window and held out his *Ausweiss* for identification, said good evening to them as we picked up speed. I hadn't realized how long I'd held my breath; now I let it out and it seemed to never stop coming. Ulrich laughed. "Nothing," he said. "Just a couple of old farts; should be in bed. Nearly everybody wants to protect the Fatherland. Pepperidge, everything, believe me, is copasetic."

I grunted, I remember, and then began to tremble in my corner. They wanted to be heroes and maybe they were, but if we got caught, it'd be my ass to fry. I thought about that. Theirs, too, and their friends. But, shit, why didn't they rescue somebody who wasn't afraid of being rescued? Mindelheim, I could see through the thin, curving space beneath the brim of the hat, was a two-light village with two or three buildings—the church and the town hall I supposed. Memmingen was larger, but we had no trouble there, either, just kept boring through that tunnel made by the headlights. "Leutkirch, Wangen, and then Friedrichshafen," Ulrich said. "Then Lindau and the border." He stepped on the gas again. Friedrichshafen sounded familiar, like Kaufering, but I was beat to my socks; it'd been a long day, and my stomach had been in my mouth every second since we'd left The Nest. The buzzing in my head got louder, and the being tired, half-high with the cognac, and just plain scared, all came together. I remember thinking that I wouldn't have minded being one of the servants who had to get up on Saturday morning and drill. They were asleep right now. I imagined our passage through the mountains we could see on clear days from Dachau. I knew we were climbing and climbing, because Ulrich was shifting gears, and it was getting colder in the car. Ulrich started humming "Dardanella" and Maria joined him. I knew it would please them if I joined in, but as far as I was concerned, if *I* was going to do any singing, it would be when I was safe in Switzerland. Maria was good. Sometimes she took harmony, and sometimes she took melody while Ulrich riffed his way through. I guess they'd done it before. I wondered who she really was and how many times they'd done this, and how many more Germans there were who were "friends." It was better not to know. I asked no questions and they volunteered no more information. I must have fallen asleep because when the car stopped, I tried to lose myself behind the seat.

Cold air came whipping in through the window Maria was opening. I had the feeling we were on top of a mountain. She took the
bundle of clothes and tossed it out into the night. "There," she said.
"No more uniform, no more number." My number, I thought, is 3003,
3003. Outside Wangen, Ulrich stopped and filled the tank from a can
of petrol he had in the trunk. That woke me up, too, but right away
I started to think of the names of the towns and villages we'd passed
through. In Dachau I guessed there were prisoners from every city,
town, and village in Germany.

I dozed off again, and when I woke it was to the sound of Ulrich's
voice: *"Achtsam!* Pepperidge, careful!" The first thing I noticed was that
Ulrich and Maria seemed to have got all stiff in their seats, like a couple of bird dogs. And they weren't humming anymore. There were lots
of lights up ahead in Friedrichshafen. "Keep that hat pulled down,
Pepperidge." Ulrich sounded as though he was going over a score with
somebody in a band. "Pretend to sleep. They hardly ever see colored
people down here, so don't worry if they flash lights in your face. You
pretend to wake up. You're some high potentate, got it? From now on,
if we get stopped, you've got to pretend to be above all this shit. Germans go for that, okay?" I said okay but my belly was skipping and
jumping as I saw the lights of the town growing brighter beneath my
hat brim.

"One more thing, Pepperidge, to stiffen your spine. It's got to be
now, this trip, for two reasons. I'm being reassigned; we don't know
when someone else will replace me. Second, we've heard that Frau
Lange is pregnant. We can't take the chance that this is a fraud.
You know some ss wives have been caught abducting babies right
out of the nursery back there. The Ordinance of September 13, 1936.
You probably never heard of it. Every ss man has to have four kids."

Yeah, I remembered it, but I didn't tell him. I wondered how
many he had; if he had any, I didn't think they were with Maria.

"Now, think, Pepperidge, if Frau Lange has a child or children,
what'll happen to you? They'll get female servants, won't they? Oh,
they might keep you on, but then again, maybe not." His voice got
low. "Do you think Lange could afford to have you running around
loose in camp?"

I was thinking, If she *is* pregnant, it's Bernhardt's—or maybe not. Maybe Dieter Lange did his duty. Or maybe she was jiving. There did seem to be a lot more babies and female servants around the ss compound lately. If Dieter Lange was looking for a chance to get rid of me, this would be the time—if Anna had been bigged. Hadn't looked any fatter than usual to me. Who would listen to me in the camp? And why would I want to say anything anyway that would make it tougher for me? Oh, God. Why was everything happening at once?

"So now's the time, isn't it?" Maria said.

"Sure looks like it," I mumbled, and it sure did, since we were nearly there and I couldn't do boodily-boo about Anna or anything else. While I was thinking, they'd been talking about going through the town to save time, and we were driving slowly down a street a couple of blocks away from what looked like the main one. Ulrich and Maria were remarking that it looked good so far, when head-lights swept up from the rear, swung to the side, and a police car pulled up beside us. There were two men in the front seat. The driver waved us down. Ulrich stopped and lowered his window. The cop in the passenger seat got out and came around to Ulrich's side; I tried to vanish into the seams of the seat. When he was at Ulrich's window, all I could see was a blotch of green that was his uniform. "What do you do, where do you go, this time of night, sir?" I was sure he was looking at Ulrich's card, and had seen his uniform, because he wasn't all loud and bullying, the way Germans can be if they have more power than you. The blotch of green was wrinkling and unwrinkling, and I could just see light poking around inside the car. The cop said good evening to Maria, and she answered in a chilly, high-class voice. The light lingered longest on me. "Please don't wake him up, officer," Ulrich said. "I have to get this man out of Germany. It's a duty I preferred not to do, so I brought a friend to keep me company. He's someone we don't need in the Reich. And someone you're better off not knowing about." The green blotch grunted behind the light, which suddenly vanished, but with my eyes still closed, I saw flashes of red from it. Sweet words: "Okay. Sorry to have to stop you, sir. Heil Hitler." Ulrich answered, "Heil,"

with Maria joining in. We drove out of Friedrichshafen in silence.
We'd gone several miles. Ulrich downed his window again. "Smell
that, Pepperidge? That's the Bodensee. Halfway over is Germany;
the other half is Lake Constance, Switzerland. One side smells just
like the other, the way land does, even if there are frontiers." I felt
a hand I knew to be Maria's on my knee.

"Mr. Pepperidge, we're almost there," she said. She asked Ulrich
in German if he was very tired, and he answered in German that this
kind of trip never exhausted him. We were going down, easing
through the night that was barely beginning to lighten.

Ulrich said, "Listen now. We have to go through Lindau and then
Bregenz—German and Austrian frontier. Germany now controls
Austria. Once in Austrian territory, we cross into Switzerland at
Lusteneau. On our last trip the border was manned by Austrians.
They're still there, but so are Germans now. We have to be more
careful here than anyplace else, and I mean *Achtsam!*" Again he
sounded like a guard at camp. "If I have to say certain things,
and do certain things, know now that I don't mean them, understand? It is a game I may have to play. Once you're on the Swiss
side, forget them."

"Oh, I don't know if I can do this," I said. I heard the resignation
in my voice. Ulrich shouted that I had to. His girl tried to calm him
down, but he said, "He's just got to, that's all." He was quiet for a
minute, then said, "Pepperidge, I know you'll do your best. I understand what you say. A man doesn't spend five years in that shithole
without losing something. That's the way it is, and that's why they're
there. But damn it, man, you never thought you'd lose your freedom,
and you did. I'm sure there were many times when you thought you'd
never get it back; now you've almost got it and you've had two hours
to prepare to take it. It is minutes away now, *minutes.*"

There was more silence, before Maria said, "If it doesn't work, it
won't be just you going back to camp—"

"Maria," Ulrich said, interrupting, "Don't." But she went on.

"Eric will go and I will go and some others as well, and the
people who need help won't get it, not from us. So don't be nervous.
Do nothing to make them suspicious, just like you did back there.

You were fine. Oh! And remember, you know no German. Eric will translate everything, if necessary." I told her I understood.

"What's the name of your perfume?" I asked.

"*Seducteur.* You like it?"

"Devastating," I said, and they laughed. The car seemed to glide to a stop at the crossing in an area of bright lights through which walked two border policemen on either side of the car. The red-and-white barriers lay waist-high across the road. Steam whiter than the lights rose from the mouths of the police.

Through his lowered window Ulrich called in German, "C'mon. Don't take all night. I've got to get back to quarters." He was already holding out his card. Maria was smiling at the cops on her side. Now, once more, I could see beneath my hat brim blotches of green-gray uniforms.

"What's the hurry, sir?" one of the policemen said.

"To complete this rotten mission and get back to Munich. What's yours, to drag ass all night?" Ulrich said. Once again, small, powerful beams of light swept through the car, coming to rest on me.

"Raise your hat," one of the cops said in German. I didn't move.

"Your hat, nigger," Ulrich said in English. "Remove your hat." I took off my hat.

"Papers," the officer said.

Ulrich said, "Give him your passport and visa." I did. I squinted at the light. Maria offered the officers on her side cigarettes from her case. They took them, checked the brand and smiled. On Ulrich's side one officer was studying my papers while the other looked at me like I had three heads. Ulrich said, "Officer, his papers are okay. Let's get this nigger out of here into Switzerland." The cop shuffled faster through the passport.

"All right! You don't mind if I check this piece of American shit, do you? You've got a job to do, I've got a job to do. Relax." He went through the passport again and checked the visa once more. "Good thing he's not one of those Rhineland bastards, or his ass would belong to us," the cop said. He snapped shut the passport on the visa. "All right, sir. Proceed. Get him out of Germany." The light on my face went out. The cop saluted Ulrich. "Heil Hitler," he said,

and Ulrich returned the salute and the words. I melted into my corner. Maria waved as the barriers were raised. Up they went, crank
turn by crank turn. I was trembling. Maria and Ulrich said nothing
until we moved.

"Not as bad as I thought," he said, and sighed. "Just think. If we
could have done this two months ago, you'd be free right now."

"It went so well back there that I don't think we'll have any
trouble ahead," Maria said. "Now Switzerland. What would Europe
do without Switzerland?" She put her head back on the seat.

A little while later Ulrich said, "Sam's waiting for you on the
other side."

"Sam?" I said, "*Sam* who was guitar?"

"The same."

"I thought he was in America."

"He was, but he came back to help Jews and anyone else who
needs it. He's got a place. You'll rest for a day or so and he'll get you
off to France. The Swiss will be kinder to you than to the Germans
who've run there. In fact, Sam's residency period has not much time
to go. He'll have to be replaced. The Swiss don't want to upset the
Germans by protecting refugees too long. If the refugees can't get
papers to France or anywhere else within a few months, phttt! back
to Germany." I was thinking of Sam with much fondness now.
He was a so-so musician but, apparently, a great person. "Fifteen
kilometers to go," Ulrich said. Then I thought of Friedrichshafen
and Kaufering: there would be camps going up there, part of the
Dachau system, according to a map I'd seen on Dieter Lange's table.

We came to the frontier at Lusteneau. I said to myself, Good-bye,
Austria, hello Switzerland, see you soon, America. I was sweating,
cold as it was. I remember the arrangement of it. There were five SS
standing across the roadway in front of the barriers. The one in the
middle patted his left hand flat down on the air, giving us the slow-
down sign, while his right went up to signal Ulrich to stop. There
was a smile on his face and he took a dainty little step toward us
even before we stopped.

Ulrich said "*Scheiss!*" at the same time I recognized Bernhardt.
Maria moaned. I pushed myself deeper into the corner of the seat.

The rifles of the four men were pointed at Ulrich; Bernhardt's pistol appeared suddenly in his hand. He aimed it at Maria who jerked back with her hands raised before her face. Ulrich braked and we all lurched forward. He climbed out slowly and raised his hands. Maria got out even more slowly; I think she was trembling. I didn't move. Through the opened doors I heard the jangle of the metal on the gunbelts of the ss. The lights were very bright.

Bernhardt said, "You made good time, Ulrich. Is my piano player all right?" Ulrich said nothing. Bernhardt jerked his chin up and the four ss moved Ulrich and Maria away from the car with their rifles; Bernhardt looked inside. "Pepperidge, are you all right?" My teeth were chattering so much I couldn't say anything. The sound of his voice was calming. "A little nervous then, Pepperidge?" I nodded vigorously. "You look dressed for Switzerland. How we'd have missed you—me, Lange, Frau Lange, and Frau Winkelmann, eh? We have another suit for you. Come on. Get out. Go over there into the office." He pointed to the building, where several border guards were standing. I think I shuffled, because my legs seemed to have a mind of their own. As I went, I heard Bernhardt say loudly, I guessed to Ulrich and Maria, "Heil Hitler," because they said together, as though they'd rehearsed it many times, "Fuck Hitler, fuck you." I must have passed out then.

I woke up on the floor of a truck. It was daylight. I was back in uniform, but the new shirt was still on under the jacket, and the new shoes were on my feet. It seemed that a month had passed since the night. There were sharp pains everywhere—my face, my whole body. My lips were swollen, my eyes half-closed, and when I moved, pain jooged from one end of my body to the other. I groaned, and one of the two guards asked did I want a cigarette. I said yes, but it came out "yepths." He stuck a Drummers in my mouth and lit it. The other guard looked at me and slowly shook his head. I couldn't tell where we were going, but I supposed to the camp, to the guard-house, and from there to the Bunker. I didn't care. I didn't mind dying then, but I didn't want to die badly; I didn't want it to hurt. I finished the cigarette and slipped back to sleep. The guards woke me this time. We were in front of Dieter Lange's house. They helped me out and into the house, and left me. Dieter Lange came down the stairs real slow. He stopped and studied me, then finished coming down.

"Bernhardt was right," he said. "He used you as bait. He would've looked very bad if they had pulled it off, but you know Bernhardt wasn't going to let that happen. Took a little while, but he's a patient man. Can you imagine, right here in the SS. Cigarette, Cleef?" I nodded. He gave me a Chesterfield. I was shaking so much I couldn't light it; he had to do it for me. I asked about Ulrich and his girl. He got a basin of water and a cloth and helped me downstairs before he answered. "Bernhardt had them taken to Friedrichshafen prison. They were beheaded there, *Execution durch Fallbeil.*"

I finished the walk up the Lagerstrasse and went back to open the canteen. I knew that soon Dieter Lange would have a replacement for Baum, some sneak to keep an eye on me. I went into the back room and opened the new carton of toothpaste. Outside, the columns flowed up and down the main street, feet pounding, dust rising.

———

Thursday, May 19, 1938

"Guess what?" Anna asked me in English. Her face was scrubbed clean of makeup; her attitude was like a saint's. I shrugged. I was washing dishes. Dieter Lange was not home. "Oh, come on. You must forget what happened. It wasn't your fault. Colonel Bernhardt should not have beat you the way he did. But you are special to him, unique, a colored jazz music band leader. No one else in Germany has one, so you make this *Lebensborn* famous for him, in an unofficial way. You're all right now. You are back home, back at the canteen, and back with your music. Don't sulk. You could be where Ulrich and his girlfriend are, you know. So, now you guess what, Cleef."

She said she was going to have a baby. She held up two fingers. Two months on the way. I said congratulations. She said thank you. That means you'll be sending me into the camp to stay? I said.

She said no, they—she and Dieter Lange—hadn't discussed that.
I *knew* she wasn't pregnant at all. *I* clean up. *I* gather the garbage.
I take care of what has to be burned, and, since I've been able,
I've gone through all the Lange trash bit by bit, as I never did before.
And I last saw Anna's dead blood cunt rag last week. The bitch was
padding herself. "And, can you imagine? Ursula's pregnant two
months also."

I said, "Oh, imagine that." So they were both going to pad themselves up to nine months. I didn't know if Winkelmann would be
happy. Since he and Dieter Lange were not friends, I didn't know
if he was a freak or not.

"Do you want a boy or a girl?" I asked.

She switched to German. "I don't care, but I want it to be tall and
with blue eyes and blond hair—even though I don't have blond hair
and neither does Dieter." In my head, suddenly, there was an empty
space waiting to be filled, and I knew nothing would fill it except
saying something that was true. I told her that her hair was lighter
around her pussy, so maybe she would have a blond kid, *if* she was
pregnant. She started to scream, but stopped. She was worried about
being heard. The saint was gone. She snatched my hands out of
the dishwater and began to push me down the stairs to my room.
She was following me down, her voice deep in her throat, calling me
names, threatening me. She said she would send me into the camp,
that Dieter Lange would make me disappear, that Bernhardt would
chop off my head. I was being backed up into my room during all
this. She suddenly quit and sat down on the steps. "Well, you see,
we *must* do something. People are wondering where my babies are,
when my babies will start coming. So." She had started to cry. She lit
a cigarette while we went back to the kitchen and the dishes. I asked
what she would do with four kids, since she didn't even like them.
She said she didn't know. Suppose, I said, you lose this one—the one
you're supposed to be having now. "And then?" she said. I asked her
did she remember the whole ordinance about having babies, that
the husband could have them by another woman? I saw that didn't
appeal to her, either. I was spieling and scheming to keep my behind
out of that camp and she knew it; but she also didn't wish to be held

down by kids she didn't want. So I told her she should have Dieter Lange make some arrangement to get a fake statement from a doctor saying she shouldn't even try to have kids anymore because she might die. She lit another cigarette, all the time moving her head up and down. I knew the spiel was sounding good to her. "Umm," she kept saying. "Umm." She put out her cigarette, stood up pulling and tugging at her dress. "Some walking, some thinking," she said, and then went out. Bitch, I thought. Everything I said she'd already thought of. I know it.

Mon., June 27, 1938

Last Thursday night Dieter Lange let me listen to the radio with him and Anna. Joe Louis was fighting Max Schmeling for the second time, and Joe Louis, I'd read, was now the heavyweight boxing champ. In camp they'd been talking about the fight for a week, throwing up their fists and laughing when I walked by, like they did after the first fight. "Oh, Schmeling's gonna kill that guy, Sunshine, you watch! That nigger's gonna get his, Snowball. Schmeling's of the master race!" All this coming from some raggedy-ass Black or Green or SS. In a fair fight, I could've whipped half those cocksuckers, but the people in this camp don't know nothing about fair.

When I first joined Mr. Wooding's band, and people kept giving me this crap about my coming from Storyville, I got into some scrapes and did so well that, for a while there, they were calling me "Pepper."

Anna set out some coffee and cake and schnapps. It was like a family, each of us with secrets put up on a shelf for the time being. The German announcer, Arno Helmers, said there were 70,000 people in Yankee Stadium. "You know that place, Yankee Stadium?" Dieter Lange asked. I told him I knew where it was, that it was practically brand-new when I left New York, and I thought about the bridge that carried you from Harlem into the Bronx and to the stadium. The announcer was describing the crowd, the records of each fighter, and how Schmeling had beaten Louis the first time. He said it was hot in New York, that Mike Jacobs was the promoter of the fight, and that now the fighters were entering the ring.

"Why does Schmeling get almost as many cheers as Louis?" Anna asked me. I was ashamed to tell her that white Americans wanted Louis to get beat almost as much as the Germans did. I pretended I didn't hear her. We settled back and waited for the bell to begin the first round.

"Louis is across the ring," the announcer said, "moving to the left. Schmeling moves back against the ropes. Louis! A left! A left and a right to the jaw! Schmeling's trying to push Louis off with his left, but Louis keeps coming! A left to the jaw, another left and a right! Another left hook to the body and a right! Schmeling is reaching for the ropes! Louis is all over him! Schmeling's knees are buckling! He's turning away from Louis and here's *Louis* with another right. Arthur Donovan is moving between them, counting . . . one, two . . . Now Donovan steps back and Schmeling advances and—*Louis!* A right that sends Schmeling to the floor. And now Schmeling is up, but—Louis! Left to the chin, another left, and another and a right to the chin—Schmeling is hanging on the ropes; Louis, another left to the head, a right to the body . . ."

I thought I heard a scream above the crowd noise, and then it was like somebody took a great big knife and sliced off the sound and the scream. The radio spit static, nothing else. Cursing, Dieter Lange sprang up to turn the dials. "What's this? What's going on?" He pounded the radio with the flat of his hand. Then he snatched his hat and ran out.

"I bet you they cut it off because Schmeling is losing," Anna said. I didn't say anything, but to me it sounded like Schmeling was getting murdered. Somehow I managed to keep from smiling, even though I wanted to jump and shout. First there was Jesse Owens and now Louis. In the first round! In seconds! That superman shit of Hitler's was taking a whipping! I bet those colored men over in camp are catching hell from the other prisoners. You'd think they'd be happy to see Schmeling take a beating. But I know those jokers; they're white and German first, prisoners second. I didn't think white folks back home would go out killing black folks the way they did after Jack Johnson beat Jim Jeffries when I was a kid. Two colored men were killed by crackers over in La Providence then. But you never know.

When Dieter Lange came back, he was mad. I went downstairs to my room. In the darkness I raised my arms and opened my mouth and screamed silently, "Yay! Yay!! Yay!!!"

Yesterday I finally found Dr. Nyassa back in *Revier* One. Nobody seemed to know where he'd been. He looked and sounded tired and weak. He was thinner. He wouldn't look me in the eye. He told me he was now under medical care; he was now as much patient as nurse. I asked where he'd been, and he smiled a little sad smile. "A long, bad story, my friend, very long and very bad." First, he told me that some of the colored men I'd seen were Africans stranded in Germany, students, one or two boxers, adventurers. But the Germans called them *Ballastexistenzen*—persons without value. With them were some of "The Rhineland Bastards," *Der Rheinlandbastarde.* These, he told me in a low and weary voice, are, or were, the children of the French colonial soldiers, the Senegalese and other Africans, and of the colored American soldiers who helped the Allies occupy the Rhineland after the World War. Some, of course, had grown up since 1918, and were among the men I saw; the rest were in other camps. How many may have gotten out of Germany he didn't know. Dr. Nyassa was quiet for a long time, during which one of the new doctors stuck his head into the room and told him not to tire himself because they were going to do some tests on him. We had both scrambled to attention and said, "Yes, sir." We sat down again. I asked him what tests, and he waved the question away. "A lot of those people, grown and children alike, were taken to clinics. I've been away, to Frankfurt, to the clinic of Dr. Otmar von Verschuer. I've been sterilized."

I jumped in my chair. To me that meant they cut off your dick. I said, "They cut—" He said no.

"They just fix it so you can't ever have children. I knew of this doctor. There's a whole program being run by people who were members of the Kaiser Wilhelm Institute for the Advancement of Science. Dr. Just and I knew many of them, like this Verschuer and Eugen Fischer." Nyassa leaned closer and whispered, his sour breath spilling over, "That goddamn Fischer, back in 1913, did a study on the kids of German fathers and Namibian mothers, *'Die Rehobother*

Bastards und das Bastardisierungsproblem beim Menschen,' 'The Bastards of Reheboth and the Problem of Miscegenation in Man.' So
these wretched Germans have been at it for a long time. Nineteenth-
century science belonged to the Germans, so they go back with this
quite a distance. . . ."

He leaned back in his chair, breathing heavily. I asked if he was all
right, and he said no. He wondered what Just would think of all this.
I asked him again what tests they were doing with him, and he said
he didn't know, because they never told the truth, and anyway, they
weren't going to do anything more to *him*. I felt so sorry for him
that I wanted to tell about Ulrich and Maria and my ride through
the night. "They have to kill me, one way or another," he said.
His voice was so low I could hardly hear him. "Whoever heard of a
Neger Biologisch? Only those people from the KWI, and just a few of
them. I can't exist, but I do. The solution is simple: I must *not* exist.
I am a life without value, even here." He got up slowly. "Well. I have
bored and frightened you. Take this. My wife's last address. If you
get out, just tell her it was too much. They've made me feel like a
frog. It would have been good to hear you play, just once. Come.
I'll walk out with you."

We went out of the building, and all the while I felt like I was
walking with one of those jokers back home who's on his way to a
fight he knows he can't win, but he has to go. *Has* to go. I didn't know
what to say. He walked me to the middle of the Lagerstrasse and
shook my hand; his felt light, even though he tried to squeeze hard.
There was no strength in it. He turned and walked, not back to his
building but around it. "Wait!" I hollered. I followed because I knew
what he was going to do. I suppose I could have stopped him.
I didn't. He knew what he wanted, and who in the hell was I to get
in his way? But he was, besides Werner and Gitzig and maybe a few
others, the only person I could talk to in camp. Most certainly the
only *colored* man. "Wait, Doctor!" I shouted after his thin, bent back.
Sometimes the prisoners stopped a fight; I'd seen that happen many
times, because a lot of people besides the fighters could get into trouble if the guards came. But if a prisoner was doing something all by
himself, something that didn't bounce back on other people, you let

him do it. It was the one thing a man could do, make the decision to walk on the forbidden grass strip, which Nyassa was now doing, even as the guard in the tower was shouting and swinging his machine gun toward him. Nyassa started to run; he moved like an old, crippled man. The gun chattered; prisoners stopped what they were doing if they were not in a column, and ran toward the sound. Dr. Nyassa jumped high in the air to clear the moat. I think he was hit a couple of times as he sailed through the air like a balled-up piece of paper, because something disturbed the smoothness of his flight. But still he flew and landed, without moving again, on the electrified barbed-wire fence, which bulged out, then back in, with Nyassa's fingers clutched tightly through it. The guard kept shooting. I thought of Revelation: "I was dead and now I am to live forever and ever, and I hold the keys of death and of the underworld. Now write down all that you see of present happenings and *things that are still to come.*"

Thursday, Aug. 18, 1938

There are now two more men who work with me in the canteen. Dieter Lange says before the year is over there will be 20,000 prisoners in Dachau, so more help is needed. I guess I should say I work with the two new men, since Dieter Lange told me it was now important that *Germans* seem to be in charge. One is Lappus, a Green, and the other is Huebner, a Witness. I check in the stock; they place it on the shelves and do most of the selling. I make sure the place is as clean as possible, but I also do the books for Dieter Lange to make sure these guys haven't got their hands in the till. But they make a nice balance; Huebner seems to be about as honest as a man can be. If Lappus has any desire to be another Baum, I don't think Huebner will let him.

There are exactly ten Africans in camp now. I've spoken to some of them. They aren't very friendly because they're scared. They've all had the operation that Dr. Nyassa had. Maybe they're more sad than unfriendly. Some I can't speak to because they don't speak anything but African. The guards call their speech "Chinese." The Africans were part of an English circus that went bust in Germany.

The German women thought them exotic, the Africans thought they were something hot, and boom! Before they knew it, they were enemies of the state, violators of the "blood and honor" laws out of Nuremberg. They all wear the black triangle on their knees and chests. I wrote down some things in German for them to learn. I know they need the German and, I think, down deep, they know they need it, too. Huebner is very good with them when they come into the canteen, which is not often.

If I am to bear witness like it says in Revelation, I have to say that what the Jews are going through is unbearable. Since I last wrote here, they've had to register whatever they own. Down to the toothbrush, the shoelaces. The Jews have had to register their businesses, no matter how small, and any Jew who has a police record, no matter how insignificant, is picked up. Can there be any Jews left? Have they been blind? By the first of the year they are to have their names changed officially to "Sarah" or "Israel." That will be like having a different color skin. Did they think this wasn't real? And now, just yesterday, Werner tells me, in Evian, France, a conference ended. It was about the Jews and which countries would take them in from Germany and Austria: not a single country, including the United States; not a country, not one. And in they come. Not only here, but all over Germany where there are camps; the tailors are still busy making six-pointed gold stars and triangles.

Monday, October 3, 1938

Last Friday at The Nest I found Moritz in a closet playing *"Deutschland Über Alles."* I was surprised at how sweet it sounded on the violin; it was very nice, and I told him so. He said it was by Haydn, from a piece he wrote for a string quartet. I said he must have been a patriotic cat. He laughed. Haydn, he told me, died in 1809, before Germany was a whole country or, he whispered, a *Reich*. During some of the rehearsal time now, we listen to the records that Dieter Lange and Bernhardt collect on their travels because, Dieter Lange says, "You can't get German Brunswick, HMV, Telefunken, Odeon, Imperial—they aren't recording jazz music anymore."

All the labels are from America, Holland, France, Switzerland, Sweden, or England. Now we have the Benny Goodman band, quartet, and trio. I read in an old British paper that he has colored— Teddy Wilson, Lionel Hampton, Lester Young, Walter Page— playing with him. Also some new Lunceford and Ellington, Red Allen, Mildred Bailey, Ella Fitzgerald, Charlie Barnet, Coleman Hawkins, Erskine Hawkins, Woody Herman, Billie Holiday, Santo Pecora, Louis Prima, Don Redman, Gene Sedric (from the Wooding band), Willie "The Lion" Smith, Art Tatum, and Jess Stacy.

After listening to Sedric's "The Joint Is Jumpin'" and "Off Time," everybody in the band had something to say about The Nest "jumpin'" or not "jumpin'." "Off Time" is interesting because, while the tempo is fast, you can cut it in half, but Germans don't know how to "Lindy," so the side is more for learning for us than for anything we can cop and play. I can do a pretty good copy of Jimmy Rushing on "Shoe Shine Swing," and, naturally, the people love to hear me do renditions of Louis Armstrong's "Pennies from Heaven" and "Confessin'." In other words, the music keeps us from going crazy, because, with each passing day, it looks like the situation in Germany isn't going to get any better, but worse, as Ulrich said, as Werner said before him. Last week the British and the French agreed to let the Germans take part of Czechoslovakia. The problem is *when*. Old Gitzig was right.

Lily Bernhardt is pregnant. I'm surprised she's alive at all, with all that piss in the tea and snot in the pudding that Gitzig served her. Now that Gitzig spends more time in camp, and gets him a little now and then, I suppose he's not doing it anymore; too risky. Besides, he's getting plenty of pretty good stuff in Bernhardt's basement to keep account of, and, if I know Gitzig, he's managing something himself. He told me, "This stuff is shit. You should see what we got in the warehouse in Munich. Bernhardt has already made a lot, believe me." He supposed Dieter Lange was doing okay, too, and he's right. His storeroom in the basement is crammed full; he's also been storing stuff in the attic, including two suitcases filled with reichsmarks and food from Anna's visits to her parents' farm. I guess there's a stash out there, too.

There are railroad tracks going into the camp now, and tracks to the factories and sheds just west. Details working there. Armaments, Werner tells me, what else? I keep saying there can't be a war, and Werner keeps looking at me, like I'm a dummy. "You know who the prisoners work for over in those sheds? Messerschmidt, Dornier, BMW, I.G. Farben . . ."

Of all the different groups in camp, the Reds remain the best organized; nobody fucks with them, and everybody does what they say. They know what's going on. They try to get their people into the important jobs, but the SS prefers the Greens and the Blacks; they seem to have a lot in common and they recognize each other, the way *we* do.

The good jobs are in the camp kitchens (which ensure a lot more, if not better, food, naturally), supply depot, laundry, bath house, property room, shoe repair shop, tailor shop (includes sock darning), carpentry shop, machine shop (in some of the rebuilt factories), lumber yard, infirmaries, library (they call it), photo shop, and paint shop. Also gardening and tending rabbits, serving in the SS houses, and, yes, playing in the camp band. The prisoners who work the details in the sheds have it easier than those who work in camp; they have contact with civilians, and the SS guards don't want to act like the shits they are when the civilians are around. Hohenberg and some of the others in the Labor Office do the best they can for the Reds, but they can only do so much. They also have some people in the Records Office. The camp police are prisoners who work under the SS; no one likes them, no one trusts them. Back home we called them stool pigeons.

Friday, Nov. 11, 1938

I've shut the door. I'm in this tiny room (the canteen has been partitioned off again) where I do the books. But now I'm writing to *you*. Those prisoners with the soft jobs, who have time on their hands and run in and out of here, are in the main section talking about the past two days, Wednesday and Thursday. I can hear their laughter and loud, boasting voices. I never had the experience, but I've heard about times like these. The crackers back home would say Moses did this and that, and old Moses would run because he knew if they caught him he'd hang. Moses could be the name of any colored man. Whether they caught him or not, the crackers would come into the colored neighborhoods and burn houses, beat up people, shit, *kill* them if they couldn't find Moses to kill instead. People ran to church or hid in the woods. People would *pray* the crackers would catch Moses and leave them alone; *they* hadn't done anything. It didn't matter to them that maybe Moses hadn't done anything, either. They just didn't want the crackers to burn their homes or to kill them. The one or two colored men who thought the people ought to fight back, quickly found themselves all alone.

The prisoners outside are talking about something like what happens back home, but instead of a lynch mob they're calling it *Kristallnacht,* the night of the broken glass. All of Germany was like the booby hatch, the ones who went nuts and the ones who watched them. They burned or tore up and looted almost 8,000 shops owned by Jews, killed 35 Jews, burned about 200 synagogues; some Jewish women were raped; nobody knows how many Jews were hurt. The papers say the Jews will be fined a billion marks for causing the disturbance.

Some say there was altogether 25 million marks worth of damage. And they are already making more room here in camp for guess who? Every Jew who can run is running, or packing up to leave. But to where?

Bernhardt's little *Einsatztrupp,* with Gitzig working the books, is already having a profitable time in Munich; they may even need another storehouse now. If Bernhardt's doing so well, I can't imagine how Goering's doing.

Anna and Dieter Lange think they're slick. I've heard them talking about how they got the doctor to sign her "can't have babies" paper. So they're getting away with it, not having kids at all. She's dumping the pad and claiming a miscarriage. A lot of times they talk right out in the open, like I was still a piece of furniture; some of the important stuff I hear through the furnace flues that come down from their room into the cellar. They talk about money all the time, where to put it. Anna thinks they should help her folks buy more land and livestock, little by little. Dieter Lange wants to make safe and secret investments, get the money to Switzerland, but he's afraid he might get caught. He's told me sometimes in his room, or down in mine, when Anna's out—when I learn the most important stuff—that he wishes all this business would settle down, maybe even that Hitler would get put out, so he could leave the SS and open a nice, fancy club in Berlin. Dieter Lange has done what he set out to do—make money. He used the SS to do it, but the SS is using him, too. He's got to be careful. So they make money on rake-offs, but can't do anything with it. Bernhardt's in the same fix, except he's a state security officer. Wouldn't be the first cop to have sticky fingers. He has valuables that Goering doesn't want or maybe doesn't even know about. Besides, Goering's a very busy man, according to the papers. No, never knew a cop who wasn't crooked in some way—stealing sex or goods or money. Saw too much of it working clubs back home and here in Germany where the uniform, the flag, the slogans, the marching, only cover it up. Sure, the German folk this, and the German folk that. Fuck the folk. These camps wouldn't be here if the folk didn't want them. And there'll be new camps in Czechoslovakia, because the Germans won't be happy with just the Sudetenland; they want the whole place.

Anna surprises me with her temper, her sex, her drinking. And her English. Only rarely now does she ask me to explain a word she may hear over the radio during a BBC broadcast. She loves to read about Hollywood movie stars in American magazines, especially Marlene Dietrich who became a U.S. citizen last year. "German movies," she says, "are all about being a good German, not romance, you know." She's come a long way from *Uncle Tom's Cabin,* and I did it. Everybody looks down on me, but I taught her English; everybody laughs at me, but they love my singing and playing; everybody despises me for being a faggot, but everybody wants to do it to me or have me do it to them. I wish I could lay this burden down, but on clear days when we can just see the mountains to the south, I remind myself how close I came, so I wait, just as Dieter Lange and Anna wait. When they're together they talk about "afterward." When Dieter Lange's with me, "afterward"

is without Anna. I think Anna, too, thinks about "afterward" without
him. Me, when I think "afterward" it's without either of them. Everybody's waiting for something, yet I don't think anybody can help
believing that things are just beginning.

Thursday, Dec. 29, 1938

Of course, we've had Christmas: big dances at The Nest, and even a
party here, for the first time in a long while. I'll remember that party,
because there were a couple of doctors who came; one was the man
who was doing the tests on Dr. Nyassa. Recognized him right away.

Ursula Winkelmann and her husband have been feted all over the
ss compound. Her pad is off! The baby is here! I can't imagine what
this Winkelmann is like that he went along. There are a bunch of
strange saps in the ss! Ursula went to Momma's a few days before
the "baby" was expected, and when she returned to the compound,
she had this baby all wrapped in pink. And her and Anna have been
cooing over that little bastard like it was really her own! (Will she
pad out four times for the bronze Honor Cross of German Mother-
hood, or six times for the silver, or eight times for the gold?) Who
knows about this? Me, Anna, Dieter Lange, Ursula, naturally, and
her husband, and maybe two or three people at *Lebensborn.*

There's a big Christmas tree in the room where the piano is.
I love the smell of it, and the decorations and lights and candles.
The Winkelmanns, the Bernhardts, the Langes, and me sang Christmas carols, me playing the piano, last Thursday. Bernhardt gave me
a carton of Players and a bottle of Scotch and patted me on the back
as if to say, "Everything's all right now," but it isn't. I've often wondered if he watched while they cut off Ulrich's and Maria's heads.
(Or could he have done it himself?) Dieter Lange gave me some
socks and handkerchiefs, but he had already slipped me a bit of that
darling white powder. He once said, "If that fat-assed faggot Goering
can use it, why can't we?" Anna gave me a book that bored me after
the first page. I put it away.

I spent Christmas alone with a goose, which I didn't eat but left
in the oven for Anna and Dieter Lange, some liquor, which I drank,

and the piano, which I didn't play. I don't mind when I'm by myself, which is something most prisoners never get to enjoy; you're alone if they put you in the Bunker, but that's hell. This is more like heaven. You relax when you're alone; you don't have to be watching what you do or say, or watching, period. I sat at the piano. The truth is, I'm not happy like I used to be with the music. I haven't found my real self in it since May. Just ricky-tick, tinky-tank stuff. My fingers don't play what I think I hear. I can't seem to make music out of the way I feel. I keep thinking there's got to be a new kind of music to explain this shit I'm in, because music expresses every kind of experience one can imagine, but I can't pump it out of myself, and that makes me afraid; if I don't have my music, really don't have it, then I don't have anything. It's bad not to have any-thing. You wind up doing what Dr. Nyassa did. Please, God. Help me.

Monday, January 9, 1939
    Typhoid epidemic.
    Typhoid, and everybody's scared, so The Nest has been without in-person music for a couple of weeks, to make sure none of us brings to it what's been knocking off prisoners in the blocks. The doctors and nurses from the *Reviers* have been giving shots and medicine day and night. Inmates lined up in the cold. Rivers of snot, shit, and saliva. Prisoners working on the sewers. Clean! Clean! the guards shout. Wash! Cleanliness is next to godliness. Wash! Don't drink from here! Don't drink from there! Smoke—black, oily, smelly—boiling out of the crematorium. In the SS compound, where the sewer system is good—except where some prisoners may have sabotaged it—every-one is boiling water; everyone is checking for the red spots and the runny bowels, waiting for the weariness that doesn't end. There's not a lot of running from bed to bed right now out here, let me tell you. Over in camp, those that're well have to help those who aren't, and prisoners are being switched from their regular details to the mess, cleanup, and crematorium details. If this is with less than a good heart, it is nevertheless good insurance; you never know when you

might get sick and need help. From one end of the camp to the other, the smell of shit and burning bodies seems to have frozen right in the air.

When we're not boiling water and scrubbing the house from top to bottom, me and Anna are smearing alcohol and disinfectant over everything. The house smells like a vat of chlorine, and I'm sure every house out here smells just the same. I think the smell of vinegar and dill is better. Dieter Lange is off on another trip, but one I think he went to, instead of being sent on. Maybe he's hoping Anna will get sick and kick the bucket, maybe that I will, too. Anna needs me to help clean, and the canteen's closed, anyway. Anna's as strong as one of her father's plough horses, and I'm in pretty good shape myself. Nobody's visiting these days, either. Afraid of catching something. (Which is why Anna hasn't been fucking with me. She's afraid she might catch something from me, and I'm afraid I could catch something from her. I'd punch her in the jaw if she tried anything funny right now.)

Well. All this gives me time at the piano, and that's good because I don't have to go over scores. Instead, I'm trying to think up new music and find new ways to make it work, like planting the rhythm in space instead of leaving it alone. It's nice, playing while Anna sews upstairs or sleeps. (Sometimes when she comes down she says, "That was nice. What was it?" Or, "That sounded like glass breaking in the middle of winter. What was *that* supposed to be?") Being alone gives me a chance to think about things, too, like when I told Werner about Ulrich and Maria. He just shook his head, and asked if Maria had given her last name or where she was from. I told him I didn't know. Then he wanted the exact date, which I gave him. I still think he's writing things down for later. Funny how we all think there will be a "later." He told me that some of the colored men had died, some more had come in, and all were put in the same block with the Jews. All had been sterilized, he told me, by x-ray; two, he believed, had been castrated. The thought of that made me shiver. He said they just slit the sacks and take out the nuts, sew up the sacks, and you sing alto instead of like Paul Robeson— unless they. . . . Then he asked if I understood all that was going on.

Before I could answer, he started to give me a lesson in civics. Another one.

Things were very bad in France, he said, where fascist Frenchmen were exerting more and more power, which the working people could hold in check for just so long. (I wondered if there weren't fascists everywhere; there seemed to be a lot of them in Germany, so I thought it'd be only natural for them to be all over.) When the French and English backed down over Czechoslovakia, a lot of French officers resigned, and so did some people in the British parliament. Werner called the French "shits who can't be trusted"; they managed to drag the Americans into their front in the last war because they couldn't handle it themselves, but that's the way they are, he said, good in the kitchen, superb in bed, and cowards on the battlefield. I asked him, "Even the workers?" and he stopped short for a second, and then went on like he hadn't heard me. Werner was mad that day, last week, the first of the new year. What a way to start it.

I feel most sorry for the gangs that have to clean up the snow and ice. They slip and slide with their boards fastened together, their shoes wrapped in rags if they have no arctics, and most don't, their bodies bulging with old sweaters and pants, two or even three jackets, rags wrapped around their heads to protect them from the cold. They know the only way to keep warm is to move, so they have this little dance: slip-slide step-step shuffle, shuffle-step-step slide-slip, then shovel-lift-throw, and start all over again. They are the only ones who hear the music; it's like watching a dance chorus in a movie without sound.

Wednesday, February 8, 1939

It's so cold we've put up the porcelain stove in the living room. It burns wood we have brought to the back, where I split it. We don't get as much coal as we used to, and when we do get it, it's soft coal, coke, and doesn't heat as well as the hard. The porcelain stove works just fine, but I hate taking out the ashes. Ashes make dust that I have to wipe up. The one good thing about winter, Dieter Lange says, is that he doesn't have to buy ice or worry if I'm going to forget

to empty the pan under the icebox. We have cold boxes attached
to the kitchen windows. Whatever we put in the boxes freezes like
rocks. The cream is pushed out of the bottles of milk we set out
there. Sometimes the bottles crack. The meat looks like the parts
of bodies I hear the SS doctors are dissecting. Of course, that may
just be jailhouse gossip, of which there is an awful lot in camp.
For example, Huebner was telling me about an ASO who came in
fighting with the guards all the way from Frankfurt because he
claimed his idiot kid had been taken away and killed. Threw him
in the Bunker right away and proceeded to whip his ass every hour
on the hour, twenty-five strokes, and still he fought. One day the
prisoners near him didn't hear him anymore, and a detail came in
to wash out his cell. Where did he go? Up the chimney, they say.
The Reds are still snooping around because, as Werner said, "A man
can come in here and be crazy, but *nobody* can be *that* crazy without
good reason." Nobody knows the man's name. Werner believes
almost everything; I wonder how it is that he's not crazy, too.
You got to shut out some of this shit and believe it's jailhouse
gossip in order not to go nuts.

Monday, March 6, 1939
    General mobilization. The German government is talking
war with Czechoslovakia, the rumor says. Mad because the Czechs
haven't rolled over and given up like the British and French want
them to. The English are calling up people, and in camp, Jesus Christ,
there are prisoners who want to volunteer to go to war. Can't be the
"later" everyone's been hoping for, war. Well, they've been talking
about it coming for a long time. I'd imagine if The Nest was open,
and it will be next week Bernhardt says, there'd be the same old
saddle-up, flag-waving, give-me-some-pussy-because-I'm-going-
to-war bullshit.
    The second day the canteen was open after the epidemic was over,
a colored boy came in wearing the black triangle of the asocials.
Actually, he was just on the dark side of high-yellow. I didn't
know this until Lappus called me from the office and said a young

colored prisoner wanted to talk to me; that was when I met him.
"You're Mr. Pepperidge?" he asked. He spoke first in German and
then repeated in English. His English was okay. And it wasn't
British English, either. Before I could answer—and I wanted to
answer quickly because no prisoner called another "mister," and
I didn't want him to be laughed at—he said his own name was
Pierre Braun. I said hello in English and led him away from the
customers, who were not buying as much as talking about the
possibility of war with Czechoslovakia. It stinks in the canteen in
winter, and everyone tries to get as close to the little stove as possible. Five feet away from it there's no warmth at all because of the
bodies packed around it. Pierre looked about fifteen. He could have
been my son. He was a skinny kid with big eyes that I thought must
once have been very bright. He had a tic on the left side of his face.
His hands were long and thin. There was something about him that
made me want to put my arm around his shoulder. To comfort him.
To stop the tic. To bring brightness back into his eyes. He seemed
very sad.

"Well?" I said. He kept looking at me. Like a kid, too.

"Somebody told me you were an American." In this place that
could be anybody. Oh, Christ, I'm thinking. How come he knows
American English? I'm curious to know how he got here, who he is.

So I say, "Yeah, that's right."

He holds out his hand again and I take it, and we shake for a
second time while he's telling me, "My father's American, too.
He was an American soldier. My mother's German—from Mullheim
—the Rhineland. I got my father's English from her. And I studied
it, so if we ever went to America . . ." I drop his hand. He cocks
his head and looks at me, a question in his eyes. He sees I know.
"You know about the Rhineland Bastards then?"

I pat his shoulder. "They, they . . . ?"

He nods his head. "Yes. They did that to me and sent me here.
It's happening not only to black Rhinelanders, you know." I don't
know why, but we're whispering.

"I'm sorry," I say. "What can I do for you?" He hunches his shoulders.

"Just tell me about America when you can." After a minute he adds, "My father never came back. He never sent for us. My mother was mad." And here it is.

"How old are you, Pierre?" I ask him. He tells me fourteen. I ask where he works and he tells me the disinfection hut. That's near the north wall. The epidemic must have been hell for him. Then he has to go. I tell him, "Stop in any time except Saturday. We'll talk about America." He grabs my hand once more and shakes it and thanks me.

Huebner is about five years older than Pierre. I hadn't thought about that before, how many young Witnesses there are here. I wonder what Huebner will do when the next Witness roll call takes place. Will he step forward and renounce the Witnesses, or stand in place? I think he'll stand still, and I guess that's why I like him.

Thursday, March 16, 1939

Gitzig came over Monday. Hadn't seen him in a long time. Said Bernhardt was busy in Vienna and Lily was visiting relatives. He had the house to himself for a little while. He looked good: good clothes and shoes. He didn't even seem to look as much like a rat as he used to—well, not quite as much. We talked about how big the SS compound had grown, and all the women and the babies. He said any SS man worth his salt was going to have a nice nest egg by the time all this was over. I asked what he meant by "by the time this is all over." He told me the plan was to invade Czechoslovakia on Wednesday, since the Czechs were so slow to hand over the land Germany claimed. And later, they'd take the whole damn thing. "So," he said, "that information I told you to take to Werner . . . a safe bet, eh? And don't forget, Poland next. But I suppose by now they've got all their people out." I told him I didn't know. He had a problem, he said. "You remember those radio parts I told you about, how we ought to save everything? Well, I put together two." Somehow I couldn't imagine Gitzig the swindler being able to do that. "I got one complete radio in the camp," he said, "and all but one tube of the second. It's all wrapped." I waited. "Take it to camp. Give it to Werner."

I was surprised. "Werner has a radio?"

He laughed. "I know many things you don't know I know. Werner knows how to use it." He saw that I was not anxious to do that. "They don't search you when you go through, Pepperidge, come on. There are people waiting for that tube." I asked where he managed to get the parts and he said in his travels, and laughed again. "I'd have taken whole radios, but how in the hell could I get away with that? Bernhardt would have my ass in the Bunker like sixty just to start with." Gitzig knew I was on my way to the canteen.

"Right now?" I asked him.

"The sooner the better," he said. "They want to know what's going on with Czechoslovakia." (German troops went into Bohemia and Moravia yesterday.) I asked what would happen if they searched me this time at the guardhouse, and he said, "It's your ass, I suppose. Even Bernhardt couldn't save you. And they'd *make* you tell them who you were carrying it to, who you got it from, and then they'd make Werner tell, and the game would be up." He shrugged. "That's the chance you take, Pepperidge. What do you say?" I said all right. He slapped me on the back. "That's the spirit. This thing can't last forever." I told him I thought he only stole, swindled, or pissed in the tea, and he said he still stole and he was a better swindler than Bernhardt—who didn't have to swindle or steal because he was a licensed ass-kicker and could do anything he damn well pleased—and besides, the whole business was a swindle with the fucking Nazis; he knew because it takes one to know one.

Right now it was merely a matter of who was going to swindle who and for how long. He was hedging bets. I didn't understand. This prick was in no position to make choices, just like the rest of us weren't. But I said, "At my expense."

He hawked some snot and said, "Who the fuck you think carried in all those other parts?" I told him I was wondering what was making him so *stark* all of a sudden, and he said he had a family he wanted one day to be proud of him. He'd never mentioned family to me, and I told him so. Over his face came a slow smile. It actually made the ugly sonofabitch look handsome. "I'm going to have a child. I mean, a woman is going to have a child by me," he said.

"One of those country-girl whores," I said.

"No," he said. He loved this woman and she wasn't a whore.
He was still smiling when he said, "I put my life into your hands,
Pepperidge, but I'm so happy I have to tell someone!" He leaned
very close and whispered, "A woman out here." I jumped away from
him like he had a nasty cottonmouth snake in his hand.

"An SS wife?"

He just grinned—shy-like—and nodded his head. I started to
ask him if he was crazy. Then I realized that this stuff was probably
happening all over the place. Shit, in a twisted kind of way it was
happening to me. But the business had to have started with the
woman. No calfactor would dare approach the wife, daughter,
mother, cousin, aunt, or grandmother of an SS man. Talk about
leaving this place in a hurry, that would give you the right ticket.
Well, Gitzig and me were in the same boat, except in my boat beside
Anna were Ursula and Dieter Lange. Maybe the husband never did
enough homework. Maybe, after a while, being the wife of an SS
officer was like having the clap or worse, and the women got sick of
it. I took a good long look at Gitzig, who was still grinning. Had he
wondered which side his goose would slowly be cooked on if the
baby looked like him? I saw he hadn't. I just shook my head. It was
plain to see that Gitzig was in love, and that never allowed you to
look over the consequences when your love came down on the
wrong side of things. The sonofabitch had joined the human race.
I took the tube in without trouble and gave it to Werner. It was like
carrying in a can of sausage for him, no trouble at all.

Thursday, March 30, 1939

There were new tuxedos for us when we returned to the Pussy
Palace. No doubt from the wardrobe shop of another Jew who'd
managed to get out or who was in a camp somewhere. The tuxes
are midnight blue, not black, and smell so new that there couldn't
be a single typhus germ trucking in the seams. After all those weeks
in Dieter Lange's house and the camp, it felt good to be back.
One problem, though, and it's Moritz. He's got blues deeper than

Duke's "Mood Indigo," blues deeper than the color of his tux. After the first set of our first night back last week, I pulled him into a corner. Bernhardt knew music, but he didn't *know* music. I mean, he couldn't tell when someone was off unless they were way off. But I could, and I knew Moritz was off. I'd heard him play that fiddle long enough to know. I knew it wasn't his love life; he had some real Berlin *Leder* among the *Lebensborn* workers, and I was happy he was happy. It was something else. All this time, he finally told me, he was hoping to get himself bought out of camp, but somehow his family could never get the money together. Then, during *Kristallnacht,* some of his family vanished. It was the worst time ever for Jews, he told me, and something had changed in the way he was now treated in camp. When he marched out with the band to have an inmate punished, get a whipping, or to be hung on the Tree, the guards spat at him and kicked him and called him names—which they'd not routinely done before. It was like he was the one going to punishment. So he was afraid, and I couldn't do anything to help him, and that's what was wrong with his playing. Then he cried. And I held him. That was all I could do. He heaved up and down in my arms, his lousy perfume sneaking up my nose, until, slowly, he came to a stop and blew his nose on a rag.

———

Tuesday, April 4, 1939

I slipped down to the disinfection hut today with a pack of Drummers (I don't think he smokes, but he can trade them), a bar of chocolate, and a can of sausage for Pierre Braun. I thought I might talk with him about America. Yesterday Anna gave me a three-year-old *Saturday Evening Post.* On the cover was a fat colored woman who looked like Aunt Jemima. She was bent over an open oven basting a turkey. She wore a head rag. Sitting close by on the floor was a long-headed little colored boy. Reminded me of my auntie's house back home when I was a kid.

I get to the hut without any trouble, look over at the garden, and I see Pierre there with Hohenberg. Hohenberg, with the stiff dick that never goes down. And the way he's close to the kid, the look on his face, like he's hungry for something, scares me and makes me mad at the same time. I don't think about it twice. I just go over and tell Hohenberg to get the fuck away from the kid and leave him alone or I'll kick his ass. The look on his face makes me know he's up to no good. I can see the kid doesn't know what's going on. Maybe he's never been approached before. Usually the prisoners stay away from disinfection hut workers for fear of catching something. Anyway, that's the way I saw it: Hohenberg trying to take advantage of Pierre. I chase his ass right out of there. He knows I'd managed to take care of Baum; word gets around, or even if it doesn't, the prisoners could guess at the sequence of events.

I pick up two rakes and give Pierre one so we won't be standing around doing nothing. That's the quickest way to get the guards on your ass. I ask how he's been, if his health is all right, if he's heard from his mother. Everything is all right with him, but he's not heard from his mother and won't because it's forbidden. He asks me why I was mad at Hohenberg, and I tell him the camp is filled with men who haven't had a woman in years, so the prisoners turn a little bit queer with each other. Young prisoners they tried to make into women. They bring gifts and sweet-talk them; or they beat them up or black-mail them. They do all sorts of things. I tell him I have cigarettes and food for him, but I wasn't trying to slick him into anything; tell him I am queer myself, so I know what's going on. I am thinking he might draw back a bit when I tell him, but he doesn't. He says he isn't like that at all and just didn't think about the way it is in camp, but now he understands. He asks how I got that way. All the time we're raking dirt and mixing it with pig shit to fertilize it. Tell him I didn't know, I just am, and had been in America. So I get the conversation around to that and I can tell he feels easier. I ask where his father had come from and he says St. Louis. Do I know it? I say I don't, but I know a little something about Kansas City in the same state. A lot of very good musicians lived there. Did his daddy play any kind of music that he

knew of? He doesn't think so. Was St. Louis a nice place? I tell him
no. A lot of colored people had been killed there in race riots.
He wants to know what those are, and when I describe them he asks
if I'd ever been in one. I laugh because if I knew one was on the way,
I'd run. Do they have those everywhere in America? No, I tell him,
but they have enough. It isn't easy for colored people back there.
His daddy made his mother believe all that stuff about democracy
and every man being equal to the next. I tell him, though, that there
are some pretty nice places. If a colored man knew the ropes, New
Orleans was a fine place with lots of good spicy food. I think then
of a steaming bowl of gumbo and nearly cry. And Philadelphia is all
right, and New York and Chicago, I tell him. I can see him brighten-
ing up. They don't do there what they are doing here? he wants to
know. Of course, I tell him no, and give him a scowl like a father
would in answer to a silly question. Lots of colored people in those
cities, I tell him.

Harlem, he wants to know about. I rake for a minute, then tell
him it is the place every colored person with gumption or get-up-
and-go wants to be. Because of the tall buildings? He'd seen pictures.
I laugh again. How can tall buildings help a man get along? I ask
him. You know better than that, I say. It's just that people do things
in New York that they don't or won't or can't do anywhere else. Like
Berlin, then? I start to say that depended on what you wanted to do,
but I say instead, a little. What are colored Americans like? he wants
to know. I am a little sorry I'd started this, but at the same time, it
feels good to tell him about things, like a daddy would. They're like
your father and they're like me. They're like Joe Louis—and I wait
to see if he knows about him. He does. Pierre grins. And like Jesse
Owens. He grins again. They're poor and a very few—very few—are
rich, but not rich like white people are rich. Do they work in factories and stores and on the trams and buses? I rake out a new furrow.
No, I tell him, but both the men and the women work very hard for
little pay. So then he wants to know how they earn enough money
to save and get ahead (which is every European's goal). I have to tell
him that colored people don't own any factories and damn few stores
and running the trams, trains, and buses is what white people do,

that and all the neat, clean jobs. Then I rake and don't say anything more, because I'm thinking, Shit! How *do* we get by? Anyway, it's time for me to get on back up the street to the canteen. "I have to go now," I say. "We'll talk again." I collect his rake and set them against the fence and steer him back toward the disinfection hut. If the guard in the tower is watching, I know he's thinking I probably outtalked Hohenberg to get me some booty. I slip the stuff from under my jacket down into his shirt. Then I think of something, and I say, "Wait a minute." I need a little more help. I pick up a rake again and with the end of the handle draw this into the dirt:

When I finish, I tell him, "Press your hand on it, right between those two things at the top." He's wondering what it is, and I say, "Go ahead. It's colored American magic. It'll protect you from any- thing bad." He's got a stupid look on his face. "Pierre. Do it!" He bends to his knees and presses the earth right between the sideways crosses at the top of the sign for Loa Aizan, who protects whoever wears the sign from evil spirits. Pierre looks at me sort of funny, like what's going on with this guy, then he goes to the hut and I start up the street. I march right up into Werner's block. Being a block leader doesn't seem to be such a bad job at all. I mean, Werner doesn't have to rush out of bed, bolt down his food, and march off to work and back singing as loud as he can. Not bad at all, just looking after things and seeing the others behave, and collecting information. He must see something on my face because he looks edgy. I don't even say hello. I tell him to tell everybody, especially that goddamn Hohenberg, to leave that Braun kid alone if they want to stay healthy. Werner's looking at me like I've gone nuts. Then he grins. Then he laughs, pats me on the shoulder and says he'll tell them, don't worry, he'll tell them.

Monday, April 17, 1939

Another April, another bunch of baby bastards, the same old SS all dressed up, the girls who look the same as all the others, the same looks at each other ("I'm *really* off to war now, honey, so . . ."), the same thinning out of people just past the middle of the second set. Only thing different was we were playing more slow drags because this shit in Czechoslovakia was serious business, Bernhardt said last Friday. He showed up with Anna. His own wife's sick a lot with that baby she's carrying. Sure ought to be used to it by now; been carrying seven months. Bernhardt, he don't need excuses for anything he does. Anyway, Dieter Lange's away clearing up accounts at the other camps. He's now going to be responsible for just the ones in Bavaria and Linz, and Mauthausen in Austria. That may come to thirty or forty small and large camps, I heard him say to Anna, if all the plans are put into operation. Last month, though, he had to get rid of seven prisoners at other camps because they were dipping in the till. I guess the same way he got rid of Baum. I wondered then just how many camps there were going to be when these crazy Germans got finished. Sure, everybody's glad the epidemic is over and that the mess in Czechoslovakia doesn't look *too* bad for now. But I guess before long there'll be some Czechs in the camp, just like there are some Austrians (and they still ain't stopped coming). On the stand, we've played the numbers so often we can just let our minds fly out of the Pussy Palace. Moritz was sounding better, more like himself, but still a little off. I was more worried about myself, because I knew I'd worn out my vocals. I wasn't with them anymore, and I knew I was right when I'd catch somebody in the band looking at me and then look away quick just when I thought I was faking up a storm. Well, they'd become pretty good musicians.

That was last weekend.

This past weekend, Moritz wasn't in the truck when it stopped to pick me up. I asked where he was, sick? Moritz hadn't ever been sick. Nobody answered me right away. The guards smiled at each other, but said nothing. Franz, while lighting a cigarette, drew a finger across his throat, blew out the smoke, and turned to watch the road. We could talk while we dressed. We were always alone then.

Somebody at The Nest had squealed on Moritz's leather boy. They took him to the Bunker. They had Moritz stand alone on the Dancing Ground after the evening roll call. This was Thursday night. (I hadn't gone to the camp Friday morning, because Anna got a bug up her ass about spring cleaning, so I hadn't heard anything—not that you always will.) Then they marched him into the Bunker, got his violin, and made him play while he marched. "Marched to his own tune, straight up," Teodor said, chewing a sandwich. He snorted. "He knew it was the end for him, crippled for life, or dead. He's marching across the Appellplatz and he breaks out with this *'Air.'*" For a minute I thought he meant a fart. But he meant a *tune*. Then, he said, Moritz started a dancing march, bouncing to his own music.

I asked what the hell he was playing, and then Fritz broke in. "They say he was playing some Jew shit—*'Hava Nagila'*—and the guards began to beat at his legs, but he kept on playing and marching, even when they started on his body and his head." (All stories like this are pieced together. One prisoner sees this happen, another sees that happen, and others see what they see, and eventually the story gets put together.)

I asked if the tune meant anything to make them beat him up. Alex said, "Let's rejoice."

Danko said in a voice that sounded like he'd run a hundred miles, "From Palestine." The Reds finished the story, put the final touches on it because the prisoners clean up all the messes, and those that belong to Werner's gang report to him. It seems that Moritz's leather boy was already naked on the whipping block. They gave Moritz the whip. By now they'd smashed his violin. He threw down the whip. They took the leather boy off the block and strapped Moritz to it. The leather boy didn't throw down the whip. He flogged Moritz to death, although twenty-five strokes is supposed to be the limit—for small things, like leaving camp without authorization, saying rotten things about the government, or keeping certain articles or tools. For a couple of prisoner queers, all the rules went out the window. Then the guards flogged the leather boy to death. Werner's people said it was a mess. So I had another bad weekend at The Nest. It was so bad that Bernhardt wanted to know what was wrong. I told him we needed new material, and he said okay. Then he took Anna by the arm and led her out of the hall, I suppose to the cottage he uses back on the far side of *Lebensborn*.

Sunday, April 30, 1939

Earlier I was upstairs with Dieter Lange and Anna listening to some records. No doubt that jazz music is changing. They'd been calling it "swing," but it's still jazz. Wonder how come they call Benny Goodman the "King of Swing?" He could be a "Duke" or a "Count," but not a king. Dieter Lange's got just about everything Fats Waller ever did, and Billie Holiday, too. I enjoy playing the records when Anna and Dieter Lange aren't around, so I can relax and think about the way the music's being played. When they're around, Dieter Lange's always saying, "That's jumping!" or "That's swinging!" What a pain in the ass. I've never liked people who couldn't blow a halfway decent fart, but who run off at the mouth about this musician or that one, or what's being done with the music and what isn't. Sometimes, whether they're home or not, if I hear something in the music, I'll try to work it out on the piano my own way.

The Germans just kicked another few thousand out, over into Poland. That would be like kicking black people out of New York and Philadelphia and Chicago and sending them to Mississippi. Who the fuck would want to go to Poland? The Jews are not allowed to take whatever they have left with them, and once there, they can't leave, and they have to live in certain places. How do they live? Their jobs were here, in Germany. Dieter Lange says Hitler told everybody how it was going to be in his book, *Mein Kampf,* but nobody believed him. I listen to the prisoners talking about the Jews—and they don't mind my being there—as if I would naturally agree with them. Ha! With these bastards? They never ask me what I think, and I never tell them. I'm not dumb. They *hate* Jews, nearly all the prisoners, even many of the Reds. "The Jews controlled the banks until Hitler took them back. They control the banks of the

world." Really? I think. I never thought of it one way or the other.
Some of the Jews I knew were gangsters or ran pawnshops. "The
Jews took over our schools, the theater, wrote all the books, and
squeezed all the Germans out of the retail business," the prisoners
tell each other. I didn't know anything about that, not having spent
all that much time in school back home, and certainly none in
Europe. And I didn't read that many books; never have. In Germany,
and I guess everywhere else, you can't tell a Christian from a Jew
in a store or anywhere else. On Saturdays it was true that you saw
Jews going to their church, but the very next day you saw Christians
going to theirs. In Berlin show business, I knew Jews and Christians
and couldn't tell—shit, didn't give a damn—which was which. As far
as I knew, one club owner was as bad as another. Theater was something I didn't know about. So when the prisoners talked about the
Jews just taking over everything, I wondered how come the Christians were too lazy to write the books, do well in the retail business,
run the banks and schools and other things? It was all a bunch of
bullshit, what they were saying, and I knew it, and down deep they
did, too. They just wanted to get rid of the Jews to make themselves
feel more important. I could see that from where I stood in the peck-
ing order back home. I got tired of all those stupid white people
thinking they were more important or better than me. If the Christians have it in so much for the Jews who "stole everything," why are
they bringing in Gypsies as fast as they can? Gypsies don't write shit,
as far as I know, and not only don't they own any banks, they don't
even use the motherfuckers; and they don't want to have much to do
with anyone who isn't a Gypsy. Bullshit, bullshit, bullshit. The world
runs on it the way a car runs on gasoline.

I thought about this business and what it would be like back
home if white people in the Congress passed a law that would do
to colored people what German laws are doing to the Jews. I mean,
if the laws were *everywhere* back home, not just the South and some
small towns around the country. Would we just pick up and march
into prisons? Would we say, "Yazzuh, boss," and march off to another
Poland? All twelve million of us? How could we ever hide, pass for
white, unless we damn near were? (I guess after all this time there's

got to be a few million who've slipped over the line.) Who would
send us money to help get away and to where? Probably Africa,
but I don't know anything about no damned Africa, and wouldn't
want to go there, running around with a bone in my nose, or a plate
in my lips, like in all the pictures. Who would hold conferences to
figure out a way to save us? Conferences didn't save those Jews, and
my guess is, push come to shove, white people would prefer Jews to
colored people, anyhow. Sometimes when I pass a bunch of Jews
and hear quiet, secret laughing, or under-the-breath singing—not
those work songs but something harder and deeper—it reminds me
of colored men on the chain gangs that you pass on the roads in the
South, and I know that the Boss-man, the Cap'n-suh, German or
American, hadn't yet managed to completely kill the spirit.

Last week Pierre told me that when he got out—when *we* got
out—he wanted to go to New York. I asked about his mother,
and he just hunched up his shoulders and let them fall down.
He's mad, I think, because she can't write to him. And she let them
carry him off without a fight. Says he couldn't live in Germany anymore after what's happened to him, and when I told him again that
America wasn't a bed of roses, either, he said he'd take his chances,
that it's better than this. I agree.

Pierre has a fine, well-shaped head. He's always close-shaven,
working in the disinfection hut. Other prisoners can have a little
hair on their heads, but not enough to make a nest for lice. The
gas Pierre and the other prisoners use to clean clothing and spray
prisoners is very strong, he told me. Sometimes he has to go outside no matter how hard it's raining or how cold it is. The good
thing, he says, is that he's sure no bug in the world wants to be
bothered with him. He still has that tic. Pierre seems glad to see
me, but to get to him is like moving between two worlds. I can see
what his is like, but he can't understand mine because I haven't
told him all about it, of course. I mean Dieter Lange or Anna.
I did tell him about the club for the ss—that's where I get the
sandwiches and other things I can sometimes give him. He wanted
me to explain jazz music and I told him there is no explaining it;
it just is.

Pierre likes to play "Suppose." "Suppose we get out of here."
(He always says "we.") "Maybe next week. What would we do?"

"First," I say, "supposing we had money, we'd get the first train out
of Dachau to France, Paris."

He smiles.

"Then we'd find rooms in Montmartre. There are a lot of clubs
there where they play jazz. And I have friends there, Freddie Johnson
and Ruby Mae Richards, and I think there'd be a guy there who
played in my band at the ss club. We'd have fun in Paris."

"And then?" He's waiting for the America part, but I'm not in a
big hurry to get to it.

I say, "I also have a friend in Amsterdam, and I know some
recording people in Madrid, but maybe we'd go to London, so you
can see that, too."

"I would like that," Pierre says.

"Then we'd take a ship, a Cunarder."

"Do they let colored people on those ships?"

"Yes, and not the back of the ship, either. They're great big things.
You wonder how they can float."

"I'd be afraid," Pierre says, but his eyes sparkle.

I think about "Suppose" down in my room. The next time we play
it, the ship will be coming into New York harbor.

I heard footsteps upstairs. They were Dieter Lange's. "Cleef? Cleef,
I'm coming down. We should have a drink." He was on my stairs
now. "It's been a couple of weeks, Cleef. Anna stayed to help Ursula
with the baby." Clump, he came, clomp, he came, until he was at my
door, in his pants and undershirt, holding a bottle of schnapps.

I hate Dieter Lange. Sometimes I wonder how I can hate him so
much and still be alive. I think I hate him enough to drop dead from
it. I wouldn't hesitate one second to kill him, kill him in ways even
the ss couldn't begin to imagine. Thing about it is he knows I love
living a helluva lot more than I hate him. I've had these thoughts
before, I know, but I can't get rid of them. They keep going round
and round in my head like a trapped rat trying to find a way out.
I think sometimes when we're together, me and Dieter Lange,
that I should just *kill* him. To hell with what comes next. I could.

It wouldn't be hard. He's got all puffy and soft, and so deep in shit that he's scared of everything. He can only relax with me. The power he has over most other people is shit. We both understand that. It wouldn't be at all hard to kill him, but then what? Even if I could do it without laying a hand on him—gather some of his hair and make a potion, get a black rooster (from where?) and vinegar (plenty of that around here), write down his name seven times, split a fish and fill it with black pepper, sew up the fish with black thread and hang it in the yard, chop up bits of his or Anna's hair real fine and put it in his food so that his stomach gets tangled up and he dies; or grind up glass in his food so it feels like no more than a bit of gravel or dirt, like you find in spinach or lettuce, and let him slowly bleed to death; or make a doll of him out of his clothes and hair and fingernails, say the words, and stick him with pins—then what? I'd never be allowed to stay in the house alone with Anna. Would Bernhardt take me in, me, his exotic, one-and-only jazz *Neger?* Hell, no. Because Dieter Lange's his fall guy. Every Nazi has a fall guy between himself and disaster. We called them front men or beards back home.

Monday, May 15, 1939

I think the tic on Pierre's face comes slower now, but it's more violent, like one part of his face wants to rearrange the other. I can tell he's embarrassed by this because he doesn't talk as much and listens more. He is also confused because he doesn't know what's happening to him. I miss Dr. Nyassa. I trade goods for sulfa pills with the senior in *Revier* One. He's been real top dog since Dr. Nyassa killed himself. The pills don't seem to help Pierre. I think the problem's nerves, but I don't remember what they did for tics back home. Everyone knows it's bad business to try to get to the doctors. They always think you're malingering. You have to be just about dead to get excused from a detail. And even if you got into the *Revier,* you might not ever get out. They do things there. Better Pierre should have a bad tic than a bad death. I think that spray they use to kill lice is bothering him.

The flower gardens are ready to bloom. You'd think nature would say, "Uh-uh, not *here* you don't." But the blooms are coming, as they do every spring. I get a funny feeling about that, like the way you feel back home when a chain gang grows out from beneath a grove of magnolia trees. The Amper River flows fast now, and it is thick and dark. I'd like to be a leaf or twig riding its surface right out of camp. And now the prisoners, like small armies, march to their details inside and outside camp, singing more brightly. Dust doesn't yet rise from beneath their feet, but it will in a few weeks' time; it's only May and the ground is still damp. To the quarry they march and it, after all this time, still looks untouched, they say; and to the swamps to continue to drain and plant; and to the gravel pit to gather the stones to make the roads and campgrounds smooth; the 4711 clears the sewers or lays new pipe; and details march to the SS compound to build new houses, clean the streets, put up lights, build new roads; to the SS barracks that are always being enlarged; to the farms, the factories, the warehouse construction sites; to the forests to cut and haul trees. They go singing as if they were on a holiday or the most decorated of Hitler's legions, in step, uniformed in their chain-gang stripes, their striped berets, arms swinging. They are so many and look so mighty marching, that a stranger might wonder how so few guards could ever contain so many, many prisoners.

Wed., May 31, 1939

"Well," I'm saying to Pierre as we pretend to work the garden as part of the garden detail. "Well, the Cunarder would come into New York harbor, where we'd see the Statue of Liberty—"

"With the torch held high? I read about that," Pierre says. His face brightens for a minute. Being out in the sunshine seems to make him feel better.

"Way, way high, Pierre. And then the ship would pull in beside all the other ships from all over the world, there in the Hudson River, the West Side, around 42nd Street. Then we'd go through customs, show our papers."

"But I don't have any papers, Mr. Pepperidge."

I hadn't thought about that, but I say, as we continue "Suppose,"
"Don't worry. In England we'd get a Nansen passport for refugees.
They'd let us in, all right. I'm an American, and you're—well—we'd
get some adoption papers in England, too, so we could say you're my
boy. We could ask them to fix the papers that way."

"Yes," Pierre says, smiling, "I could be your son until I find my
real father."

"I'm sure we could do that," I say.

"And then?"

"Then? Oh. After we finish customs, we'll take a taxi to Harlem.
That's the section of New York where colored people live, remember?"

"No white people?"

"Here and there, yes. I don't know about *now*, though. They may
have all moved because white people don't like to live near colored
people. We'll check in at a rooming house on 135th Street for a few
days to get our bearings. Try to look up some old friends, play a few
numbers and maybe hit—the numbers is like a lottery, you see, and
we'd need some money because we'd want some sharp clothes. You
can't go around Harlem looking just any kind of trashy way, you
know, especially if you're a musician. When I was in Berlin, I heard
about a lot of new clubs opening up in Harlem, so maybe it wouldn't
be too hard to find a band to play with."

"All right," Pierre says. "We've got new clothes. Do we go to church?"
"Church!"

He looks puzzled. "Yes, church."

"I—well—if you want. There are some grand churches in
Harlem." He's right, I think. We ought to go to church. "Are you
Protestant or Catholic?" I ask.

His eyes twinkle and he leans close and whispers, "I think my
mother is part Jewish."

I look around to see if anyone heard. No. The other prisoners
are busy. "Well," I say. "I've heard there are black Jews in Harlem.
They, the ss, they don't—"

"No. I'm not a fool. I see what's happening with the Jews."

The tic that comes just then is fierce, like something has grabbed
his face and is trying to twist it off. Pierre's eyes are like those of

someone looking from behind a glass door for help. Then it passes, and from the slump of his shoulders, I know "Suppose" is over for the day. I think of the other workers from the disinfection hut. They are all slow-moving dumbbells to me, shuffling, eyes drooped like drunks. It has to be that stuff they use. Sometimes you can smell it near the north wall sharper than the smell from the crematorium. Didn't Loa Aizan understand that this was evil? I thought of Hohenberg; he was the only person I knew in the Labor Office. Could Gitzig do anything for me? I didn't think so. Werner looked after his own, but demanded favors from everyone else.

"I . . . I never heard of black Jews . . ." Pierre says. He seems to be waiting, the way people wait for a sneeze to come. When the tic doesn't come, he sighs and without a word, turns and walks to the disinfection hut, his arms almost motionless at his sides.

I went to Werner anyway. I told him Pierre was sick and needed to be, I thought, in the fresh air. I planted myself in front of him. He'd done me some favors, but I'd done him more because I was in a position to do so. The barracks was empty.

"The quarry?" he said. "Fresh air out there."

"No!" I was surprised he'd said that.

"Swamp?" What was going on? He knew how frail Pierre was.

"Not the swamp, Werner, the garden. Can you do it? *Will* you do it?"

"That's for old guys and the priests," he said. He wouldn't look me in the eye.

"But he needs to be out there to stay alive," I said.

Werner walked to the window and held his hands behind his back. His silhouette was not as square and hard as when we first came here. There was a bending in his shoulders, and his white hair sprayed off glints of silver in the light. The block was empty and quiet. I studied his back and waited. It was all crap, this ritual, and I suddenly knew that's what it was even though we had never gone through it before. The only other thing I'd ever asked for was to keep Hohenberg away from Pierre. Without turning around, Werner said, in a tone I'd never heard before, "I think we can work it out."

I waited for him to turn, smile, and pat my shoulder. He turned. I could not see his face clearly with the light behind him.

"What's in it for me?"

To give myself time to think I started to say "What?" But I'd heard him all right. In a voice that was low but with meaning as loud as a thunderbolt booming at my feet. All the sounds that I knew were outside seemed to burst right through the walls; all the smells of the place that it would never, ever, be rid of, even in midsummer, when the doors were open and the bedding was hung between the blocks for airing, became heavy, funky, bad, and I had the feeling that Loa Aizan was now at work.

I said, "Anything you want, Werner, that I can give you." Every homosexual I ever knew believed that every other man down deep was also queer, for a minute, an hour, a lifetime. The situation varied. But I was surprised.

"In here, then," Werner said, his voice squeezed, his movements jerky. I followed him from the living room into a corner of the dormitory away from the windows. He didn't look at me. He didn't have to. I knew his eyes were half-closed, hard, and hot. The first-timers, no matter how much you helped them, were brutal, in a hurry to begin, and in a bigger hurry to finish, because they were ashamed of themselves and despised you, even in the best situation, which this was not. Always they seemed to have lost what they never knew they had, except some idea of themselves as *men,* and always they put the blame for what they did on you.

"Do you have grease or something like that?" I asked.

He walked quickly to his bunk, rummaged through a bag and hurried back. "It's pomade," he said. He still didn't look at me.

I took it and did what I had to do, then helped him. He was breathing hard, but wasn't quite saluting. He was hot enough, but he was also afraid. Not of being caught, but of losing, he thought, a part of himself. I kneeled and took him until he was almost saluting the back of my throat. Then I taught him. "Oh, that *hurts!*" I said. Of course, that's what he wanted to do, hurt me for what *he* was doing. He wasn't, but it's always wise to let them think they've done what they never admit they wanted to do in the first place. It didn't take Werner long. I grabbed his cock, which was fading fast and squeezed as hard as I could. "This isn't going to be a habit," I told him. I kissed him full on the mouth, uncoiled my tongue inside. He made believe he was trying to get away, but something more within him than within me made him stop and submit with soft groans and wheezes. He knew then that *he* had not fucked me; *I* had fucked him. (And I did feel that I could have said "Now me" and he would have.) Between men and men and women and women and men and women there's always that, and that is why, I suppose, there is the play-acting to make it look like something else. When I released him there were tears in his eyes; the hard gray of them was now just mist and fog. As I left, he was returning to the window in the living room, and I could see that his shoulders were bent more than ever.

That's how Pierre got to work in the garden.

———

Thurs., August 24, 1939

Dieter Lange walks about the house humming. He is cheerful. He pinches Anna and she jumps and giggles and slaps him, not hard, on his back or chest. He says he's in line for another promotion, which means an even larger house, and that means more space for the goods that are now crammed tightly into the cellar bins, in the attic, and in the closets. His buddies gather and they huddle around the radio, listening to speeches and the news. It's all about Poland. Poland this and Poland that. Danzig this and Danzig that. Who gives a damn about Poland? Too much like Russia for me. I did hear about a colored guy in Warsaw name of George Scott, who played drums and accordion. Don't know if he's still there, but if he is and I was him, I'd haul ass out of there on the first ship. The Germans mean to get Poland, just like Gitzig said, and no fooling about that. That means more goods for Dieter Lange. He thinks Polish hams are even better than German, Polish vodka better than Russian. The problem with Poland is England and France. But Dieter Lange's friends don't think they want to fight, since they didn't fight over the Rhineland or Austria or Czechoslovakia.

Why now? And anyway, the Germans were better trained. Look what they had done in Spain. The war was over down there, thanks to the German training and the German air force. What had the English done? Nothing. The French? Nothing but run up and down their Maginot Line, in which they'd hide if war came.

So Dieter Lange's buddies drank coffee and schnapps and had me play while they sang marching songs. They seem very pleased that yesterday Germany and Russia signed a treaty, but in camp the Reds had a helluva fight because some of them said Russia had sold out. A bunch of Reds were taken away. Bernhardt said they were to be "canned goods," whatever that means. I don't think I want to know. Bernhardt said the commander of the camp had not yet been able to find the radios he knows the prisoners have somewhere. Otherwise, they wouldn't have known what was going on. There is a kind of electricity around the compound and also in the camp.

My main concern is still Pierre's health. I get him as much fresh fruit and good food as I can, as often as I can, hoping that will strengthen him. And I bring him the clean socks and underwear that Anna has given me. How much more can I pay anyone for a clean job for Pierre? And with what? Werner's got two strikes, and I think he knows it. The first for knocking me down in front of Karlsohn and the second the way he made me pay for Pierre's fresh air. *Fresh air.* Good Lord don't charge nobody for fresh air, but Werner did. Something will work out. It's got to.

In our "Suppose" game we now live on 137th Street. And I have a small band. We play in a little walk-down club on Seventh Avenue, the same street we stroll down on Sunday. I couldn't give him the name of the club, of course, and he didn't insist on one. (I hope they're still strolling up and down Seventh Avenue.) We were going to go to a synagogue, but Pierre says, "I wouldn't know what to do. We never went at home." So, instead we go, all dressed up, to a Methodist church where the choir romps and people clap in time to the music. "I like that," he says, because I'd sung "Let My People Go" for him, the way they do it in church, and "Amazing Grace," which he knows in German. He hums that right along with me as we bend over the garden.

"But I need a job in New York," Pierre says.

I want him to have a nice job, but something he can really do. I ask if he knows French, and he says he does. I can see him as a maître d' at one of those snooty clubs in Harlem where they're always trying to put on airs, like white folks. I can see him in white tie and tails. He is a good-looking kid and maybe he can meet a rich woman that way, too. I explain the job to him and he likes it; he wants to do it. Besides, it will leave him time to study.

"Study? For what?"

"I want to be an engineer," he says.

I think of The Cooper Union downtown. I don't know if they take colored, but we can find out. If they don't, we'll find a place in New York that does, that's all. I tell him I think that is a good idea, since it might take a long time to find his real father. Germany, I tell him, is small compared to the United States, which is three thousand miles wide and two thousand miles long. He can't believe how big it is. Then I tell him Russia is even bigger. I've seen the maps. I love to see his eyes widen when I tell him things like that. I can see he is impressed by how much I know and how much traveling I've done. It makes me feel good.

Then he says, "I don't understand something."

"What?"

"Why you, an American, are still here."

A drizzle starts, and gray clouds, big rolling balls in the sky, seem to slow and open up. The drizzle grows to rain. Pierre waits. I don't know where to start. I play "Suppose" with him so questions like this won't come up. "You'd better go in now, Pierre. We can talk about this another time. Not now."

"You never want to talk about it."

"That's because I told you already what I am. It's against their law— if they catch you. Besides, it's boring, Pierre. Very boring after six years."

"Six years! Will I be here that long, Mr. Pepperidge?"

I could cry. "I don't know. I really don't think so. Maybe the war will change all that." We stack the tools. The other prisoners are going to their alternate tasks without a wasted motion. "If the war really comes and Germany loses, we can all go home."

"But I thought," he says in a small voice, "you and I would go to your home together."

The rain is coming down steadily now, cold German rain. I say, "Yes, yes. But we'd tell your mother first."

"No!" he says.

Sunday, September 3, 1939

The band didn't play at The Nest this past weekend. Germany was on full alert and the army had been positioned on the Polish borders. The week before, everyone in the compound was at the camp loudspeakers. The "black" radios in camp were probably running all the time as well. Last Thursday Hitler broadcast his peace terms to Poland, but the very next day, at 5:30 in the morning, he said over the radio that Germany had invaded Poland thirty-five minutes earlier because the Poles had attacked a German radio station on the border at Gleiwitz and at several other locations, too.

This morning, because France and Britain have a treaty with Poland, they said they are at war with Germany. Today, the SS guards wore full battle outfits and looked meaner. Groups of prisoners strolled down to the *Priesterblock;* others crowded into the canteen, but I couldn't tell how they felt about the war. Some, like me, must have hoped that it would bring them freedom; some, as before, must've wanted to join up and gain freedom that way; others were as quiet and still as the weather, which was gray and sticky, even with the wind that came off the mountains now and again, carrying sharp drops of rain. To piss on Austria and Czechoslovakia is one thing, but France and England make it a different crap game altogether. The world won't stand for Germany filling these camps with Frenchmen and Englishmen the way it let them fill with Jews, Gypsies, Austrians, Czechs, and now, I suppose, Poles, and that might save us. I hope to God it does.

Sunday, Sept. 10, 1939

We've been listening to the radio, naturally. Sometimes at night, Dieter Lange hooks up the shortwave he got from somewhere, and hopes it doesn't interfere with the camp radios in the offices. We listen for short periods and then he shuts it off. We catch the English broadcasts—there's nothing we can make out coming from France. Anna translates the English for him. If she doesn't understand she turns to me. I throw out something. The British have mobilized; so have the French. Dieter Lange is not happy, but Anna tells him the situation could make them rich, very rich. He tells her that then she'd only want more. She always wants more. Then she tries to calm him down. I know he wants out; he's never been in anything this big. It scares him.

It was strange at The Nest this week. Every guy in uniform was exuberant. No mistake, though, there's a shit storm coming.

Today in camp Pierre asked me what the war would do to our plans. I told him I didn't know. I was pretty annoyed, because here I am trying to get him some kind of job out of the winter snow and cold (they'll be starting the garden harvest next month) and he is thinking about a future that may never be, now that the war's come. I'd run out of patience with him, and was about to draw him up short, when he said he was being assigned to help build a greenhouse so there'd be fresh vegetables for the officers, and he would work in it. He showed me the assignment slip. I was so ashamed of myself and so filled with relief I said, "Whenever this mess is over, we'll do just what we've planned."

"Thanks, You Guys," I whispered.

Thursday, Sept. 29, 1939

So much has happened that my head is swimming. It's like being drunk. Poland is smashed. The Russians seem to be working with the Germans; they're taking over part of Poland, too. And Poland is knocked out the way Joe Louis knocked out Schmeling.

After dinner last night there was a knock on the door and who's there but Bernhardt, carrying a small box and all spiffed up in a uniform so new I could smell it. He and Dieter Lange and Anna joked and drank coffee and ate cake. I finished in the kitchen and went down to my room. I was there a half hour before Dieter Lange called me up. Anna was not there, but I could hear her moving around upstairs. I stood across from them and waited. It looked like something bad. I couldn't really tell because Dieter Lange's face showed no expression, and Bernhardt's was the same as always, fixed with a little smile.

"Now we're at war," he said. "Berlin says all bands not within camp boundaries must be German military bands, or those whose members are German civilians selected by the *Reichsmusik Direktor* himself, Heinz Baldauf." He sighed. "Cliff Pepperidge and His Wittelsbachers are no more. Immediately."

I'm sure Bernhardt thought he was saying it lightly, but it came across like doom cracking through the house. Germans do not have a light touch. I glanced at Dieter Lange, who looked at me briefly, then his eyes seemed busy looking for something in the room. "Your musicians have been notified and will just settle back into the general prison population, which in fact they never left." His smile widened a little. "Your good life will continue here with the Langes and the canteen. Can't beat that, eh? And I won't have to worry about subversive elements at The Nest trying to spirit you away. Times will change and maybe we can go back to the old routine, eh?" He crossed one leg over the other, his boots reflecting a high shine. "We will have bands with the best musicians in Europe, won't we, Lange?"

"Yes, Colonel, and perhaps we can even invite the great bands from America to entertain in the Reich."

Bernhardt nodded and then said, "But first, we will hear those musicians in France—Johnson, Lewis, the gajo, Django Reinhardt."

"Naturally," Dieter Lange said.

"I have a special task for you," Bernhardt said to me, uncrossing his legs. "I have spoken to Lange about it and advised him to do the same. The labels on all my records must be changed."

He pointed to the box he'd placed on the table next to his chair. "It's filled with labels from German record companies—Brunswick, Electric, Telefunken, Imperial, Gramophone. Remove all the old labels. For example, if you have an Ellington record with 'Mood Indigo' on one side and 'Black, Brown and Beige' on the other, you substitute Brocksieper's 'Tea for Two' and 'Polka Polka.' But make

a chart so I'll know when I pick up a Wagner, I'll really have Benny
Moten, something like that, *nicht wahr?*" Before that business with
Ulrich, Bernhardt and me had an easy relationship. He joked and
I laughed; he rubbed my head and I smiled; he said the music was
great and I smiled a bigger smile. But I always behaved like he was
the crook running the club, and he knew it. Since Ulrich's death,
I'd behaved with him like a whipped dog, and he knew that, too.
It was supposed to be that way. I told him I understood with a "Sir,"
and he said he'd have the records brought over tomorrow.

I went back to my room, already missing The Nest. I'd miss
our time in the kitchen, the good food there, the workers, the girls
who came in their best dresses for the Friday and Saturday dances.
I was already missing the hungry and sometimes loving way they
looked at the young *Siegfrieds* in their dress uniforms, missing
the smell of flowers in the spring and summer, the clean wind
through the opened windows, the sight of civilians on the streets
we drove through, the shop windows, the parks, even the crying
babies. And the rehearsals when we played anything, tried anything, before we got down to the numbers we'd actually play that
night. And I would certainly miss the tuxedos, white shirts, and
shining black shoes. For a few hours they had helped us to believe
we were not really what we were—prisoners without hope of release.
What would happen to Danko? The Gypsies were suffering more
than the Jews or the men in the Prisoner Company. Alex—what
would happen to him? And Fritz, who had learned to whip the
cello like a bull fiddle? Where is Franz to play his licks on the
drums now? Who would now appreciate Ernst's flute playing?
And would Oskar only play his harmonica in a corner of Block 13
when he wasn't on some detail that would smash his spirit? And
Teodor, what music would he write now and who for? No need to
worry about Moritz and that sweet violin, or about Sam, who was
long gone in another direction. A band leader looked after his
musicians, even though he might not like them. They'd looked to
me for direction, ideas, and what Mr. Wooding called "execution."
But this is a different time, a different place, and it's every swinging
ass on his own.

Now I'm back to one benefactor, Dieter Lange, or maybe two, with Anna. But Dieter Lange is afraid and Anna is unpredictable.

I am lucky, still. The Polish prisoners and civilians are entering camp now. They're like the new boy on the block; the guards must beat them up, show them who's boss. Everyone in camp breathes easier because they are beating up the new guys, but that will last only a little while. Then the guards will be back beating everyone's ass, as usual. The Polish boys they call "doll boys," *Pieple.* Poor kids. Some of those bastards have already buggered them; I've seen a couple of kids who walked as though they were riding a horse, it hurt them so bad.

I was in bed and couldn't sleep, listening to the trains rumbling out to the factories and warehouses. Sounds carry far in this place. Sometimes you know the trains are bringing prisoners, or taking them out. I was thinking this when I heard Dieter Lange coming downstairs. I was surprised. He wanted me to come up to the kitchen and make some coffee, which meant he wanted to talk. I didn't know if it had to do with Bernhardt's visit or not.

He sat at the table with his head in his hands. It was three o'clock and the fall darkness was so close it felt like a suit of clothes. When the coffee was ready, he signed for me to sit down at the other end of the table. He reached over and patted my hand. "Don't look so worried," he said. "I couldn't sleep. You hear the trains?"

I said I had.

He slurped his coffee.

"Too bad about The Nest. You liked it?"

"Sometimes." We'd talked about this before. I said, "What's the matter? What's bothering you?"

Dieter Lange pushed his cup aside. "I'm not getting the promotion," he said. "They're giving them all to the *Waffen* SS, not the *Allgemein* SS. The war."

I looked at him over my coffee and listened to the small sounds in the house: floors creaking, wind against the windows, dogs barking far away outside. So the armed SS, not the general SS, would get all the breaks. That ought to put all the camp guards in their places, but it probably won't. "Now you don't have so much responsibility," I said. "Isn't that good?"

He half smiled. "That's good, yes, but the promotion . . . well, it might have given us more protection, you understand." He rubbed his face, and the bristles of his beard gave off a rasping sound. "But you're right," he said. "Too much responsibility isn't a good thing here. Already I'm going crazy, moving the pieces." His hands were flat down on the table, fingers spread. Dieter Lange looked at them. It was cold in the house. He sighed. "The Poles are coming in, you know." His voice fell to a muttering. "The Poles come in and to Mauthausen we send the Pinks, and to Hartheim in Linz in invalid vans we send the crazy ASOS. We send the Jews to Poland, and if they have room at the subcamps, we send them there, all to make room here. Around and around it goes, from camp to camp to camp."

Dieter Lange was feeling sorry for himself. "That's not your worry," I said, and it wasn't. "That's the camp commander's head-ache."

He raised both hands and let them fall back to the table. "You know I must have some idea of the numbers so I can stock the can-teens in my jurisdiction, Cleef. You know that." There were tears in his eyes. "First Germans, Jews or not, then Austrians, now Poles, and it's too late for there not to be Belgians, French, and whoever else gets in the way. Round and round and round," he said softly, "and Anna doesn't understand the strain."

I leaned across the table and spoke quietly to him. "Dieter, Dieter Lange. If you don't get hold of yourself, Anna will have it all. You'll be in the booby hatch and Anna will have the money and take all the stuff to her father's farm. If you keep showing this weakness, she'll tell Bernhardt to get rid of you, of *us*. I told you before, you got yourself and me into this mess, and you've got to get us out. The only way to do that now is to do what you have been doing, and stop all this goddamn whining. Are you a man or a fucking faggot?" I stood up. "I'm going to bed. You woke me up so I can listen to this crap? C'mon. Get hold of yourself."

I went downstairs. I could hear him shuffling around in the kitchen, from the table to the sink; then I heard him go slowly up the stairs. Sometimes Dieter Lange needed talking to in a hard way. Anna cajoled. She often buried her impatience beneath a pretended interest and listened to him, mining every complaint like a jeweler with that thing to his eye used for diamonds. I wondered, as I often have, how it was that a man like Dieter Lange could hold in his hand the life of a man like me.

So it's me and You again, God. You riding that sad train with its bells of brass ringing for clear passage into hell; You with a bunch of Polish prisoners in the boxcars. Will You send them like that in the middle of winter, too? Can You see me? Can You hear me through the sounding silence that is Your response to the prayers that climb up to You? Can You hear the prayers of the Gypsies, the prayers of the Jews, the ASOS with their curses, the criminals with theirs, the politicals? How can You not, if You are there? You have heard the cries of the Polish boys; where are You? Isn't there *something* You *must* do? Have You no more good Loas to send us? You know, sometimes, *most* times, I think You are not there at all, that You are snake oil, that You are a vision that comes with cocaine. I've been in Your desert with its serpents for more than forty nights; in fact, I have suffered this desert more than forty years, it seems to me; I've been embalmed in the salt of fear for longer than forty days. The dead drift through my sleep— are they with You or with the Other Guy? And I see the shapes of those yet to die, crowding like clouds on the horizon. The sky is filled with them. I hear the music as they march down the 'Strasse:

> Ta-dum, ta-dum; ta-dum, ta-dum
> ta-dum ta-da-da ta-dum, ta-tum

The sad weak music of a harmonica, a drum, and an accordion. Marching to the gallows, the Tree, the Bunker, the rifle pits where sound splits the silence like a pointy-nosed dog barking once or twice or three times.

> Were You there when they crucified my colonel?
> Were You there when they crucified my Menno?
> ooOOO—sometimes it causes me to tremble, tremble,
>   tremble. . . .
> Were You there when they crucified them all?

Were You there when they crucified Herr Ulrich?
Were You there when they crucified his girl?
ooOOO—sometimes it causes me to tremble, tremble,
    tremble. . . .
Were You there when they crucified them all?

Were You there when they crucified Nyassa?
Were You there when they crucified Moritz?
ooOOO—sometimes it causes me to tremble, tremble,
    tremble. . . .
Were You there when they crucified them all?

Ah, so. Nothing. I am still in my room and Pierre is still in his block, You willing. Dieter Lange and Anna still pound each other (can't You hear them through the furnace flues?), and in the camp someone is dying in great pain that You will not ease; someone is hanging himself; someone is hungry and whimpering beneath a blanket whose warmth never was; someone is crying; someone is running away (bang! bang!); someone is cradled in the steel arms of the crematorium, which will soon be rebuilt by the priests; someone is locked inside a van whose destination is Hartheim Castle; someone is released and will report to his nearest police station for his homecoming; someone is on his way to work in a war plant, and someone is on his way home from a war plant; a German soldier just got killed in Poland; twenty-five Polish soldiers just got killed by a German machine gun; a baby was just born, and its grandmother just died. My music is wounded and it bleeds my life away. It won't JUMP and SHOUT, do You hear me? It won't SWING and SWAY. . . and I can't get a sign that You hear me. I asked for a sign a long time ago. Your train done stalled? Didn't You talk to Moses? Didn't You talk to Jesus? Didn't You give Saul the sign that he should be Paul? How come You talked so much *then* and ain't sayin' shit now? So I *ain't* Your sweet, smiling Christian, Your kick-my-ass Witness, your *Rabbiner* Jew; so I only talk to You when the Amper River's at flood tide like the Jordan, when the blues open up to nothing like a rotten fishnet. Say what? Faith is *what?* Hahahahahaha. You think You slick. But You know better than to show up down *here*. Germans eat Your ass for lunch, jack! You so chickenshit, You sent Your son down here and them *other* Germans nailed His ass to the cross, didn't they?

You just snake oil squeezins? If not, please help me take care of Pierre. Please?

Saturday, November 11, 1939

Dieter Lange came up behind me this morning while I was cleaning the house before going to the canteen. Anna had gone shopping in Munich to get some new clothes. "They almost got him!" Dieter Lange whispered, as though someone was hiding in the house. "Almost got him!"

"Got *who?* Who's *they?*"

His eyes were bright and he was all up in my face like when he's drunk and he whispers, *"Wie steht es?"* How about it? *"Hitler!* They almost got Hitler, with a bomb in Munich, Thursday night!"

I snapped the dust out of my cloth. To me a miss was as good as a mile. I didn't know what all the fuss was about. "But who did it?"

"Some Red carpenter in Munich. They got him."

"But who else? You said they."

"Just him, as far as I've heard. But it shows that people don't want war and they want to be rid of Hitler. So maybe the next time they'll get him, eh? And maybe that's not too far off." He walked around the room, his hands behind his back. "You know I'd let you go if we got out of this mess. I'd give you the money to get back home. I really would, Cleef."

"I'd sure appreciate that," I said, but it wouldn't happen. He knew it and I knew it. White people fulla shit, especially when they run a place like Dachau. He stopped walking right in front of me and held my dusting hand. "What's the matter with you, Cleef?" He gave me a close look, as though he might find something in my face that he'd missed before. "You've been . . . *nicht heir* for over a month now. Are you sick?"

I looked at him. I didn't know what he was talking about. I said, "What do you mean?"

He raised his arms and moved them slowly up and down like he was a bird on the wind. "You just *flott machen* all the time, maybe like you had some cocaine?"

I released my hand and went back to dusting. He watched me and said, *"Achtsam,* Cleef, *bitte, Achtsam,"* then he went upstairs to his office.

When I finished, I shouted to him that I was going to the canteen and left. I didn't wait for him to answer.

It was another Armistice Day, ha-ha-ha, to celebrate the war to end all wars, except the one that just began. Ta-ta, da-da, de-dum . . .

"Hey, Sunshine!!"

I stopped and turned around. I'd passed through the *Jourhaus* gate. Sergeant Rekse, his *Schaferhund* straining at his leash, was shouting. I didn't know why.

"What do you do, why do you skip like a little kid? Are you nuts, Pepperidge? You want to wind up in the Hartheim wagon like those other niggers went out of here this morning?" Skipping? I was skipping?

I whipped off my cap. "No, sir."

"I'll tell your mother on you!" he roared, laughing, rolling back on his heels. He rubbed my head for good luck. The shepherd he'd brought to heel snapped his head from me to Rekse and back again, its tongue hanging out. Would Rekse never forget that visit by Ruby Mae?

"Get going, Pepperidge, and get those marbles out of your head. They're glass, you know, and can be broken."

I thanked him and replaced my cap and walked quickly away, up the west-side path, into the stiff, cold wind. I lowered my chin to protect my throat even though the sun was shining. But would Pierre be gone? Would he have been one of those "niggers" on the wagon ride to Hartheim?

We used to gather on this side of the camp to hear Hitler's speeches, which were broadcast over the loudspeakers hooked up across the moat on the SS side. The moat is outside the wall on this side of the camp. Now there are walls with electric fences on top. I could see the rooftops of the factories, hear the banging and clanging of work going on inside them, the hum and screech of machinery.

I was almost never on this side, but I could marvel now at just how much the prisoners had done since I first came. Down at the end of the camp the sun was reflecting off the glass of the new greenhouse. Oh, Pierre. A group of prisoners pulled a wagon loaded with the dead from the *Reviers* and the morgue.

Then I was at the northwest corner where the small north road bisects the smaller west path, where the gates lead to the inferno the dead don't feel. Or if they do, they can't say so. The greenhouse stood before me; to its right was the garden, then a space where rabbits were raised for SS *Hasenpfeffer* and for Luftwaffe pilots' jackets. Then the disinfection hut where Pierre had worked. Above all this was the north watchtower with its sliding glass windows, its machine gun, and the guard with his rifle. I stood there with my pass at the ready to show any guard, and watched the prisoners wheeling barrows of rich black dirt from a huge pile into the greenhouse. The prisoners were all white, untouched by that soft golden color that was Pierre's. My stomach began a slow cold slide downward. I moved forward a few steps. Maybe the sun was shining too brightly, or the cutting wind was blurring my eyesight. "Oh, Pierre," I whispered. I looked at the pile of earth, then saw a shovel and a pair of blackened hands, disembodied parts, moving in a slow steady rhythm, filling a barrow. I walked to where I could see who the shoveler was. It was Pierre! He saw me and winked and smiled. I smiled back and felt the wind sharper on my face where it met the tears. I waved and turned away toward the 'Strasse. Why were my footsteps heavier than before? Would Pierre be in the next group to Hartheim? Would it be easier for me if he was, or even if he'd gone this morning? There would be no more "Suppose," no more worry. It would be over and done with. I felt I was walling up something inside me that no one could touch or reach from now on, that no one could hurt. Dieter Lange could be in me, but not in that place; Pierre could "Suppose" me, but never again would he be able to touch that place, because it was my sanctuary, my church, the grove where Loa Aizan, forever watchful, now rested.

I skipped up the 'Strasse humming. In answer to the smiles, the circles drawn on the sides of heads, I muttered, "Fuck you. Fuck you."

Sat., December 8, 1939

That carpenter Dieter Lange told me about, who tried to blow up Hitler, is in the Honor Bunker. His name is Eller, but that's a fake.

There are now supposed to be two Englishmen in the general population. Don't know why not the Honor Bunker, where, the gossip is, they've got the president of Austria and some big shots from Czechoslovakia. I wonder how those people live there. I wonder what they think when they look between the poplar trees and see the rest of us. Are they keeping notes, too? Will they tell what happened? Hell, they're probably thinking the same thing I'm thinking: better them than me.

I have finished putting new labels on Bernhardt's records, and also on Dieter Lange's. Of course, I played them all again as I was doing that, just to make sure I had the right labels for the right records. In the canteen, Huebner, Lappus, and me handle the Christmas rush. The prisoners with their sorry bits of money or camp chits buy the shitty items Dieter Lange stocked for them. The only good things are what Lappus has made—little lampstands and walking sticks and jewel boxes—and the SS guards want them for next to nothing. Other items are starting to come in. Mineral water, biscuits, candy, tins of fish and meat, but hardly anyone can afford these things. Sometimes groups put up the money, and each man gets just a taste. The packages from home and the *Hilfe* are coming in steadily. They usually do around Christmas. Sometimes I think Christmas was invented to help bad people do something good once a year.

For Pierre I have a pair of wool socks, brand new, and a sweater Dieter Lange gave me. The Langes plan to stay at home this Christmas—which means work for me. Not only the house and the cooking, but they want to have a party or two as well. Who will entertain? Guess who.

Sunday, December 9, 1939

Sundays are nice for me now. I don't have to rush around after a Saturday night at The Nest and, while the canteen is often busy since the prisoners don't work, there's still a lot of time to drift around the Appellplatz and talk to people I don't see very often. Some prisoners go down to the *Priesterblock* to church, and others visit friends. Today I introduced Pierre to Willy Bader who wears number 9 on his uniform. So he came here 2,994 prisoners before I did. And almost 13,000 prisoners before Pierre. He used to be good friends with Werner. I don't know what happened. Bader seemed to know something about Pierre, but I suppose if you're a colored man in a place like this, everybody knows, or thinks he knows, something about you. (The bad thing about walking around the 'Platz in the summer are the boxers—who don't box, thank God, in cold weather. They put on shows for the SS. When I walk by, they call and whistle and holler "Choe Louis!" "C'mon fight, Choe!")

The work in the greenhouse is hard, but comfortable, Pierre says as we walk and talk. In our game of "Suppose" he has finished his engineering studies. He has a girlfriend. She has rippling blond hair, he says, and I tell him, "Not in America you don't." So I have to explain that shit to him, and explain and explain, but somehow he can't seem to get it, and I wonder, as I have done before, if we should continue to play this game. Then I look at him, see his tic, think about the way things are with his mother and how he'll probably never see his father, and I decide that some things just ought to have a good ending, because life's so goddamn shitty, and I feel sorry for him all over again. But not as sorry as before, 'cause he's just not going to get into that place any more. Besides, he just doesn't look as well as I thought he would. I think, He's going to die. Pierre is going to die, and if he knows it, he never says it. After meeting Bader, he says he wants to go back to his block, 24, and find a place to sit down. He is tired. "Mr. Pepperidge, I also have great pain." That is the first time. I don't suggest that he go to the *Revier*, and I don't think it ever crossed his mind. The last medical place he went to hurt him, and he is hurting again, with pain he can feel in his body this time, as well as in his mind, which, I think, won't ever leave. God never tells you how much time you got. And neither does Loa Aizan.

Sunday, Dec. 24, 1939

It's early. Dieter Lange and Anna aren't up yet. It's so early that I don't even have to check the furnace. I can tell it doesn't need shaking or stoking right now, so I'm writing. It's so quiet, it sounds like the pencil is making a lot of noise.

Last night, long after dinner, Dieter Lange called me up and sat me down at the kitchen table and we had a couple of drinks. He was already high; he'd gone in the afternoon with Anna to an SS party. She was upstairs sleeping it off, but he wanted to go walking in the snow. Nothing I wanted to do, but he insisted and was starting to get mean about it. So we bundled up. He wanted to go to the camp. It was snowing soft, slow, great big flakes. "I want you to appreciate how lucky you are, Cleef. You've been in a funk lately. Maybe you're sick again? You don't think so? Well, I hope not." We plodded on through the snow that was quickly replacing all that the snow commandos had removed earlier. Ahead, the lights of the camp seemed filled with dots as snowflakes flew down past them. Dieter Lange exchanged greetings with the guards on duty at the *Jourhaus* gate. They joked about the weather, *lustig Weihnachtened* one another. The guards even patted me on the back and offered me a drink from the same bottle they were drinking from. I was feeling better than I had when we left the house. It all looked quite pretty. Neat and regular, squared, arranged, like those little toy villages the kids settle in cotton under the Christmas tree. Peace on earth, good will to men. I saw a group of prisoners standing at attention on the Dancing Ground, stiff as icicles, the snow building on their caps and shoulders, creeping up around their shoes. What had they done? "See that?" Dieter Lange said. "You could be one of those. Look, look at those barracks, those blocks, and think of those poor bastards in them trying to keep warm. Tonight, whatever they find that burns they can put into the stoves. And tomorrow night—" he broke off as we turned down the 'Strasse and Gypsy singing drifted up the street in a sad, soft language I didn't understand. But I understood the tone, like you can't hear blues and not know that there is sadness up front, or tucked in between smarty-pants lyrics. Dieter Lange stopped, so I stopped. We listened. And in a dot of light reflected by a snowflake, I saw, or thought I did, a small flash that could have been a tear on his face.

Then we started to move again, into a frightened, whispered swell of sound from the other blocks: *Stille Nacht, Heilige Nacht . . .* And I almost said, "Let's go to 24," but I didn't. Pierre had my gifts, and I couldn't trust this weeping, juiced-up, shit-packer. How can you ever trust people, really, who cannot, deep down, hear you because they're so busy listening to themselves? Dear God, right then I wanted to trust somebody. But Dieter Lange was not that person. We walked and Dieter Lange sniffled; he kept saying, "See, you have it not so bad." And, "Cleef, maybe, next Christmas . . . ! Maybe." We tramped back up the 'Strasse, back through the guardhouse gate, and home. When I was downstairs, I thought of the camp all soft under the new snow, the way it always looked under new snow, like frosted gingerbread, as though it could not be what it really was. And I knew, as I always had known, that when Dieter Lange woke up, he, too, would be the same. How could one drunken walk through camp on a Christmas Eve change anything? I just hoped I wouldn't have to fight him off the booty later on.

———

Wednesday, January 3, 1940

"What can be the matter with my little Cleefie?" Anna said. She'd tried to come down the steps quietly, but I knew it was her. What was she doing down here? Dieter Lange hadn't gone out. She pushed open my door and stood there in a rumpled silk slip through which the light from upstairs outlined her thick body. "Cleefie?" I had a more than passing acquaintance with that tone in her voice. I said nothing. I was nervous. They'd been recovering from a New Year's Eve party, then a New Year's Day of eating and drinking and running upstairs for a couple of hours, then running down and back up. Feeding, fucking, and drinking.

I know what is going to happen, and I say, "No." Anna is close to my bed, reaching down for my wrist.

"Come," she says.

They are bored with each other, I think, but it's never been this bad. Do they think if they pound and probe each other long enough and hard enough they will forget they hate and fear each other? Is that what they've been trying to do these last two days?

"Yes. Oh, yes. Dieter sent me. He has some very fine cocaine for you, and we can all celebrate the New Year. Come, Cleefie."

She grips my wrist in a hand that feels like damp warm dough. "We will make you well." From upstairs Dieter Lange's voice booms down the stairwell, "Come, Cleef!"

"No," I whisper, but Anna has pulled me half out of bed with one hand and is yanking at my dick with the other. "No. No!" The blankets are off. She pulls me to my feet, laughing softly, the way hunters do when they lift a rabbit or bird they've shot. She crushes the silk of her slip between our bodies. She smells sour through her tired perfume. I think then that I will take a walk, go away, not be with them, not be the plaything they can bend, stick, lick, and suck.

In the "Greeting Room" of the *Jourhaus* the guards are beating the prisoners who have just arrived, teaching them the "Saxon Greetings," hands behind the head, leaving the body an open invitation to violence. I stroll around, spitting in the faces of the guards. They do not notice. I climb upstairs to the room where I met Count Walther von Hausberger and later Ruby Mae. Reckse sits behind the desk; his feet are on it. He's asleep. I take his pistol and shoot him, but there is no sound and he remains as before. I go back down and open the files and rip the papers and let them fall like snowflakes; somehow the pieces never reach the floor.

The Bunker is dark and cold, a long square tunnel. It smells of blood that hasn't been cleaned up; it's a slaughterhouse, more fit for animals than men. I float down the corridor. The doors to the cells are three feet from the floor; they are like pens for animals. Down the corridor I go, seeing behind the bars wounded, beaten men who look as though they should be hanging from hooks. I answer a scream with a gentle "Sshhhh . . . " but the scream does not stop. It seems to urge forth other screams and moans. Three guards drag a prisoner out to the courtyard. They joke with each other: "This one will be like grape jam in the morning." I will the guards to die. They do not. The wooden doors bang open and they enter the courtyard. I make the sign of Loa Aizan, but He says, "Shit, Clifford. It's too late for that joker."

"Come on now, Cleef. That's a good boy. This is very fine stuff. That's it, a quick little snort. Zooom, eh? This foolish talk of being a plaything. . . ."

In the *Wirtschaftsgebaude*. The Records Office. Labor Office. Political Office (Bernhardt and Gitzig). Storerooms. Showers. Kitchen. Camp Police Office. I start fires. I rip papers. I let the showers run. I reassign Pierre to me. I assassinate Bernhardt. (How can I harm Gitzig?) In the kitchen. I see monstrous rats in the thin red water of the great cooking pots. I throw real meat and then turnips, cabbage, and potatoes from the ice room into the pots, which hang on hooks before a row of fires that look like the entrance to hell. More meat! All the small fires come together in a big one. I imagine that the flames can be seen all the way into downtown Dachau. How I love the smell!

Across the way, on the wind-ripped Dancing Ground, I urge the twenty men standing at attention, held like actors in the floodlights, to return to their blocks before they freeze to death. I kick the dogs and their guards. "Thank you, Pepperidge," the prisoners say (everyone knows me), but they don't move. I enter the canteen and find Pepperidge in his little cubbyhole of an office. He sits on a box writing under the light of a coal oil lamp. "What is it we're writing?" I ask.

"A very long letter." He doesn't pause; he doesn't look up. He is thin. That makes him look taller than he really is. He has a squeezed, tender face, and eyes with very long lashes that darken the room with the belligerent sadness of having known too much. The stinking kerosene smoke mixes with the vapor of his breath. I look at him and I want to cry. I want to put my arm about him and make that hawk/wren look the gaze of doves.

"To whom are we writing?"

Now he looks up, raps his teeth with the stub of the pencil. His fingers are like slender brown worms that have dried in the sun. "I do not know," he says. "Maybe God."

"I see," I say, but he's returned to his feverish scratching.

We are a tangle of bodies emitting stink and liquids. I am hurting, therefore I want to hurt; even while crying, I want to hurt, then to wound; even more, to kill. I try to kill her as he's hurting me, but Anna doesn't mind; the slow, terrible frenzy in my head freezes with the realization that she is to pain what sugar is to flies. "Stop that goddamn crying!"

The Infirmary is quiet now, except for the whimpering that dares not grow to a moan. The duty orderly drinks Dr. Nyassa's brandy. I piss in his cup and stir it with my finger. The orderly ignores me, swallows and swallows with great loud gulps. I draw syringes to full with morphine and inject the worst-looking patients. It's the least I can do, but they continue to whimper in both buildings. I check the morgue and find no one I know. There are more bodies these days. They'll have to make more room.

Werner and Bader sit in the Red block and are not talking, not even listening to the radio. All the Reds have been down in the mouth lately. I would like to be friends with Werner again, but that business will always be there between us. What I don't understand is if the Reds can be so good at organizing and running things in here, why didn't they do it out there a long time ago? Then maybe none of us would be here. We have all been captured by the politics of ourselves. The Nazis have let us know what we're really like. They are men and women, too, just like us. But they have dared, with terrible success, to take politics beyond the thin invisible line of whatever morality men think they have won over the beasts of the field. This must be what the Reds are pondering in the charged silence of their block. I sit there in the emptiness between the two men and finally ride the silence of the other, brooding Reds out to Prisoner Block 7.

I enter with both fear and admiration. In the center of our hell, many of the prisoners—the Pinks, the Reds, the Purples, the Golds, even some of the Greens, Blacks, and Browns—have said in word and deed, "Fuck Hitler," for personal reasons or larger ones. Who knows? Who cares? They lie in their chains, the presumption of something larger than individual manhood, a pride as fierce as their hatred of their captors, stilling the expressions of pain that must reside in their swollen limbs and crushed flesh. *("I* am the baddest motherfucker in this place.") There is order and quiet here that transcends even that in the political block. These punishment prisoners await the next scheme, the next murder of an SS guard, the next slaughter of each other, the march to the gallows to music.

"Gentlemen," I say.

"Fuck off, nigger." This in bored voices.

"I would like to play some music for you." I conjure up a piano and await their permission.

"Fuck your music. Get out!" They rattle their chains, hawk up snot, and hurl it at me with the precision of marksmen.

"I am"—the word is clumsy in my mouth—"a comrade."

The block is filled with real and mouth-made sounds of breaking wind. They bounce their chains on their wooden planks; the sound grows to an ugly basso crescendo and I leave. It may be a very good thing that they are chained up.

In Block 15 are the Jews with their stars; starred because their second triangle—red or green or black or pink—is inverted over the first gold one to make the six points of David's star. They are made to suffer so much. A few of them pray in Yiddish or Hebrew. The others cannot wait for God's good intercession; they know they have to look out for themselves. I see that some have the blank look of men who realize, too late, that this experience is one they could have avoided had they believed what they saw going on. They are exhausted, these men. Working the quarry and the gravel pit in winter is consignment to death; anywhere they work is consignment to death. The slightest untoward word, look, movement, from one of them is reason enough for even the most reserved guard to kill him on the spot or slowly, as his mood takes him, without fear of reprimand from his superiors. With a few exceptions, other prisoners, equally doomed, ease their slides to hell by being as vicious as the guards. The Jews are the niggers of Dachau and in all the other camps where they are found.

I dump an armload of challah onto a bunk; I set down a huge vat of matzoh-ball soup, far better than Aschinger's pea soup, and call them to eat. No one hears me. I tell them another conference has been called at Evian, and this time all the nations in the world will, after arranging their freedom, accept them without quibble and stake them to a new start. They will be as many as the sands on a thousand beaches. No one moves. The observant among them sit quietly, already bent in subservience to the Messiah, for all this is His will, His doing, and the purpose will later be made clear. The others discuss the prisoners who are secret Jews who will have nothing to do with them. Some say, "Good for them." Others call them traitors. But no one will give them away; no one will trade a name for another day of life. Pierre's name hasn't come up. They look at him and know for an absolute certainty that he can't be one of them. He is a Negro, or part of one. Loa Aizan must be smiling.

Pierre lays in his upper bunk in Block 24. His face seems a different, unwholesome color, like slate that dogs have shit on.

"You have finished engineering school and tried to find your real father but haven't, and now you're ready to marry your girlfriend— and no, she's not blond. Where would you like to live? 555 Edgecombe Avenue? Why not? The top floor, of course, where you have a marvelous view."

In his sleep Pierre seems to smile. He hears.

"You work downtown and ride the 'A' train there and back. Your wife is a teacher. Yes, there are a few colored teachers in Harlem. She, too, has gone to college, you see. You are very happy and hardly ever think about Germany or your mother and real father anymore. Me? I just keep on playing. It's too much fuss having your own band, though. Running around getting those jokers together for the road or just making them be on time for work in New York. And somebody's always complaining about the money, and how the uniforms wear out so fast because they're so cheap. So I play for somebody else. Maybe Teddy Wilson has left Benny Goodman. I *know* Teddy made good geets with Goodman. Geets? That's money,

son. No, no, I don't live with you. I live down on '37th Street, where
I think you and me thought about living once, remember? Nah,
young people don't need no old folks soaking up their space. But you
and your wife come to see me and I have dinner with you all every
Sunday when you come home from church. Usually fried chicken,
mashed potatoes, gravy, string beans, biscuits, lemonade, and strawberry shortcake for dessert. Your wife is a very good cook." I pass
Pierre the platter of chicken. He crunches into a thigh. The sound is
like music. "Then you know what happens? AhhHHH! you guessed
it. You bigged her. You're going to be a father and that'll make me a
grandfather! Hotdamn, Pierre, hotdamn!"

Pierre now looks very tired, like maybe he's having a bad dream.
I tell him it's going to be all right, that he's not going to die from
those X-rays they gave him. He can't die.

"Why not let him sleep with us?" Anna whines. I picture her waking
and wanting to jump at the Woodside again.

Dieter Lange is half asleep, but he says again, "Go, Cleef." To
Anna he snarls through his drunkenness, "You want someone to
come to the house and find him up *here?* Stupid woman! No! You
like doing it with him, eh? Well, no! And that's it! Go, Cleef. Give
him the last of the cocaine."

"Well, at least he ain't all queer like you," she whines. Anna is
drunker than a hundred skunks, but I'm at the door, aching front and
back; then I'm diving downstairs to draw water for a hot, or at least
warm, bath, but "ain't all queer" lingers in my aching head. Country
girl. Didn't know shit when they first met, except that those farm
animals always climb on from the back, and maybe she thought
that's where the action was. And got to like it. Wouldn't be the first,
man or woman. And Dieter Lange made her believe that doing it
in the hump was the only way to do it, until she tangled with Bernhardt who showed her the front-way bliss. Please, let me remember
this when I wake up.

It's good that Block 24 is right next door to 26, where the priests
and ministers are. Where I met Menno. I can hear Loa Aizan

chuckling: "Fools. So what did your God do for you?" He shouts over my shoulder. But they all seem to be thinking or talking softly and seriously. About the rabbits they're caring for, or the garden in good weather, or the other easy jobs they hold, or how to get Commandant Loritz to allow them to have a chapel, or how to get those colleagues who'd not been brought here to push their congregations to send more packages, or how to conduct an ordination in secret, with monstrance, crozier, oils, silk mitre, and so on. They are also concerned about measures they can take to secretly get their rations at camp and packages from home so they will not have to share with other prisoners. They need their strength to minister to the inmates. Should they post guards at the door to discourage the hungry? Loa Aizan is grinning. He must know that many of these are honorable men who have spoken out against the National Socialists. But then he lets me know that places like Dachau make honor regrettable. These men thought it would be rewarded, like in the movies. Instead, they were brought here, where honor is a burden. They are like everyone else who is here, Loa Aizan whispers. They want to survive, to live.

"All ye who are heavily laden . . ." I start. I stop because these men are pleased that it is the Polish priests, arriving now in great enough numbers to be segregated in 28, next door, who will be taught how to build the new crematorium, replace the wooden one with stone. German humor. They do not see that, I can tell. "This time," the men of God are saying, "the crematorium will last." I think, They are always reconstructing death, these Germans, even their priests, who anoint the constant journey to it with oil and wrap it in the linen of consoling words.

The bodies are stacked outside where the weather is as efficient as a hospital morgue. The chimney exhales its thick, black, oily smoke; the fuel source is endless. The *Sonderkommando* detail here need never worry about warmth. These ovens, made for baking bread and stoked with coke, give off constant heat, and the prisoners have come to enjoy it. The bodies outside are naked. The clothes have been removed and washed and sprayed and stacked, ready for the new prisoners. The stacks of bodies remind me of the photos of the

Great War, with the dead piled sky-high along row upon row of trenches. They didn't pull gold-filled teeth during the Great War; they do here. The bodies are brought in and dumped to the floor where two men pry apart the jaws; one takes pliers, rips out the gold teeth, and dumps them into a bucket. Then another group hauls the body to the oven, where yet another has already pulled out the "sled." They deposit the body into it and slide it inside the oven, into the leaping, curling flames that attack it with the speed of a nest of frightened snakes. The oven door is closed. A prisoner shakes the grate with a long metal rod. Body ashes, mixed with snapping, sputtering sparks, tumble down into the pit. The ashes are shoveled out; the finest of them into the urns, which are haphazardly affixed with names and numbers; the heaviest of the charred bone fragments, including the skulls that may have cracked with the heat, are pounded into smaller bits and wheeled outside in barrows. This bone and ash will be used to make smooth the Appellplatz, the Lagerstrasse, the east and west roads, the paths to everywhere, and to fertilize the gardens that will bloom again in spring.

How efficient this gruesome assembly line is. The prisoners work in silence, exclaiming only if a tooth is difficult to pull or when fire snatches at the hair of a body before it is pushed farther into the oven. I think of Albrecht Dürer's *Apocalypse* and of *Hansel und Gretel.* All right, witches, here is your oven. What is there for me to say in this place? The decay that brings the worms takes too long; the *Sonderkommandos* only hasten decomposition, for, as Dieter Lange said, "The pieces have to be moved." This is the last movement.

The water is warm enough. I sit and let the juices that have dried on my skin come loose and slide into the water. The Langes' snores rumble down through the house like small trains rocking over a trestle. The compound is between sleep and wakefulness. It is close to the hour when the guards change watch. A truck whines down to the SS barracks.

Four floors and a basement for the enlisted men of the SS. Where there was nothing when I first came, there is now this great edifice

to house our tormentors, a parade ground, and an arched walkway.
Here they hang up their whips, clubs, and guns, those instruments
of power, without which they are just like us; and here they kick off
their boots, remove their long coats and jackets, and loosen their
tunics, symbols, like armor, of power. Here they shower and play
snap-ass with their towels; they play cards, farts, and the radio.
Here they must think over the day (or night) and consider the weak
and troublesome. Here they must plan, these men of Himmler,
the guardians of the state, the manner in which their victims should
be dispatched. Rules are nothing. *They* make and are the rules, and
they know the prisoners know that. In these plain rooms they
scheme to get to know the officers' wives or daughters or sisters
better; how to get into town to sleep with girls (or, often enough,
with each other); how to visit the cabarets in Munich. They wonder
how well the war will go, though there's been little action so far.
Some have vowed to seek transfers into the fighting SS; some have
not, because here the prisoners can't shoot back.

I hear them talk. I listen to their thoughts rustling from room to
room down the narrow halls. Our keepers are very plain people who
believe strongly that the law is the law, and it is their law—police
law—which is always designed to serve the big people, never the
little people. All these men (one for every 150 prisoners, the same
for all the other SS at all the other camps) and their families—how
is it that all of Germany does not know? How is it that an entire
nation slumbers so easily?

I clean the tub and creep down to my room. There will be no early
risers this morning.

Monday, Feb. 12, 1940
Winter fits the camp like death. The wood details trudge out
and back; the snow commandos do their frozen dances. The cold
makes the eyes water and then freeze as the tear leaves the socket.
The uniforms grow stiff on prisoners who have never stopped moving and sweating. For all the dogs about, their turds never remain

longer than it takes the nearest prisoner to clean them up, sometimes with their bare hands. The dogs sit on their haunches and seem to be smiling; the guards laugh. The entire camp seems to have one single, all-consuming drive—to stay warm.

Werner intrudes, enters my tiny office in the canteen with the vague apologetic motion of a debtor; there is something urgent in his manner.

"Your friend," Werner says without further ritual.

I think for a moment.

"The boy, Braun," he says. Werner is impatient. I wait. "He just barely made roll call this morning. We had to prop him up. I don't think he's going to make it tonight."

I have not had the chance to see Pierre in over two weeks. He was weak then, and the prisoners who work with him in the greenhouse were doing his share of the work. We didn't talk much. Talk seemed to tire him, so we didn't even do a line or two of "Suppose." I had nothing to give him.

"Of course," Werner says with a shrug, "there's nothing anyone can do. It's plain the boy's dying. Perhaps it might have been best to let him go to Hartheim with the others."

"Ah," I say. "I wondered how it was he didn't."

Werner shrugs. "We got Hohenberg's people to mark him DIKAL—not to be shipped to another camp."

"For me?" I ask. Werner turns aside. I examine what is not quite my surprise. One is always discovering something new in camp.

"For you both," he says. More briskly, he says, "You want to see him? Better do it now." He speaks like a man paying off a debt.

It takes me a few seconds, but I say, finally, "I can't," and Werner leaves. Then I start crying, but I tell myself that it's more for me than Pierre; he can't get into that place I've closed off. No one can, anymore. "Suppose" was for him, but it allowed me to think of possibilities, gave me my anchor back, and, after all, death in this place is catching.

The day passes slowly. I will linger in camp until evening roll call. Uhlmer, Lappus, and Huebner move about preoccupied by the rumored shifting of prisoners from Dachau and the *Selektion.* Jews will go to Poland as usual; Witnesses to who knows where. Huebner

is still not saying what he will do when the *Bibelforschers* roll call—
more consistently rumored now—will be made. It's been a long time
since the last one. I still think he will refuse the offer of the state.
He has been like a real Christian who, lost, stops in a jook joint to
ask for directions. If they empty some of the blocks, it can only be
to refill them. Who's next?

In winter the daylight speeds by, on its way to a longer night.
The details march in singing to the music of the band, to *Rosa-
munde,* the air above them filled with vapor from their breath that
trails out behind them. Some moan with the soreness of their throats
and they try to muffle the slick slide of mucous that chokes them
and produces the wracking coughs. They begin filling the 'Platz, as
orderly as soldiers. I watch from the window as the roll-call officer
speeds his people through the frozen ranks. I cannot see the place
where Block 24 gathers. The prisoners stand like dirty blue-striped
icicles. The roll-call clerks, SS, and block leaders, check off the
numbers. The floodlights become brighter in the galloping darkness.
The band falls silent. The prisoner clerks on the roll-call detail move
from squad to squad where numbers are checked. With the sun
gone, the wind hurtles through the Dancing Ground and the prayer
of every man is almost written in fire in the blackness above them:
Let everyone be present and accounted for.

The counters are back to the SS *Stadie.* Now I see why he looked
so familiar; he is Karlsohn, and he is dressed for combat. He struts
over to the roll-call officer, salutes, presents the papers the prisoner
clerks have given him. The officer, too, is in war dress, as is a squad
of soldiers. This, of course, is just in case they have to pursue a prisoner. A small truck, its exhaust uncurling white ribbons, idles nearby.
Every roll call, everything is prepared for the *Hasenjaged,* the SS
chase for escaped prisoners, the rabbit hunt. The officer barks at
Karlsohn, and Karlsohn returns the salute, whirls away shouting at
his squad. They leap into the truck and it shoots off into the 'Strasse.
Twenty thousand men remain motionless under the lights. Their
prayers haven't been answered. Someone is missing.

We wait for the shots, but none come. I can see the men in the
rear ranks closest to my window. They are shivering. The light from

the moon, which is rising fast, glistens on the snot running from their noses. The evening meal will be late. I return to my office and unpack a box of canned snails and a box of Mahorca tobacco and some Yugoslavian cigarettes, Dravas. I arrange the little packets of salt and pepper Anna has put up for sale. The camp food has no seasoning and the salt and pepper are luxuries the men buy, or trade their socks for, or bread, or whatever else of value they have. The floodlights are still on, the prisoners still in ranks, I see, when I peek out the window again. The sirens haven't gone off, which means the prisoner is presumed to be inside the camp. I can feel the hate in those still, frozen forms. Whoever is missing, though recovered tonight, might be found dead in his block in the morning, hanging from a beam in the shower. What melody can one find in such a sight? Which chords to use? The silence is frozen in place out there, and two hours have passed. Dieter Lange will be sending out for me soon; he doesn't know I stayed. But now is not the time to close up and cross the 'Platz to the house.

There comes then, sharply through the frigid night, like a single trembling note, the sound of the truck. It skids off the 'Strasse and onto the 'Platz, stops before the roll-call officer. Karlsohn jumps out, salutes. The squad lifts a long bundle, a rope trailing after, out of the truck and dumps it before the officer. It is a body. The rope seems to be trailing from its neck. I hear my heart beating in my ears; it is so strong and steady that I think it must last forever. Same steady beat, like a drummer who knows the number's going to be very long, with extra choruses. I know, though I cannot clearly see from my vantage point, that the body is Pierre's.

"Achtung!" The roll-call officer roars angrily into the PA system. Men already at attention try to move their frozen bodies to a higher level of attention. "Caps off!" Twenty thousand men snatch at their heads, remove the battered striped berets. "Caps on!" Another storm of motion and the caps are on again. *"Absperren!"* The floodlights wink off. I hear the prisoners' footsteps pressing haphazardly over the creaking snow. In the moon-lightened darkness the men mill about to see who was brought in. They surround the body. There is sudden movement. Can they be kicking him? Him, who made them stand

two hours in freezing cold, perhaps miss their evening meal, and go hungry to their blocks?

I turn out the canteen lights and slip on my jacket, and as I go carefully down the iced steps, Werner comes slowly toward me. "It's the boy," he says. "He hanged himself in the back of the greenhouse." Werner walks with me to the body. In the light falling across the front of the Dancing Ground from the *Wirtschaftsgebaude,* and in the moonlight, I see Pierre's face is frozen in a massive, final, twisted tic. The rope has disappeared halfway into the flesh of his neck. Spit and gobs of snot reflect bits of moonlight. I wipe it off with my sleeve. The prisoners would have spit on Jesus. And so would I.

"Well . . ." Werner says.

I say nothing. What's there to say?

"They'll be coming to take him to the morgue." He sighs, turns, and walks toward his block. I kneel beside Pierre to finish wiping him off. Suddenly there is someone beside me. I look up. It isn't Werner. It's Willy Bader. He unties the rope, straightens Pierre's arms along his sides. I hear the creak and roll of the wagon and the stomp-warming feet of the men assigned to pull it. Bader waves them away when they are upon us. We move to the head. "I go with you," is all he says. The *Koppeln* huddle together. "Where do you go?" they ask.

Bader glances at me and I tell him, *"Baracke* X. What's the point of the morgue?" Bader tells them what I've said. They tell Bader to bring the wagon back to the morgue, the *Totenkammer.* We lift Pierre and place him carefully into the wagon, then slip ourselves into the harnesses. We pull through the protesting snow. The wagon, the Moor-Express, is ten times heavier than Pierre. We struggle down the 'Strasse, then turn and go past the disinfection hut, the rabbit hutches, the gardens, the greenhouse, and through the gate to the crematorium. We are sweating when we arrive. Bader speaks in a low voice to the commandos, who look at me and nod. After, Bader guides me out, back to the wagon, and we pull it to the morgue. "Good night," he says. I shake his hand.

Mon., April 15, 1940

The kids move unsteadily about the house, Lily's and Ursula's. But the war's really all people care about now that the army has taken Denmark and part of Norway. Already we're getting cases of sardines and Danish cookies; already Anna's got maps of Copenhagen to study. Goebbels is on the radio all the time now.

I am here in my clean uniform, serving coffee and cake, but I seem to be watching them from that secret place that's just mine, like a place at the bar between sets the bartender shoos people away from. "That's Cliff's spot, man." I mean, I see them and they see me, but I am really far away, in my own spot, seeing them through mirrors. I can't say what I see, but it is something so bad it makes me sweat and think of the evil Loas: Agarou Tonnerre, Babako, Bakula-Baka, Ogoun Badagris, and Baron Samedi, who is the Loa all Loas do business with at the end. They will claim all these women and all their children forever and ever.

And I hear in these women's voices, behind their cooings and cluckings, the pretentious tones of plantation wives or jailers' wives. Miss Ursula, Miss Anna *("Gott! Gott! Mein Gott!"),* I've heard your wet sounds, your cocaine sighs, your schnapps-sick moans. Is an asylum any different? Here you are in your pretty print dresses, in your pretty pink-and-white houses, but your husbands wear black (death) uniforms and brown (shit) shirts.

This morning, as we waited for the garbage truck to come down the street, I saw Gitzig. He waved and came over. Up and down, calfactors were taking out the garbage or ladders to begin the spring cleaning—windows, porches, outside walls. Some were tending the flower beds to ready them for blooming. The air was warm and soft for April, and the sky was blue.

"You don't look so good," Gitzig said.

I shrugged. What was there to say?

"This spring, it will go," he said.

"The war? I thought it was going already."

"Not the way it's going to go," Gitzig said.

Of course, he wanted me to ask what was really going on, so he could tell me how much he knew and how he was involved in it.

Instead I said, "That kid is starting to look more and more like you, Gitzig, lover man, Gitzig."

He turned and looked up and down the street. "Do you really think so, Pepperidge?"

"So," I said. "Blackjack. It *is* yours."

"Sometimes," he said, "when I'm with Bernhardt, I turn and catch him studying me. And I think, He knows. Lily wouldn't tell. He just knows."

"Shit," I said, "if he wants her to tell, he can make her. You know that. But the little fucker looks just like you."

"It really shows through, Pepperidge?"

"To me, yes. From the first time I saw the kid. But I got different eyes than white people, you know." I wanted to put him at his ease, but he was already nervous. He wasn't talking about no love now. "What're you doing these days, Gitzig? You haven't asked me to take anything to Werner lately."

"That's because I heard you and Werner don't talk too much now. What happened? You want to tell me?"

Tell him Werner packed my coal in exchange for a favor for Pierre? Why? How could that help me? Maybe Werner's nature turned on him. Maybe that pussy at the Puff was just too worn out for him. Who knew, shit, who cared anymore? Yet I felt that since I knew Gitzig's secret, he wanted one of mine in return. In jail everything was up for *Valuta*, trade-price, exchange, barter. *Valuta* was also insurance: If you tell on me, I'll tell on you. That way, no *Verzinken*, no betrayal.

"Never mind, Pepperidge. I can guess. The Reds are just like everyone else." Gitzig patted my shoulder. "It's okay. What am I doing? It's like being back in Leipzig, back in the business again. I've been working on ration books and foreign money—counterfeit— because Bernhardt has to get his. So all this is for Denmark and Norway, and already being put to good use there, you know. Soon, Holland, Belgium, Luxembourg, France." Gitzig offered me a Players. "I do good stuff, Pepperidge. Looks and feels like real. The Swiss eat it up. I can make Bernhardt rich, so what if his wife has my baby? He doesn't love her. He loves money. All these cocksuckers are like that. It's the money. So, more countries, ration books, and money; bet your bottom pfennig on that. I think I'll be around for a while. In the outside world, Bernhardt would be nothing next to me. All he is now, like the rest of his pig SS-SD-Gestapo, is a god-damn crook in a uniform."

Gitzig was shuffling around like a boxer in his corner. A taste of the good life had changed him, put some fight in him and took out the rat. The good life and love. I didn't imagine that Gitzig had spent any time lately with Lily if Bernhardt suspected anything. Maybe that's what got him steaming. I hoped he wouldn't get reckless.

The garbage truck was not far away now, and Gitzig went back to the front of the Bernhardt house. The street was jumping and voices called out. Shit. It was spring and it was getting warmer, and you didn't have to split wood or bring in coal or coke and take out the ashes anymore, and the German army was crushing everything in front of it.

———

Sun., June 23, 1940
    "Es blitz!"
    "Blitz Schnell!"
    "Blitzkrieg!"
It was on the radio two hours ago. The French have signed an armistice with Germany. The *"Blitz"* did it. Zing, whing, bam, boom, and it was the English into the sea, the Belgians, Dutch, and Luxembourgers on their knees in the middle of bomb-blasted cities, then *"Blitzkrieg!!"* around the Maginot Line and *voila!* France fell over as though it was a cow hit on the head with a sledgehammer.

Could all the food have gone to the army? There seems to be a shortage in camp. Which is good for Dieter Lange's new brand, Krieger. He had the labels printed in Munich. Not like these regular store labels that look so cheap. We pasted his labels on the outside of mayonnaise jars and put the stuff inside—cabbage soup, beet soup, turnip soup. The new label with the big blond warrior-Viking assures the prisoners that the stuff is okay, 100 percent Aryan. Have to be careful with the Krieger brand, though. It's not approved by the camp director's office, and it's not too tasty. But they move when there's a shortage of food, and as Dieter Lange says, our prices are right. Next, we're going to try chicken soup, but that's going to cost. Dieter Lange has to hire some women out on his father-in-law's farm to kill, clean, and cook the chickens. Women who can be trusted. Or who're just plain dumb. There's already the payoff to various guards in charge of the prisoners who move the stuff.

The details that march out to the civilian plants, though, eat okay. Can't have those prisoners falling out on the job in front of civilians while they're making guns and plane, truck, and tank parts.

Dieter Lange and Anna have been arguing all weekend. He has to go to Paris. He wants to see how many goods he can reroute from Les Halles to his canteens in the Bavarian camps. She wants to go with him. I can't imagine Anna walking along the Champs-Elysées. *Anna Lange?* All that money must be burning a hole in her pockets. Dieter Lange's, too. Of course, Anna won. She will go with him.

The Dancing Ground was filled with prisoners taking the sun earlier today, taking the sun and exchanging news about the war. Will England be next? How long will that take? Between a couple of the blocks a small group of prisoners listened to a flute player. The man was doing Bach, what else, and he made me think of Ernst. I watched the man lipping and breathing into that battered, tarnished instrument with such love I could have cried. Some of the prisoners did. Once I looked up and in one place the sky seemed bluer than anywhere else, like there was a hole in it. I watched the hole in the sky and listened to Bach. And for just one minute, things weren't so bad.

Huebner was not in the canteen today.

Thursday, July 11, 1940
They think I don't know. They talk in low voices around the table when I'm not in the kitchen, and when I'm there, they hardly talk at all. I could put the pieces together for them, but they still wouldn't know what's really going on, because they aren't supposed to. No one is.

Last Saturday, after two days in the Punishment Company, Gitzig was taken to the rifle range and shot dead—after they had made *Hackfleisch* out of him. On the range they tied him to a post and began shooting from his feet up.

Just before dawn Sunday morning, Lily Bernhardt, carrying her baby, was led to a cottage beyond the rail sheds and was strangled from a rafter. It was hot in the shed. They just tied a rope around her neck while she cried, drew it tight, and pulled it over a cross beam. In the blocks they did that very slowly. The prisoner sweated and the SS called the strangling a "sauna." They placed the baby in Lily's arms and put a rope around its neck, too. Gitzig was buried, Lily and the baby cremated. Different places, different times, of course. That bothered me like a sticky piece of lint on a dark suit, because, maybe, Lily and Gitzig and their baby might have been the most natural, the most—somehow, in some way—honest accident to happen here. Lily, fragile, birdlike, and unloved, pushed out of the nest Bernhardt was crowding with his women (of which, besides Anna, there were many, as befitted his station), kept bumping into Gitzig and must have seen something no one else ever saw in him, and then things happened. How? When? Did Gitzig ever confess to adding ingredients to the iced tea and the tapioca? Later, how did she tell him the baby was his? But she must have told him. And then he told me. The fool was happy! What did she tell Bernhardt when he asked about that baby? What was his response? How patient a man he must have been. Having horns grown on his head by the ugliest prisoner Dachau must ever have seen only made him more reserved. It was money he was after, I guess, not prestige. Revenge must have been an orderly thing, scheduled in due time, when Gitzig had finished his cataloging, his engraving, had in fact finished his life, which he was realistic enough to have guessed, no doubt.

Ah, but there was the question of Lily's revenge. How many people stand up to an SS colonel with the kind of story she had to tell? Not to tell it was never her plan, I bet. Maybe it had nothing at all to do with poor Gitzig.

Colonel Fritz Bernhardt transferred to Lyon. All that the Langes know is that Bernhardt is there and Lily, the baby, and Gitzig the

calfactor are gone. They do not have my grapevine. But they can
guess. Dieter Lange hopes he is now safe from those nasty whims of
Bernhardt's; Anna breathes a bit easier, too, even if she's still got the
itch for him. Women seem to go for dangerous men like him.

My news came from the Reds with their contacts inside the
Punishment Company, the rifle range commando detail, the crematorium commando, and so on. I'd bet bottom dollar that Bernhardt
knew all along about his wife and Gitzig, but he needed Gitzig then.
Poor Lily. I suppose there was no place for her to run to. I'm just
happy Bernhardt is a jazz music freak. And that he liked Anna well
enough to leave us all alone—her, Dieter Lange, and me. Well. The
Langes can guess, or just make it their business not to know. Ain't
none of my business anyway.

So when Dieter Lange finally gets me alone and says, "Bernhardt's transferred to France. His wife is gone and his servant's gone
and his house is closed up. What do you think of that?"

I say, "Is that so? He's in France? Everybody wants to go to
France these days. And Gitzig, where could he be, what could he be
up to? Surely, something with Bernhardt, wouldn't you say?" But I
can't fool Dieter Lange; he knows I know something, but he doesn't
know how to make me tell it.

"They say he's divorced his wife," he says, "and had his man sent
to Buchenwald. Might talk too much here, you know." Dieter Lange
sighs. "Anyway, we won't have to walk on eggshells around here now.
A transfer may be a good thing for Bernhardt's career." Yeah, I'm
thinking, and for yours, too. Not good having too many crooks working out the same kitchen, especially if one is cooking your wife all
the time, and you know it but don't want to do anything about it.

Anna is more direct when she gets me by myself. "He could be a
mean man, Fritz Bernhardt. He could hurt you. Well, you know. Look
what happened to those people who tried to get you away." Anna rolls
her eyes. "True, he may be in France, but I believe that's only to get
ready to do in England what he did in Austria, Czechoslovakia, and
Poland, but worse! And if anything's happened to Lily, I don't want to
know about it." She looks at me hopefully, as though I might say something. But that's not going to happen. Not in this life. "Do you believe

he divorced her?" I shrug. "Was there anything going on between Lily and that Gitshit? C'mon. You talked with him. He was your friend. He nursed you when you were sick that time, remember?" I shrug again. "Just as well Bernhardt's gone," she says. "He wasn't coming around too much. Busy, he said. And things, well, they changed."

Tuesday, Nov. 12, 1940

Listen to Goebbels and the Germans are kicking England's ass; listen to the BBC and the English are kicking Germany's ass. One thing for sure, though: English cities are catching hell, so everyone believes Goebbels. They think maybe the invasion of England is on the way, or better, that England will quit like France. The Germans would like the war to be over. They don't understand why the English won't quit.

Not quite two weeks ago the English bombed Berlin for the first time. At night. You would have thought a colored man walked into a meeting of Kluxers and punched one in the jaw the way the Germans carried on. What did they expect? Then, two nights after that, the English came again.

This past Sunday Hitler spoke on the radio. He swore to destroy English cities, burn them to the ground. Huebner is now in Mauthausen, working in the quarry with other Witness details. Each such commando lasts about four months. Then the SS marches them right off the top of the quarry. Splat. Splat, splat. Huebner was a good man, but good don't count for shit in these camps. Anyway, you were okay by me, Huebner.

Yesterday after the noon meal, a bunch of Poles were lined up on the Dancing Ground. Lappus said they were officials. They looked scared. I'm sure they would have traded the "P"s on their uniforms for anything else just then. They formed up after a roll call and marched north on the 'Strasse. To the northeast of the camp is the swamp, and mostly Jews work that detail. The Poles weren't going out there to help the Jews. Beyond the swamp is the rifle range, the Schiessplatz, where prisoners are shot. The Poles marched north, and we waited for the sound of gunshots to carry back to us on the wind.

We always waited, but because of the distance and the way the range was built—halfway down into the ground, what they called a *Kugel-fangen*, a bullet catcher—we didn't always hear the gunfire.

While we waited, the first French prisoners climbed down from the freight cars that had been pushed onto the siding near the south-east side of the camp. They straggled to the quarantine hut. If Pierre were alive, he'd give them uniforms that had been deloused and had "F"s sewn on them. *(The pieces go out, the pieces come in, and all they amount to are lots of dead men.)*

Thursday, April 24, 1941

It started Monday. A big *Svina Exkursiona*, the prisoners call it, was set for Tuesday and Wednesday. *Reichsführer* Heinrich Himmler was to visit.

Visits by the big shots, even SS big shots, are good, because no one gets beaten or killed just before, during, or after them. And the food isn't bad, either, even though the prisoners don't get the pigs that are always slaughtered just before the big shots are shown into the prison kitchen. On the other hand, the camp has to be made spotless to give the impression that prisoners always live so neatly and are always so clean.

The rain started Sunday night, and on the way into camp Monday morning I could see mud and puddles, and I knew the canteen and the blocks would be filthy by the end of the day. How were things to get cleaned and stay clean until after Himmler's visit?

The same as always. More ashes and dirt on the 'Strasse and the 'Platz. Shoes off at the door of the blocks, the canteen, all the buildings. It rained all day Monday, into the night. After dinner, Dieter Lange said I should do things around the house on Tuesday and Wednesday morning. Himmler's pig visit would be over by noon Wednesday. This was just in case one of the officers wanted to show off and be cute with the *Schwarze Amerikaner*. I have to say that sometimes Dieter Lange does try to keep me out of harm's way.

Tonight he told me and Anna about the visit and how Loritz and his staff stood out there in the rain in the middle of the 'Platz until

Himmler's car, with the license plate SS 1, drove up. This was after Himmler had inspected the SS guards near their barracks. From time to time I threw a small log into the porcelain stove to knock off the damp chill. Anna began to snore softly. Dieter Lange shrugged and continued with his cognac. Himmler came and Himmler went, the shrug said. Of course, he wasn't one of the big shots in camp, so he missed a lot of what was going on. As usual.

But he had always understood, and so did I, that the things he did he could only do because no one paid much attention to him as long as he did his job. He helped out the SS kitty and his own pocket, of course. And he was going to Paris to see what else he might do to fatten his wallet.

I hate going downstairs when the weather is damp and cold like this, and Dieter Lange and Anna hate going up to their room, but at least they have each other to stay warm by. Dieter Lange thinks Himmler came to look over the problem with space. Germany invaded Greece and Yugoslavia on the 6th, so here we go with more pieces.

Fri., May 16, 1941

Dieter Lange and Anna are due to return from France tomorrow. They have been gone a week. Somebody put a bug in Dieter Lange's ear that they should go before the middle of June because he just might be busy soon after. He told me this one day while we were rearranging the attic for more space. (The cellar, which now has a strange smell, could not hold even a straight pin, it's so full.) He looked worried when he told me. "The pieces," he muttered. "The more they capture, the more pieces to feed." He grunted. "And the more money to make. But where can I put it all, where? Where to put it." Then he said, "Now Laufen, now Tittmonig, the pieces . . ." He was talking to himself and moving the cans and jars and links of dried meat as though they were checkers or chess pieces.

I know that parts of Dieter Lange sometimes fly away from him like crazy notes break out from keys you never intended to touch. His life is too much for him. He was a small-time hustler, pimp,

faggot, but through the ss he'd become much more: the canteen
supply officer for at least thirty camps for which, to which, and
through which he has to "move the pieces." He has to keep two sets
of books (one for the authorities and one for himself) and watch the
prisoners who work for him or have them watch each other. What
he needs is a colored jazz musician who owes his life to him in each
of the thirty-odd canteens in his charge, not just me in Dachau.

Like everyone else, Dieter Lange now prefers Witnesses. Next to
a colored musician, they're pretty good workers. But they don't last
long. They are among the fastest moving "pieces."

I'm glad the Langes went to Paris again. I thought it might be
good for Dieter Lange. He might run up on a solution for moving
and hiding his money, which I bet my last dollar is what's really worrying him. I don't want him to get sick or go nuts. If I am going to
live, I need his help. No Dieter Lange, no Clifford Pepperidge.

Half of this week I spent in the canteen going over the stock and
records. I can always eat the canteen food, the good stuff that Dieter
Lange and me keep hidden from Uhlmer and Lappus. The problem
was the bathroom. The Reds didn't want me to use theirs and neither
did the Greens, who weren't far away. Both thought I should pay—
with cigarettes or canned food or sweets—just to take a shit or a piss.
They didn't used to mind so much, but now everything is so crowded.

The nights with their floodlights and train-rolling, the banging
sounds, the occasional shot off in the distance, the "sporting" on the
'Platz when the guards made some poor prisoners run around and
roll on the ground while dogs snapped at them for hours on end,
could not bring deep sleep. I never spent a night in the canteen without thinking of the time they brought in Pierre's body.

The rest of the week I spent at the house, cleaning, gardening—
and playing for hours at a time. The piano is way out of tune; sounds
spongy and the pedals are too loose. But I played. Not trying to work
out anything. Just keeping close.

Something's going on. It's like before the invasion of Poland.
No trains have come into camp carrying new prisoners; they arrive
empty and go out filled with finished factory work, rifles, and parts
for all kinds of things I don't know a damn thing about. Those trains

pull out two and three times a day, and the prisoners who work in the factories go around the clock in three shifts. The guards whisper among themselves. Piles and piles of new prisoner uniforms have been uncrated, so we all know the camp will get even more crowded.

Tuesday, June 24, 1941

Oh, shit!

The Reds are in as much of a stew as they can be without drawing too much attention to themselves. Germany invaded Russia on Sunday and, according to the radio announcer, is roaring unmolested through it like some ancient Teutonic giant. For everybody it must be like doing a crazy solo in a great big band with row upon row of brass, reeds, and sidemen doubled up everywhere. When will this solo end? How many more bars to go? What, another chorus? What, another and another and another . . . ? No coda in sight? Another bar of a melody that none of the prisoners wants to dance to anymore (though they must, of course)? When does this blues piece end? 'Cause that's what it is, a blues to end all blues, your soul getting soggy and coming apart like bread in water. Can't put no name on these blues. But the people who ain't prisoners like it, the SS and the civilians in the factories and warehouses between the compound and the camp. Everywhere you can hear German marches and Germans marching—in the camp, outside it, over the radio and the public address systems. Oompah-bah! Oompah-bah! Crash! Cymbs! A roll of snares! Trumpets! Bugles! Trombones! Kettle drums! Bass drums! The Germans in their various uniforms. Even coal miners have them.

Every prisoner who enters the canteen has a story. "Russia falls in three weeks," says one, a Green.

"Ah, no," says an old Red, one who will be going East to help finish some new camps in Poland. "*That* symphony won't be played again, not this time."

German Greens and Blacks stand up the most for the German army, which "drove the English into the sea, trampled the Belgians, Dutch, Danes, Norwegians, Poles, and French. Germany will extend from the Seine past the Volga."

"And you'll still be a child-molester!"

Rumor and gossip and argument and sometimes fact meet in the canteen like people in a train station, but the weight of fact shadows the movements of the 20,000 slaves and their 500 SS guards: The French did give up and the English took a helluva bath, and the hope that they together—or singly—would kick Hitler's ass and see us released just *"durch den Kamin fliegen gehen,"* just went up the chimney like the smoke from another burning cadaver. For whatever the Reds feel or want, how can the Russians, who so quickly sold out almost two years ago, defeat a blitzkrieging army that at this very moment is practically at the main highways to Moscow and Stalingrad and Leningrad? Never mind that the English are still raiding the north with their planes and bombs.

"Stalin bought time!" some of the Reds now argue.

"And divided the East with Germany! Naive! Crooked! And now the devil's getting his due!"

"Trotskyite!"

At home they shouted at me for breakfast the other morning, like I was some kind of slave. (As much as we'd done together.) Made me mad, but I brought it on myself; they got used to this old coon doing his Sambo show with the cooking and serving, just to keep his ass out of, if not the oven, another camp or even, if you want to put lick-back-to-lick, this camp, on the other side. I spoiled them, and now they need me. Wasn't that what the old coon wanted? Yeah, man, it was, and I do live, and not badly, either, while a whole lot of other folks have kicked the bucket, gone up the chimney, got shot while escaping, taken the *"Fantomas"* to Hartheim. So I don't complain. I just get mad.

For Dieter Lange the war in the East means problems, complications, the movement once again of the *Stücken.* But he's at least in a better mood since he and Anna returned from Paris. I imagined them there: Dieter Lange in his SS black or gray, his black boots and all that pigeon shit they wear on the collars, his cap, his figure tall and getting thick, his hair graying, his faded blue eyes trying to appear nonchalant instead of tired, cunning, and trapped, his stride slow and careful, not calling attention to itself; and Anna in a flowered dress, girdled, her face made ruddy with rouge and powder, those carefully watched haunches rolling against the restraints. How wonderful Paris must have seemed. I'm sure the French hated them.

Dieter Lange brought back news: Ruby Mae is supposed to be in Portugal. Willy Lewis got to Switzerland. Freddie Johnson is in a camp here in Germany. Josephine Baker is still in France. Django Rheinhardt is playing constantly. Bricktop's been gone since a month after Poland. We laughed because we knew that was the second time the Germans had sent her packing. So, I thought as he was giving me the news, he got around. Probably told Anna he had business. I wonder how she spent *her* time on this visit.

The "hot" stuff back home, Dieter Lange told me, was "Cotton Tail" and "Don't Get Around Much Anymore," both Ellington pieces, and "Brazil" and "That Old Black Magic." For a while, while Anna visited Ursula, we put the Eastern Front on the shelf and played the records he'd brought back and drank and talked of Paris and Berlin, which they'd visited on the way back. There are bomb shelters there now.

He ran up to the attic and came back with a sweet-smelling box. "For you," he said, and opened it. Lingerie, dangerous-looking stuff, too.

"I never wore that," I said. I fingered it; it was soft and smooth. It almost whispered.

He smiled, closed up the box. It was clear he was going to keep it hidden upstairs. "First time for everything," he said.

I said, "Yeah, well, we'll see, won't we?"

He acted like he hadn't heard me.

Sunday, Aug. 3, 1941

I hear Hohenberg got caught with a *Junge*. In one of the storage rooms in the *Wirtschaftsgebaude*. Everything works until you get caught at it. Hohenberg had a group of Pinks who worked in his office, and everyone knew why, but enough got to be enough; Hohenberg got to have too much power, even for a German inmate. They say Karlsohn caught them. His name ought to be *Hurensohn*, whore's son. Caught them like salamanders riding each other in a pond. Well. I never thought much of Hohenberg after he tried to take advantage of Pierre. Even after he arranged for Pierre to work in the greenhouse I didn't like him, because Werner was the man who really arranged it. So Hohenberg has the usual six o'clock *Kalter Arsch* appointment tomorrow with the end of a rope. He will march out to the sad playing of the sorry-assed band to become another cold ass. Dead. They might as well order us to stop breathing as to stop fucking each other. They know that. It's just that this time Hohenberg is that periodic reminder.

If Uhlmer is supposed to be watching me, he doesn't have the time, any more than I have to watch him. The war in the East means work: more inventories to keep for the camp and for Dieter Lange; more timetables to move goods from his storage in Munich and his father-in-law's farm; more bribes to pay to guards, drivers, and people I don't even know about; more Krieger products to slip between the approved stuff. The new prisoners from France, Belgium, and Holland haven't yet grown used to prison food. What money they have they spend for our soups, the salt and pepper bags, the bootleg cookies and candies. When they run out of the packs of cigarettes, they buy the little bags of mixed tobacco and dried lettuce leaves we also sell. Uhlmer must be doing pretty well; his uniform's always clean and neat, and he always wears socks. But he could say the same for me or for Lappus, who, though not as well turned out as us, certainly doesn't dress like the average prisoner. Lappus is still nice to people. Uhlmer has been acting like a capo. He will, like Hohenberg, hang himself, and I will be more than happy to help.

More doctors have been sent here. The prisoners have built a foundation for something huge that was rolled up and set between Blocks 3 and 5, and the doctors are recruiting more prisoners to work in the *Reviers*. At first there were volunteers. I can't figure what was offered to make anyone here think that volunteering would be good for them. Nobody ever saw the volunteers again. The SS say they were sent home, just like they (the SS) said they'd be. But now everyone who comes into the canteen believes that as far as the doctors and that thing between the blocks are concerned, the air is getting thick, dangerous, *Dicke Luft,* especially with the rumors of what's going on with Jews in the East, where more and more of the older prisoners are being sent to work with engineers. Why are only Jews being sent East? Hi-de-hi. If it's only Jews, then it's got to be bad. Every prisoner goes the other way when he sees the clerks and doctors from the Infirmary strolling up and down the 'Strasse or the 'Platz.

"Wer ist an unserem Ungluck schuld?" the Jewish capo shouts. "Who caused all our misery?" The guards watch, smiling, as the Jews march out to work, and later march back. The marching call is always the same. The marching Jews, in step, shout back *"Die Juden! Die Juden!"* (Left, right, left.) Sometimes I think I can hear a strange echo, when the answer could be "The Negro! The Negro!" Then the Jewish columns run into SS guards, whose day isn't complete until they shout *"Dir gefallt es hier? Was?"* The guards ask because the Jews have insisted on living. "Do you like it here?" In other words, "Aren't you dead yet? Damn you, die!" Then I think of a long broken column of men who are Negroes.

Everyone's saying the doctors working in that thing are doing experiments. Mostly on Jews, Gypsies, Pinks, and Blacks.

Sat., September 13, 1941

So it's taken longer than three weeks. It's not over in the East. So what? There's not a guard or prisoner who doesn't believe it soon will be. We saw the first Russian prisoners of war this past Monday. (No one knows why they were brought here, but everyone thinks it's not good for them that they have been.) They say they were marched all the way from Russia after the first battles. They sure looked like it. They didn't march, they staggered in, dirty, stinking, hungry, thirsty. The guards were hitting them and shouting, in Russian, *"Bistro! Bistro! Bistro!"* "Hurry! Hurry! Hurry!" and the Russian soldiers, an ugly shit-colored mass drifting toward quarantine, were calling out to anyone, "Please give me bread, please give me bread," saying "bread" in both Russian and German so no one would miss the meaning. *"Daj chieba, Brot, daj chieba, Brot."*

The prisoners who were on the Dancing Ground as the Russians passed, and who had with them a crust of bread, a cigarette butt, a half-rotten piece of fruit, passed these along as sneakily as they could. Some of them got caught and were hauled off to stand in chains against the *Jourhaus* wall until their own punishment could be selected.

I have to be more diligent about gathering writing paper. It seems to be getting scarce. Right now there's plenty of glazed paper the SS sometimes allows prisoners to have for their windows in the winter. Since it's just the end of summer, I managed to get a few rolls to store.

Dieter Lange came home late and woke me and Anna up and made us sit with him at the kitchen table. He slid some glasses to us and brought from a shelf a bottle of French cognac.

"Well, now we're in the shit," he said.

It was about midnight, and through the window I could see the gray mist slowly rolling down the street, blotting out the streetlights every once in a while.

"What's the matter?" Anna asked.

Dieter Lange sighed. He had been drinking, a lot, before he came home. "We've got an SS Colonel and an SS General Major to deal with now. And it's best you don't know who they are. In fact, they warned me not to tell who they are." He poured drinks for us. "They seem to know everything about us and about the business, your father included." He sighed again.

"They want to—" Anna began.

"Improve things, Anna. That's what they say." He stared at her while she twirled her glass on the enamel tabletop. I drank and pushed my glass over for more. Sounded like the way gangsters back home did business. Just muscled their way on in. And the gangsters in Berlin, back in the days when I wouldn't have looked twice at Dieter Lange, were just as bad. Maybe even worse.

Dieter Lange poured me half a glass and waited for Anna.

"Well . . ." she said. "Looks like they want to take over. Just how would it work? They're not going to turn us in? What do they want? How much? When?"

"Starting now," he said. "What we have we keep. We put back in that souvenir shit, they get us some cheap beer and alcohol, which they will have cut and mixed, and since Himmler's about to make whorehouses in the KLs legal, we'll control the *Bordellschein*. We just tell them what we need and they'll see we get it." Dieter Lange turned partly away from us. "They haven't decided how much money they want from us. They have to look at the figures first." He drummed his fingers on the table. "There was nothing I could do. These are *Nacht und Nebel* people; they can make you disappear in the night and fog. They are also Ploetzenee Prison people, where they're invited to dinner after watching a few people lose their heads."

"Let them have it all," Anna said.

"That's not the way they want it," Dieter Lange said.

"They need a front," I said.

Anna said, "How do they know?"

Dieter Lange shrugged.

Bernhardt, I thought. Part of a big plan to squeeze money out of turnips; maybe like Krupp or Siemens, a great big European company store for all the slaves. I didn't mention this to Dieter Lange because, at least for the time being, he was, deep down, happy that he didn't have to move the "pieces" by himself or lay his head on the block. And maybe he was already planning to turn over Anna and her father, if push came to shove.

The radio announced that Kiev had fallen with the capture of two-thirds of a million Russian soldiers. I can't imagine such numbers. The BBC says only that the Russians have suffered heavy losses.

Did I tell you that they call that thing near Block 5 the *Himmelwagen?* A Dr. Rascher is doing research for the Luftwaffe on high flying. Pacholegg works for Rascher as a ward clerk. He's an Austrian Red who was in Poland before coming here. Ghosts dance in his eyes. Pacholegg says the rumors about that thing are true. I know just a little about this Rascher. He lives in the SS compound with his wife, Nina, and their three children, all of whom were "born" when she was in her forties. This I told Pacholegg. It is common knowledge among the SS wives, Anna says, because half of them don't want or can't have kids. So they kidnap them or make deals through *Lebensborn*. A lot of these bitches can't afford to point the finger at anyone else.

Pacholegg may let the ghosts dance in his eyes only when he talks to me, the way Gitzig used to, spilling out all his secrets. I don't know why people do this with me. Is it because I'm an American, even if a Negro? Or do they look at me and see a witness? How can they know? Anyway, the *Himmelwagen* is a decompression chamber. The TPs, as Pacholegg calls them, are strapped into a parachute harness. "They give them a helmet, sometimes, so they feel like a pilot. Then they vacuum the air out of the chamber." Pacholegg talks in a plain, low voice without emotion, as though from memory. "Then the Test Persons die. Horribly. While we watch and take notes. The TPs beat and tear at themselves, you know, pound on the walls and shout and scream. The pressure on the ear drums must be terrible. And their lungs are ruptured, you know. At 30,000 feet of pressure, they last thirty minutes; it's clear that for only ten minutes are they functioning anywhere near normal."

Pacholegg blinks, but the ghosts remain. "Once Rascher did an autopsy on a guy whose heart was still beating. He'd passed out from the pressure. That prick Rascher examined him quick, said he was almost dead, took him down, and cut him open. And watched the heart beat. I looked in there, too. It was like a wiggly little animal without skin."

Pacholegg shudders. "Well, I've had it worse, you know, in the East, with Russian POWs, near Minsk." He had been arrested in Vienna, then sent East to help build more camps. He says he knows nothing about the rumors of the shooting of thousands of Jews in Treblinka.

I light another cigarette for him, a real one, rich in dark tobacco, a French cigarette. Pacholegg tells how much the Germans hated the Russian soldiers for putting up such a fight, even as they were being defeated, and how the order came down to execute every Russian captured—as quietly as possible.

There was a large stone house in the woods—"a white birch forest," says Pacholegg. It was an examination-interrogation center, they told the Russians. One by one the soldiers were led into a room—there were four rooms with high ceilings in the house. The soldiers were led forward to booths for questioning by German soldiers who asked the Russians their names, and as the Russians gave them, they were shot through the head by riflemen concealed in the ceiling. Each room was soundproof, so there were four at a time. Name? Bang! And ten minutes to clean up before the next group of four Russians came in for "questioning."

I ask Pacholegg what he does at the *Himmelwagen* tests.

"What can I do?" he asks me. "I strap them in. I take notes. I clean up after, me and the other clerks and nurses. The TPs make a mess, you understand. After a while, you don't mind so much death, you know."

You wouldn't think it, so slight a man, so scared-looking and quiet, like something under a rock you've just kicked over. He's one prisoner who doesn't mind having his hair cut so short all the time, because he's afraid of lice.

Monday, Dec. 8, 1941

Balamabama! Whoampabam! It sounded like an explosion going off on the steps leading down to my room, or a fight. I couldn't imagine what was going on. I almost did the number right in my underwear. I jumped up. First thing I thought was they had caught up with Dieter Lange and we were all going to the Bunker and maybe worse. Oh, that noise was flying down the stairs and my door flew open and Dieter Lange pulled my light string before I could. Anna was hunched up right under him. "Cleef! The Japanese bombed the American Navy in Hawaii! Come up and we'll listen to the radio some more. C'mon."

Upstairs Anna made some coffee. It was after midnight. Dieter Lange said the first reports had come in hours ago, but nobody believed them. "I thought when they said *Tagesbericht!* it had something to do with that BBC report of the big Russian counterattack," he said.

"Do you know exactly where is Pearl Harbor?" Anna asked me, and I said no. I only knew Hawaii was somewhere out beyond California; it's where the ukulele comes from. I put some wood in the stove. Dieter Lange looked worried one minute and confused the next. I wasn't sure what I felt. Why would the Japanese attack America?

"So, Dieter," Anna said. "What does it mean? Is it good or bad? Japan is—"

Dieter Lange interrupted her. "Japan is a German ally. Like Italy." He shook his head and got up to pace. "No good. The Americans will come in now." He stopped pacing. "Maybe good. End the war. We all go back to civilian life. Cleef goes home. We are all fine, after a while. So."

"But there will be much more fighting, Dieter. It won't be so easy to go back to civilian life." Anna now seemed puzzled.

"And if the U.S. is in," I said, "then I'm an enemy alien—"

"Things will be the same as now," Dieter Lange said quite simply. "Exactly the same. You've been here so long under the PC warrant, I'm sure they won't change your status, so forget that."

We sat sipping the coffee and listening to the radio. Dieter Lange kept working the knobs, but there was nothing more. I thought of Pierre and smelled the sea and the rusty, stale odor of the wet steel of ocean liners. Inside, I think I smiled; inside, I thought I saw in both their faces, another shade of fear. And I was glad, the way you are when you know something, finally, is settled; the way you know that, when you play one note, another precise note must be played for the first one to make sense.

———

Wednesday, January 14, 1942

I am back. Hope left me. Just got up and hauled ass. Then the blues came stomping in like Dieter Lange drunk and looking for the booty. I just gave up. Beat. Tired of being a witness, a slave for the Germans; of the Langes, of the years, of the war, the whole fucking, stinking war; of the dying, of holding on to the best of the worst that has been my life. I never had the blues so long and so hard. Something was going on inside. Going on far away, down a long road overhung with big dark trees, something like a little kid you can barely see, he's so far away. When I was feeling most blue, I could just see this child, and I guess I reached out, grabbed him, and held on until he grew bigger and closer and finally climbed back inside me. Here I am again.

I am always a big hit in the lingerie. For Dieter Lange and then Anna and Ursula. I looked better in it than any of them would have. It felt good, too. Anna and Ursula made up some new games for us.

I have seen a few more colored men in camp. It's the strangest thing to notice a colored face sticking out among all the white ones. Stuck smack in the middle of all this white craziness. I don't want to feel sorry for them. Sorry requires energy, giving up a little of yourself, whatever you can spare; maybe that's what happened to me before; maybe it even makes you weak, I don't know. But even strong white men are niggers here—until a colored face appears—and then, except for the Jews and Gypsies, no one else is a nigger anymore. Even so, the prisoners play the awful game with each other. Some of the latrine signs read: *Nur für Polen; Nur für Französen; Nur für Ukrainishen,* and so on. Might just as well be For Whites Only like back home. Anyway, these colored guys don't look American to me. Something about them, some way they walk and gesture, some way they stare back at me. I feel no pull toward them, as I did with Dr. Nyassa and Pierre, but they weren't Americans either; they were more than that and maybe, to them, I was, too. Shit. I know the only reason those men are here is because they're colored. The only reason. Even so, it's hard to keep up with anyone except the older inmates who haven't been sent East. I know it's important to have friends in a place like this, but I'm past that. A friend is just a piece to be moved or destroyed, and one way or another, they take you with them, or bits of you.

Some of the Blacks and Greens have been allowed to volunteer for the Russian front, even while the Russian soldiers keep staggering into camp. The SS used to laugh at prisoners who wanted to volunteer to fight. Things must not be going so good in the East. I heard from Bader that the people in Dachau town have been complaining about the sight of the Russian soldiers straggling through the streets, so trains will now be used to bring them directly into camp. Bader now has Hohenberg's job and makes up the details that work for the civilian companies in the factories just outside the camp. I'm happy for him because I once heard he was going East. Bader's a good source for news.

With the furnace going and windows closed in the winter, the smell in the cellar seems to be getting worse. I asked Dieter Lange to look around the storeroom and he said he had; nothing was spoiled. He didn't know what the smell was. Leave him alone, he said. Mind my own business. So what if I have to sleep down there? That's the way he went running off at the mouth, but I know what it is now.

While Dieter Lange and Anna were shopping in Munich, I opened the lock and pushed inside his storage space. It seemed to me that even the dried meat that was hanging there smelled awful. I found the place that smelled quite by accident. I'd gone through cartons and boxes and metal containers of crackers and biscuits. One more to check. It didn't lift easily, and I thought, Uh-huh! I left it in its place and moved stuff from around it. Whew! I was growing afraid to open the tin when I'd cleared the area. I thought there might be a head in it or some other part of a body. I was shaking I was so nervous. When I shook the tin, there was a rattling sound, so then I knew there wasn't a head. Why did I think that? In this place with these people, why not? Yet I didn't want to think that Dieter Lange was so much like the rest of them. But what was in the tin that smelled so bad? I pried off the lid and turned away from the stink that shot out. I tipped the tin toward the light and the rattle became like stepping on deep-laid gravel. I held my breath and looked inside, but I couldn't tell right off what was making the sound. I picked up a wood file and dipped it inside and brought out two or three dull-looking pieces of metal. I took them in my hand and looked at them; one was solid, the others hollow with ragged little wires on them. I rubbed them on my clothes. They got a little brighter, a little more . . . gold. I dropped them as soon as I realized what they were and what remained in the foot-high tin. Gold teeth! My first impulse was to jump, but something, I don't know what, made that impossible. I just sat there, petrified. After a while, I picked them up and put them back inside the tin, then, with the file, I reached in and stirred the teeth, the bits of rotten flesh and bone.

This was all that was left of 5,000 people? Ten thousand? I got up and went to my room and lit a cigarette and blew the smoke all around. Then I had another one. When I was finished with that one, I got some chlorine powder and poured it in the tin and shook it up and replaced the lid. A colored musician with a mouth full of gold or a diamond stuck in a tooth, like Jelly Roll Morton, wouldn't have lasted long in this place. I put everything back and locked up the storage space. I could see Dieter Lange (and maybe his new partners) melting down gold teeth and fillings and stashing the brick away until it became safe to take it out. For a second I saw that little boy way down the road, but I made him come back where he belonged.

From now on there will be more free time in camp. Improve morale, get more work out of the slaves. That's the word. And there is the whorehouse, sanctioned by Himmler himself. That's to improve morale, too, even if it doesn't hold down the spread of the clap and syph. This new place is bigger than the old Puff.

Radio London says the Russians claim they have trapped and are killing the soldiers of fourteen German and Rumanian divisions. Goebbels said on the radio, "What does not kill us makes us stronger."

There is something about news like this that gives me a feeling like warm sun you can't see because of the fog.

"So, Pacholegg," I say when I see him and another Infirmary detail in a corner of the canteen where they are smoking and avoiding the other prisoners who come in. (Or maybe it's the other way around.)

"So?" he says and turns away. I think this is because he doesn't want the others to hear him talk about the work they are doing in the big black tank over there. Kohler, who has that same look in his eyes that Pacholegg has, looks the other way; Kohler has already told me about the other experiments. The more they are forbidden to talk about these nasty things, it seems, the more eager they are to do so— if they can do it without getting caught, of course. So Kohler doesn't know that Pacholegg talks and Pacholegg doesn't know that Kohler talks. And then there's Neff.

I shrug and continue marking down the prices of the carvings the prisoners made for Christmas for the SS. If these don't move within a week, back in storage they go until next Christmas. I pause right there. Who knows? There might not be a next Christmas in Dachau. Then, revenge. That's why everyone wants names, and that's why names and deeds are forbidden to be discussed. To hell with that. We all want revenge. It is like strong, hot soup with a tumbler of cognac thrown in.

We know what needs to be known. Rascher and his decompression chamber, Schilling and his malaria research for the Afrika Korps in North Africa—for this the Test Persons get inoculated with a serum, then they are shot to see if their blood has coagulated.

Neff, another Rascher orderly, works with the doctor on a second air force experiment, which makes it look like Hitler still imagines the Third Reich running from the Atlantic to the Urals, and from the Arctic to the equator. (Maps have appeared in camp and are marked, then whisked away again.) Neff's work is on Arctic weather. Rascher wants to determine how much cold people can stand. "At first we just put people naked out in the cold behind the fence and splash water on them every hour," Neff says with a shrug. "The test is nothing. Not controlled. We take temperatures at the start and at the end; then, if they're not dead, we revive the TPs with warm baths." He pauses. "But now we've got a big vat and a bunch of Russian TPs."

"Why don't you shut up?" Pacholegg says.

"Why don't you make me?" Neff answers.

They're up snarling and straining like dogs. I retreat to my cubbyhole. An old Red pushes between them, pats them on the shoulders, and shoves them off in different directions.

Something's going around. I hear it whispered: *Sonnenaufgang*. It's from the Reds and it means victory is coming over the German army and fascism. Maybe that's why everybody's so touchy. Hope. The possibility. A future where there wasn't anything before. Don't mess up, but start remembering the names.

Dieter Lange tells me that Goebbels and Baldauf have formed a big swing band, Charlie and His Orchestra, to play over Berlin Radio. For the morale of the military. Freddie Brocksieper plays drums.

They play Gershwin, Dorsey, and Miller—and change the titles of the numbers. The *Zazou Junge*, the kid jitterbugs, are still raising hell in Hamburg, between visits by the British fliers who also like to say hello to Essen, Bremen, and Berlin, of course, as well as a few other places. Me and Dieter Lange listen to Charlie on the radio. Pooo . . . They've written in most of the ad libs. The music's got as much swing as a wet firecracker. Not nearly as swinging as we were at the Pussy Palace.

Sunday, March 1, 1942

There are men in this place whose faces make you want to run away from them. But you can't. You're afraid to ask them what's wrong. You don't want to know more than you already do. But you *do*. You want to know if things are worse than you know they are or maybe a little bit better. You sometimes believe you know everything that's going on but the camp with its blocks, factories, officers' compound, SS barracks, and outside work areas are far too large now. Before, you could never know anything for sure; now it's impossible.

Herbertshausen is now a *Schiessplatz*, too, but I never heard of it until Werner and Bader took me on a walk around the 'Platz yesterday. I knew there had to be some reason for it, because you don't walk around the 'Platz in March unless the sun has made a mistake and come out. And for the past few days the sky has been gray, spitting snow and rain sometimes. It's so gray that you begin to think that God's doing something up there He doesn't want you to see, or that maybe Loa Aizan has closed up and gone off on a binge. The only thing above that's not gray is that curling smudge of black from the crematorium; when the weather's like this, it flattens out over the camp and the smell drills through everything.

Werner and Bader, who now seem to be on speaking terms, probably because of whatever's happening in the East, have heard that Laufen and Tittmoning have been designated ILAGs, internment lagers, or camps for enemy and neutral civilians. They told me they think I will be transferred to one of them. My heart jumped! But . . . wouldn't Dieter Lange know how things work better than they do?

Maybe, they said, but in case things did change, they wanted me
to know that the SS is systematically killing the Russian prisoners.
Well, everyone knows that. The Russians are mostly assigned to the
quarry so they can die one way or the other. But they are so tough,
many of them have made little hearts out of quarry stone, and they
wear these around their necks to show the SS their hearts are just as
hard. The prisoners call these guys *Steinerne Herzen*. The Germans
know. Last fall, the SS lined up 6,000 at Herbertshausen and killed
them all. The Reds in the Herbertshausen *Sonderkommando* who
were allowed to live after the burials reported the shootings. Werner
and Bader said they had no documents for this, but the graves could
easily be found. Why do they tell me this? So that, if I did get transferred, I could pass along the word somehow. Would I do it? I said
yes and hurried back to the canteen where it was at least warmer
than outside.

Wednesday, March 25, 1942

Two weeks ago, there was the sound of trucks grinding through
the streets of the compound. It had just turned dark and it was close
to dinner time. I had left the camp early to work at home, and I was
ready to serve dinner when the trucks came. There was a pounding
on the door and someone calling for Dieter Lange. Up and down the
street there was shouting. Dieter Lange does not like to be disturbed
at dinner, but he jumped up and ran to the door. "What? What's
going on?" Whispering. "Oh! Oh!" Dieter Lange said out loud,
which made Anna run to the door, too. More whispering.

I waited in the kitchen. I could see the headlights of the trucks,
which were lining up one behind the other in the street, their
engines running, the steam from their exhausts floating up the sky.

"Get dressed warm, Cleef," Dieter Lange said when they came
back. Anna was right up under him. "They need you people out here
to help with the evening meal in camp."

I asked what was the matter. He and Anna exchanged a look and
he shrugged and said a lot of people were sick.

"From what?" I asked.

"They don't know, but they don't think it's serious," Dieter Lange said. He was now at the closet pulling out gloves and a thick scarf. Anna was chewing on her bottom lip. I knew it had to be something bad over in camp, like another epidemic. I never once thought they were going to take all the servants out and shoot us. The officers and their wives had gotten too used to us for that.

Anna jumped to the bread box and began slicing bread and hurriedly placed some bologna in between. "Boots," she said to Dieter Lange, "he will need boots. And an old sweater, Dieter. It is very cold and still much snow."

I went downstairs to dress, putting on two pairs of underwear, socks, and a lumber jacket I wore when I worked outside. I put my prison jacket over it. Beneath my cap I put on a hood I'd made from Anna's old stockings. Then I returned upstairs and put on the boots. I shoved the sandwiches in my pockets and pulled on the gloves. "Try not to go near the prisoners in the blocks," Anna said. Dieter Lange said nothing. But I knew if there was an epidemic over there, he would quickly find a trip again to take him away from here. I looked out the front-room window and saw the calfactors standing like statues in the road in front of the houses where they worked.

"Go. They'll pick you up," Dieter Lange said. Anna pulled her sweater tight around her and it seemed just then she was getting heavier.

I went out. There were lights on in all the houses along the street. Guards were shouting, the engines rattling and humming. "Get in the trucks. All prisoners, get in the trucks. Hurry, hurry!" The voice came over a loudspeaker. The guards, their long coats bouncing around their legs, pushed the servants into the first trucks and sent them off, and the next group and the next, until I was pushed in myself, out of the wind, which was steady and sharp, and bit through everything. "Hurry, hurry! You miserable, soft-life shitters, hurry up!" The trucks vibrated, creaked, and rumbled through the snow and ridges of ice. I noticed Captain Winkelmann standing at the front of the line of trucks. He seemed to be in charge of this business.

Guards at the back blew on their hands and lit cigarettes. "What's going on?" someone whispered. "Typhoid," someone else whispered.

"Not again," another said. "Yes," still another said. "I work for one of the camp doctors. It's typhoid all right." So the talk went as the truck crunched over piles of frozen slush, skidded this way and that, and got up enough speed to rush through the *Jourhaus* gate, where the guards waved us across the roll-call yard, made bright as day by the floodlights. There the trucks slid to a stop, and we were bullied out of them and into formation. Men not dressed as warmly as I was began to shiver and softly stamp their feet. The guards shouted for silence and, with their leashed dogs bounding and snarling, herded us into two groups. I was resenting all the shouting, pushing, and cursing, the goddamn dogs, but I knew it was a luxury to get mad; the general population went through this several times a day. Who were we to get uppity when we all knew that a prisoner who let anger show got the crap beat out of him—and that was the mildest punishment!

Then we were trotting in formation up the steps into the kitchen in the *Wirtschaftsgebaude.* It was deliciously warm inside and smelled of food. We looked at each other and smiled. Maybe this wouldn't be so bad after all. The prisoners who were wearing *Holtzpantinen*, wooden shoes, slipped, regained their feet, balanced themselves carefully, and continued to skate along the tile floors that were fast becoming wet and dangerous. Soon we were lined up before the long row of sparkling stainless-steel food containers hooked above ovens. Each container had a number, and they were huge! I wondered how many men it took to carry one. My group was broken down into three smaller ones, and mine was sent to stand before the container marked "29." Twenty-nine! That was way at the end of the camp, the last block on the east side, if this was for Block 29! There were twelve of us, and I could now see that we would use long wooden handles to carry the container. These were six inches square and rounded at the places where they had to be held. Our eyes flashed and flickered from one face to the next. Six of us on each side, but could we lift, let alone carry, that huge, hot kettle of food?

"Bereit . . . heben . . . ! Heben!!" Down along the ovens men were grabbing hold, fear and panic already plain on their faces. We, too, grabbed the handles at the command to lift, and tried to force the

container up and away. It didn't move. In shock, we glanced at each other once again. I was sweating from fear and too many clothes. Up the line, out of the corners of our eyes, we saw the SS start down, beating, punching, kicking, and suddenly men who only a moment before couldn't lift their containers freed them from their places above the ovens, and began staggering toward the doors. As the guards approached, we got our vat off its hooks and began sliding, skating, stumbling toward the doors being held open by the guards. They popped us with their clubs as team after team scampered out and steam leaped from the containers into the night sky. There were only two steps to climb down, but they might have been twenty feet apart as we maneuvered down, wheezing, whining, and panting. Behind us, as we gained the ground, we heard a cry, more cries, of anger, despair, and fear, then shouts followed by the bang of metal on the concrete steps, and soup came washing down under our feet, but we hadn't stopped. The dropped container banged once or twice more and then its sound was lost among the curses and screams of men, and the barking of dogs.

Before us we saw, and behind us we heard, these curious beasts shuffling and clomping and moaning, all the legs and the bright metal containers reflecting the lights of the 'Platz where we were slide-skating toward the 'Strasse, a guard at each end of the pole. We struggled to hold the container high enough to keep it from bouncing on the ice and snow. It seemed to take an hour to cross the roll-call square. My legs trembled. Someone behind me was crying (I was the second man on the left pole) and someone else kept saying, with each step or slide, "Oh, oh, oh." The men at the front and rear positions were easy targets for the guards. It helped not to look up, to just somehow in the dark feel the steps of the man in front of you and match your own to his, to find your own music to struggle to. So unless we caught one of the blows, we only heard them land, followed by the muffled reactions of the prisoners. "Ow!" "Oh!"

There seemed to be three teams in front of us, judging from the SS shouts and curses and the reactions to them, but most of the teams were behind us. Our efforts, the dying heat from the containers, and our fear brought the sweat to our bodies like sheets of warm water. Our clothes would freeze on us. I called my legs back from going off on a solo. We couldn't stop to wipe away the sweat. I tried not to feel or think. I felt the weight biting down in the side of my neck, then my shoulder. I felt we'd gone another hour, but when I glanced up, I saw we were just passing the canteen! The first building after the square! My heart flew away and my stomach fell to my knees. I'd never make it. By the time we got between Blocks 1 and 2 I'd be dead.

"Stop!" one of the guards in front called. "Set it down. Change sides! Hurry! Hurry! Useless pieces of shit. You! Move, nigger!" In a frenzy we scuttled around, lifted the container and struggled off again. I felt a little better. We were gaining on the team carrying the container for Block 30, one section of which had become another *Revier*. I looked around and saw that the "30" team was letting their container slide along on the snow, and as much as the guards were beating them, they still couldn't get it up. We shuffled and skated past them.

Behind us, panting and groaning and singing, we heard a group of Jews. I wondered how many men were on their poles. Surely they had come from their block, 15, because if they didn't get their own food, no one else would get it for them. The guards wouldn't let that happen.

There is no mistaking the sound of a club against a human skull, and the "30" team in back of us was getting more than its share of clubbings. Fear and pain, fear *of* pain, will make a man do almost anything. It wasn't long before we heard the "30" team right behind us, and the "15" team not far behind them. We switched again between Blocks 3 and 4, and in the dim lights of the block entrances, I saw tears, sweat, and snot on the faces of the men in my team. My heart was pounding in my ears; it felt like it would tear loose. We lurched forward again and somehow we seemed to have found each other's rhythm; I could feel the coming together, like a bunch of musicians. The crunch and wheezing of the teams behind us seemed to be falling away. Then we were changing at the Punishment Company block, 7, and starting up again. On the next change, between 11 and 12, I looked behind. Some teams had reached their blocks; others continued down the middle of the 'Strasse.

The crematorium smell shifted to our direction, and that may have goaded us on, for the next time the guards said to change, we just kept going, fueled by the momentum of our pace and by the fact that we were midway to 29. I wondered about the men who did this twice a day. Now there were breathless whispers among the team. "C'mon, pick it up. Faster. Aren't you as tough as the guys who live here? What are you, *Kaminfutter*, chimney fodder? Show a little courage. Don't be a Señorita. C'mon, put your back into it, we're more than halfway there." We were sounding like horses that had been at the plough too long. We encouraged, coughed, panted, prayed, talked to ourselves. But our container was now bumping and scraping the ground, and each time it did, in fright, we forced it back up and struggled on. We strained to see the block numbers. We switched between Blocks 23 and 24 in the section called Moscow and Warsaw.

The north watchtower loomed tall and white before us. Was the guard pretending, fixing us in his sights, pulling the trigger? There was then the point at which we knew we were going to make it, being so close to the tower. I could feel a surge of power along the pole as we leaned toward 29, moving to our right. Block 25 crept backward, then 27, and we were at 29, where the block leaders were waiting and the prisoners who were able, weakly waved their enamel bowls and beat them with spoons. We struggled up the steps, through the doors and into the building, which stank of shit and vomit. We set down the container and fell to the floor beside it.

We had done it!

About 400 of us hauled food for three days and then, because the SS feared we might contaminate the families we worked for, we were carefully examined and sent home. Gangs of new prisoners from other camps and Russia replaced us.

———

Saturday, April 18, 1942

New and bigger signs have gone up in the latrines:

> *Nacht dem Abort, von dem essen*
> *Hande waschen, nicht vergessen.*
> After the latrine, before eating,
> Wash your hands, do not forget.

The prisoners hardly have time to do anything—wash, shit, or eat. Work, yes; everything else is *Schnell! Avanti! Rasch! Ein biss rascher als sonst! Wenga! Wenga!* Hurry, hurry, faster, a little bit faster. . . . So shit gets in the water and everyone gets sick.

The Langes were glad when I was finished carrying food. I noticed they didn't get too close to me for a while, which was fine with me. The canteen stayed closed, so I did things around the house.

The fertilizer truck has just left a small pile of gray ash for mixing in the soil. The past couple years I haven't been so squeamish about shoveling it. Now I just whisper to it, "Who were you?" Or "Who were you guys?"

I've begun the spring cleaning, taking time out to lay in my bed and look at old magazines when the Langes aren't around. Anna's down in the dumps. I talk to her in English, but she's not interested anymore. So I say, "Inefay ithway emay. Uckfay ooyay. Itchbay." She doesn't know if she should smile or get mad; I smile so she should know what I said was harmless. She's got something on her mind besides the war, the big-shot partners, and all the scheming and hustling.

Dieter Lange was right, of course; I will not be moving my rusty-dusty from Dachau to any other camp. He visited Laufen and Tittmoning. Says they are filled with people who are naturalized citizens of the U.S., Canada, England, and South American countries. He found an American Negro in Tittmoning, a painter. There are a few colored men there. Dieter Lange pulled out a piece of paper and read, "Josef Nassy. From New York. He had been living in Brussels when the war caught up with him. The commandant over there likes him. Helps him get his painting stuff."

"Oh?" I said.

"No, no," Dieter Lange said. "He's married to a Belgian woman."

"You're married, too."

"Shut up, Cleef. Don't be smart with me."

I shut up and wondered what kind of life this Nassy was having. Dieter Lange explained that the men in those camps had problems with their passports or were resident aliens when the Germans took over. "But their status is being honored," Dieter Lange said. "There are even Jews there who aren't headed for—you know—the East."

There was something like a little hole in our talk then. I knew there was stuff he'd heard about what was happening in the East, besides the war, and he knew there were things I'd heard. The prisoners weren't the only "pieces." The SS guards, too, were moved from camp to camp as the need arose, or as some, especially the officers, felt their careers could be improved in another camp. Rumor said the new camps in the East offered the fastest chance for promotion, and jokers like Eichmann, Loritz, Remmele, Zill, Hoess, Koegel, and others had gone far up the ranks when they went to them. Maybe Dieter Lange was like me in this case. I'd heard a lot of stories about what the Germans did and were doing, but the stories coming in on the grapevines through prisoners being transferred from camp to camp were the kind that, if you believed, you also had to know the train had gone off the track carrying you with it.

Dieter Lange shook his head. I wasn't going to say anything unless he did. Something like this was so dark and bloody that whatever words you used to describe it were just the introduction to a composition that could never be finished. Dieter Lange shook his head again. He said he didn't understand why Winkelmann wanted to go East. But Winkelmann was old for a captain. In the East he might get ahead fast, if nothing happened to him first.

Sunday, May 17, 1942

The Winkelmanns have left. Dieter Lange said he told Winkelmann not to let himself get caught by the Russians because they were doing to the Germans what the Germans were doing to them.

Winkelmann said don't worry; he wasn't going to the front, but to a camp in Poland called Auschwitz, a big place with many smaller camps attached to it. There were important things going on there that should warrant quick promotion, Winkelmann said. Dieter Lange said he just grunted when Winkelmann told him that. When Dieter Lange, Winkelmann, and some others went into Munich for a farewell party, Anna, Ursula, and me had one of our own. Now I think I will miss Ursula. With her around I learned things I never knew, couldn't even imagine.

Fri., July 17, 1942

Goebbels had said that he was going to get even with the British for bombing Germany by punishing the Jews. There can't be a person in Germany who doesn't know what's already being done. Radio London said Americans bombed German bases in Holland on the Fourth of July. To which Dieter Lange said, "Hmmm, hmmm." It's more dangerous than ever to listen to London, but naturally, Radio Berlin is saying only good things or that things are not as bad as we may hear. You have to listen to the outside to know what's really going on.

Haven't seen any of the colored prisoners in a while. Dead or transferred?

New camp rule: Only German prisoners can beat other German prisoners. Well. All the camp police are German. The block leaders, seniors, secretaries, capos, and so on are mostly all German, too. Like Uhlmer in the canteen. He's handling all the whorehouse passes for Dieter Lange—but I still handle the money at the end of the day. Next in line come the Austrians, then the Poles, who could make good Germans *(Eindeutschungfähig)*. Same old shit. Everybody sticks together except colored people, and they don't because everybody else makes sure, one way or the other, that they can't.

Anna started moping around after Ursula and her husband left. Feeling sorry for herself, I guess. Also, she's back exploring the joys of the wine closet, and I don't mean just the wine.

John A. Williams

Sunday, August 23, 1942

It was very pleasant today. Everyone strolling around the camp, *spazierganger.* Here and there church services, the Catholics, the Protestants. Why not? There are 2,000 priests in this place. How many ministers I don't know. The priests and ministers both are called by the SS *Kuttenscheisser*—robed shitheads. (Prisoners with dysentery are called shitters—*Scheisser.*)

On days like this the Russians walk around and whisper about *Der Rasche Gang des Onkel Josef,* while they hunt down and exchange *Kippen,* cigarette butts. That means Stalin's Red Army is beating the shit out of the Germans.

There are a couple of places in camp called *Interessengebiet,* where the prisoners go to barter. Cigarettes and tobacco are the main forms of exchange. I don't know who decides the rate of exchange or how or why. It does no good to argue that last week the rate was lower. When the food hits rock bottom—like now—with turnip and beet tops and dandelion greens and one piece of bread served day after day after day, the canteen does good business—if the inmates have money, of course. Then there're the bartering places for those who don't. Today the *Valuta* is:

> 1 loaf of bread = 30 – 50 cigarettes
> 1 dead cat *(Katze)* = 20 cigarettes
> 1 small dog *(Hund)* = 30 cigarettes
> portion of soup = 5 – 6 cigarettes
> suspenders = 3 cigarettes
> 1 slice of a sausage = 1 – 2 cigarettes

Blocks 15 and 17 are being cleaned out again, which only means that Jews are going East to make room for more Jews coming from the West—France, Belgium, Holland, Luxembourg.

Thursday, Nov. 26, 1942, Thanksgiving Day back home

Oh-oh! Oh, boy!

I just got my paper out of Dieter Lange's storage because he's going to clean out everything that's not in cans or jars. Just in time, too.

He's now moved all the boxes and canned goods out to Anna's father's farm. I think they plan to bury stuff, including the gold teeth.

He's keeping the dried meat because there are food shortages in camp, and this time they're bad. They seem to be bad everywhere. A train transport from Danzig rolled into camp with 600 prisoners, Poles and Russians. There had been 900 when it started out. A ten-day trip. No food. Six corpses chewed down to the bone. Bad? It's worse than that. And Dieter Lange has heard that scrip will replace money in the camp. That word came from his big shots, he said. "Who the hell can use paper play money?" he said.

There are other things going on. In July the Americans had bombed Holland. Eighteen days ago they landed in North Africa! And the Russians have surrounded the German army at Stalingrad and are killing the soldiers and starting an attack of their own! Hitler said on the radio: "We knew the fate that awaits us if we lost, and for this reason we have not the remotest idea of a compromise. We have always had the Jews as internal enemies and now we have them as external ones." Got news for that joker. It ain't only Jews lookin' for his ass; it's the whole damned world. So what does the great leader do in return? Why, he takes over the rest of France.

And Anna drinks.

And Dieter Lange drinks. They drink and talk, him and Anna, about the idea they had while in Paris.

"We would go to France and from there to Portugal. Spain was out. Franco might have sent us back, but Portugal is neutral. Now France is out. We would have had Anna's father send us whatever he could make on the sale of things, you know. . . ."

"No," I say. "I don't know. What was supposed to happen to me?"

I drink, too, and get so mad my blood bubbles like spit on a hot stove.

"That's why we didn't do it," Anna says, the lying bitch.

"Yes," Dieter Lange says. "That's why."

Lies, all lies. I have the feeling that they want to climb on my good side and stay there. I think about the time off they gave me after hauling food during the last typhoid epidemic, the good word they put in for me with Dieter Lange's new partners. There is something more than sex now and music (which I'm not playing too much of) and watching Uhlmer and Lappus; it's my being American, colored but American, and maybe, if push comes to shove, I could put in a good word for them. Yeah, I would. In a pig's ass.

So I take myself another drink and hold up the glass in a toast to them for their kind thoughts and say, "Shit. I don't believe you. Shit."

Sunday, Dec. 13, 1942

The Langes were quiet and hung over when I left them this morning to go to the canteen. The guards at the *Jourhaus* were kind of evil, but the camp hummed with the talk of the raid last night. Everybody wanted to know if anyone else knew more than they did. Prisoners who'd come from the French coast or Holland or Belgium or camps in the north were familiar with the sound and rejoiced in what it meant.

A siren had sounded. It was the first time a siren like that had ever gone off in the compound or the camp. I crept to the window above the coal bin and peered out. Pitch black. No streetlights. Nothing.

I had been lying in the dark, my mind just one big hole, not able to sleep, wrapped in the darkness that opened dark doors that led softly, quietly, to deeper darknesses, considering for the first time, really, *Freitod,* suicide, and also thinking from some other, strange, removed distance, how silly that was, to have such a thought, when it was looking like Hitler had got both his balls in a nutcracker. But you wanted the Russians to hurry, the English, the Americans; you wanted the Germans to fold and step up and take their punishment. The sirens kept howling, echoing in the darkness. Then they fell silent.

I heard a long, low rumble, like Loa Aizan or maybe God snoring, but there wasn't a space in the sound; it just kept getting fatter and fatter, louder and louder, closer and closer, mightier and mightier, and then I could hear little spaces in it the way you can in vibrations. I felt the earth and house shiver, heard the glass in the windows whine. Air raid! I thought. Air raid! They are coming! Where, where? Munich, yes, Munich. Blow the motherfucker to bits.

Make dog meat of the people. Leave a hole a hundred miles deep where the city used to be.

Light began to slip into my darkness. The sound of the planes grew shorter and thinner, then thinner still, and weaker, and the night began to breathe again. The sirens didn't come back on for two hours.

So everyone wanted to talk about the raid.

"They're coming," everyone seemed to say. "The *Kuhtreiber Luftwaffe.*" The American cowboy army air force. It was coming. For a moment nobody seemed to mind that all they were eating right then was carrot greens in warm salted water and sawdust bread.

Monday, Dec. 28, 1942

Dieter Lange said it himself: "The way things are going, the next Christmas we celebrate a little bit the American way for real, eh?" It was Christmas Eve. We had decorated the tree, eaten, opened presents, and were drinking and playing records.

"Why do you talk like that?" Anna asked. "You know what they could do to you if they heard."

"You never minded before," he said. "A fact is a fact unless it's too close to home, is that it?"

"So," she said. "What do you and your Colonel and General Major plan to do about the situation? And does whatever you do include me?"

I was drinking pretty good myself, and I said to Dieter Lange, "She knows too much for it not to."

"Who asked you, big mouth? You forget yourself."

"So do you, you faggot," I said. The Christmas tree smelled pretty and I felt reckless as I threw myself into the middle of this drunken, nasty storm. Once it was just me and Dieter Lange who were so dangerously tied together, then Bernhardt, who had the upper hand, and Anna who also had a hand up, then Ursula. Now it was just the three of us and those two ghosts of Dieter Lange's; but they did not create the presence, the unending threat, that Bernhardt had. I smirked at him.

"You nigger queen," Dieter Lange said. He was growing red in the face. "Bitch."

Anna laughed. "Sometimes."

"You shut up, too." He filled his glass again and drank half of the cognac it contained. Between him and Anna, it was going fast. "You know I could have you both killed like that!" He snapped his fingers.

Anna laughed again.

Dieter Lange slapped her.

The Americans are coming, I thought, and went over and knocked him on his ass.

Anna laughed once more. *"Meine Held,"* she said. "My hero. Be careful of the tree."

Dieter Lange got to his feet and rushed me. I pushed him away. He looked puzzled. "Go to bed," I said. "Don't beat up your wife at Christmastime."

"Or any other time," she said. "Let's put him to bed and we can stay and talk."

"I don't want to talk," I said. We started up the stairs with Dieter Lange.

"Du Dreckneger," Dieter Lange mumbled, *"hau ab."*

"You shit Nazi," I said, *"You* fuck off."

I pushed him onto his bed, then went to the attic. When I came back down, Anna saw what I was holding and she began to giggle. Dieter Lange saw, too, when we rushed into the bedroom, and he shouted, "No!" But when we jumped on him and began to pull off his clothes and put on the lingerie, he didn't struggle so hard, it seemed to me.

I pulled off my clothes and Anna pulled off hers. Dieter Lange said no again, but I don't think he meant it.

Thursday, January 7, 1943

He came in roaring and stomping like a tank, throwing his cap, coat, gloves, and scarf on the floor, ripping his arctics off and hurling them against the wall of the foyer. He grabbed off the wall the picture of Hitler everyone has in his house and threw that on the floor, breaking the glass. Himmler's picture was next. Dieter Lange stomped on it until the shattered glass sounded like grains of sand beneath his feet. He kicked the remains of both pictures from the doorway through the living room. He pounced on the piano and beat it with both fists. He kicked chairs and sent them bouncing. He picked up the poker and wound up to throw it through the window, but Anna jumped on his back and, as he was shrugging her off, he seemed to get hold of himself. I stayed in the kitchen where I was waiting to serve dinner. Right then my name was Wes, and not in that mess, whatever it was.

"Cognac, Cleef!"

I grabbed the bottle I'd uncorked for dinner, filled a glass, and gave it to Anna to give to him, the way you'd give the lion tamer a hunk of meat instead of giving it to the lion itself. Dieter Lange groaned and his eyes watered with anger.

Krieger brand goods are no more, not here. There are food shortages all over Germany, not just in the camps. The Colonel and the General Major, Dieter Lange said, grinding his teeth, had directed that all KL canteen goods be diverted to the civilian population. Therefore, commandeered were all the services, supplies, and equipment of all camp canteen provisioning units. Supplies provided by canteen officers as individual vendors would now be compensated at the rate of 50 percent per item. The present rate of production, however, was expected to continue. Supplies ready for distribution would be gathered at a new central warehouse in Munich. Because it was necessary to maintain high public morale, this would not be disclosed for the present, as in the directive concerning the use of human hair in mattresses.

Dieter Lange was imitating his General Major, I took it to be, reciting all this like a prissy Prussian.

"It's the scrip," he said. "And the black market. They can check you too good with scrip. The black market, it's still real money—and good rates. They know what they're doing. It's people like me who're getting fucked and there's not a thing I can do."

"Pass it on," I said.

He was blubbering and snatching at his food like it was raw meat and he was a Doberman. Anna sat straight up and watched him carefully. I kept the table between me and him. "Just cut what you pay those women to cook and clean and pack those jars, and what you pay the guards. Tell them the same thing your partners told you. What can they do, what can they say?"

He rolled his eyes at me. I used to know about this kind of shit. A joker hires you for a date at one price. When you're finished, there's all this who-struck-john about the size of the house, or the house this or that, so it turns out that the money isn't anywhere near what you were told in the first place. What do you do? Don't take it, or take it and remember? You know the band leader got his before dividing the rest. So, yeah, pass it on. I've seen some bad fights over short money and two or three musical careers cut short, too. "They didn't tell you not to pass it on, did they?"

"I was going to do just that," Dieter Lange said. He smiled for the first time since coming home.

"Then why were you so mad, Dieter?" Anna asked.

I turned to the sink so she wouldn't look at me.

"I didn't think they'd cheat me so soon and so much, but however you figure it, that's what they're doing. They took over the operation all right. After you've done everything and delivered the goods right into their hands."

"War is hell," I murmured.

"What?"

"I said that's right. They can go to hell."

Dieter Lange passed the bottle around. "Listen. Everybody's getting ready." He held up his hand and rubbed his thumb across the fingers. "Everybody."

"Yes, and we've got ours, too, haven't we, Dieter?"

She was making sure, but he was slow to answer. "Yes, yes." Anna smiled like someone with a pat hand you're not supposed to know about. Most of the stuff they had was somewhere on her father's farm—or better be.

"So," she said, "let this go."

But I said, "Everybody's getting ready for what?"

They both looked at me. I just wanted them to say it, that things weren't going so hot: that business with Hess almost two years ago, the air raids coming deeper and deeper into Germany, the Cologne raid by a thousand planes last May, the slaughter at Stalingrad, the landings in North Africa by the Americans. Hell, we all listened to the radio in the dark, spinning dials, picking up London. Anna never saw the congestion in camp, which now held five times as many prisoners as it was designed for; she didn't see the bodies piled up beside the morgue or in ditches near the train sidings or thrown against the four sides of the crematorium. She didn't know that a prisoner found with a single louse on him went to his death like the signs said: *Ein Laus Dein Tod!* Typhus was typhoid's shadow. She closed her ears and mind to the sounds of the trains clanking in, mostly at night, with more "pieces," or clanking out for destinations in the East, the most recent being a load of Gypsies. Someone told me the guitar player Danko was among them. They let him keep his git so he could play for the rest of them on the trip. No one ever talks much about what they're doing to the Gypsies. I'd thought poor Danko was long dead. The place is as big as a city, and inmates hear last month's news only today.

"They allowed me to keep the name Krieger," Dieter Lange finally said. "Who knows, maybe after, when all's calm again, I can really go into business with it."

Yes, I thought, drinking along with them, so they can stick you with the rap when *Gotterdammerung* comes. No, they don't have to tell me why they think everyone's getting ready. I know. No Franz and Heller comedy here.

On average, we finish two bottles of cognac or something else just as strong every night when Dieter Lange is home.

Sunday, Jan. 31, 1943

Werner, who now seems less whipped, and Bader, Pacholegg, and Neff from the *Revier,* and some others, gathered in a corner of Block 1, where the Family is located. The Reds still want me to know things in case I get a break and get out. They never listen. That's not going to happen. Dieter Lange said so, and in this case I believe him. Still, they say, it's possible.

Pacholegg spoke first. The Schiller malaria experiments have been canceled, and anyway, it looks like the English and Americans are running the Afrika Korps out of Africa. The TPs who've not recovered well from the injections have vanished, and the others have returned to their blocks. The rule is that if the TPs survive the experiments in good shape, they're allowed to live; if not . . .

Neff says Rascher is in the final stages of the Arctic experiments. One Russian survived, but Himmler ordered him killed anyway. "We had a Jew, a Gypsy, and the Russian, who I don't think was Jewish. The usual stuff. The life jackets held them up. The water was 29° centigrade. We had gauges on their heads, stomachs, and in their assholes. People die quick when the head's chilled, the medulla and cerebellum. We always find up to a pint of blood in the cranium during the autopsy, or Rascher does."

Neff's voice was soft and slow. His glance kept falling on me.

"These were turning blue quick. They held hands. Rascher said to make them stop, but their grips were too tight, like they were already frozen together. The Russian kept hollering, 'Today us, tomorrow, you.' Rascher paid no attention. He expects such statements when people are dying. I had the feeling that holding hands made them last longer. And so did Rascher, but the Jew and the Gypsy went almost together. The Russian—all their names are locked in Rascher's files, as usual—after two and a half hours responded fully, but you know, there was damage inside. We begged Rascher to give him a shot. The Russian laughed. At three hours and fifteen minutes we pulled him out, covered him, and he came back all the way. What to do with him? Did the survivor rule apply to Russians? Rascher contacted Himmler's office directly. Himmler said the rule did not apply to Poles, Russians, or Jews. A *Kommando* from Herbertshausen told me they marched him out, all alone, and shot him, but not before he said again, 'Today me, tomorrow, you.'"

I said, "I heard from another assistant there were women."

Neff nodded. "They were used to keep the men warm. From Ravensbrueck. Rascher even had two men and two women fucking at zero degrees. Right after, their temperatures rose right back to normal."

Bader said, "So every pilot who gets shot down in the North Sea is going to have a *Nutte* along to revive him?" He snorted.

"You watched?" Werner asked.

"Of course. We all did. We had to monitor the gauges. Listen, that's not as bad as decompression. Four hundred Arctic tests, maybe ninety died. The rest, mainly Russians and Jews, on Himmler's orders, were killed."

Sometimes you can see men trying to remember. Those people of the Family who were there, got up and walked one by one to the window, lit cigarettes, if they had them, or mooched them from someone else—not without grumbling from the donor—and asked Neff and Pacholegg questions:

"Exactly how many Russians in the experiments?"

Neff and Pacholegg looked at each other.

Pacholegg said, "We work different shifts for different doctors. It's hard to say."

Werner said, "Hundreds, surely. Thousands?"

Neff said, "Maybe two thousand, but that would include talk of the work of other doctors."

"Which ones?" Bader asked.

"Well, in addition to Rascher, Schiller, and Deuschl—you know Rascher also developed the cyanide pill. For suicide or execution," Neff said.

"Grawitz," Pacholegg said. "He does stuff on infections."

"Fahrenkamp. He works with Rascher," Neff said. "And Dr. Blaha, he's a Czech, also does some things with Rascher. What, I don't know. But if you have a tattoo that's not a number and fall into his hands, it's too bad."

"Finke and Holzloehner—"

"Siegfried Ruff," Neff said, interrupting.

"How can all this be going on right under our noses?" Werner said.

"If we knew, what could we do about it?" one of the Family asked. "Nothing."

I looked outside the window. The 'Platz was empty. Shit, it was cold out there. In winter, free time was time to sleep, on the floor, sitting in a corner, anywhere but the bunk, unless you had doctor's orders. The men walked around beating the rhythm of the doctors' names into their memories. They would have to remember a long time; how long, no one knew. I had only to remember until I could get here, now, with pencil and paper.

Neff and Pacholegg sat there after the Family had broken up. They smoked the cigarettes they'd been given with a leisurely sadness, pausing to look at them as though they might speak. I said, "You remember stuff like that, what you told us?"

Pacholegg shrugged. "I can't forget it."

There was a space between us and the others, the space you feel between yourself and someone with a disease you could catch. These two, and others who worked with them, knew too much. They knew they were going to die, be bundled off to the Bunker or trucked out into the gray mist of a new day to Herbertshausen; no six-in-the-evening public hanging for them. They'd not been caught committing a crime like stealing food or trying to escape or fucking another inmate or getting fucked by one; but like so many of the *Sonderkommando* details, Neff, Pacholegg, and the other assistants were branded. Maybe that's what their cigarettes told them when they looked at them.

I said, "Like me. I think I can't forget things, either."

"No," Neff said. "You're a musician. You remember things. There's a difference. And that's why you're here. That's why we say things to you. You're an American."

It is such a wonder to me, this "American" thing, the faith these jokers seem to have in them, the Americans, the respect, the hope that it will be the Americans, finally, who rescue them. (They would take the Russians, too, but only if they had to.) In the abstract, the American army cowboys, the Statue of Liberty, Franklin Delano Roosevelt, the Four Freedoms they talked about on the radio, have worked on the prisoners like a slow electric current through the forbidden foreign broadcasts, shocking them with possibilities. And to many of them, even those who once laughed at me, I am the symbol of all these things. Most of them don't know what America is really like, and probably wouldn't care as long as the truth didn't disturb the dream.

You learn something every day. The Prisoner Company was always for the toughest guys. Now the PC holds some of the Blacks who used to belong to the *Zazou* jitterbugs and to the Edelweiss Pirates; the Pirates ran away from conscription—but got caught. And also there are what are called the *Meuten*, anti-Nazi gangs touched with a little Red.

How did I learn this? From the canteen I watched a *Postenkette*, a ring of guards, empty Block 7 and march the prisoners to the siding where a boxcar waited, empty.

"Russian front," said a young runner for the SS who'd just got some cigarettes. Then he told me who those kids were.

All the Prisoner Company inmates wear the *Himmlerstrasse* haircut—bald except for a strip of hair running from front to back—and have the targets painted on the backs of their jackets. "*Kanone Futter,*" the runner said, jerking his thumb toward the boxcar into which the kids were climbing, the targets on their backs rippling as they moved. "*Wurst Fleisch.* They'll have the Russians in front of them and the SS behind them."

Monday, March 29, 1943

For two weeks they came, day and night, the RAF and the Americans. I didn't know there were that many airplanes in the world. Down they came from the northwest, shaking loose clouds in the daytime and stars at night. It was like someone drawing a bow across a tremendous bass fiddle. The target was Munich, of course. We didn't need Radio Berlin to tell us that. I wondered if Schwabing was still there, the university where the students—or some of them— had called for a revolt against the Nazis and were executed for it, the Englischer Garten, the Marienplatz. I just wondered. Didn't matter a piece of shit to me whether they were or not. As for the students, it took them a long, long time to get brave, but maybe they belonged to another generation. Maybe.

From here and Mauthausen, even until now, details were gathered and put on trains, buses, and trucks. Sometimes they marched along Dachauerstrasse all the way into Munich to dig out unexploded bombs and bodies everyone knew were under the bricks and stone because they smelled. Or hauled away the shattered buildings. Or repaired the water and gas lines, the electric wires. Or made it possible for Siemens and BMW to continue making stuff for the war. Or laid new track for the trains. Could they say no, these men who were half-starved, who fought off typhus and typhoid, brutality, injustice, bigotry, prejudice? Those who came back said some of the people spat on them, while others offered them crusts of bread or half cups of ersatz coffee.

Many didn't come back; the *Himmelfahrtskommandos,* the bomb disposal details, they went to heaven. In bits and pieces and a loud noise they didn't even hear. And the ones the walls fell on. And the ones who just died in Munich instead of Dachau because that was where their hearts quit. And the ones who walked away, their filthy *Drillich,* striped uniforms, easy targets for the aging SA overseers and SS, who made believe they were Russians.

Friday, May 14, 1943

The camp is quivering. Everyone wants to talk about the war, the victory, the *Sonnenaufgang,* and *Zukunft,* the time after the liberation. But the guards are touchy and evil. The prisoners who are able, talk of these things in whispers, move away from approaching guards like small, quick waves of water.

As the winter at Stalingrad when the Russians turned back the Germans had been the most fierce in half a century, so this spring has been the coldest in memory. The *Himbeerpfluckerkommandos* haven't been sent out to pick raspberries. These are the sick and weak. Way out among the raspberry bushes, when a decent spring comes, and the earth has been enriched by who knows what, the SS orders the shooting of the prisoners and reports they tried to escape. That's the *Kommandoaufgel.* The capos just march out the details to an isolated place, usually north of camp, kill everyone with a shovel, a club, an axe—whatever's handy—and return the report to the SS detail officer, "Command dissolved."

We haven't had anything on our shelves for two weeks. Uhlmer and Lappus have been detailed to rifle the Red Cross packages and whatever else gets into camp. Potato soup and sawdust bread make up dinner. Sawdust bread and hot water passing for coffee are for breakfast.

Wednesday, September 29, 1943

Goddamn, oh, goddamn!

In mid-June the Allies—I think that means mostly Americans—landed in Sicily! And Italy surrendered three weeks ago! Each bit of news like that was like a loaf of fresh, real bread. Speaking of which, Dieter Lange and Anna have been slipping tins of stuff back from her father's farm. And fresh meat.

Oh! I felt like playing the piano and singing, making a joyful noise, but I'd have to fight the Langes. They're drunk most of the time now when he's around. And they spend a lot of time on the farm. Probably getting some hideaway ready. Ha, ha, ha!! Forgive me. It's just too exciting to write sometimes and besides, Dieter Lange and Anna snoop around a lot now. I have a large cracker tin that I store you in, wrapped in a raincoat. There's a corner space in the cellar ceiling where you just fit. Now I have all the pages together. Pardon the crayon.

Back in May there was news of a big fight with the Jews in Warsaw. The grapevine now carries word of riots at a couple of camps in the East where Jews are being killed. They say there are whole towns in Eastern Europe where there are no more Jews; they've all been killed, and they are doomed in Dachau, just like the Gypsies. That's what they say.

The grapevine. Prisoners come here from about thirty-five camps, Dieter Lange says, when he's raving about moving the "pieces," and inmates are transferred from here—those that live—to about thirty-five other camps. Sometimes they're sent back to the camps they came from. Really moving the pieces.

———

Sunday, October 17, 1943

"I'll be glad when you're dead, you rascal, you; I'll be glad when you're dead, you rascal, you . . ."

The tune just climbed into my head a few days ago as I was walking home from camp, just climbed up there, pushed a few things around, and made itself comfortable. It comes in different rhythms: the Dead March, slow and heavy; or the bounce and tinkle of a ragtime piece; or the up and down of a Pine Top Smith boogie-woogie; or some old stiff Paul Whiteman ballroom number where the rhythm is like somebody scared walking on cracking ice; or some banjo or guitar-driven, foot-stomping Dixieland beat.

I see Loa Aizan blinking in time to whatever rhythm "Rascal" plays in. Sometimes I think I hear God humming it to Hitler, then Dieter Lange or Anna will say, "What's that tune you're humming?" And I say, "What tune?" When I catch them looking at each other a certain way, I know I've been humming it and get hold of myself. But it always comes back.

We're down to Greek and Yugoslav cigarettes. Forget the salt and pepper packs. Food is so scarce there's no need for them. One of the priests sells lengths of rope to be used as belts. Does good. Another guy sells little squares of paper to roll straw, potato skins, grass, or anything that will smoke like a cigarette. Dieter Lange and Anna don't care anymore about making cigarettes to sell out of whatever is handy. "Scrip is shit," Dieter Lange says. "Stop that goddamn humming, Cleef. You're driving me crazy!"

What's doing good is the whorehouse. It's in the storeroom where prisoners' clothes are kept in the *Wirtschaftsgebaude*. There are mountains of shoes there, and pants and jackets and things, and even though they've been disinfected, the place smells like bodies rotting in the shade. Lappus and Uhlmer at first liked taking care of the passes and handling the scrip because they thought they could get a little pussy once in a while, and maybe they did. Now, they don't seem to like it as much. (Not the pussy, the job.)

A good-looking pros is a rare thing. Maybe it's because good-looking women can always find someone to look after them. The times I've been over during the hours of business, it was hard to tell if the women had ever been good-looking. The good lookers are usually snapped up by the SS. The so-so by the block seniors, boss capos, straw capos, and on down the line until what we get are what you wouldn't look at twice on your drunkest night, no matter how much you wanted to "jelly-jelly." Women who were selling before they came to Dachau (and maybe that's why they're here) I guess make up about half those working. The rest just want to stay alive, especially if they are Jews or Russians or Poles or Gypsies.

Women prisoners live outside the wall in a couple of blocks, in another enclosure. Most work for the SS officers in their homes, watching kids, cleaning, cooking, and shit like that. Most of the women capos and SS guards are dykes, big as men, bass at you in a minute, mustaches creeping on their upper lips. Some of the women inmates brought little kids with them and others have had babies in the camp. Gitzig is the only man I knew in this place who was happy to claim he was a father. I don't think I hum "Rascal" when I see this. And I don't know what happens to those babies and kids. It's only the fucking that people care about, men and women. You would think that would be the last thing the prisoners think of. But it's the first, right up there next to food. I am thinking about every woman I ever heard of who fucked for a drink or a good time or to feed her kids or to keep a job or just to be with a guy.

Sunday, Dec. 19, 1943

Christmas next Saturday. Bitter cold. No wood for the stoves. Now is the time of *Nix Travacho, Nix Camela.* (That's a mix of German and Spanish.) No work, no food. Food? A pig wouldn't touch the shit coming out of the kitchen these days. So the weak get weaker. Now they have wagons to carry the food vats down the 'Strasse. Most prisoners aren't strong enough to carry them anymore. The strongest men are the ones in charge of things. They aren't thin. They look almost as healthy as the guards. Cocksuckers. You notice them right away.

In the canteen, where we burn old cardboard cartons when we have them, you hear again the stories from the blocks of the *Leichen-*

zuchter, the corpse growers, inmates who don't tell when another prisoner has died so the dead guy's food rations can be used. In winter it takes longer for the dead guys to stink, so you naturally hear more of these stories in cold weather than you ever do in summer.

Good men who are strong don't last here. I mean jokers who are strong in the usual ways, good fighters, or they have powerful faith, guys you can trust, like that. Once in a while you hear a story of a man who turned on the guards or just plain said no to something that would hurt other prisoners. Of course, the man is killed. The guards wonder how such a person could behave that way, because these camp guards recognize strengths through training and instinct, and maybe they are even jealous or afraid of them. The KLs are designed to break strong men like Werner and Bader; they are either broken or bent (in ways that are not obvious), made into capos or block leaders or runners; and they serve the SS as sort of "decent" men other prisoners work well for. They are watched very closely.

Then there are the quiet, shuffling, watchful men who never look you in the eye, maybe because they fear what they might see or what might be seen in *their* eyes, who whine and snivel, steal, grow corpses, do almost anything for food—*food*—who know when to work hard and when not to. They move through their days like they are walking through a bayou filled with cottonmouths; they survive the way moles survive, or rats, or anything else that lives in dark, underground holes. These inmates are inconspicuous, which is, for survival, the best way to be here. They grow a toughness I can't describe; it's slow, smooth, and colorless—or colorful if need be, like some lizards. You can't really call them hustlers or operators since you know they want only to live. Their hustle—yes, their lives —depends on not being noticed, on not being seen in uniforms that are too clean or shoes that are too good, on appearing to have become exactly what the Germans (it's easy to forget, and shameful too, that there are many German prisoners here as well) wanted— the hidden, quiet parts of some awful machine. But I'd sure hate to see a world filled with such people when the war is over. People forget pain, laugh at it when it stops hurting. I want them to remember.

There are only a few names for the strong—*stark,* "Kong," *chlopak*—but a whole bunch for the weak, names that've come since Dr. Nyassa flew to the wire: *Zaramustafa* is what they call Muslims from Yugoslavia, and *Muselmann* is for prisoners so weak that they look like they're praying all the time. Then there is the *Schwimmer,* whose arms float around to help him keep balance as he tries to walk, and *Schmuckstuck,* "a jewel of a guy," which means he's a goner, he's so weak. There are dozens of names. Everybody jumps on the weak until, finally, the SS makes *Selektion*—on the detail, in the blocks, at random—and the shuffling marches begin to the rifle ranges or to the wagons lined up for transport to Hartheim Castle. (I am well-known to the guards; they see my face from a distance, so they know I "belong" to sort of a big shot. This continues to be a good thing, a very good thing, otherwise I would have been fertilizing flowers by now.)

And practically everybody who isn't with those poor bastards feels they deserve to die because they let themselves become weak. What bullshit. And what a bad time to go. The Russians are almost in Poland. The Americans are in Italy. Every night and day when the weather is good, a German city is bombed to hell. So I wonder why aren't these prisoners rising up, like those Jews in Warsaw or some of the other camps we've heard about? I know: Fuck the Jews. They had no choice, like the Gypsies. If the machine does nothing else, it will make Jews and Gypsies disappear as though they never existed in the first place. *We* will wait, though, even if they kill us one by one and empty the whole goddamn place. But each prisoner believes, with all his heart, that *he* will not be on *Selektion,* that he will get by, and that by next Christmas he will be free. Merry Christmas, diary.

Tuesday, January 11, 1944

Yesterday Dieter Lange took me up to the attic and pointed to one corner the farthest away from the stairs. "Tear up the floorboards from there when we need it," he said.

I know they have been trading tinned goods and preserves for small bags of soft coal and bottles of coal oil for the stove they now have in their room. I have no heat in mine. The whole house smells of kerosene.

There is no more coal to sift for in the ashes from the furnace, and the ice on the windows is so thick you can't see outside. It takes a whole day to thaw out the food we have in the window box.

The piano keys play thick and sad, like they are pounding in deep snow.

The war, especially in the East, is sucking the life out of Germany with each blast of freezing wind rushing from the Alps.

The best-dressed, best-fed prisoners are those who work in the munitions factories adjacent to the camp. For the war effort. And these are the "Pearheads," the *Birnkopfer*, the guys with the training to work the machines over there with the civilians.

Nothing has changed except there are more prisoners. From 180 men to a block there are now over a thousand—three, four, and sometimes six to a bunk, with three rows of bunks. There are 2,000 men in Block 30 alone.

In the canteen they talk of the bastards with dysentery who can't get to the bathrooms because they aren't working or because of curfew. They climb out the windows to shit on the rooftops. Neff has told me that some men are so weak that, to avoid punishment for messing themselves, they crap in their food bowls and then try to clean them out so they can eat from them. That's another cause of typhoid. And all the signs about louses don't help; that's why the typhus.

I used to think of the canteen as being like a barber shop back home, where jokers gathered to gossip, get news of people they knew, make a quick trade, or play the numbers. No numbers here, though, just "pieces," and they have driven Dieter Lange crazy. He goes through the motions. The canteen is bleak, gray, and cold. Anything we get on the shelves lasts only a few minutes, if it can be eaten, but usually we're out of stock.

One day some inmates were gathered around the stove, in which there was no heat whatsoever. It just made them feel there was heat because what they surrounded was the stove. One of them had an old magazine. They were playing "Eat." He opened the pages slowly, and when there was a picture of a steaming plate of food, beautiful cake, or something else to eat, the first one to jam his face into the page got to "eat" it. The pages became wet with spit. Uhlmer could not watch; Lappus was amused. Like me, they weren't starving, were merely a little bit hungry most of the time. And cold.

The Russians reached Poland almost two weeks ago. Oh! That sounds so good! I'll be glad when you're dead, you rascal, you.

Bader says that sonofabitch Karlsohn and other SS guards his age have been sent to the Eastern front. (Please, you Russians, don't miss!) They've been replaced by wounded or sick soldiers from there, and even some civilians from the town.

Waiting. We're all waiting, like for some lover to come, only he hasn't said exactly what time or what day; but you know he's coming because he's sent you little notes from North Africa, Sicily, Italy, and almost every day from Russia. Imagine—I'm forty-four and still looking for the best loving ever! Freedom! *Freiheit! Befreiung!* Liberation!

And across the 'Strasse the doctors still work, stacking the dead like logs, and we stare at them. They have nothing to do with us. They are just "pieces" lost in the shuffle.

Saturday, March 25, 1944

The SS replacement soldiers from the Eastern front have sometimes talked of troop trains being put on sidings so trainloads of Jews can be hurried to the camps there. When they're asked why, the soldiers, almost every time, say nothing and draw a finger across their throats.

There are some things I don't understand about this war, like how come the Germans are invading Hungary now. I thought they were aces, Germany and Hungary.

The Langes are having some terrible arguments. Anna wants to go live on the farm and Dieter Lange doesn't want her to leave him. Then he should come with her, she says, but she knows he can't. All that talk about afterward, when Germany won, he was going off on his own to do this, and she was going off alone to do that. Now they're afraid one will get to whatever they have stashed away before the other one can. The General Major and the Colonel aren't letting us get anything for the canteen, and Dieter Lange knows they've conned him good and he can't do one damn thing, though he tells me he's been trying to pry goods loose from the ILAGs like Laufen and Tittmoning. Wonder how those colored guys are doing there. I wonder if there are any more here. When there are, the other prisoners call them *Zulukaffer*. Since there are always new prisoners who don't know me, I am a *Zulukaffer*, too—but I am Dieter Lange's *Zulukaffer*.

I've been with Anna. She likes to dress up, put on lipstick and perfume now, and we dance to records. Acts like she's Brunhild. Cries in bed. Tries to get lost doing it, it seems to me. She's getting strange. She'll start a conversation and then break off to stare at something like it will remind her of what she wanted to say. I wait and wait until finally I have to say, "What?" or, "What were you going to say?" That makes her furious. I try to get her to speak English, but that's a waste of time.

And I've been with Dieter Lange. With both it's like maybe that time will be the last time. But Dieter Lange gets so drunk he's useless. He's so busy, busy, busy, brushing off this or that, complaining that things haven't been cleaned or the figures I give him don't look right or Anna doesn't put enough starch in his shirts. He's like a damned fussy old woman one minute and a drunken pig the next. They drive me crazy, the both of them.

They say Dr. Grawitz is doing new experiments with Gypsies. Pacholegg and Neff say that's true.

Nobody wants to ask what. Nobody wants to ask why, with all the talk of the Allies landing in France soon.

"Causing new kinds of infections, then trying to cure them," Pacholegg says.

It's very muddy outside and the men are strapped to the rollers, crushing gravel into the mud. It is something to do.

"Seeing if people die drinking too much sea water," Neff says.

Still nobody asks why.

Friday, April 14, 1944

The flower beds are being turned, the earth raked. Suppose the blooms turn out to be little bodies of prisoners, just swaying in the breeze.

During the winter we all noticed that the smoke from the crematorium *never* stopped coming out. It was like a factory, running all day and all night long. That many people dead, many more gone, yes, Another Man Done Gone, without so much as a good-bye or a prayer.

Anna has noticed that the wives with children seem to be vanishing, leaving. "Running like momma and baby rats together," she says. If she had kids now, she could use them as a passport out of Dachau to the Black Forest. Or her father's farm.

Some of the women out here, and there must certainly be some, would have fallen out if they'd known about those eighty Jewish kids who came in last week from France. I heard it from Werner, who now seems to have found the old purpose to his life. The oldest kid, he said, was fifteen, the youngest eight, and they knew they were going to die because their parents had been killed in Buchenwald. They put the kids in Block 7, and a few days later they were transported to Hartheim, and probably were damned glad to go after spending time with some of those hard cases. Eighty kids, eighty small "pieces" Dieter Lange wouldn't have to worry about. Younger than Pierre.

You would think if a killer was told, "Stop killing, the cops are coming," the killer would stop. But no. I think this place, Germany, is like a sanctified church, where the spirit takes hold of one person, then two, three, or four catch it, then the whole church, and nothing stops the dancing, singing, and crying until somebody falls out and cracks his head or everyone's just too exhausted to move any more. Sometimes, even the people who've fallen out still quiver and shake on the floor. Never liked sanctified churches. Always scared me.

Friday, May 26, 1944

They're coming, but it's taking forever. The days seem like weeks, the weeks like years. We've even gotten used to the bombers going and coming. They seem to have little to do with us except for the companies of *Himmelfahrtskommandos* that march to the trucks to dig bombs out of Munich's belly (while singing "Lili Marlene," which they hope will get them some bread with marmalade, maybe a cup of tea or coffee from a civilian). We want the planes to come, not by the thousands, but by the hundreds of thousands—but every time they come, a mess of prisoners goes into Munich to die. Why the hell can't they bomb this place, bomb all the camps, destroy the factories and rails everywhere, since the prisoners are dying anyway?

My mind seems to be on the *Zukunft*. This year, God, this year. Loa Aizan, please, now. I'm forty-four, but I feel like ninety-four. Will I still be able to play? I know the music's changed. I can guess what the colored musicians are doing with the music from what I hear the German bands play on the radio. But how are they doing it? What keys are they playing in, what chord changes are they making, what times are they playing in? Colored folks fuck with white folks' music, turn it inside out like you do a worn-out collar. But will I be able to do that? Fingers gone all dumb, the piano my enemy, just sitting there all out of tune, daring me to take some licks at it. Mr. Wooding, wonder how he's doing, if he's got hold to what's going on. Instead of whining and carrying on when I was in touch with Willy Lewis, I should've been talking about music. I listen to "Don't Sit Under the Apple Tree," "Dear Mom," "The White Cliffs of Dover," "Moonlight Becomes You," "When the Lights Go on Again," stuff like that and it all sounds soft and tender. Young and sweet. Slow-drag stupid. Stick your head out the door for a minute and smell those human steaks cooking and you know ain't nobody singing the right songs. Not for this shit.

Thinking like that brought me back to the piano and to some of the things I was doing before I had the band at *Lebensborn*, when I thought I heard all kinds of things where I hadn't heard them at all before. I didn't even ask if I could play. The Langes are always drunk anyway. They just sit there fussing, him saying she took too much of the hooch, or her saying he's drinking too fast. Just waiting for the news, just waiting to pick up Radio London or Armed Forces Radio on the shortwave. Dieter Lange got him a new set so he could catch it all, including a station called the Voice of America. Said, "Everybody out here has got one or if they haven't, they know where they can listen to one." So they can know which way to jump, I think.

The first time in a while back on the box, when I wasn't feeling so sure of myself, I slid into "Yellow Dog Blues." Playing was like sticking my fingers in Karo syrup, but the more I played, the more the piano loosened up, the more it became less spongy, kinda friendly, like it knew what I wanted to do. I tried on "Muskrat Ramble" and "Tiger Rag." "I Ain't Got Nobody" seemed a natural since I knew that piece backward, forward, and sideways, and then some. I think Dieter Lange and Anna calmed down a little, because I didn't hear them fussing. I felt old-fashioned, but I just punched the keys and kicked the pedal into "I Surrender Dear," and then feeling like to hell with it, jumped into "One O'Clock Jump" and "Moon Glow," but damn, even *I* didn't know if it was going to land on its feet. It did. "Body and Soul," and my skin grew a few goose pimples. That's a dark number with a lot of addresses on it. Then I did some of the things that came over Armed Forces Radio—"Gee Baby Ain't I Good to You," done by a pianist I never heard of, Nat Cole, and Ellington's band (new one, I think), ripping with "Take the 'A' Train." Then a really swinging band doing "Apple Honey." Woody Herman, I think. Big, *big* band, lots of brass. They don't play too many colored bands, and the singers are white, too, folks named Crosby, Sinatra, Haymes, Como, Eberle, women like Jo Stafford, Helen Ward, and Helen Forrest. Not too many vocalists like Jimmy Rushing, the Ink Spots, Ella Fitzgerald, or Herb Jeffries. It's a special day when they play those singers.

I tried another number I'd heard, "This Time the Dream's on Me," and just to give Anna and Dieter Lange a little something, I threw "Blue Skies" at them. It didn't take. Besides, it's not much anyway. Some of these white-boy tunes you just can't do anything with but let them die, because they aren't songs, just tunes. Russian white boys are different. On Sundays sometime you hear them singing in Blocks 6, 20, and 22, where most of them are segregated. (It's funny using that word with white people, *Absondern, Rassentrennung.*) If you could sing blues in Russian, those jokers got it. Maybe that's why I didn't like Russia when the band went there with Mr. Wooding —what those people suffered was too close for comfort. In the canteen the Russians are the only ones look like they don't want to kick my ass at first sight. But then, I got my stare when some of these jokers been pissed on all their lives walk in and right away pull that European-type cracker shit on me. Number one, they haven't ever had no colored man look at them like that in their life, and number two, they look at number 3003 on my jacket and figure I know something about staying alive, and I see them thinking, If *he* can do it, so can I. But they don't know the arrangement for that number. Well, sometimes I wonder about it myself. Anyway, the more I played, the better I felt and the better the piano sounded. To hell with anything else but that.

It's yesterday I really want to write about.

Dieter Lange has been away checking the camps at Augsburg, Kaufering, and Allach, so I've spent the time in the canteen. Anything not to be stuck a long time alone with Anna, not that Dieter Lange gives a damn anymore. In fact, it seems to get him hot if he thinks I've been with her.

So I'm at the canteen window when the morning roll call begins, before six, the sun not quite up. I never risk sleeping when roll call starts; never can tell when some guard might take a notion to see what I was up to. I always get up and watch the prisoners march down the 'Strasse with breakfast, see them like chickens without heads, dressing, making their beds, washing, eating, all in half an hour, and then rushing into formation on the Dancing Ground, just row upon row upon row of stiff, striped men in that flat, gray light that everyone hopes to see again tomorrow. The slow-rising sun throws thin shadows from the poplar trees that square the camp. Once they were just sprigs stuck between an occasional white birch tree; now they stand like spears with their handles jabbed into the ground. The count comes in, block after block. Then the details are ordered to march out. The capos wait for their men.

No one moves.

I don't understand what's going on. For a minute, I think maybe I hadn't heard the command. I stare past the backs of thousands of men to see the expression on the face of the ss officer in charge. But I can't see it from here because now they have to use all the 'Platz, which covers a large area. So I imagine his face, imagine him looking at the loudspeaker like maybe there was something wrong with it.

"Alles heraus; im Gleichritt . . . Marsch!" he calls again. "All out; in step . . . March!"

There is no motion. Every man I can see on the 'Platz this morning looks like something strange growing out of the earth. It is so quiet.

The roll-call officer backs away from the loudspeaker and his assistants huddle around him. The guards on the 'Platz hike their rifles to the ready. The prisoners aren't going to work! The roll-call officer and his men are looking at a group of Russian officers from Block 6; I can barely see them from the right corner of my window. Two or three roll-call clerks scurry back and forth between the Russians, whose spokesman seems to be a ramrod-stiff oldish guy, and a couple of block leaders.

Willy Bader is escorted to the roll-call officer, who is looking mad now, scowling at the Russians. He goes nose to nose with Bader, maybe asking him what the hell is going on. Bader gestures and shrugs and points to the prisoners, then to the Russians. The Russian officer marches out, turns around to face the prisoners, and leans toward the loudspeaker. "Go to work," he shouts in bad German. His voice carries tough. "Do not sacrifice yourselves for us."

Later I find out the Family and the International Committee had told the inmates not to fall out for their work details in protest over the rumored plan to shoot ninety-two Russian officers. Thirty thousand for ninety-two.

But still the prisoners don't move. I wonder if they would have done this a year ago. Certainly not two years ago.

The roll-call officer marches off to the *Wirtschaftsgebaude.* He returns within minutes as trucks filled with ss from the barracks roar through the guardhouse gate and park with the back ends of the trucks facing the prisoners. There are machine guns in them with men already crouched to fire.

The sun behind the gray lends a kind of silver shimmer to the scene. Is it really happening? Still nobody moves. The ss reinforcements, hundreds of them, spread out, ready. The roll-call officer again gives the command to fall out and march away, and as before, there is no movement.

The Russian officer wants to speak to Bader; the roll-call officer agrees. The Russian is insisting, Bader is arguing, but the Russian finally wins. He shouts to the prisoners, "Comrades, march off! Good-bye!" The Russian's name, I find out later, was Lieutenant Colonel Tarassow.

Bader speaks to the roll-call officer's assistants. One of them speaks to the officer, and he gives the order to march out again. This time the striped forest moves, and even as the details march off, singing loud as usual, the ss begins to herd the Russian officers into small groups and leads them away. By now the sun is way up. It seems the prisoners have left something behind that took years to grow.

That was yesterday and the rumor was true. The ss shot them all.

Wed., May 31, 1944

Dr. Rascher is in the Bunker. His wife's been sent to Ravensbrueck. Because of the experiments? Ah, no. Because they lied about "their" kids. Pacholegg thinks also that with the Russians moving fast out of the East, and the Allies moving up Italy, and with the talk, talk, talk of invasion across the English Channel, maybe somebody wants to close Rascher's mouth. What about the other jokers? Pacholegg provides an answer to why the experiments continue. If the results look good, he says, maybe the American, British, and French pharmaceutical companies will lease the patents. It's all about money, like with the sulfa drugs.

Tuesday, June 6, 1944

The news we've waited so long for . . . the invasion! It started last night when the Americans landed in France. Rome fell about the same time. Dieter Lange has not left the radio in almost a week.

Sunday, June 11, 1944

Yesterday the bombers hit Munich again. From Italian bases this time. Dieter Lange says he heard on the radio that there were 750 bombers. "That fat-ass, Goering, doesn't fight, doesn't send his men to fight. It's the anti-aircraft guns he wants to use instead. Why does he save the planes?" he whines.

Turns out there was a *Wuwa*, a secret weapon, after all. It's a *Vergel-tungswaffen*, a get-even bomb. And they started dropping it on the English last month. Goebbels tells us this, and so does Radio London and Armed Forces Radio. The British call them buzz bombs. Dieter Lange is angry because Germany waited so long to use them.

Thursday, July 20, 1944

We got the news in the darkness in which we sat listening to the radio. This news came from Radio Berlin: Somebody tried to kill Hitler with a bomb. The report said he was alive. Dieter Lange took his mouth off a whiskey glass long enough to say, "You can't trust them. Maybe he's dead, and if he's dead—maybe it's over. But some of the generals don't want it to be. Sometimes I think the goddamn generals are worse than Hitler." The announcer gave a bunch of names of generals with Hitler who were wounded. Nobody got killed? We'll see. (I'll be glad if you're dead you rascal, you.)

Anna said, "Damn it, they *missed!*"

The Russians are 100 miles from Warsaw. Prisoners again pull out the maps. "The Russians are here." Pointing. "The Allies will come this way in France." More pointing. Every prisoner is a general and a prophet. The war will be over in three months, five months, two months, ten months; Germany will quit day after tomorrow, next week, the first of the month—but not before they kill everybody. Some of Werner's people went missing, and while trying to find out where they might be, he ran into this: When the trains come in to the sidings now, the SS asks all those who are university graduates or who speak a few languages, to step out. They will act as interpreters. This is an important task, say the SS. And of course, always willing to be special, not one of your ordinary people, they rush forward gladly. Then they are marched out to the rifle range (instead of a special campus barracks) and are shot dead. Werner's people saw this, so they, too, were killed.

Bader told me that in addition to "regular" inmates, there are now almost 8,000 women here, nearly half of them Jewish, plus 300 German civilian workers who have been charged with some crime, and 4,000 more from assorted countries. "And," he said, "You're not the only American anymore. There are nine more down in Block 24. They're American pilots. Shot down. They're to be moved to an officer's POW camp. There are 685 other prisoners of war also waiting for transfer, to a *Stalag*. There are only 262 Gypsies left . . ."

His voice drifted off. It was warm, a nice day with dust floating lightly in the air, kicked up by the marching details, the camp work. Not too much wind, and it was blowing from the east, so the smell from the crematorium wasn't bad. Details were hauling away the bodies outside the *Reviers* and those beside the railroad tracks. You look at the corpses and think of the Americans, British, and Russians coming day by day a step closer, and you wonder if they will arrive soon, or if the Germans with their *Selektions*, which seem to be more frequently random, will succeed in making more prisoners vanish up the chimney, or through the doors of Hartheim Castle in Linz, or out on the rifle ranges. There isn't a prisoner who doesn't wonder about this.

These are the only realities: securing food enough to stay alive, having energy enough to avoid *Selektion*, and doing both successfully enough to enjoy liberation. There persists the fear that for revenge, the SS will kill us. They *must* kill us. They exist to kill us. Though there are many thousands more of us to kill, this seems not to be of great concern to them. The machine pistol and the machine gun and the areas in which we are confined make it as easy as shooting a bunch of small animals trapped in a barrel.

But now you see, even in the eyes of the *Muselmänner*, a distant, sharp little light that wasn't there before. The most irreligious pray to somebody, to something. *Heilbare*, "recoverable," is the way every prisoner wants to appear at *Selektion* or *Taufe* time. "*Weg von heir!*" is the word at the approach of a guard, a capo, or someone you don't know and who might be an informer, a *Zinker*. "Get away from here, out of the way of trouble!" "Not now! Don't fuck up *now!*"

You can almost hear some giant unseen clock ticking to every train that rolls in, to every puff of thick black smoke the wind snatches from the chimney, to every number called at the morning and evening roll call. I keep wondering what the world will be like when this is all over, when the inmates of this great insane asylum get free of their keepers. And what about the rescuers who've waded in blood to save us? The world will be, I think, a very crazy place.

The half-planted and half-tended flower beds have bloomed with their multitude of flowers; how silly they look now.

Sunday, August 6, 1944

Who can believe the stories from the East? We know they want to kill us, but out there the stories describe a symphony of killing— with rhythms and numbers and with the finest industrial instruments—in the killing camps, the *Vernichtungslager:* Treblinka, Belsec, Sobibor, Chelmno, Riga, Vilna, Minsk, Kaunas, Auschwitz-Birkenau, Maidanek, Bergen-Belsen, Buchenwald, Mauthausen. Oh, there are hundreds; I can't recall all the names people mention. How are they killed, the Gypsies, the Jews, the Russians, Poles, French, Dutch, Italians, Austrians, and so on? Bullets, car gas, and the kind of gas, in more powerful doses, that Pierre used to disinfect clothes, Xyklon B. Five thousand a day, 10,000, 20,000 . . . off the train and into hell, to music, naked (something queer with these Germans—killing and nakedness together, sex and killing). In a strange way, you get used to what happens here. I mean, that's the plan, to get you used to it. But what happens in the slaughterhouses that brings these men here with a look in their eyes like a bullet just missed their heads, is a thing I can't begin to imagine. Yet they are here, with their stories of digging up bodies to burn or move, or planting seedlings of trees where acres of bodies have been buried. But that means the Germans who did and who do and who order and who allow these things to happen know exactly how murderous they've been. If even Dieter Lange starts shaking when he talks about what he's heard and seen, God help us all. Oh, it'll be quite a world afterward with all the lynchers. They won't get caught; they never get all the lynchers, because they don't want to, because the sheriff protects his deputy, the judge protects the sheriff, and the church-going business people and politicians protect the judge.

How can this meal be served to me? I didn't ask for it. All I *ever* wanted was to play my music and be happy with someone I liked who liked me. Now look at this world these white folks have made. Jeeeee-suss.

Wednesday Night, August 16, 1944
Yesterday morning, on the French Riviera, American, British, and French soldiers landed near Nice and Marseilles. ("I'll Be Seeing You . . .")

———

Saturday, October 21, 1944
Paris was freed in August, and the rest of France is coming loose, too. The Russians are in Prussia. Some of the American cowboys are inside Germany, or what's left of it. Radio London, Armed Forces Radio, the Voice of America, all say the bombers and fighters never stop flying from England, Italy, and now France. And everyone who has been into Munich says it looks like it's been hit by ten earthquakes.

Luxembourg is free and the Germans have been pushed into northern Italy. Was it the accumulation of these things that made me dig up the address of Dr. Nyassa's wife? Did these events force into my hand the name of Mulheim, where Pierre came from and where his mother, bitch that he said she was, may still live?

There must be some connection between the war, the way it is going, and my daydreams of being back with musicians who are exchanging stories about the Club 802, the Clef, the Amsterdam

Club in New York; or lying about the Petit Chaut in Constantinople, the Weiburg Bar in Vienna, the Flea Pits, the Paraquet Cabaret, the Casino de Paris, the Tabariss in Holland. They would tell me their stories and I'd tell mine, and we'd laugh and drink and maybe they'd call me Pepper instead of Cliff because I'd lived through this. And we'd talk about the down-deep prejudice of white men everywhere— home, France, Turkey (even if not so white there), Belgium, Italy, Germany (of course!), and how they made Louis work so hard he busted his lip and that changed his sound because he had to play on another part of his lip. . . .

I daydream and dig up addresses. Dieter Lange sweats fear so you can smell it. Anna is sick and he won't help her; he wouldn't mind if she died. The doctor says her symptoms are of typhoid. I nurse her, wash her, clean her, feed her. There's no one else to do it. I put cold cloths on her head, check her temperature, and listen to her whining and crying and moaning. I check the redness of her spots, give her the sulfa pills and clear soup (like the prisoners get, but hers is made from something besides water and salt and turnip tops). Dieter Lange doesn't come near her. If it were safe to go check some other camp he'd have been long gone, but there's no point. The house smells of shit. Opening windows doesn't help.

What else doesn't help is Hitler. He offered peace, but Roosevelt, Churchill, and that bad-assed Joe Stalin already done said "Unconditional surrender." I guess that means give it all up. What it also means is Germany has lost but just won't quit. How many times did I see bad jokers start fights in clubs, clearing out the tables, spilling drinks, making women scream and men holler, only to see Mr. Bad get his ass kicked, if not his face slashed? Nothing feels better than to see a bully get his. Must be human nature, to see Mr. Bad get his ass kicked good. Now it's Germany's turn. *Now.*

But I attend this *frau,* this farm girl, whose only discoveries in the world have been money and fucking. That's all. If she got religion, it was for one lousy stinking second. She lays there, the autumn air blowing with a slight chill through the windows I've opened; lays there watching me do things for her, her eyes filled with thanks, her fat little hands lingering on my arms and wrists. Anna has no friends. Ursula is gone and Lily Bernhardt, who kept her distance anyway, is dead. The sewing circle that made swastika flags broke up a long time ago. If there are still *Kaffeeklatsches,* she hasn't been invited to one in over a year, and she hasn't held any probably because no one would come. Anna Lange is a prisoner, too.

She tells me of her life before Dieter Lange, when she lived on her father's farm south of Esterhofen, not far from Dachau. An only child, like me. Her parents hated her because she was a girl, not a boy, and her mother couldn't have any more children. A boy would have been of more help. She took care of their small herd of cows, milked them, brought them in and out. She hitched the horses to the plow and drove them and walked in cowshit up to her knees. She helped care for the crops, planting, weeding, harvesting. When the harvest was in, read the magazines from Munich and Berlin and went to the movies.

Then came these SA and SS officers from Munich looking for a place to build a camp. Good Nazis. Dieter Lange kept coming back. Anna's father had voted for Hitler. He liked what the Nazis said they would do for Germany. Hindenburg had his turn and failed. Things would go better with Hitler in office. So how could he refuse Dieter Lange's request to marry her? And she, anyhow, was dying to get away; even the town of Dachau was bigger than Esterhofen, and Dachau was just a ways from the big city, Munich. Queer? She didn't know what queer was. She had no friends even then to talk to about such things. Not even in school, which none of the kids liked. She watched the animals until her folks chased her away (just like I thought). She got hot watching them and knew something should have been happening to her, too. So, then, Dieter Lange.

He wasn't very good-looking, but neither was she. He'd come from Berlin, though, and talked about the bright lights and the clubs and the entertainers, and he flattered her mother and father and made them feel that they had a son after all, one who was an officer, too. She knew they couldn't understand why he wanted her, but what could they say? What could they do? And since the camp would be for criminals, he would see that they got the help they needed to run the farm and make it prosperous. That he promised. And he kept his word.

He liked to fuck, Dieter Lange did, in the behind, which at first
she thought was all right, though it didn't do much for her. She
questioned him. He said that was the way all the Catholics did it to
please the Pope and to not have children. In those days, who could
afford to have kids, and she didn't want them anyway. There was too
much life to be lived. Sometimes she got him to do it the other way,
but not nearly enough, which was why, of course, she got involved
with Bernhardt, who could do it half the night without coming up
for air. And he had that reputation; he would fuck anything moving,
the more unusual the better. He showed her lots of things. He teased
her about how much she wanted to do it and wondered why Dieter
Lange wasn't doing his work at home. Then she began to wonder. So
that day she came home and I was fighting with Dieter Lange over
the records I broke and that slap I gave him, she knew what was up.
Finally. She was glad that she had helped to make me, as she'd told
Dieter Lange, not all queer.

I told her, as she lay there (this was a couple of weeks ago, but
she's still down—the typhoid takes nearly a month to break), that
I never liked doing it with women. I didn't know why. I just didn't.
Always? she wanted to know. Not *always,* I said. You know, when
you get to that age. Why, that's what I meant, she said. Then she
said, Oh, dear.

She then wanted to know how we had met, me and Dieter Lange,
and I told her about Berlin back in the old days and how he was a
small-time pimp and confidence man—and queer—who used to go
to the clubs for one thing or another, and how he'd always send me
drinks and try to talk to me. Berlin, I told her, was full of queers
then, but they began to melt into the woodwork when the Nazis
came in, even though so many Nazis were themselves freaks. I put it
to her that she was queer and she smiled. You mean Ursula, she said,
and I said Yes, Ursula. No, she said. She just liked doing something
different. But you liked her, Anna said. You liked doing it to her.
I know. I could tell. She had a nice behind, I said. Not like mine,
which is a little bit too much, eh? she said.

"Get some sleep," I say. "I have to go to the canteen."

"Why doesn't Dieter come and help look after me?" she asks.

"He gets the medicine," I say.

She cries herself to sleep.

Friday, Nov. 24, 1944

Back in the spring there was what I called a roundup. It was like a *Selektion*, only the SS were forming labor battalions to go work on the Western Front. Whatever they did wasn't enough, wasn't shit, because the Allies came anyway. Now they're forming another labor battalion. Somebody said they're doing this in all the camps. Nobody wants to go now. In the spring it was different. But now the whole American, British, Canadian, and French armies are fighting in Germany. Any *Haftling* who looks halfway healthy is going West, and those *Zinkers* and rats and hustlers and SS runners and everyone else who has managed to eat regularly and can carry a shovel— Uhlmer from the canteen included (Dieter Lange told me to choose between him and Lappus)—will get a taste of war. And that may be their last taste of anything, because the Germans will throw even their own kids, yes, little boys, into the fight to save the Reich. The prisoners ain't gonna be nothin' but sitting ducks.

Yesterday was Thanksgiving. We listened to all the Thanksgiving stuff on the radio. There was even an American football game broadcast from Italy.

Anna is able to get up for a little while at a time. If she were in the camp, she'd probably be dead by now.

Tuesday, December 26, 1944

A late Christmas present. Big bomber raid about a week ago. Bader says Elser (Eller?) was killed in the raid, but I don't see how, because they say he was in camp, not Munich. Maybe they just decided it was time to kill him. Elser was the guy who tried to kill Hitler two months after the war began.

The Germans got back into Belgium and, according to Radio Berlin, kicked the shit out of the Americans. That was another *Blitzkrieg*. Through the mountains. More German bullshit! It's *got* to be.

I write in my room. It is bitterly cold. There's only the little kerosene stove going up in their bedroom. Now Radio Berlin is saying "counterattack, *successful* counterattack." The Allies are saying "heavy fighting, heavy fighting." This would have been the Christmas every prisoner wanted, with liberation around the corner. Not now. Everyone's afraid the Germans have pulled another rabbit out of the hat, like the buzz bombs, that maybe they'll take back everything they've lost since June. Now we know where all those labor battalions went. Maybe Uhlmer will never come back, so it'll be just me and Lappus in the canteen, where what we have to sell isn't worth buying, not even with scrip.

The gas chamber that was being added to the crematorium is finished. Me and Bader slipped around the stacks of bodies with the help of one of the *Sonderkommandos* to see it. He was grumbling, because now there'd be more work to do and maybe not so many men to do it. The smell was a little bit more powerful than the stink of the dead lying all around; that wouldn't last. On the door, lettering read:

> *Zu:*
> *Gaszeit:*
> *Auf:*
>
> In:
> Gas time:
> Out:

Then a skull and crossbones and an arrow pointing to a handle. Under these was:

> *Versicht! Gas!*
> *Lebensgefahr!*
> *Nicht Offnen!*
>
> Danger! Gas!
> Dangerous to life!
> Don't open!

The place looked like a shower, with tiled floors and walls. Bader whispered, "So now a little bit fewer transports to Hartheim, eh?"

Tuesday, January 2, 1945

A few nights ago I heard a noise on the steps leading to my room. I knew it was Dieter Lange and I sat up to curse him out. He came through the door with a crash, carrying with him the rancid odors of sour sweat, bad breath, and liquor. He felt for me. I started to shout, and then there was a second of pain and nothing else. As soon as I woke I felt the pain in my face and I knew it was swollen. My pants had been torn off. My insides hurt so much I couldn't take a deep breath. The cocksucker had raped me.

I called him those things right to his face, yes, I did: you dirty, stinking, low-life sonofabitch, sneaky, no 'count German white trash, shiftless, chickenshit Kraut, pickle-sucking Nazi dummy, two-bit shitbag, motherfucking slimy . . .

Anna tried to shush me, but I told her to shut up.

You nasty, funky, trifling, shithead queer, dried-up old fruit, freak, sissy, you worn leather asshole . . .

I took his neck in my hands. Anna pulled at me and I shoved her away over the linoleum floor that was cracking with the cold. Dieter Lange was still drunk, his eyes half-closed. Slobber dribbled out of his mouth. He looked like he wanted me to kill him. What a start to the new year.

It wasn't any of my goddamn fault that his General Major and Colonel got caught in the big black market that covered Europe from Poland to France. The Munich paper was open on the kitchen table with their pictures in it. "That's them! That's them!" he'd cried when I staggered up the steps meaning to kill him, whatever else happened, just kill him deader than dead. And as he ran from room to room, me chasing him and trapping him in the kitchen, he said, "They're coming next for me!"

"You gonna be one dead Nazi when they find your ass!" I was throwing chairs and shoving the table, and I picked up the stove poker and swung at him with all my might. He jumped back out of the way and I hit a rack full of glasses that exploded into fragments. Anna screamed. "The Gestapo can have your stinking ass when I'm through with it, you pork-pushing, shit-packing punk!" He fell into a chair, and that's when I wrapped my hands around his neck. "Fuck me like I was some kind of pig . . . " I said, thinking how good it felt, having his neck in my hands, and in their embrace he tilted his head backward, as though to make more room for me to squeeze, but I hadn't started to do that yet.

Anna threw her arms around my waist and pulled, her feet making screeing and cracking noises on the broken glass. "But it's almost over, Cleef. Please, don't."

That was true. The Americans had pushed the Germans back and were advancing, ready to cross the Rhine. I didn't stop because Anna asked me to; I stopped because she reminded me of what I already knew and because, if the Gestapo didn't come for Dieter Lange, if they stopped with the big shots—and everyone likes to hate big shots—then Dieter Lange would remain my ticket to survival. Not so if they got him—or I killed him. If he lived, I remained Dieter Lange's nigger; if not, I was a dead nigger. And with the Germans in retreat again—what the Poles called *Zirkus Plechovi,* the metal circus —the guards were scared, ready to kill, especially an American who didn't have a gun, like me, for example.

I stood a moment looking down at him, catching my breath. With a whimper, Anna tugged once more, as though she'd read my thoughts. I knew just then that whatever happened outside the house, no matter how Dieter Lange behaved toward me out there, or even Anna the rare times she went out, I, The Cliff, was the strongest person in that house. I drew back and slapped Dieter Lange out of his chair. "Bull rape me, will you? Because you're scared, you do that to me? Because your buddies got caught and you lose some money you knock me out and joog me like I was a corpse or something? What is *wrong* with you fucking people? Just how crazy are you, to make *everybody* in the world hate you? Come near me again . . ."

I told Anna to make me some coffee. She started, then paused over Dieter Lange. "Fuck him, bitch. *Coffee!*"

Sunday, January 28, 1945

I stared at Dieter Lange and Anna Lange last night when the BBC announced that the Russians had liberated Auschwitz and found—shit, what can I say? We'd heard the rumors for a long time and now knew them to be true. The Germans behaved as though they didn't have one single thing to do with Auschwitz, or even Dachau. I said, "Just wait till they find all the other camps." Then they looked at me like they were seeing me for only the first or second time. Slowly, fear climbed up in their eyes. I watched it, thought of the way death, the cruelest kinds of death, and sex, the more unusual the better, seemed always to go together with people like the ones I was staring at. It was a luxury brought only by the prospect of Germany being ground under, thinking like that. I had lived in the middle of it for almost a dozen years, heard about the edges of it every day, and yet only news that this place was done for allowed me to think of how big and how evil it all was, the kind of evil they couldn't begin to imagine when preachers talked about it in church.

Friday, February 16, 1945

The Allies bombed Dresden; the place is still burning. Thousands died, burned to a crisp. Fried. Baked. Barbequed. Good. Great.

Dear, *dear* God. Oh, Loa Aizan.

I think I have the syph. These sores on my butt. *In* my butt. That rotten sonofabitch. At dinner I told them. Dieter Lange said it's probably nothing. I cussed him out and asked who had he been fooling around with, anyway? He said nobody, but he lies. I can tell he's lying. Anna said Dieter Lange wasn't sleeping in her bed anymore. I said it was too late for that. Dieter Lange said he'd have someone come and look at me, and I said who could look at me and not know what had been going on all these years between us? He said the same doctor who'd done the *Lebensborn* papers for them. Anna wants an examination, too. I think Dieter Lange already had one and is on medication.

"Pears" are rolling now for reasons the guards never thought of two or three years ago. Yesterday the "pear" belonged to a man who got caught stealing a rag from another prisoner to replace his own, which he'd used to wipe his behind. After he used it, he washed it out. After three months it was worn out. He needed another. He stole one and his "pear" rolled. Twenty-five lashes used to be the punishment for petty theft.

Diary, could I become rich selling you piece by piece for toilet paper? Then could I buy some magic cure for this?

Sunday, February 25, 1945

I leave Lappus to run the canteen and I walk around the Dancing Ground and up and down the 'Strasse. It's cold and windy, but, like everyone else, I keep waiting for that good thing to happen. It's in the air. A fool couldn't help seeing it. The Family and the International Committee have gathered and have posted lookouts at the door of Block 1. The Blacks seem to have huddled closer to the SS guards, like the Greens. But the guards are mostly old men now and some are even civilians. It's plain they'd rather be somewhere else. The Family and the IC are just as concerned with maintaining the routine as the guards. No work today. Everyone is inside, out of the cold, wondering if the rumors of still another typhoid epidemic will turn out to be true. Maybe the rumor was started by one of the groups to keep the guards away from the blocks. Maybe not. Now there is always talk of a rebellion, of guns that are already in the hands of the IC or the Family, of knives and clubs, of battle positions.

The big problem is food, getting enough of it and sharing it to try to keep people alive until liberation. If I brought food in, it wouldn't last but a second. There are just too many starving jokers stumbling around here. In the old days when I brought food and things in for Werner or for Pierre or to trade, it was different—you didn't have to worry about 30,000 other people trying to snatch it out of your hand. I miss those old days, sometimes, when I felt I was a part of things, the *Widerstand,* the resistance, hauling around radio parts, passing on information from Gitzig to Werner. Now it's every man for himself.

I find no one to talk to. Besides, it's too cold to talk for long outside. I return to the canteen and take one of the sulfa pills Dieter
Lange's doctor gave me. I suppose he gave them to him, too. What a
shabby little man. He just pulled me apart and flashed a light up
there and tskked. He's probably seen unimaginable things so often
that he's used to them. He just said, "Yes, that's what you have,
syphilis. Take these four times a day with water." Then he left. I feel
like a leper. I've never had a disease before, not even the clap.

When I get home, I take the piano stool and break it apart and
make a fire in the stove. I take the plate of boiled potatoes Anna
fixed for me and sit beside it. Dieter Lange is bent over the radio.
I know Anna doesn't want me in the kitchen, and him neither. She
sits on the other side of the stove, pulling her fingers and mumbling
something about going home. My mind is a thing watching me trying to think. I feel so tired, so weak. When I finish writing this, I
have to check my hiding place. Dieter Lange's bin is empty. Just a
few sausages hang there with mold growing on them. They smell
rotten. But maybe it's me I smell, or Anna, or Dieter Lange. It's hard
to tell who or what is smelling these days.

Thursday, March 15, 1945

Now I believe what I've heard. Werner came into the canteen
today with a woman SS guard. Oh, he seemed proud of her and she
was giggling and carrying on, and they were touching each other.
Well, what can I say? This close to the end and he's got an SS girlfriend? And he's been working with the International Committee
and the Family? Seems to me he's got his dick on his mind instead
of his thinking cap. But who am I to mark the changes in other
people?

Anna tried to leave yesterday, but she was brought back because
she fell down in the mud and couldn't get up. Drunk. Dieter Lange
doesn't know what to do with her. All she needs to do is start
screaming about two faggots with syphilis and there'll be a black
"pear" and a blond "pear" rolling at six o'clock that night. Stupid
bitch. Who would miss her if she turned up dead?

Sunday, April 1, 1945

Yesterday the sky was blue except for a few big white clouds. A bunch of American planes marked with white stars with red balls inside them and red tails, dove out of the sky with a noise that made the ground shake. They were heading toward Munich along the railroad tracks. They zoomed low and then high, turned sideways, went up, and came back again. They were sparkling silver. Then German planes appeared out of nowhere to chase them.

I was just outside the camp when the racket started, on my way home where I was thinking of burning the top of the piano for heat. All the SS and their runners in the *Jourhaus* ran out to see. The planes roared and whistled up and down the sky, then flattened out over the camp, making noise like rolling thunder, their guns yammering and pounding, their engines howling, until they flew out of sight over the horizon. Enlisted men, SS officers, wives, calfactors, civilians—we were all watching this business in the sky, the vanishing, the thundering, the climbing up into the clouds and diving down again. The machine guns sounded like drummers practicing on snares at the far end of a great big empty hall. All the sounds flew far away, but left the echo of a promise to return—a whine, a growl, something. And then an American plane came roaring out of the west behind the factories with a German plane right behind it. The German plane didn't sound like the American plane—more like a long, sharp whistle—and its guns went *Poom! Poom!* Tatttaaaattttaaaaat! The American swung up in the sky in a big loop and came down right behind the German. The American plane was skidding back and forth like a wounded bird, but man, the American sounded like he was doing the Mammy-Daddy roll on that German's ass and wasn't going to quit. Then he tried to pull up, but only skidded off to the north. Now the German was trying to climb up into one of the big clouds, but it seemed like he hit an invisible wall, and then smoke came rushing out of his tail. He started to nose over and then began a run down the sky, leaving smoke like a big pencil streak against the blue. Flames jumped out. I heard people groan. I heard myself shout "Get out!" Then, "Jump!!" At that moment it didn't matter that he was a German. People were shouting, *"Fallschirmspringen! Fallschirmspringen!"* Parachute!

Parachute! But the plane seemed to be drawn faster and faster to the ground. It went through a cloud and marked it with a black, whirling streamer. I almost turned away, and maybe what kept me from doing so was a sudden blossoming of white with the sun sparkling off it. The American! His plane had been hit, too, and he'd had to use his parachute. There was a faint explosion to the north, but everyone's attention was on the German plane whining through the air in a long steep angle that carried it out of sight behind the horizon east of the camp. There was a crumping sound. It shook the earth delicately. I thought, He's gone. Not up the chimney, but down the stack.

The American was drifting north of the camp, toward the rifle ranges. His plane had gone down, without smoke or fire. Two trucks filled with ss from the *Jourhaus* drove out of camp through the factory road and turned north. How great it would be to capture an American pilot! they said. Nobody I could notice was going to see about the German. There was nothing new about jokers being burned up around here.

The airplane fight gave us something to talk about at home, a chance to break the nasty stillness that had closed in on us. I could not burn the piano top. Just couldn't. Not even to spite them, to dare them to say something so I could curse them out. Anyway, the house wasn't quite so cold now, and really, since the compound guards brought her back that day, Anna hasn't treated us so much like lepers.

Dieter Lange was grumbling over a big bowl of soup with a little meat but mostly turnips and cabbage made thick with flour, that the Americans had shot down another secret weapon, the *Dusenjager*, the jet fighter that had crashed. "The buzz bombs only make Hitler feel good," he said. "And the jet fighters can't protect us here. You saw. The American shot him right in the ass."

"Isn't he talking bold these days?" Anna said.

"Everybody's talking these days," he said, "and some are doing more than talking. You'll see."

"And what does that mean, Major Lange, what does that mean?"

"It means not everyone is going to sit still and take the blame for things Hitler and Himmler and Goering and Goebbels ordered done. That's what it means."

Anna slid a look toward me.

"You better take more time to cure your syphilis instead of trying to think up schemes," she said to him. "Look where your scheming has got us."

"Shut up, you tub of lard."

"Oh, shut up yourself, you queer."

I said, "Why don't you both shut up and listen to the radio."

God. Every night it's like this. Dieter Lange hasn't been away on a trip because he's up to something. I know him. And, besides, now that Anna's tipped her hand with that running away, he's not going to let her out of his sight.

The sound of a car stopping quickly in front of the house made Dieter Lange unplug the cord to the shortwave radio, which he kept hidden in a closet. He pulled some clothes over the radio and closed the door and walked to the window. He was scared. And so was I. What was on Anna's face was not fear, more like she was expecting to have some of her problems solved.

Bam! Bam! Bam! Bam! I said to myself, Oh, shit. Dieter Lange's face went white. The General Major and the Colonel and now us. Dieter Lange went from the window, whose curtain he hadn't even had time to push aside to look out, to the door, his face clouding up like he was going to cry. He managed to open the door and an SS sergeant saluted and shouted, "The *Jourhaus* duty officer, Captain Baugh, wishes the use of your black, Major, at once, please."

Understanding that he wasn't to be led away to have his head chopped off, and also that there was a duty officer involved, Dieter Lange demanded to know for what purpose.

"To help, sir, with the American pilot who got shot down this afternoon."

"Ah hah! You got him then?" Dieter Lange said.

"Yes, we did."

"An American who doesn't speak English?"

"Oh, he speaks English. He's a black man like your black and speaks no German, of course."

"Oh! Is that so? But you must have someone there who can translate."

The sergeant came close to Dieter Lange and said, "Captain Haug would like to show how well we treat prisoners, even black ones."

"And there aren't any in the camp?"

"Not worth showing, Major."

"But what do you want my calfactor to do?"

"Just to make the pilot feel comfortable."

An ugly grin spread over Dieter Lange's face. "Ah, the captain wants to get points with the cowboys for a little later on, eh?"

The sergeant grinned. "You said that. I didn't."

"I'll join you," Dieter Lange said.

The sergeant looked uncomfortable. "Captain Baugh said, in case you said that, there are already too many people in the interrogation room, sir."

"Let him change clothes and take him then."

I could not *imagine* it. A Negro riding one of those mighty machines, a Negro who'd shot down a German plane, a secret-weapon plane? Who'd floated through the sky to land safely out in the fields? What would they do to him? These thoughts and others raced around in my head as we sped to the gatehouse in the last light of day.

My third time. There'd been Count Walther von Hausberger, then Ruby Mae Richards, and now the pilot. Up the stairs again (which meant they hadn't beat him) and into the same room, which was filled with cigarette smoke and SS men.

Even in clean rags I must have looked a sight. He stared at me out of the cozy-looking, wool-lined leather jacket. His gun holster was empty. His wool-trimmed aviator cap sat cockily tilted to one side and a little back on his head. He looked like a boy, only a little older than Pierre but in good health. He was smoking and I think he was a little afraid; the smoking helped him to hide it. There was a little blood on his face and his left cheek was swollen, like he'd bumped it or been hit.

"You work with the translator. Make this man feel comfortable, eh?" Captain Baugh said. I guess it was Captain Baugh. "Who he is,

where he's from. In a friendly fashion. See if he's hurt and needs
a doctor."

"Hello," I said in English.

"Hello," he said, squinting up, trying to figure what was going on.

"Can I please have a cigarette?" I asked the captain in German.

As I was lighting it the pilot asked, "What kind of camp is this?
Are you an American? What outfit were you in? What do they
want? I'm a prisoner of war, you know, and an officer."

I said, "I know. Are you all right? Not hurt or anything from the
parachute jump?"

"No. I'm okay," the pilot said.

"They want to know who you are," I said. Captain Baugh smiled
approvingly.

"Captain Homer Harrison, Jr., serial number 628-93-47, Protestant. Blood type, O. That's it, mister, name, rank, and serial number. That's more than I'm required to give these cats. Who are
you?"

Captain Baugh approached holding out his hand. "Captain
Harrison."

The pilot, suspicious, shook Baugh's hand briefly, then turned
back to me.

"Clifford Pepperidge, from New York," I said. "I'm not a soldier,
I'm a prisoner."

"What's that you're saying?" the captain asked loudly, moving
toward us.

"I just told him I wasn't a soldier." The translator verified this
with a nod.

The young Negro pilot and I stared at each other. He said again,
this time to the captain, "What kind of camp *is* this?"

The translator spoke rapidly to the captain. "Tell him it is a camp
for criminals," the captain said. Everyone stared at the pilot.

"Criminals?" the pilot said, looking at me. I didn't answer.

Then another officer leaned forward and spoke in German,
"Where are you flying from? Since when does the American air force
have black pilots?"

The translator spoke.

Harrison shook his head. "I told you," he said. "Name, rank, and serial number. Blood type and religion were free. That's it. Nothing more." To me he said, like they weren't in the room, "Where are we? How close to or far from Munich?"

"Dachau," I said.

"How far from Munich?"

"About fifteen miles."

"What does he say? What did you say, Pepper-ah?" the captain asked before the translator could speak.

"He wanted to know where he was and how far from Munich." While they were talking, coming up with the next questions, I said to the pilot, "This is a concentration camp." I saw that meant nothing to him.

"Why are there so many dead people just laying around? I saw them. Are those cemeteries out there where I came down?"

I said, "Yes."

The translator rolled his eyes.

"What does he say?" Captain Baugh asked.

"Make way," someone in the rear of the room said, and the bodies moved apart while an SS man leaned forward with a bottle of cognac, a glass, and a sandwich. The pilot looked at me. I looked at the captain, who nodded, and said, "Let him eat and have a drink. The Luftwaffe people will be here to take him to an officer's prisoner of war camp. I think they'll want to know just how he shot down one of our best planes. He doesn't have to be frightened. The war's almost over. Remind him he was treated well in Dachau and that Captain Hans Baugh was his interrogation officer." The captain winked at me. "You understand."

"Can I talk with him, Captain?"

"Why?" Captain Baugh seemed to be tired and resigned. "What about?"

"Because he's a colored man," I said, because there really wasn't another reason.

"I think not. He doesn't need to know anything more about this place and I think you would tell him, no?"

I didn't answer. "But can I stay until they come for him?"

"No. He'll be all right, and even if that was not to be the case, it'd do no good your being here. That's all." He told the sergeant who'd brought me to take me back.

The pilot was eating the sandwich and drinking, his eyes jumping from me to the captain. "What's all this about?" he asked.

"The German air force people are coming to talk to you about shooting down that plane—"

"That ME 262?" His face broke into a great, beautiful smile. "You saw that? Messed *up* that cat, man. Another jet kill—"

The captain interrupted. "What's he talking about now?"

There was a look of wonder on the translator's face as he said, "About the plane he shot down. He shot down one before."

A growl came from the men in the room.

To Harrison I said, "They won't let me stay with you till they come, so good luck. Uh—when will it be over?"

He looked sharply at me as though I'd turned suddenly into a spy. He drank and held my eyes and took a deep breath. "Okay. Aybemay ootay, eethray eeksway. Orefay at eethay ostmay. Ancay ooyay akeit-may?"

"Esyay," I said. I didn't know I looked that bad, but I nodded and held out my hand. He shook it, then the sergeant took me away.

The Langes were waiting up for me with a piece of sausage and a big glass of schnapps. I told them all about it, answered what questions I could, even the one about when it would be over, and I laughed at them. I felt like Gabriel warming up on his horn. But I wasn't feeling so good. Had they poisoned me with the schnapps? I drifted downstairs and pulled the blanket over me and curled up. Just tired, I told myself. You hold yourself together for a thousand years with threads and strings of hope, and when somebody who should know tells you it's going to be all right soon, maybe the strings start breaking, pop, pop, pop.

———

Thursday, April 19, 1945

Yesterday in broad daylight, they made General Delestraint take off the uniform he insisted on wearing and shot him dead. On the 'Strasse near the Appellplatz. He thought . . . I don't know what he thought. But the Family and the International Committee, which have become Resistance Committees, or some jokers who belong to one or the other, or maybe both, say he was told he was going to have a shower and then join the honor prisoners in their Bunker. He must have known that was bullshit, if that's what they told him.

He was a rigid, proud little man. He once told me in the canteen when he wanted a pack of Bleus (which of course we didn't have), that the best soldiers he ever commanded were Senegalese during the Great War. ("They had no illusions. They knew they were in France to die for France.") Thing is, after the ss shot him, they left his body there in the dirt for a couple of hours before they took it away.

I haven't been in camp since then. It's getting dangerous, and I still am not well. Neff tells me to get out and stay out because it looks like we've got typhus going around again. The ss and their camp police are like kids who must have a last taste of candy, except in this case, it's not candy, but killing; they can't seem to stop. "Let the *Kuhtreiber* come," they say. "We'll show them the wild west. Bang! Bang! And we don't have to worry about Rosenvelt anymore since he died last week." Roosevelt was a president I never even knew much about.

The prisoners are mainly confined to the blocks. There are too many of them for the ss to guard outside, with the few men they have left. And the ss are afraid of large details because some ss have been murdered. I think of a can of meat left too long in the sun, the way it can swell and then explode.

The airplanes with the red tails—how wonderful yet sad they make me feel, because I don't know what happened to Captain Harrison—fly over almost every day now. It's like being greeted by a neighbor from down the street or Loa Aizan looking things over.

Every prisoner with any sense knows, or thinks he knows, that the camps have been liberated in Poland, that Bergen-Belsen is free, and that Buchenwald was liberated ten days ago. The 3,000 prisoners the

SS was trying not to be caught with there are all dead on the siding just outside the east wall of *this* camp, stinking like hell in the fifty box-cars that brought them here, says Bader. Bader's people do the count. Bader is busy these days, keeping peace and getting some kind of final tally on who is dead and who is alive, block by block. Resistance group people (who announce themselves as such) are coming out of the woodwork now. What or how Werner fits in, I do not know and don't care too much to know. Prisoners who have lived for months in holes beneath the blocks or in the eaves of the blocks have crept out.

Tuesday, April 24, 1945

Oh, Captain Harrison, your two weeks are up; now we have to work on the next two. Damn!

Nuremberg, Hessenthal, and a dozen camps to the north, including Flossenburg, have been liberated. Next stop, Berlin, where the Russians already are. The news comes in static bursts over the radio. Anna sits blubbering, her legs swollen, her feet puffing out of her shoes. Dieter Lange is in and out. "Yes, it's typhus," he announces. "No point running to your father's farm," he shouts at Anna. "The Americans will be there in another day or so, if not already." She cries and holds out her arms to him. He spits.

The compound seems empty. No flower beds turned. Few cars and trucks. Few people out under the gray April sky that often opens and lets loose rain. I think at night the mothers and children go, in trucks if they can, on foot if they can't, hoping to get into the town and from there as far away from this place as possible.

We don't sleep, we doze in chairs, coming awake in the night when a truck or car glides down the street with slitted blackout lights. Alarms go on and off, crying down the night like children lost in the darkness. Even in the house, the smell of burning flesh invades through the cracks, and I think of the bodies that have been thrown every whichaway, like store dummies. Nobody cares. Nobody moves them. They are just there, from one end of the camp into the compound.

We have been hearing guns a long way off, soft as though they meant us no harm. Last night they seemed closer, a little louder, a lot

meaner. Dieter Lange has been running back and forth to the
Jourhaus for orders and news. Like the way he was in the old days,
cutting a deal here, a hustle there. Evacuation orders, he says, are
coming. The camp will be destroyed.

"What do you mean, 'destroyed'?" I say. "How can you destroy
the camp?"

He does not answer. He tries to look wise, like only he knows the
secret.

Anna says it. "You mean *kill* all the prisoners, leave *30,000* bodies
for the Americans to find? Is Commandant Aumeier crazy?"

Dieter Lange shrugs. "I have nothing to do with these things. I
run the canteens, and that is all. You know that is all I've ever done."

I laugh and nibble at my boiled potato. The house is silent and
cold. No sense listening to the radio. I don't know about Dieter
Lange and Anna, but I can almost see them coming, red tails blazing
in the sun, tromping through German farms and along German
roads. Out in the street the SS, the old men in and out of uniform,
the kids, and the wounded troop by for the changing of the guard,
singing the sad "Lili Marlene." What must the prisoners be thinking
to be still singing in the camp?

Saturday, April 28, 1945

It's hard to find paper. They're cleaning out everything in the
camp, the compound, the factories. Everywhere. And running
around like chickens with their heads cut off. Burning records. Every
day there are fewer guards; they just seem to vanish. Probably burned
their uniforms and slipped away in civilian clothes, which are price-
less now. You'd think they were made of gold. They aren't even trying
to feed the prisoners in the camp, Dieter Lange reports. They have
to do for themselves for food—buy it, steal it, take it from somebody
else. Bodies are stacked up beside the moat, in the 'Platz, in the
'Strasse, along the outside walls of the crematorium, and just inside
and outside the electric fence. The SS officers' wives have all gone,
some west to Augsburg to surrender to the Americans, and others
south to avoid both the Russians and the Americans.

Americans. Will they be black or white or mixed up? I don't think mixed. Will white American soldiers look after me the way Negro ones would? And if they don't, what do I do? Great God Almighty, what if nothing's changed? C'mon, Cliff, whatever else has changed, you know *that* ain't changed. The whole world is looking for Americans to save them, and I don't know that they will.

I am going south with Anna tomorrow. Dieter Lange has arranged for us to go with a women's group. We won't have much food; two boiled potatoes each. Going may be safer than staying around here because there are supposed to be committees in the camp with arms to stop the guards from killing off the prisoners. That will start a war. The ss wants to empty the camp or leave corpses so the Americans can't know what they really did to us. Dieter Lange thinks the guards are crazy to want to kill more pris-oners now, but it doesn't matter to him, he says. Of course it doesn't. He'll be gone. He's got money, civilian clothes, and papers, and he's not taking Anna, and certainly not me. Anna's on her own. She knows and Dieter Lange knows that I'll leave her as soon as I can. She's so weak she can hardly walk. We'll make a good couple for a little while. Me shuffling because of the infection, and her hobbling like some baby elephant. We'll go with the third group of women prisoners. She should keep her mouth shut and stay with the prison-ers, Dieter Lange says, shaking his finger in her face. She's been cry-ing and pleading with him, saying she can't walk all the way to Allach. There are no vehicles, Dieter Lange tells her, and besides, Cleef will look after you. Cleef is not my husband, she cries, and he shouts maybe he's not, but he's fucked you often enough. I think, why now? Who cares now who she's fucked or been fucked by? I am mad at Dieter Lange and I wish I was well enough to kill him. Look at him! Thin as a piece of old wire, his face wrinkled and worried and stubbled with a dirty gray beard, his muddy blue eyes sliding back and forth from her to me and to the window . . .

Yet if not for Dieter Lange, I would be dead, like those other colored men, the Africans from the Cameroons, the *Mischlings,* like those thousands and thousands of Reds, Russians, Jews, Gypsies, Witnesses, like all those thousands who were in the way. I needed him like God needs the Devil, like Loa Aizan needs Loa Baron Samedi. I would not rather have died. So we used each other, Dieter Lange and me. He liked tight places and a chocolate lollipop and jazz music. I liked living, being alive, and I lived better than the prisoners in the camp and sometimes better than those who worked out here. He could have taken my life as easily as he took me, even if he feared the consequences. If I was made into something less than human, I lived. If he gave me syphilis, I lived. If he enjoyed my humiliation and suffering, I lived. Living is everything. Death is shit. Death is smoke going up the chimney without one single note of sorrow being played or sung to mark your passing. Death in Dachau is rotting in the swamps, flying to the electric fence, bleeding from broken, beaten bones in the Bunker, being mauled by the dogs, shot by the SS, drowned by them, hung by them, beheaded by them, starved by them. And then they pull your gold-filled teeth before they burn you and spread your crushed bones and ashes over the Appellplatz or use them as fertilizer for flowers. In Dachau, death is escape, they always said, and maybe it is. I don't know. Life will keep me walking until I find the Americans, but I have to rest now. I'm not a youngster anymore, and I don't know how far we'll have to walk. I hope it stops raining.

* * *

Dear Bounce,   *October 18, 1986*

It was great talking to you and Justine again! And Liz is in college! Wow! It's been that long since I saw you? Did you pass along my greetings to my man Tank? I'm sure the teams you're putting together will do fine. You worry too much. You're probably secretly glad not having a son who's an athlete, the way college and pro sports are now. I know I am. But you know more about that than I do.

I've now finished reading the diary you sent—some package! I will try my damndest to get it into the right editorial hands, but do understand that we have a severe generic problem in this business. But I won't quit trying, trust me. I am grateful that you thought to send Clifford's diary to me. Imagine that old soldier keeping it so long and then giving it to you.

During all these years, there must have been many African Americans passing through, not to mention those in the army. He sure has repaid the brothers who didn't waste him when they could have. He must have seen something in you he had not seen in the others. I can dig that. Strangers trying to pierce the consciences of one another by sight, maybe vibes, in a world stranger than we can begin to imagine.

The diary is a heavy thing, Bounce. Bet you a sideline ticket on the fifty the next Super Bowl that they'll be celebrating that war from the invasion of Normandy until its end—without looking too hard behind or between the lines. People don't know, and probably don't care, about the black people in those camps, not that there's any honor in having been in one. You wouldn't wish that on your worst enemy. But here it is almost fifty years later and people are just beginning to learn about outfits like the Red Tails, the 2221 Regiment, and dozens of others.

I got real curious and looked up some of the names Clifford mentions. Freddie Johnson did get camped, but he was freed in an exchange in 1944. Willie Lewis got to Switzerland, where he sat out the war. A guy named Arthur Briggs, trumpeter, who Clifford doesn't mention, played with Johnson and got out of Europe one step ahead of the Germans. He says the International Red Cross may be located in Switzerland, but it was then German from its chitlins out. I heard that Valaida Snow got camped, too. Ruby Mae Richards died in Paris in 1976. Sam Wooding died just last year in New York at ninety. During the Depression, while Clifford was in Dachau, Wooding dropped out of the music scene and went to the University of Pennsylvania. He graduated in 1942 and then taught music. One of his students—you guessed it—was Clifford Brown—"Brownie." Doc Cheatham is still wailing; he was in Wooding's band, too. His chops gotta be made of titanium. Saw him in New York a few months ago. I think he wears a rug, but there's nothing phoney about his playing.

I wonder what happened to Clifford. If Cheatham and Wooding lived so long—like so many others who were camped—isn't it possible that The Cliff could have lived long past his diary? Couldn't he right now be playing at some tiny little club in one of a dozen European countries? Or could he have gotten back, given up music, and gone into something else? But surely he would have been rediscovered by all those black musicians who've been going to and from Europe since the end of the war.

And if he came home, I think he loved his music too much to have ever given it up, especially when he could have teamed up with guys like Eubie Blake and Cheatham and become old royalty.

Had to run, but I'm back. This guy Joseph Nassy. I've seen some of his paintings in a little synagogue in Philadelphia. He was Jewish, born in Surinam. His father was Dutch. They lived in San Francisco, Los Angeles, and then Brooklyn, then he moved first to England and after that Belgium, where the war caught up with him. He was a naturalized American and a radio engineer who loved to paint. After the war he managed somehow to gather all the paintings he'd done, so they were available after he died and went on a tour across the U.S., Israel, and Europe. He was in an internment camp, where the Germans tried to live up to international standards.

A friend of mine conducted a search for Ethiopian Jews who were reported to have been in the Bergen-Belsen camp. Some had been taken to Europe for study even before World War I. He checked archives everywhere, including Israel. There he was told by an archivist that the Ethiopians had not become Jews until the 1975 Law of Return, so they wouldn't have been registered as such in the camps or on the Holocaust lists.

Dr. Nyassa's buddy, Ernest Just, had a best friend, a German, Dr. Max Hartmann. In 1949, with a couple more good guys, Hartmann compiled a rap sheet on his colleagues who'd worked with the Nazis on all kinds of experiments. What I don't know is what happened when he turned that list in. (Probably not much.) I'm not sure, but from what I've read, it seems that Just was doing work—some of which involved changing the sex of worms, without the DNA charts that Crick, Watson, and Wilkins later came up with. You probably already know that Just's forebears were German immigrants to the U.S.

I've met a lot of guys who were in the army in Germany during the war, and they all say that the Germans they met wanted them to kill and capture Russians, not them. Hey, if I'd been a German then, I'd probably have said the same thing, given what they did to the Russians.

Getting back to Clifford, I can't imagine, though I've tried to, how I could have survived in that place. He was lucky he had his music, his German, and his body. I thought the Germans would have done things to black people that they would not have done to others. Maybe they did and that's why there's no record, so far. It is hard not to think of James Howard Jones's Bad Blood: The Tuskeegee Syphilis Experiments, *while reading sections of the diary. There wasn't a lot of fuss when that book came out. How different are we, then, from the Germans from whom we got so much? As you know, one of the German defenses at Nuremburg was that a lot of their crazy experiments were conducted here first.*

It's time for me to quit this letter before I really *let loose. I'll be checking in with you regularly. You and Justine have to settle in for the long haul, because you* know *no one is going to be eager to hear Clifford play these* blues.

—Jayson Jones

BIBLIOGRAPHY

BOOKS

Bar-Zohar, Michael. *Arrows of the Almighty*. New York: Macmillan, 1984.

Bricktop and James Haskins. *Bricktop: The Exuberant Story of a Fabulous Life*. New York: Atheneum, 1983.

Chorover, Stephan L. *From Genesis to Genocide: The Meaning of Human Behavior*. Cambridge: MIT Press, 1979.

Davis, B., and P. Turner. *German Uniforms of the Third Reich, 1933 – 1945*. Sydney: Blandford Press, 1986.

Dawidowicz, Lucy S. *The War Against the Jews, 1933 – 1945*. New York: Holt, Reinhart & Winston, 1975.

Delauney, Charles. *New Hot Discography: The Standard Dictionary of Recorded Jazz*. Edited by Walter Schaap and George Avikian. New York: Criterion, 1948.

Des Pres, Terrence. *The Survivor: An Anatomy of Life in the Death Camps*. New York: Oxford University Press, 1980.

Döblin, Alfred. *Berlin Alexanderplatz*. New York: Fredrick Ungar, 1961.

Eckardt, Wolf Von, and Sander L. Gilman. *Bertolt Brecht's Berlin: A Scrapbook of the Twenties*. New York: Anchor/Doubleday, 1975.

Engelmann, Bernt. *In Hitler's Germany: Life in the Third Reich*. New York: Pantheon, 1986.

Gold, Robert S. *A Jazz Lexicon*. New York: Knopf, 1964.

Gun, Nerin E. *The Day of the Americans*. New York: Fleet, 1966.

Hilberg, Raul. *The Destruction of the European Jews*. Chicago: Holmes & Meier, 1961.

Kogon, Eugen. *The Theory and Practice of Hell*. New York: Berkley, 1980.

Lee, Ulysses. *U.S. Army in World War II: The Employment of Negro Troops*. Washington, DC: Office of the Chief of Military History, 1961.

Levi, Primo. *Survival in Auschwitz*. New York: Collier, 1961.

Levi, Primo. *Moments of Reprieve: A Memoir of Auschwitz*. New York: Penguin, 1986.

Lifton, Robert J. *The Nazi Doctors: Medical Killings and the Psychology of Genocide*. New York: Basic Books, 1986.

Major, Clarence. *Dictionary of Afro-American Slang*. New York: International Publishers, 1970.

Manning, Kenneth R. *Black Apollo of Science: The Life of Ernest Everett Just.* New York: Oxford University Press, 1983.

Müller-Hill, Benno. *Murderous Science: Elimination by Scientific Selection of Jews, Gypsies, and Others in Germany, 1933 – 1945.* New York: Oxford University Press, 1988.

Myers, Gustavus. *History of Bigotry in the United States.* New York: Random House, 1943.

Peukert, Detlev. *Inside Nazi Germany: Conformity, Opposition, and Racism in Everday Life.* New York: Oxford University Press, 1980.

Plant, Richard. *The Pink Triangle: The Nazi War Against Homosexuals.* New York: Henry Holt, 1986.

Proctor, Robert N. *Racial Hygiene: Medicine Under the Nazis.* Cambridge: Harvard University Press, 1988.

Ramati, Alexander. *And the Violins Stopped Playing: A Story of the Gypsy Holocaust.* New York: Franklin Watts, 1986.

Reitlinger, Gerald. *The Final Solution: The Attempt to Exterminate the Jews of Europe, 1939 – 1945.* Northvale, NJ: Jason Aronson, 1987.

Rothschild-Boros, Monica, C. *In the Shadow of the Tower: The Works of Josef Nassy, 1942 – 1945.* Irvine, CA: Severin Wundermunn Museum, 1988.

Rubenstein, Richard. *The Cunning of History: The Holocaust and the American Future.* New York: Harper Colophon, 1978.

Seghers, Anna. *The Seventh Cross.* New York: Monthly Review Press, 1987.

Shirer, William L. *The Rise and Fall of the Third Reich: A History of Germany.* New York: Crest/Fawcett, 1962.

Zwerin, Mike. *La Tristesse de Saint Louis.* New York: Beech Tree/Morrow, 1985.

OTHER PUBLICATIONS

"Concentration Camp Dachau." Brussels/Munich: Comité International de
    Dachau, 1978.
"Concentration Camps Fail to Still Lips Praising God," *Consolation,*
    vols. 21 – 27, excerpted from the Watch Tower Society's files. New York:
    Watchtower Bible & Tract Society. Sept. 12, 1945 – Jan. 16, 1946.
The Holocaust. Jerusalem: Remembrance Authority, 1977.
"Keeping Integrity in Nazi Germany," *Awake!* New York: Watchtower Bible &
    Tract Society. June 22, 1985.
"The World Since 1914: Part 3: 1935 – 1940," *Awake!* New York: Watchtower
    Bible & Tract Society. April 8, 1987.